FIREBRAND

Also by Georgia di Donato
WOMAN OF JUSTICE

Firebrand

Georgia di Donato

Doubleday & Company, Inc., Garden City, New York
1982

ISBN: 0-385-15886-6
Library of Congress Catalog Number 87-47860

For my parents
Helen and *George Townsend*

AUTHOR'S NOTE

In this novel three of the major characters are fictitious: Amanda Lamar, Tom Maynard and Carl Gerhardt. The Pacific Northwest has generously provided a large and varied cast of historical figures who share the stage. Among those best remembered for their roles in shaping the destiny of Washington state in the late nineteenth and early twentieth centuries are: Colonel Alden Blethen, Erastus Brainerd, Horace Cayton, Mary Kenworthy, George Cotterill, Anna Louise Strong, John Considine, Mark Reed and Sol Simpson.

The author has brought fictional elements into the lives of these historical figures: Certain dates, places and events have been altered for dramatic purposes. For instance, anti-Chinese riots are historical fact—but they took place earlier in time than the actual confines of this story. Some imaginative elements also occur in the portraits of the Seattle *Times,* the *Post-Intelligencer,* the *Union Record,* the Clough-Hartley Mill, the Slade Mill and the Simpson Lumber Company.

FIREBRAND is, then, a work of fiction inspired by historical facts, merging historical people and events with actions and events that *could* have happened.

Georgia di Donato

FIREBRAND

Prologue

On December 24, 1916, Amanda Lamar was escorted from the courthouse to a third-floor cell at the King County Jail. Leaving the busy traffic of brightly lit corridors to enter the gothic gloom of prison felt only a shade more painful than the long walk past fellow journalists—colleagues and rivals—with whom she had covered the events of an entire generation. Now it was *her* event which others had come to record. She met their eyes bravely, not wanting their pity, and with an undefeated lift of her chin, answered in a clear, resounding voice the questions which flew from all sides. Having spent most of her life seeking answers, it was not in her nature, even now, to remain silent. Let the world know why she was here. And how she felt about it. Let them know it was not the end, but only the beginning.

"Hey, Firebrand!" A photographer leaped in her path. "How about a smile for your old pals?"

She smiled.

"Do you think you got a fair trial?"

"If I had, I wouldn't be here."

Her characteristic gesture of defiance drew a sympathetic laugh. She had sat through the trial feeling helpless while her fate was determined by the prosecutor's cleverness, the jury's confusion and the judge's lack of compassion. Yet, she was expected to be grateful that she had been found guilty only of sedition. For had it been treason, the defense reminded, her future would have been very bleak indeed.

But what could be bleaker, she asked herself now, than to be thirty-seven years old, alone, bereaved, and behind bars?

"How do you feel about it?"

"Raped."

A bulb flashed in her face. She didn't flinch. There was a stigma, a shame in being at the mercy of one's enemies. And like a rape victim, she knew she had done nothing for which she should repent.

"Then you're not guilty?"

"Certainly I am."

Guilty of defending my beliefs, of loving the wrong man. Guilty of risking all I've ever worked to achieve. God, what a question! Didn't my journalism as "Firebrand" lead men to their deaths?

"What will you do while you're in prison?"

"Ask the state. I belong to them now." Time. That was the special terror.

"Will you retire when you get out?"

Retire? What a frightening word, a dead-end.

"Never. I'll only retire when I'm buried."

A spontaneous wave of applause was abruptly silenced as heavy doors swung shut behind her. Now her tight smile disappeared, she let herself falter.

The deputy accompanied her in silence to the cell reserved for special offenders. He seemed embarrassed to find himself in charge of a prisoner who had once come to this very cell with him, as a visitor on a mission of mercy. He averted his eyes and repeatedly cleared his throat while removing her handcuffs. She thanked him, wondering why he pretended not to know her. Perhaps it was because she no longer had an identity. Or maybe there was a regulation that prisoners were not to be spoken to. At any rate, he was anxious to hurry away, after first locking the barred door behind him, then the solid door which sealed off the block. The finality of iron connecting with iron echoed in the vast dead space which surrounded her cell. No sounds penetrated the walls, no sunlight filtered through the high recessed window.

This is to be my entire world now, she thought. This is to be my universe. It contained a cot, sink and toilet, a table and chair. To this she added a small bundle which someone had thrust into her arms without explanation, and which the deputy had hastily checked and let her keep. Opening it, she discovered that the necessities for a reduced life had been given to her—a towel, toothbrush and comb. Tucked between the folds of the towel, she found a notebook and pen. Surprised, she laughed aloud, exulting in the echo of her own voice. Then she let go the flow of tears which had been suppressed far too long. A sensitive guard, or even a sympathetic stranger— someone had slipped her the tools for survival. Someone believed that she must carry on. She would sleep, and then she would begin to try and live beyond the walls of her cell, through writing; her mind, at least, would escape to freedom. She wouldn't belong completely to the state after all.

Only a week had passed, but it might as well have been a month, or even a year. There was no need to measure the hours and days, for there was nothing to fill them. Only when a clean towel was delivered, and the soiled one removed, did Amanda realize that she had a means of calculating time. Lined in with the towel was a newspaper, the first reading material to reach her. She eagerly consumed every word, especially the articles which had been written about her; then she became immediately depressed. Why did they speak of her in the past tense, as though she had died? Tears of self-pity needed no coaxing, but when she reached for the towel to dry her eyes, a heavenly fragrance escaped. There, nestled in the middle, was a small bar of expensively wrapped soap. Courtesy of King County? Not likely. Why would *I* get special treatment? But from whatever its source, she accepted gratefully another memento of civilized society, a sign that her work had mattered.

The following week passed more easily. Now Amanda's dull routine was enlivened by a certain element of suspense—would another gift arrive? She was not to be disappointed. With her fresh towel came this time a slim volume of verse. Again amazed, she turned the pages, only to discover that they were love poems, each one expressing passion and desire.

She tried to think who could be her benefactor. This book of verse changed things—it suggested that her anonymous friend was more than an admirer. Perhaps it was even someone she knew. A familiar ache began to gnaw. Was she opening a wound from the past?

An embroidered lace handkerchief arrived next—and with it a brief note. It said only: "Those you have conquered will never forget you."

Amanda read it in puzzled frustration. It wasn't exactly a message of love, but almost a warning. Yet, it contained a feeling of both, a sense of ultimatum. Why doesn't he say who he is? She now knew who she *wanted* it to be.

She could envision him walking through the door, and though she dared not hope for the impossible, all reason was drifting away. If wanting could make it so, he would be with her now.

Suddenly, Amanda's thoughts were jarred by the clamor of bolts sliding, doors opening, footsteps in the corridor. Someone was coming! In another second the massive door which sealed off the world would open. Was her long wait to be over at last? With a trembling hand she rose and straightened her hair.

PART ONE

Gold Fever

1896–1898

Chapter One

LIFE began for Amanda, not in the year she was born, but on a rainy July day in 1896, three thousand miles from home, when she had just turned seventeen. As she waited impatiently in the crowd on the shores of the Willamette River, she saw only a landscape of adventure stretching beyond the Oregon gloom to infinity. The taste of salt on her lips was the taste of freedom.

Finally the gates swung wide and she found herself caught in the sudden flow of bodies. As they rushed the pier, Amanda felt released, exultant at the sensation of being out of control. What better way to make a fresh start? And once aboard ship, there would be no retreat.

Oblivious to the warm drizzle, to the fact that she was conspicuous in white summer clothes, she cared little that all the other reporters were sensibly enveloped in raincoats. There had been no time to find out what to wear for a voyage on the Pacific, and if anyone had told her what Portland weather was like in the middle of July, she wouldn't have believed them. All that had mattered was getting the assignment, and as far away from Washington, D.C., as possible. Distance alone seemed to ensure that failure and pain would be left behind. How she welcomed the company of strangers—no advice, no reprimands, no disapproval. Her life of independence had begun.

Fellow passengers swept Amanda along the pier until at last a wedge of space appeared before her, through which she could see *The Puget Queen*. She stopped. It looked exactly like its name, a squat coastal steamer, battered by years of service. So *that* was it.

Unsinkable, she hoped. Visions of sailing up to Seattle on a graceful three-masted schooner evaporated. Still, going on a tub was far better than not going at all.

Suddenly she realized that the crowd had come to a standstill. She squeezed ahead, nonetheless, until she could see what the problem was—a line of men blocking the gangplank. In fact, they had formed a human chain, with legs planted apart, their eyes of steel defying anyone to pass. They made no threatening gestures, they simply stood in ominous silence, as if they knew that their presence alone conveyed a message. Amanda noticed that her colleagues, for the most part, wore the mildly annoyed expressions of those whose experience was so vast that they were beyond feeling either fear or excitement. If they did, they didn't show it. But perhaps, inside, they, too, marched to a steady drumbeat in their chests.

Curious, Amanda moved ahead for a closer look. The men did not appear to be armed. They wore plain work clothes, and their tired, weathered faces looked as if they were prepared to wait forever, as if they had spent their whole lives waiting.

She opened her notebook to a clean sheet. But before she could formulate a question, the men suddenly raised their arms in unison, as though someone had commanded at gunpoint, "Hands up!"

Amanda's expectant smile froze. My God! Can I believe what I'm seeing? She stared in bewilderment. Every one of them was mutilated.

The man at the end of the line was missing a right hand and several fingers of his left. Her eyes moved quickly. Next to him stood one whose arm had been severed at the elbow. Then a fellow whose arm was completely gone. And on to the end of the line without exception.

"That's close enough!" It was the huskiest of the men who had spoken. His muscular upper arm tapered into a smooth rounded knob where his forearm should have been.

Amanda took another step. "It's all right," she assured, her wide brown eyes open and innocent. "I'm a reporter."

"I said—stay back!"

She hesitated, not used to being rebuffed. Seldom did her full-lipped smile fail to soften an exasperated male, but it failed her now. These were men beyond feeling. That's what the war had done, she decided, remembering how her uncle, who had lost a leg in the Battle of Winchester, had later resolved his depression by taking his own life.

"Are you veterans?" she asked sympathetically, looking at the man who had ordered her back.

"That's right," he replied with a dull laugh. "*Our* war was with the Slade Mill up in Aberdeen."

"Oh, you're mill hands!" Snickers from the others made her aware that she had spoken the obvious. "I've heard about accidents in the lumber mills, but I never imagined . . ."

"Accidents! You hear that, boys?"

He was answered by a rumble of disgust down the line.

"We're shingle-weavers, and shingle-weaving isn't a trade, it's a battle—where human flesh is staked against a pair of teethed steel discs that whirl around two hundred times a minute, not caring whether it cuts wood or cuts men! It gets everybody sooner or later. And you say accidents!"

"I didn't know. I'm terribly sorry."

"Sorry, she says!" His response scorned Amanda's sympathy. "Me too. Because we'll never work again. And we have no pensions."

"Come on, fellows," one of the reporters called out. "This is a special sailing for the press. Let us aboard!"

"Hold on!" The mill hand extended his muscular stump, which had the desired effect of producing an immediate hush. "We don't care who you are. Nobody gets on *The Puget Queen*. Blood is in this boat," he said, gesturing toward it. "*Our* blood. It was built by Slade. And if we don't get our pensions, we'll make sure it never sails again."

"Don't take it out on us," another reporter protested. "We're just doing our job, like everybody else."

"Wait a minute!" Amanda found herself saying. "If what he says is true, we shouldn't go aboard."

"Just smile and look pretty, Red," the reporter called out with a smirk. "Leave the decisions to us!"

If there was anything Amanda hated, it was references made to the color of her hair. But even worse was the implication that she didn't need to think. She stared serenely at the amused faces, her outward calm betrayed by burning cheeks. "I still say it's not right. Anyway, *I'm* not going to set foot on that boat."

Her defiance aroused another protest, and the crowd began to take sides.

"Thanks, Red, we're much obliged," said the mill hand, his mouth twisting into a downturned smile. He extended his left hand.

Amanda grasped it firmly, looking him in the eye. "I have a name. It's Amanda Lamar."

"Gustav Johnson," he replied, suddenly bashful.

She could feel his strength surging through her, despite the fact that he had only a thumb and forefinger with which to grip.

"After I gave up an arm, I figured I might as well donate a few fingers to the lumber trust," he joked.

Amanda detected the note of bitter pride, and felt a rush of compassion. "I wish you luck, Mr. Johnson. I hope you get what you want."

"Are you going to write this up?"

"Nothing can stop me."

"We'll watch for it. What paper are you with?"

"The New York *World*. If you give me your address, I'll see to it that you get a copy."

"You can send it to me in care of the Aberdeen post office. Just put Gus Johnson. That's good enough."

"I will, thanks. Now, if you don't mind, I have a few more questions . . ."

Amanda's words were lost in the scream of a siren. Heads turned as a police wagon came careening down the street and swung onto the pier. Hoofs echoed on the planking, parting the crowd, then drawing it along to witness the excitement.

While the mill hands attempted to stand their ground, a half dozen policemen jumped down from the wagon, clubs in hand, anticipating resistance. Without warning them to disperse, they seized the demonstrators and attempted to apply handcuffs. Only then did they discover that fewer than half the men had both wrists intact. This did not, however, earn sympathy. Just the opposite. The police reacted in anger, as though they were embarrassed by their assignment, and felt they were being made fools of.

Just as the mill hands were being pushed into the wagon, one of them stumbled and fell. When Gus Johnson made a quick gesture to assist him, a nervous officer brought his club down full force on Johnson's head.

"Watch out!" Amanda's scream was too late. Gus Johnson pitched forward, the impact of the blow sending him sprawling on the dock. Blood poured from his mouth and ears.

Amanda rushed over. "Mr. Johnson!"

Suddenly, she felt a restraining hand clamp onto her arm. And a voice commanded, "Don't do that!"

Spinning around, she found herself facing a wild-eyed young man whose horrified expression caused her to stop in confusion.

"Why not?"

"Do you want to get yourself arrested?" His eyes were round behind studious-looking glasses.

"But a man's been hurt!"

"Don't you understand?" He tightened his grip. "There's nothing you can do!"

As soon as she stopped resisting, he relaxed his hold.

"There. That's better." In a nervous gesture, he ran his fingers through thick curly hair. "Take my advice, and don't get mixed up with labor disputes. If word gets around that you're pro-union, you'll find yourself in a lot of trouble."

"What about *him?*" Amanda turned in time to see the police lifting the limp form of Gus Johnson into the wagon. The doors were quickly slammed shut. She looked at the young man helplessly.

"I know. It's rotten. But that's the way things are. It's the times we're living in."

Amanda studied him curiously. He appeared to be close to her own age, yet he showed not a spark of rebellion.

"Well, 1896 isn't the Dark Ages. Seems we should *do* something about it, not just sit by and watch people get beaten up."

He shrugged, his eyes straying unabashedly to the curve of her bodice. "Well, I guess we'll be sailing. You *are* going, aren't you?"

She nodded, suddenly self-conscious, and glanced down quickly, wondering if the rain was shrinking her dress.

"Good." His face cracked into a relieved smile. "See you on board!" Then he turned into the crowd and was gone.

Impatient now with the delay, the passengers squeezed up the gangplank. But the push to board was slowed by the purser, who was taking his time checking each name against his list. Amanda guessed that he was under orders to detect potential troublemakers who might try sneaking aboard pretending to be reporters.

When at last it was her turn, she gave her name and produced her ticket.

The purser looked her over with the practiced eye of a seaman. "Mercer Girl, eh?" He grinned.

She ignored the comment. A Mercer Girl was someone looking for a mate.

"Traveling alone?" he persisted, glancing down the passenger list. "Or with your husband?"

"With a newspaper," she replied.

"You're a reporter?" He whistled. "You sure don't look like one." He gave her a frank appraisal. "That makes you the only lady reporter aboard. In fact, the only *lady* aboard. So, if you have any problems, just come to me." He handed her the key to her cabin, then followed her with his eyes as she brushed by.

"A real beauty," she heard him proclaim loudly for her benefit. She walked purposefully, hoping to discourage him.

It was becoming a familiar situation. Throughout the long journey by rail from her home in Washington, D.C., all the way to Portland, Oregon, she had been besieged by gentlemen offering to protect her from the wickedness of the world, especially when they heard that she was bound for the Pacific Northwest. All agreed it was no country for women, populated mostly by roustabouts, lumberjacks and drifters, with a harsh environment of mountains, forests, rain, fog, bears, mountain lions and hidden tribes of natives. Why else would Asa Mercer have had to buy the passage for all those young eastern girls, promising them husbands and homes if they would be willing to come to Seattle? It proved the point. Girls had to be *paid* to marry a man from the Northwest and settle there for good. Amanda had met no one who would accept the fact that she was a reporter on assignment, sent to cover the arrival in Seattle of a thousand Chinese immigrants, an event which was expected to have serious repercussions. Her traveling companions warned that she would either be tricked into an unsavory marriage or end up in a brothel, unless of course she would allow them to show her the ropes, as they put it.

Amanda was not discouraged by these predictions, but only by not being taken seriously. It aroused her indignation to think that a woman alone by choice was still frowned upon.

When she located her cabin she saw with relief that her one small trunk had already been deposited. Finding it there like a friend from home was reassuring. It showed that even in the wilds of the North-west, timetables were kept, destinations reached, life continued.

She closed the door and looked about her cramped quarters—her home for the next three days. She thumped the mattress. It was hard, reminding her of the cot at school on which she had slept every night for the last three years—until her expulsion. But that was too un-pleasant to even think about. Memories of the strict discipline of Cedar Ridge would soon fade. Even the disgrace of not graduating would be forgotten. The other girls were going on to college, which Amanda didn't envy in the least. How much better to work and have a life full of adventure. Turning away from the bunk and guilty feel-ings, she found herself facing a small mirror. Leaning close she stared at her reflection.

"Who do we have here?" she asked aloud. "A real beauty!" she answered, mimicking the purser. Then in a dramatic voice she con-tinued, "Ah, Manka, are you truly one of the great beauties of the world, beside whom Lillie Langtry pales like faded wallpaper? Poor thing!"

She stopped with a sudden frown to see if a closer scrutiny would reveal any of those tiny melancholy lines which always seemed to en-hance the faces of actresses. But try as she would, she could find no character or suffering written there, only the soft golden fuzz of im-maturity. All those encounters on the train with older men had left no visible mark whatsoever. Yet, when she gave her age as twenty, no one ever questioned her. Why say she was seventeen if she didn't look it? There were enough problems in passing for twenty.

Removing her straw hat, she shook the moisture from her curls, the damp tendrils clinging to her cheeks, then twisted her hair into a bun on the top of her head to add height. Not that height was needed. Amanda was taller than most women—and many men as well. Friends at school had told her that she was the only tall girl they knew who didn't go around with her shoulders hunched. And why should she? Blessed with a perfect figure, there was no reason to slump, she reasoned. Why not make the most of it? Nonetheless, she scowled into the mirror in self-criticism.

"That purser must be crazy," she told her reflection. "Your eyes are too far apart. Nose too long, though straight at least. Lips too fat. No, not fat—full. Don't be so hard on yourself!"

Although Amanda had not inherited her mother's graceful beauty, she was attractive in a fresh, wholesome way which suggested that she could take care of herself. Still, she found fault with her appearance. Instead of being grateful that her skin didn't burn, she longed for her mother's fragile complexion, freckles and all, aware constantly of what she considered to be her own shortcomings. It was hard to avoid these painful comparisons, for her mother, Temperance Smith, was a much admired woman. Admired not only for her beauty, but even more so for her accomplishments. And it was in this respect, more than in physical appearance, that Amanda felt the subtle pressure to compete. And now I've let her down, she thought, as the pangs of guilt again intruded.

Judge Smith, as her mother was known professionally, was one of those rare women who had managed to excel in a field dominated by men. Undeniably she had had help getting started, but nevertheless her accomplishments were her own. Inspired by her father's distinguished career as a federal judge who had served under Lincoln during the war years, Temperance Smith had been the first woman judge to ride circuit in the West, appointed by President Ulysses S. Grant. She had been determined to have a career of her own, advancing solely on her own merits. Later, she had been fortunate enough to marry a man who had actually allowed her to continue her work. Lucius Lamar, a United States senator, had been proud of his wife. He had been the perfect husband and father; but of course now he was gone. And Amanda, instead of being a comfort to her mother, had so far brought only disgrace on the family.

Never mind, Amanda consoled herself, I'll make it all up somehow.

Amanda had always been a rebel. Her resistance to authority had exasperated the nuns at Cedar Ridge, whose patience finally gave out when her infamous article—the first she had ever submitted for publication—appeared in the New York *World*. It was worse than blasphemy, it was heresy, the nuns decried. Any student who would publicly proclaim that religion was outdated certainly did not belong at Cedar Ridge. So, only one month short of graduation, Amanda had been expelled, and her diploma withheld. Even her mother's reputation had not been sufficient reason to show leniency. Despite her disappointment, however, Temperance had pleaded with Amanda not to rush off, fearing that the *World* only wished to exploit the talents of a youthful rebel. Seventeen, she said, was far too young to be on your own, much less begin a career. But Amanda had argued stubbornly, and finally left against her mother's wishes. Now, stuck with an impulsive decision, there was no turning back.

The shriek of the whistle jarred her thoughts. Three short blasts, then the sudden throb of propellers beginning to turn. Quickly tying a scarf around her head, Amanda was glad to leave her cabin and join the others hurrying to the upper deck.

The steamer was moving now, churning up the water as they maneuvered out into the Willamette, heading northwest to meet the Columbia. Bracing herself against the breeze, Amanda drew deep breaths. The dampness carried a smell of creosote and fresh-sawn lumber from the mills across the river, each one marked by a pyramid of pale yellow sawdust. Her skin felt sticky as large raindrops settled.

Small fishing crafts scuttled out of the way as they steered into mid-channel, but the schooners kept to their lanes, trusting *The Puget Queen* not to cross their paths. It seemed that nothing would disrupt the busy commerce of the Willamette River. Tiers of vessels waiting to be stowed lined both shores. From her vantage point, Amanda could see stevedores lowering fresh-cut boards into the cavernous holds, while others guided unwieldy lengths of unbarked trees sixty or eighty feet long through large loading ports cut into the ships' hulls at the bow and stern. She watched fascinated at the skill required to thread the logs through the ports. What if the cable snapped and the logs came crashing down on the workers below? After seeing the injuries which the mill hands had suffered, she imagined that the stevedores were no less vulnerable.

As they picked up speed, the gray images of the Portland harbor gradually receded. But the sawmill complexes continued to ride with them, rippling the shores in a jagged chain, one after the other, feeding a constant stream of schooners until every deck was loaded to capacity. Watching them glide past, she wondered how much blood was being spilled to make it all possible? As if in reply, mournful whistles signaled their arrivals and departures, answered by the cries of gulls wheeling with the wind.

When the dinner bell sounded, Amanda lingered at the railing, her appetite suddenly gone. Conversation and laughter drifted off as the passengers moved inside. She was glad to have the deck to herself and a quiet time to think about what lay ahead.

At this very moment, somewhere out in the Pacific, another ship was steaming eastward, filled with Chinese immigrants destined for Seattle. In a few days the two boats would meet. Did those poor Chinese guess what was in store for them in the raw, forbidding Northwest? If white workers were abused, what hope was there for the Orientals? They couldn't possibly know that they were the center of controversy, that reporters from all over the United States were flocking to greet them because of rumored opposition to their arrival. And by the time they found out, it would be too late to turn back. Just like me, thought Amanda. Except for me it's an adventure, for them it's life or death.

The rivers converged, the mist turned chilly, and Amanda went down to her cabin. A tray had been left at the door. Surprised that the steward would have been concerned that she was absent from dinner, she carried it inside. Suddenly she was ravenous. But to her great disappointment, all the tray contained was bouillon, crackers and tea. Immediately she realized it had been assumed that she was seasick! Regretfully she imagined that everyone would think, how typical of a female to get sick the minute she steps aboard ship.

As soon as she finished eating, Amanda stretched out on her bunk. She had no intention of going to sleep so early, but within moments she felt her body growing heavy. The springless mattress, obviously designed for penitents, dredged up memories she wanted to forget, transporting her back against her will to the long nights at boarding school. Can the past ever be escaped? she asked, her thoughts drifting.

Suddenly Amanda found herself surrounded by open sea, her bunk heaving, as though riding the waves. A swift current swept her along, the water became increasingly turbulent. Amanda clung to the sides of her bunk, only it was no longer a bunk but a boat. Feeling that it was about to capsize, she tried to steady the craft, but her efforts were futile. Flailing the air helplessly, she tumbled overboard, landing with a painful thud.

Jolted awake, Amanda found herself not in the water, but on the floor. Stunned, she struggled to her feet, wondering why she couldn't stand up straight. Was she still dreaming, or was the floor of her cabin at an angle? A strong shudder abruptly righted the ship, then there was no movement at all. The engine had been cut. An instant of silence was broken by the wail of a siren. Then the sounds of doors opening, the quick thunder of running feet and shouting. When Amanda found the companionway jammed with passengers, she joined the stampede to the upper deck.

It was black outside. Amanda had no idea how long she had been asleep, but she saw that almost everyone had rushed out in some frantic stage of half-dress. Many were wearing unbuttoned shoes, with raincoats and jackets hastily thrown on over night clothes, as though they expected to abandon ship. Fighting her way through the confusion, Amanda headed for the bridge, from which the captain was shouting orders. But no one dared approach, for the crew had armed themselves with rifles. Panicky reporters attempting to unlash the lifeboats were ordered to stay clear.

"Take cover!" the captain shouted. "Lie down on deck!"

Everyone immediately obeyed.

"My God, what's going on?" Amanda gasped aloud as she crouched down.

"Lie flat!" commanded a voice next to her.

Amanda did as she was told, then turned her head cautiously. The same young man she had met earlier was lying a few feet away. Only this time he wasn't wearing his glasses.

"It's me again!" she said in a loud whisper, thinking perhaps he couldn't see her.

"I know it is, dammit!" he whispered back. "Do you want to get yourself killed?"

Amanda could feel the soft thud of her heartbeat as her chest pushed against the deck. "Is it a mutiny?" she asked, her voice trembling with excitement.

"We rammed a log boom!"

"What does that mean?" Then, in exasperation, "Why are we whispering?"

Suddenly shouts could be heard from the blackness beyond the steamer. The captain was holding a lantern aloft, illuminating the dark waters on the starboard side, while his crew kept their rifles trained over the railing. A boat had pulled alongside. Amanda raised her head slightly, straining to hear the angry exchange. But only the captain's words could be distinguished.

"We're not involved in your strike!" he barked. "The law's on our side. Now get that goddam log boom out of the way, or we'll open fire!"

Amanda glanced at her companion and quickly lowered her head.

"Don't worry," said the young man. "The strikers can't do anything to us. It's the captain's responsibility."

"If we sink, it won't matter whose fault it is!"

"We won't sink. Boats are always getting rammed by log booms. Usually by accident. This time it was done on purpose."

A shot rang out. Then a muffled cry from the other boat, "You bastards!"

A tense stillness settled over the deck.

"That was a warning!" the captain shouted hoarsely. "Next time we won't miss."

"You can kill every one of us!" Amanda heard the voice quite distinctly now as the smaller boat drew closer. "You got reporters aboard, so this time the world will know the truth. You won't be able to lie and say that *we* attacked *you!*"

"You did attack us, you sons of bitches!" cried the captain. "You put a hole in our side! We have a right to defend ourselves!"

Amanda raised herself to a crouching position, then cautiously stood up.

"What in God's name are you doing? Get down!" The young man's voice was frantic.

Ignoring the command, Amanda stepped over bodies to reach the bridge, her heart wildly pummeling her chest, and climbed up, despite scattered warnings from the other reporters. Hearing the commotion, the captain whirled around.

"What's this girl doing here?" he rasped.

"Captain, I only want to help," her words came in a rush. "Tell the strikers that I'd be willing to go with them, to cover their side of the story, on condition they let you continue to Seattle."

"What's she talking about?" he demanded, looking at his mates to supply the answer.

"I'm offering myself as a hostage."

"A hostage?" he repeated incredulously. "She's crazy!"

"Why? What's wrong with that?"

The captain turned in anger to his men. "How in hell did she get on board?"

"I'm a reporter, like everybody else," she managed to say with dignity.

But the captain's shoe-leather face showed no signs of softening.

"Let me see your credentials," he demanded.

"I don't have any, but take my word for it, I'm with the New York *World*."

"No wonder!" he spat the words. "That's an anti-American paper!"

"Anti-American? Because it speaks for the common man? That's— baloney!"

"What's more, any paper that gives over its front page to a little know-nothing like Nellie Bly, oughta be put out of business!" His lip curled in scorn. "Don't waste my time."

One of the strikers called out from the boat, "Let her come with us and we'll order the boom out of your way!"

"She's not going anywhere!" he thundered in reply. "I'm responsible for this ship and every passenger on it. If I turn her over to anybody, it'll be to the police!"

"The police! What have I done?"

"You're a radical. And I don't allow radicals on my boat!"

"Look at me. Do I look like a radical?"

"You're in with the strikers!"

"Then put me off!"

"Oh, that would suit you fine, wouldn't it? I can just picture what you'd write!"

Suddenly Amanda heard a familiar voice from behind. She turned to find her new friend beside her once again.

"I'll vouch for her," he said. "She's not a sympathizer. She's never even been to the Northwest before."

"Who the hell are you?" The captain glowered, holding his lantern aloft.

"I'm Tom Maynard. Doc Maynard's grandson."

"Well, I'll be damned. Now, look here, son, why do you want to defend this girl? You'll get yourself into a lot of trouble."

"But I tell you she's all right. We're friends. I've known her for ages."

"Ever since you got on board last night, that right?" The captain raised a sly brow. "All right, Maynard, I'll make you responsible for her. Just remember, if she kicks up any more fuss, your career as a reporter will be over—I don't care if you *are* Doc Maynard's kin. That clear?"

"Yes, sir."

"Now get outa here. And take her with you."

Amanda frowned.

"Come on!" Tom Maynard took her firmly by the arm. "Don't argue."

When they reached the deck below, she turned to him with a satisfied smile. "He called me a radical, didn't he?"

"I don't see what's so funny. He could have you arrested!"

"On what charges?"

"Anything he wanted. You know, lumber isn't just tree-cutting. A lot of the bigger mills own the ships they build, like Slade owns this one. If the captain works for Slade, then you don't want him for an enemy."

"I don't give a hoot," she teased. "After all, I've got *you* to look out for me."

She watched his Adam's apple rise and knew she was making him nervous.

"It will be a pleasure," he said, swallowing. "What's your name?"

"Amanda Lamar. And it *is* my first time in the Northwest. How did you know?"

"I guess I was just saying whatever came into my head."

"Well, don't think I'm inexperienced," she said, holding his gaze to see if she could make him squirm. "It won't be easy looking after me. I'm not the sitting-back type."

"I can tell."

"And of course I'm going to write about all this, whether the captain wants me to or not. So be a good fellow, Mr. Maynard, and tell me what's going on."

"I don't know any more than you do. Now let me take you back to your cabin, where it's safe."

"Safe? What do you think's going to happen?"

"Fireworks," he replied. And before he could explain, a burst of gunfire ripped the air.

"Keep going!" Slipping an arm around her waist, Tom swept her along before she could protest. As they ran she could hear scrambling on the deck above. Another volley of shots rang out. Then silence. They stopped running.

Amanda's hand flew to her throat, as if to still her pulse. She stared at Tom in horror. "What was that?"

"It'll be all right." He tried to sound convincing.

"All *right?* Sounds like somebody's been shot! Let's find out!"

"Look, Miss Lamar, we probably fired at the strikers' boat, so just stay put. When we get to Seattle, you can do as you please. But not now."

"Does the captain have a right to shoot strikers or sink their boats?"

"Of course not. But you can't stop him, so don't try. I'll feel greatly relieved," he pleaded, "if you would go back to your cabin, lock your door, and go to sleep."

"And what about you? What are *you* going to be doing?"

"Not a thing," he said, his voice suddenly hopeful. "So if you're afraid to be alone, I'll be glad to stay."

Amanda raised a brow. "Mr. Maynard, if I were a man, would you have made that offer?"

Tom looked at her helplessly. "If you were a man, dammit, I wouldn't have done any of this!"

"Dear Emma," Amanda wrote. "Well, here I am aboard *The Puget Prison,* locked in my quarters, and at a complete standstill. And though our mission has been thwarted (temporarily, I hope), I wish you could be here to share the joys of drifting on the Columbia. Boarding school was like a frolic in the meadow compared to this. The captain is a worse tyrant than any Mother Superior, and deserves to be overthrown. When he yells, his breath is strong enough to carry the coal. But he did pay me a compliment—he called me a radical!"

Amanda scribbled page after page, not caring about her penmanship, feverishly bent on getting it all down. And while she wrote, she took delicious pleasure in imagining how Emma Goldman, her friend and idol, would be filled with admiration. Only a firebrand like Emma could truly understand the necessity for taking risks to defend a belief. She had already decided that her letter to Emma would be the perfect form for her article, one which the *World* would be sure to appreciate. They, more than any other newspaper, had always been sympathetic toward Emma Goldman's activities, even when other papers questioned her motives. Every time Emma was arrested and jailed, usually while asserting her right to free speech, the *World* treated her fairly.

Although she considered Emma to be her best friend, they knew each other only through correspondence, which Amanda had initiated while still a student at Cedar Ridge. Emma had been a link not only to the world outside the school, but to a world of independence and rebellion, very different from the one in which Amanda had grown up.

Suddenly Amanda was distracted by the sound of the engine beginning to turn. She jumped up and peered through the porthole, clearing a circle in the steam with her finger, but all she could see was blackness and the far-off pinpoints of red and green running lights from the tug. Evidently it had pulled the boom out of the way. She debated whether or not to sneak up on deck, but finally decided not to. Tom Maynard seemed like such a nice well-meaning fellow, and he was so obviously taken with her, it would be a shame to get him into trouble.

Amanda awakened to gray daylight. Her small window framed an unrelieved portrait of open sea, with the thinnest of lines separating ocean from sky. They had reached the Pacific. Just knowing that she was sailing the same water that lapped at the shores of the Orient was a dizzying thought. She dressed quickly.

"Feeling better?" the steward asked when she entered the dining room.

"Yes, I'm fine. Thanks anyway for leaving the tray."

The steward nodded. "Your table is over there, where the older gentleman is sitting."

Amanda felt a twinge of disappointment. Her eyes swept the room, but there was no sign of Tom Maynard. Why did she have to be paired with such a portly old man? He appeared to be fifty, at least.

"Ah, Miss Lamar!" He made a half-rising gesture. "I was afraid I'd have to make the entire journey without a table partner. Blethen's the name, Colonel Alden Blethen." He smiled expectantly.

"Glad to meet you, Colonel." Amanda extended her hand in surprise. "How do you know my name?"

"There are no secrets on a ship, my dear." He gestured impatiently. "Sit down, sit down, you look half starved. Best thing to do is eat. Don't try to ride out the waves on an empty stomach." Blethen spoke as one who clearly valued his own opinion above anyone else's.

He was a stocky, powerfully built man whose head appeared to be disproportionately large due to a ring of untamed curls recently tossed by the wind. Bright beady eyes missed nothing, and an ample smile showed he felt he had little to hide.

"Even though I know *you,* my feelings are greatly damaged by the fact that you seem not to have the slightest idea who I am. Why is it I make no impression whatsoever on any of the pretty young girls?"

Blethen whipped up his napkin with a flourish and tucked the corner into his collar. Then seizing a knife and fork in each hand, he appeared ready to wage war on his breakfast.

Despite his admission of hurt feelings, Amanda did not believe for a minute that he was at all serious. She found herself smiling.

"What did you think of all the excitement last night?" he asked. "I don't mind telling you it cost me a card game. When we hit that boom, the best hand I ever had went in all directions!"

"Didn't you go up on deck?"

"And get trampled to death? Good Lord, no. I'm too old for that. The only sensible thing to do was take a shot of whiskey and go to bed. And that's exactly what I did."

"But didn't you hear the shooting?"

"Shooting, was there? Doesn't surprise me. I've been through this sort of thing before. A great fuss over nothing. Then it's all over and life goes on."

Amanda stared in wonderment. Imagine being so worldly that even life and death could be taken in stride!

She leaned across the table. "I think someone was murdered!" she said.

"Oh you do, do you? Well, I'd be willing to bet it was all bluff. At least that's what my sources tell me. Anyway, it's nothing to worry your pretty head over."

Amanda sighed. Pretty head! She would have to shock him. "I tried to offer myself as hostage, but the captain wouldn't agree."

"I know all about it," he replied matter-of-factly. "You should never take unnecessary risks. However, I don't mind telling you that your action was much admired. You put the boys to shame."

"I did?" Amanda flushed at the thought that people were talking about her. She glanced across the room. A number of heads were turned in her direction. She quickly looked away. "Oh, dear!"

Colonel Blethen chuckled. "Don't worry, I'll keep the pack at bay. As you know, it's my good fortune to be assigned to you as an escort, so I'm the only one you'll have to put up with."

"Escort?" She stared at him blankly.

"You mean your mother didn't tell you?"

"My mother?"

Blethen groaned. "We seem to be going around the mulberry bush. I'd better explain. Your mother is an old and dear friend. Although we don't see each other often, we stay in touch and keep up on what the other is doing through friends. And of course through the newspapers, our best sources of information." He paused. "Now don't look so distraught. Better to be stuck with the old colonel than to arrive in a new city alone."

"I'm not distraught—just surprised." So, her mother hadn't disowned her after all, but was actually worrying! Poor Mama. Amanda's feelings of stubborn anger began to mellow. There was a certain satisfaction in having everyone worried about whether you were going to survive, or what you were going to do next.

The steward arrived with a steaming platter of kidneys and scrambled eggs. Amanda helped herself to a small amount, then Blethen took a heaping portion.

"Yes," he sighed. "I suppose getting me as a chaperone is a bit like finding yourself betrothed to a fellow of the parents' choosing."

"I don't mind, really," Amanda quickly assured him. "It was very kind of you to offer."

"Well, I didn't exactly offer. I was asked."

"Then we're both stuck!" Amanda began to smile.

"Quite true. Shall we try to make the best of it?"

"Why not?"

"That's a girl! Now, eat up. A good breakfast followed by a brisk turn around the deck should put some color in your cheeks."

Amanda glanced at the porthole just as the first drops struck the pane. "Rain again!"

"Ah, rain! The great tree-maker. Without rain you don't have trees. Without trees you don't have paper." Blethen lowered his voice in the manner of one divulging a deep secret. "And without paper we'd all be out of business." He gestured with his fork, taking in the entire dining room. Then he stabbed a kidney to give emphasis to his words.

Amanda listened eagerly, hoping he was about to launch into the subject of the lumber industry. But it appeared he was prepared to say no more.

"Are you a newspaperman, then?" she asked, encouraging him to continue.

"That I am. A veteran, you might say. I've owned so many papers that I've forgotten the names of half of 'em. Buy and sell, sell and buy. Sold my last paper for a quarter of a million and lost every penny in the panic of '93."

Amanda shook her head in amazement. "Bet you felt like jumping out of a window!"

"Not me! I have tiptop credit. Matter of fact, right this minute I'm on my way to buy the Seattle *Press-Times*. It's bankrupt and I'm going to save it. I forgot to mention, that's a passion of mine—buying up bankrupt papers." He scraped his eggs against a piece of toast and took a mouthful.

"Isn't that an awful risk?"

"Bet your boots. I'm a born gambler. Now eat up, food's getting cold."

Blethen trudged around the slippery deck undaunted by the blowing rain, head bent against the wind. He kept a firm hold on Amanda's arm, steadying himself with each roll of the waves, all the while cautioning her to watch her footing. She walked beside him dutifully, thinking how clever he was to go around saving bankrupt newspapers and making so much money that losing millions didn't even faze him. Now *that* could be even more exciting than reporting!

When they had made one complete revolution, much to her relief he abruptly ducked inside. Shaking the water from his clothing, Blethen led the way into the saloon, inviting Amanda to follow. She was amused to notice that it was much more crowded than the dining room. Blethen hailed a few acquaintances, then marched directly to the only empty table in the room, which appeared to be reserved for him.

He ordered a whiskey for himself and a sherry for Amanda, which he explained was a good tonic.

If only Mother could see where my chaperone has brought me! Amanda smiled to herself.

"Your mother is a fine woman." Blethen seemed to be able to pick up her thoughts. "I read of her exploits in the Indian Territory when she served as a circuit court judge, long before you were born, of course. But I didn't have a chance to meet her until after she had married your father."

Amanda thought she detected a hint of regret. She wondered how long it had been since Blethen had last seen her mother, or if he knew that her father had died.

"Felt terrible when I heard that Lucius Lamar had passed from this world. What a great shock. He never seemed as old as he actually was. Carried himself like a man half his age. And a splendid senator, too. What a loss that was, for everyone."

Amanda nodded. The memory of her father was fading, sketchy. Yet, he had been dead only three years. Perhaps without realizing it, she had put him from her mind, blaming him for her years in confinement at Cedar Ridge. Had he lived, she could have talked him out of it. But no. He had died at just the wrong time.

"Your mother tells me that Joe Pulitzer at the New York *World* has taken you under his wing and is sure he's found in you another Nellie Bly. Is that true?" he asked with a twinkle.

There was Nellie Bly again. Although there were other female reporters, few had made the impact of that adventurous lady, whose round-the-world trek in seventy-two days had kept the papers enlivened with incredible reports. But though the *World* had financed the expedition of Nellie Bly, they had not seen fit to finance the expedition of Amanda Lamar. Her assignment was strictly on a trial basis. Which meant that she had to prove herself the first time out, otherwise she would not be given another chance.

"I don't know what Mr. Pulitzer thinks of me," she admitted. "All I know is, the *World* accepted the first article I ever wrote. It was about the future, and it was called 'No One Knows Where.' "

Blethen nodded. "Your mother told me. Alas, I missed the article, but I hear it caused quite a stir."

"Well, it stirred up the nuns at Cedar Ridge. They expelled me!"

Blethen reared back and laughed. "That's the kind of spunk it takes! If you expect to amount to anything, you have to be the type to get kicked out of school and fired from a job, at least once, each!"

Amanda laughed with him.

"Now just what kind of heresy did you preach that the good sisters found so scandalizing?" Blethen asked.

"I only said that religion as an institution was outdated, and that from my observation as a student, cloistered orders in particular were out of step with the times. But they took it personally. They called it an exposé."

"Was it?"

"Gosh, no! I didn't mention anybody by name. All I said was that no one knows where the twentieth century will take us, and that we must be prepared to change. But they were mainly upset because it appeared in the *World,* which they said was a paper that shouldn't be found in any Catholic home. And we're not even Catholics! I mean, only my father was."

"You took on a formidable opponent," Blethen said seriously.

Amanda's eyes narrowed. "Do you think I was wrong?"

"It's never wrong to tell the truth. But don't expect the whole world to love you for it." Blethen smiled. "I daresay you hit home, otherwise they wouldn't have been so upset. How did your mother take it?"

"She stood up for me, but she was hurt." Amanda hesitated, trying to decide how much she should tell him. Only Blethen's lively interest prompted her to continue. "She was hurt because they wouldn't allow me to graduate. I can never go to college."

"Oh well, is that all?" Blethen tossed the matter aside, as if it was of small importance. "Seems to me you're getting an education nonetheless."

The drinks were served and Blethen raised his glass to touch Amanda's. "Here's to the world—not the newspaper, but *your* world!"

"And to yours!" Amanda took a long sip of sherry, then found the courage to ask, "Colonel Blethen, do you ever write things that get you into trouble?"

"Every chance I get," he replied promptly.

She laughed, then tipping up her glass, finished her drink in one swallow. She could feel the heat creeping into her cheeks. "Did you see those mill hands yesterday?" she asked suddenly.

"No, I'm afraid I was the last to board, as usual. But I heard about them." He shook his head. "Rotten mess. It's all the fault of the unions, using those poor fellows to gain sympathy for their strike."

"You're against the unions?"

"Depends. When the mills go union, prices go up. That means *paper* goes up. Very bad for the newspaper business."

"I see." Amanda stared at her empty glass, suddenly confused.

Blethen sensed her disappointment. "It's hard to be a reporter and also be an idealist," he said gently. "When I was your age I thought I could change the world. Then I realized that I, too, had to survive and sometimes those interests conflicted. Now I feel grateful for each small victory. Oh, I'm not afraid to speak out—I just don't crusade any more. My expectations aren't as great as they used to be."

Amanda watched as Blethen downed his whiskey in a single gulp. Here we sit, she thought, getting drunk at ten o'clock in the morning! The sherry had soothed her insides, so that she could no longer recall the mill hands so distinctly. It was a great relief, for she didn't want to think about them any more. It was a moment or so before she realized that Colonel Blethen was speaking again.

"The important thing is that old Joe Pulitzer has given you a chance. He's got all my respect, even though we don't always see eye to eye."

Amanda smiled, but she felt a slight flutter in her stomach. If Mr. Pulitzer didn't like her story, her career would be at an end before it really began.

"He's no genius as a writer," Blethen went on, "but he knows how to inspire others, like yourself. He believes that young people bring in fresh ideas." Blethen stopped abruptly and leaned across the table. "May I offer you some sage advice on how to survive in this game?"

"I wish you would!" Amanda moved forward in her chair.

"Competition among reporters is very fierce out here in the Northwest. This is new country. Everybody wants to get a foot in the door." He lowered his voice. "Remember, you may not be the only one writing for the *World*. Many of these fellows on this ship are on their own, so to speak. They're not lucky enough to have an assignment like you do. So work fast. Don't let 'em beat you out."

Amanda nodded solemnly. The effects of the sherry seemed suddenly to have worn off.

"And another thing. Don't think too much about those poor fish with their chewed-up limbs. Nobody forces them to work in the mills —and that's the nature of the business. The labor problems in the Northwest are of interest only to the folks right here, not to people back in New York City."

"You think I shouldn't write about it?" she asked, incredulous.

"Exactly. Stick to the issue at hand. If you were sent to cover the Chinese immigration, then cover that. Don't get sidetracked. Otherwise, these boys will beat you to it."

Amanda opened her mouth to argue, then stopped. Colonel Blethen was clearly set in his ways and no doubt too old to change. She could listen to his opinion, but she didn't have to obey him.

Blethen signaled the waiter to bring another round.

"No more for me," said Amanda, pushing back her chair. "But thanks all the same—especially for the advice."

Blethen also rose. "Wait, don't run off. It's time you met your competition head on!" He gestured to a group standing at the bar. They pounced on the invitation and came over immediately, surrounding the table.

"Gentlemen, may I present Miss Lamar of the New York *World*." He went on to rattle off a half dozen names which Amanda promptly forgot, then excused himself to go take a nap.

"We wondered who you were," one of the reporters confessed as they shook hands. "Welcome to the fraternity of lunatics."

Amanda felt flattered. Maybe they weren't merely interested in staring through her clothing, maybe she could be accepted as one of them!

In the background she could hear Blethen's booming voice offering opinions as he walked out. "You cannot have a good town without a good newspaper. And with a genuine up-to-date paper, a town like Seattle cannot for long remain obscure." As he rounded the corner the rest of his words were lost.

By late afternoon the seas had grown rough, the rain had stopped, and the decks were glazed with a fine penetrating mist. Those who had eaten lunch now rushed to the railings or staggered against the bulkheads with green faces, unable to smile, but trying to pretend that nothing was wrong. Amanda lost her fellow reporters one by one as they fled for refuge, until finally she found herself alone at the fore end, defying the wind and thrilling to every swell.

Suddenly she heard a shrill whistle. Turning, she spotted Tom Maynard leaning over the railing of the deck above, and waving wildly. As soon as she waved back, he rushed down to join her.

"Where have you been?" she asked. "I thought you had fallen overboard."

"I'm afraid I had a slight touch of *'mal de mer,'*" he admitted, looking sheepish. "But I'm fine now. How about you?"

"I feel wonderful. I just *love* this storm!"

"You *look* wonderful," he said. Then he hastened to add, "I mean, you look awfully healthy."

They smiled at each other for a moment, both trying to think of what to say next.

Finally Amanda said, "Do you realize this is the first time we've met that we haven't been in the midst of a crisis?"

Tom's eyes grew round, magnified behind his glasses. "By George, you're right!"

Amanda suddenly noticed that his eyes were green. He seemed to be studying her intently, and she wondered whether his interest was due to *her,* or merely to faulty vision.

"Incidentally, that's a very nice white dress you're wearing."

Amanda glanced down in surprise. "Thanks! I was afraid the rain had made it shrink."

"Not at all—you look just like a bride!" Tom stopped in sudden embarrassment.

"Well, I'm glad you like it. Anyway, I don't have much choice. I brought all the wrong clothes because nobody told me what the weather was going to be like." She could tell from the way Tom looked at her that no explanation was needed.

"Guess what?" he said. "We're going to be mess mates!"

"We are? What about Colonel Blethen?"

"He's sick as a dog," Tom replied cheerfully. "I ran into him as he was rushing to his cabin. He asked me to take his place at the table tonight because he knew he wouldn't make it. Poor old geezer!"

"Are you a friend of his?"

"*Everybody* is. He's the grand old man of the newspaper business. Always good for a free piece of advice."

"I know. I just got an ample dose. He told me not to write anything about the mill or those accident victims. What do you think of that?"

"I guess he figures, like I do, that nobody's really interested in union news. The big story is the Chinese."

"Well, it was interesting to *me*. In fact, I can't stop thinking about it."

"Listen, we're only reporters—it's not our job to take sides."

"That's the problem—I just can't look at it that way. How can I forget about what happened last night?"

"Don't worry, it turned out to be nothing. We fired at the fishing boat, and they ran. That's all there was to it. Look, those union fellows only wanted to delay us—to show their power. They were hoping that our crew would go out in sympathy. But it didn't work."

"What do you think will come of all this?"

"I wish I knew. But let's not talk about strikes or workers any more," he said abruptly. He offered his arm. "Come on, as long as I have to keep my eye on you, let's go for a walk."

Over the next day and a half, Amanda learned a great deal about the strange new country which lay ahead, with Tom as a willing tutor; and she also learned a great deal about Tom himself. Although she tried to explain that she would be in Seattle only long enough to write about the arrival of the Chinese, he seemed determined to sell her on the merits of the town as a fine place to live.

"My grandfather was one of the founders," he admitted as they hiked around the deck. "Doc Maynard was quite a fellow. He drank too much and he lived with two wives at the same time. But he built a hospital and created a city out of the wilderness. So I think his shortcomings can be overlooked."

They both laughed.

"Do you take after him?" she teased.

"My folks are afraid I might inherit his shortcomings, not his good qualities! They keep after me to choose a profession and settle down."

"What's wrong with that?"

"Plenty! Here I am, twenty-two years old, with four years of college behind me, and I've never done one single thing that *I* wanted to do." He stopped, then asked cautiously, "How old are *you?*"

"How old do I look?"

"Twenty?"

"Good guess."

"I knew it. I'm attracted to women more than girls."

"Even journalists?"

"Especially journalists."

"I'm glad we're in the same profession so that we have something in common."

"I'd like any profession but being a doctor. I want people to know me for myself, not because I'm somebody's grandson."

"I know. It's an awful burden. Only in my case, it's my mother who's famous. And much as I love her, I can't go through life known only as the daughter of Temperance Smith. That's why I like the newspaper business—because I'm the first one in my family to take it up. It was either that or going on the stage."

"You *should* be on the stage—you'd give competition to Lillian Russell!"

"Shame on you!" she chided, amused that Tom had made himself blush. Then, she asked quickly, "What paper are you with?"

"None. I'm just free-lancing. The old man calls it indecision."

"Never mind. I'll bet that after you write the Chinese story, your family will be very proud of you. Especially if it's printed in your hometown paper."

"Not them. They expect my education to pay off big dividends. They've *invested* in me, as I'm constantly being reminded."

Amanda shook her head in sympathy. "Maybe you need to get away from home for a while. Like me. The way I see it, you have to please yourself before you can please anybody else."

Tom reflected seriously. "That's very good advice." He gave her a significant look. "You know what would please me most right now?"

Amanda didn't answer. But she could guess.

Taking her by the shoulders, Tom steered her back against the bulkhead, safely out of view of the upper deck. "You're going to change my whole life," he announced with determination. "In fact, you already have." He took off his glasses impatiently, as though he were ridding himself of a barrier which prevented him from getting as close to her as he wanted.

His owlish look was gone. He hesitated, summoning the courage to kiss her, yet fearing rejection.

"You have nice eyes," she said, encouraging him. "Green is my favorite color."

Chapter Two

IT WAS early morning when the passengers of *The Puget Queen* were awakened to four sharp blasts—the signal that they were approaching another ship.

Amanda hurried with the others up on deck, arriving just as they crossed the turbulent crust of white water marking the confluence of the Pacific with the Strait of Juan de Fuca. The ocean was behind them now as they passed between the thickly forested shore lines of Vancouver Island on the port side, and the Olympic Peninsula on the starboard. And there in the distance, dead ahead, was the immigrant ship, the formidable *George Elder,* many times the size of a coastal steamer, but proceeding at a slower rate of speed. *The Puget Queen* rolled in the wake of the larger vessel, gradually gaining on her.

As Amanda shaded her eyes against the sun, she noticed the massive stands of timber gliding by, impenetrable behind a barrier of driftwood which lay strewn in grotesque formations, like the bleached skeletons of prehistoric monsters.

"Good morning!" Tom's eager voice rang out behind her.

As soon as she turned around, he gave her an enthusiastic appraisal. "You look—wonderful!"

"Same outfit as yesterday," she replied cheerfully, making room for him at the railing.

He seemed confident, possessive, standing as close to her as possible, his hand resting lightly on her shoulder. "See anything yet?" he asked, his lips almost brushing her ear. But clearly his attention was only on *her.*

When *The Puget Queen* came abreast of the *George Elder,* instead of passing, she slowed in order to match speed. The immigrants silently massed at the railings. The Americans, appearing motley in their varied independent styles of dress, returned the curious stares of pig-tailed Chinese, timeless in their ancestral costume, wearing identical square hats and blue quilted mandarin jackets. The two sides confronted each other like players in a game, waiting for their opponents to make the first move. Inevitably the spell was broken by a dozen or so exuberant Americans who spontaneously decided to attempt communication, imagining that if they shouted loudly enough and gestured wildly enough, they could somehow make themselves understood. A few Chinese waved back. Most seemed puzzled, uncertain.

One eager man, hoping to immortalize the moment for the folks at home, scrambled to set up his camera and tripod. But his effort seemed doomed to failure, for with each roll of the ship, the camera would go out of focus. He did not, however, abandon the attempt. "Better a blurred Chinaman than none at all," he insisted with good humor.

Binoculars were passed around and Amanda took her turn. It seemed like a rude thing to do, but she couldn't resist the chance for a closer view. Slowly she traveled from one immobile face to the next.

Her first impression was disturbing. All she could think of was that they looked like prisoners. She hoped they were not fleeing one situation of hardship only to encounter another. She passed the binoculars to Tom, feeling suddenly guilty, as if she were spying through a window into the private domain of captives who were denied the privilege of looking back.

"What do you think's going to happen to them?" she asked.

"All I know is, back in '86 a boatload of Chinese landed in Seattle and were practically torn apart in a riot. I was only twelve at the time, but I've never forgotten it."

"How terrible! I hope it won't happen this time."

"It could be worse. A lot of anti-Chinese feeling has built up over the years."

"But why? I always thought Orientals were very industrious. We should be happy to have them."

"That's just the problem. They're willing to work for low wages.

Factories and mills won't hire union men as long as they can get plenty of cheap labor."

"So that's why the unions are having such a time of it!"

"And another reason why the Chinese aren't welcome is that they're too frugal. They save every dollar to buy property. Everybody's getting nervous seeing them buying up all the land. They're afraid they'll take over."

"Condemning them for working hard and saving money? I thought that's what people were supposed to do."

"It's because of the depression. Nobody wants to make room for newcomers."

"Do you think the Chinese will take jobs away from those poor mill hands with the amputated arms?"

"Not a chance, because the mill hands can't ever work again anyway. All they want are their pensions. But that's not *our* problem. Why are we being so serious?"

Amanda turned away from the railing. "It's hard to know who to feel sorry for, isn't it?"

A modest skyline of buildings materialized in the distance and grew larger, as the ship sailed past Duwamish Head and into Elliott Bay. The town appeared new, Tom explained, because most of the structures had been built since '89 when fire had destroyed the entire business district.

"We've got five thousand people living here," he said. "And more arriving every day." He spoke as if Seattle were destined to survive no matter what, thriving on its own ashes.

Then quite unexpectedly, the last ridge of clouds vanished, revealing the deeply grooved cone of a solitary mountain floating above the town, its frosted tip pink in the morning sun. Surely it was a mirage, Amanda thought, for no mountain she had ever seen was as high as this one. Or as perfectly formed.

"Yes, she's real," said Tom, enjoying her amazement. "That, Miss Lamar, is the wondrous sight of Mount Tacoma. But she's very temperamental. She only makes an appearance when it suits her." He paused to give Amanda a sidelong glance. "Not like you, I hope."

"How do you know she's a lady?"

"Because she's beautiful. And always just out of reach."

Amanda smiled. "I think she belongs to another world."

"This *is* another world," he said, taking her arm. "Better collect your things and wait for me on the dock." Then he added gravely, "And don't speak to any strange men!"

As soon as *The Puget Queen* cut her engines, the staccato chant of human voices could be heard. In her cabin Amanda hurried to tighten the straps of her trunk, her fingers clumsy with excitement. The deck shuddered for the last time as the ship groaned against the pier. Amanda left her trunk with the baggageman and rushed to join the crush of bodies jamming the companionway.

"Miss Lamar!"

Turning, Amanda spotted Colonel Blethen struggling toward her through the crowd. He smiled weakly, still looking queasy.

"No sooner do I get my sea legs than we're put ashore!" He tried to joke, then quickly added, "Have you arranged for a place to stay in Seattle?"

Amanda hesitated, wondering how she could escape without offending him. "Yes, with friends," she said unconvincingly.

"Ah, then you *do* have friends here. Good." He smiled, accepting her excuse. "I was going to recommend either the Washington or the Denny hotels. So if you change your mind, they're both good places to stay. I go to the Washington myself," he added.

Amanda thanked him for his advice and promised to convey his regards to her mother. They shook hands.

"If you ever need anything, you can always find me at the *Press-Times,*" he said.

As the crowd swept her away from him, he called out a final warning, "Mind that mob out there!"

Amanda braced herself, then started down the gangplank. Her shipmates forged ahead, eager to get ashore, for the *George Elder* was just behind them, due to dock within minutes. But no one was prepared for the reception they received from the workingmen, who converged on them with shouts and threats as if they thought the reporters were somehow to blame for the arrival of the Chinese. They chanted:

> "I'd rather be a snake by far
> Than a dirty scab like the Chinamen are!"

Many waved signs which bore hostile slogans. "Go home, John" was the most common, accompanied by crudely drawn slant-eyed faces with enormous buck teeth. Other messages were more brutal: "Rat-eaters go home," "Yellow rascals get out" and "No more scurvy opium fiends."

Amanda clutched her notebook and stared, hardly able to believe what she was seeing. Swiftly her eyes swept the crowd, hoping to catch sight of Tom, but the density of bodies, the enormous placards bobbing, the movement and confusion, all conspired to block her view, making the task of locating a familiar face seem hopeless. Nonetheless, she managed to squeeze through, dodging signs as she made her way toward the adjoining pier. Suddenly, she felt a hand on her shoulder, and turning around with an expectant smile, she found herself facing a tall, gaunt man wearing clerical garb and carrying an armful of banners with greetings printed in both English and Chinese: "Welcome to our Brothers from China." Before she knew what was happening, he thrust one of the banners into her hand.

"God bless you," said the minister with a smile, and moved off in search of another willing supporter. However, he had not taken more than a few steps when Amanda saw a burly worker seize the minister from behind, spin him around and strike him on the jaw. She heard a sickening crack as the fist connected, and saw the minister sink to his knees, eyes rolling into unconsciousness.

The worker dusted his hands in satisfaction and looked about for other prey. Amanda saw him start toward her, but before she could summon the spurt of energy needed for escape, his beefy hand clamped onto her wrist, while another hand wrenched the banner from her grasp.

"Goddam do-gooder!" he sputtered.

"Me? A do-gooder?" she echoed with wide-eyed innocence. "I'm a reporter."

The worker squinted suspiciously. "That so? Well, you better get the story straight. Them chattering round-mouthed lepers will take over every job in this country if we don't stop them! Got that?"

Amanda inspected the grimy finger he was shaking in her face. "You seem to be carrying the dirt of an honest day's labor. So what do *you* have to worry about?"

"A cut in wages, that's what. If I kick up a fuss, I'll get myself fired 'cause the boss knows that a goddam Chinaman will work longer hours for less money, and do all the dirty work. And they'll even scab when we're out on strike."

"Don't you have a union?"

The worker spat, then dragged a filthy sleeve across his chin. "What good's a union if they can't get us a fair wage? The higher-ups in this town are trying to run the unions out. Sure they want the ching-chongs to stay—cheap labor built this town. *Slave* labor!" He leaned close, breathing contempt in her face.

"Why harm the Chinese? They aren't to blame."

"No harm will come if that opium barge turns right around and goes back where it come from. We got enough slant-eyes here already."

A hollow blast from the *George Elder* ended the discussion, as Amanda felt the dock sway on its pilings with the shifting of the crowd to the next pier.

When the gangplank was finally lowered, a small number of police locked arms to prevent the workers from rushing aboard, while the terrified immigrants huddled on deck.

At that moment, Amanda noticed two nurses squeezing their way toward the gangplank of the *George Elder*. The workers grudgingly let them through, resenting the fact that they had special privilege. On sudden impulse, she hurried to catch up with them. But just before she reached them, policemen suddenly surrounded the nurses to provide escort.

"Please let me through. I'm with them," Amanda told one of the officers.

"You're a nurse? Go then," he ordered, impatient to get the women safely aboard the immigrant ship before more trouble erupted.

The nurses hurried up the gangplank, unaware that they had been joined by Amanda. The officer of the deck was waiting to greet them. It all happened so fast that Amanda had no chance to think what she would do once aboard. Her mind raced with explanations to account for her presence, but when her turn came, the officer shook her hand with a brisk sense of urgency, motioning for her to follow the others.

He hurried them to the mess hall, which he said could be used to conduct the examinations.

"I'll get the men lined up and return directly," he said, and went out, shutting the door behind him.

The nurses turned around, noticing Amanda for the first time. They exchanged puzzled glances.

"I'm a reporter," Amanda explained quickly, "but I'll be glad to assist if you'll let me stay."

"As long as Officer Crowley knows you're here, it's all right with us," said the younger of the two, looking to her colleague for approval.

However, the older nurse immediately asserted her position. "If we find any contagious disease, this ship will be quarantined. That means you, as well as the immigrants."

"For how long?" Amanda asked in alarm.

"Until the danger is past. Three to six weeks."

"What are the chances?"

The older one managed a thin smile. "You probably don't need to worry. We hardly ever examine anyone on these immigrant ships who's really ill."

"You don't? I'd think that with so many passengers there are bound to be *some* diseases."

"If they're desperately sick," the younger one said, "they usually die before they get to us."

Her companion gave her a sharp look, then turned to Amanda suspiciously. "Why are you interested in the health of these Chinese? Are you conducting an investigation?"

"Oh no, just curious."

"I see." The older one nodded primly. "Well, if you need our names, I'm Miss Bracken and this is my assistant, Miss Lovejoy."

Amanda introduced herself, then added confidentially, "I would just as soon the patients think that I'm a nurse, too. This way they won't object to my being here."

Miss Bracken's eyes narrowed. "I'm surprised you were given permission to come aboard. If there's anyone the officers like to avoid, it's reporters."

"Why is that?"

Miss Bracken's enigmatic smile spoke for her as she busied herself with the contents of her medical bag. "Why don't you ask Officer Crowley?"

"I'd much prefer that *you* tell me," said Amanda. "I have a strong belief that women should stick together whenever possible."

Miss Lovejoy smiled. "Are you a suffragette?"

"Heavens, yes! I think we should have the same rights as men, don't you?"

Both nurses looked at Amanda quizzically, but said nothing. They seemed to be reflecting on her words, as though such an idea had never really occurred to them.

The examinations progressed briskly. The immigrants filed in one entrance and out the other. Most of them received no more than a close scrutiny from Miss Bracken. Only those suffering from colds were examined more thoroughly. Amanda assisted Miss Lovejoy in segregating them from the others, a task accomplished by the use of sign language. She noticed that Officer Crowley seemed anxious that the procedure be over as quickly as possible, hurrying the men along with a forceful hand. They obeyed without question, only because it was apparent that none of them understood English. Nor did Crowley speak a word of Chinese.

"Is there an interpreter aboard?" Amanda asked him.

"Not necessary," he replied tersely. "They're in America now. They can speak English like the rest of us."

"It won't be easy for them."

"Easy? Why should it be? The kind of work they do, it won't matter whether they learn or not. In fact, it's better if they don't. This way they won't be getting any big ideas."

From then on, Amanda made a special point of smiling and speaking to each immigrant. Even though she knew they didn't understand, she felt that a calming tone of voice might ease their anxieties.

"Welcome to America. This won't hurt a bit," she repeated to each one in a friendly manner. "Thank you."

Miss Lovejoy snickered and glanced at Miss Bracken, who rolled her eyes heavenward.

Then unexpectedly, a bright young Chinese face smiled back at Amanda. "Welcome to America," he repeated after her with a heavy accent.

She couldn't be sure if he really understood the meaning of the words, or whether he was merely mimicking. But she kept her eye on him and after he had filed out, she slipped out also. She called to him as he started down the companionway, and he turned around. Amanda felt a surge of excitement. He understood!

"Only a few words," he admitted bashfully when she asked him if he could speak English.

Not caring to know how he had even managed to learn any words at all, she rushed her questions, fearing that at any moment they would be interrupted.

"Was everything all right on the voyage?"

He shrugged, smiling. "I'm fine," he said at last.

"Then nothing happened? It was a good trip?"

There was a long pause in which it seemed he wasn't going to answer. Finally he replied, "Some men sick."

Amanda nodded, understanding. "Seasick?"

"Sick with fever. In bed. Maybe die."

Amanda frowned. "How many are sick?"

He held up six fingers.

"Where are they?" she asked. "Can you show me where to find them?"

The boy brightened, nodding vigorously. He motioned for Amanda to follow him.

"Miss Lamar!"

Amanda froze. It was Miss Bracken's voice. She turned around reluctantly. Damn! What bad timing!

"Officer Crowley's looking for you," she said in a tone of reprimand.

It was a moment for quick decision. Amanda put a finger to her lips and gestured for Miss Bracken to come closer. She would have to take the nurse into her confidence. Hurriedly Amanda told her what she had just learned, watching her expression change.

"Yellow fever!" Miss Bracken pronounced without hesitation.

"Didn't Officer Crowley tell you about it?" asked Amanda astounded.

"Good God, no! That's the last thing he'd do! Don't you realize that if the ship is quarantined, they'll lose weeks of time and money? How could they run at a profit if they have to sit here in the harbor feeding a thousand men for days on end? Why, if every ship carrying yellow fever was quarantined, immigration to America would come to a dead halt."

"What are you going to do now?"

"Nothing," she replied flatly. "It's not my concern."

"Can't you tell the health department or your boss?"

"And lose my job?" Miss Bracken laughed dryly. "My boss knows what's going on. He's paid to know—and do nothing."

"Ladies! We're waiting!"

Both women turned at the sound of Crowley's sharp tone.

"This is no time to be gossiping. You're not finished yet!"

"We'll be right there," said Miss Bracken in an unhurried voice. Crowley looked from one to the other warily. "Any problem?"

"None at all," said Amanda.

As soon as he had marched away, Miss Bracken gave Amanda a sly smile. "It was smart of you not to say anything." She paused. "And you can count on me not to tell him that you're a reporter."

Amanda smiled in return. A very clever lady, she thought.

"It's easier for women to let men think that we know nothing," Miss Bracken continued in a confidential tone. "If we keep their secrets, we can survive. But if we make trouble, they'll destroy us. Why do you think these Chinese survive? Because they're like us. They know what's going on, but they keep to themselves and never raise a fuss. That's why it's best you don't write about this. Just forget it ever happened."

"I'm afraid I can't do that. It's my job to speak out."

Miss Bracken shook her head regretfully. "I'm sorry I told you so much. Now you're going to get us all into trouble."

Amanda looked at her with sudden comprehension. "You know something? I don't believe you're sorry at all. I think you revealed exactly what you wanted me to know!"

"Maybe I did," she admitted with surprising frankness. "Maybe my conscience troubles me."

"Then I'll make you a promise—I won't use your name or tell where I got my information. Fair enough?"

"I'd be very grateful." Miss Bracken held out her hand.

Amanda clasped it warmly. "You're my first friend in Seattle," she confessed in a rush of emotion. "I can't tell you how glad I am that we met!"

The demonstration had lost momentum and the crowd was thinning out. Only a few die-hards seemed willing to wait out the time it would take for the immigrants to be processed and brought ashore.

Amanda looked about the pier for Tom Maynard, but he was nowhere to be seen. Kiss and run, she thought in disappointment. How typical. She was thankful that she hadn't invited him into her cabin.

As she searched for her trunk, the musty perfume of the Orient mingling with the sweat of American overalls and flannel shirts lingered in her nostrils and clung to her clothing. She had no idea where her trunk had been deposited, and as she stood for the first time alone in strange surroundings, she felt a great wave of homesickness sweep over her. This was the adventure she had craved—why then should she long for a familiar face?

At last, in the doorway of the steamship offices, she found her trunk being used as a bench by several men who had evidently grown weary of foot stomping. Enduring their whistles and suggestive remarks, she claimed her trunk and dragged it along by one handle until she reached the street. She hailed the first carriage she spotted— a sedate black omnibus with gold letters advertising "Denny Hotel"— then waited her turn while the driver helped several well-dressed couples with their luggage.

"The only place left is next to me up front," the driver told her when the other passengers were seated.

"That's fine," Amanda assured him quickly, glad for a chance to ride outside for her first view of the city.

Suddenly a man rushed up. "Room for one more?" he asked, breathless. Amanda recognized him as a passenger from *The Puget Queen*. They exchanged smiles. The driver hesitated.

"You're not a reporter, are you?"

"Why, yes," he admitted in surprise.

"Sorry." The driver shook his head. "The Denny doesn't take reporters."

The reporter glanced at Amanda questioningly, but said nothing. He merely shrugged and turned away. Amanda could feel the color creeping into her cheeks. But she, too, remained silent. The driver shook his head. "Riff-raff," he muttered. "They're all over the place."

Amanda stared straight ahead, thinking how easily men could be deceived.

As they rode along, Amanda noticed that the town no longer looked as modest as it had from the harbor, for traffic was heavy with conveyances of every description, but mostly with delivery wagons loaded with lumber and coal.

The carriage traveled up Yesler Way, which appeared to be the heart of the business district, crossed Pioneer Square, a grassy triangle marked by a totem pole, then headed north along First Avenue. There were buildings of brick and stone, many five stories high, all constructed since the fire of '89, and looking as if they could withstand any future disaster that might occur. Perhaps Seattle was not such a small town after all. Office buildings crowded smaller shops—furniture and cabinet makers, groceries, laundries, dressmakers, machine shops, meat and fish merchants, and rooming houses. Amanda even spotted a cigar maker and a clothing factory. She also noted that the women who hurried along the boardwalks with their shopping bundles still wore dust ruffles around their hems—real frontier women, Amanda thought. Practical and down to earth.

The outer limits of downtown—five blocks in length—were marked by an abrupt end to the cobblestones. From that point on, private houses began to appear, each with a cow tethered in the yard, and all connected by a network of wide graded roads. The carriage made a sudden turn and began to climb a hill so steep that the horses strained under the load, but their footing was sure and they avoided every rut and boulder.

"Denny Hill," the driver announced as they ascended.

When they had almost reached the summit, Amanda turned in her seat to find the entire town and harbor in miniature far below. The clatter of traffic could no longer be heard, nor the whining of saws slicing wood, nor even the hum of humanity.

The driver pointed ahead. "There she is."

They had reached a plateau of sawed-off stumps and wild grasses, brambles and blossoming vines. The only building in sight was a gingerbread mansion which rode the crest of the hill with all the majesty of a sailing ship, her verandas encircling her like decks.

This is not for me, Amanda thought. This hotel belongs to the past. It *looks* like the kind of place that would discriminate against reporters, and Lord knows who else. But much as she longed to flee to the heart of town, where it was lively, violent and making history, she decided it would be more satisfying to break the rules. I'll prove that a reporter can stay at the Denny, and if they wish to put me out, they first must discover who I am.

Chapter Three

AMANDA registered at the Denny without incident, her notebook defiantly in full view, giving her occupation as student. Then, not wishing to waste a moment, she took the carriage back downtown on its return trip.

As soon as they reached the waterfront, she headed toward the pier where the *George Elder* was berthed, only to discover the gates locked with chains and a sign posted, "By Order of the Police Department."

Through the bars she could see the Chinese still on board, shuffling around the decks, probably wondering why they were being imprisoned on the shore of a free country. But the last of the workingmen were gone. A few reporters stopped to peer through the gates, then sauntered across the street to the Green Parrot Saloon to wait out the crisis. She declined an invitation to join them, afraid of missing out on the crucial moment.

"Move on there!"

Amanda jumped at the sound of a gruff voice behind her, but stood her ground as she turned to see a policeman strolling toward her swinging his club.

"Why is it locked?" she asked.

"These Chinamen are under police protection."

"Aren't they coming ashore?"

"Don't know. But if I had my way, I'd send 'em back where they come from. Now move along."

Amanda took her time. "Which way is Chinatown?" she asked.

He pointed the direction, disdaining a reply.

As Amanda set off on foot, she could feel him watching her all the way to the corner. He probably thinks I'm crazy, she thought. But how else can I find out how the Chinese feel about all this?

Chinatown began at First Avenue and rambled up both sides of Jackson Street, sprouting off into a maze of side streets and alleys. Dismal little shops with cramped living quarters either in back or above were clustered together within the boundaries of the enclave.

Amanda soon realized that she was traveling unexplored territory, a place where white folks didn't go. It seemed strange to be in the minority, to be the intruder. Yet, every time she turned a corner, she expected to find some of her colleagues there ahead of her, all having the same idea—to find out what the established Orientals thought about the new immigrants.

Smiling, she tried approaching the merchants who were standing in front of their stores, but her overtures were met with blank stares, and after several unsuccessful attempts, she realized that nobody spoke English. Was it only her imagination, or were the streets suddenly emptying?

Her footsteps echoed on the deserted boardwalks. She could almost feel unseen eyes watching her. Yet, she was too fascinated to retreat. Narrow storefronts papered with signs displaying oriental characters offered their products only to other Chinese. And in between the groceries, cafés, laundries and dry goods was an occasional mysterious window containing an assortment of herbs, charms and bottled concoctions, suggesting that medical assistance was available within. To Amanda, the Chinese seemed self-contained, a threat to no one. From open doorways she could hear rapid, excited conversation, and the clinking of pots and pans. Exotic aromas trailed her in the street, a reminder of the invisible barrier which existed between the outsiders and the people who lived here.

Suddenly a shrill cry pierced the air, then the sound of running footsteps and shouting; it seemed to be coming from the dark recesses of a narrow alley. Were they children's voices? Amanda gathered her skirts and ran toward the sounds. Just as she turned into the alley, a small body hurtled against her, knocking both of them to the ground. The impact left Amanda gasping for breath, but as she struggled to her feet, she saw that the child was a Chinese girl about eight years old, surprisingly slender to have hit with such tremendous force. The girl didn't apologize, but clung to Amanda in terror. Just behind her four boys emerged, older by several years—and white. They were armed with mud balls and slingshots, but they stopped short when they saw Amanda and pretended nonchalance.

Amanda's immediate concern was for the child. "Are you hurt?" she asked with gestures, hoping to make herself understood.

The girl had been pelted with mud. It was in her hair, on her dress and even on her face, indicating that she had turned on her assailants, attempting to defend herself.

"They put stones in the mud!" she blurted through tears. "And they got my dress dirty!"

"You speak English!" Quickly Amanda took out a handkerchief and began to rub at the stains.

The boys attempted to pass, watching Amanda warily.

"Why did you do this?" she demanded.

But as soon as they saw that they weren't going to be pursued, they skipped off singing: "Ching chong Chinamen, march along in rows, ching chong Chinamen, wash the dirty clothes!"

"Where do those boys come from?" Amanda asked the girl.

"They're truants," she replied, staring after them tearfully. "They come here when they're supposed to be in school."

Amanda shook her head in sympathy. "It's good that you're such a fast runner."

The child smiled shyly, revealing missing teeth. "If there was only one I could whip him, but not four!"

"My name is Amanda. What's yours?"

"Soo-Lee." Then she asked, "Are you a truant officer?"

"No, just a visitor."

Soo-Lee was visibly relieved.

"Would you like me to walk you home?"

Soo-Lee nodded eagerly.

As they walked, Amanda asked her if she had learned English in school. But the child replied that she had never gone to school—not because of poverty, she explained, but because her parents were afraid to send her. She had learned English when they had lived for a brief period on a farm in eastern Washington while her father picked apples. Playing with the children of the white pickers had been her only exposure to Caucasians or to the English language.

Soo-Lee's mother hid behind a curtain which separated their dark cluttered grocery store from the living quarters in back.

"Wait here," Soo-Lee told Amanda, and disappeared behind the curtain.

Several minutes passed during which Amanda could hear the mother's frantic, high-pitched voice questioning her child. Her heart ached with the thought of the terror in which they lived, where persecution was an unavoidable fact of life routinely inflicted upon them. It was understandable that they would cloister themselves and feel suspicious of strangers. Soo-Lee's mother finally emerged smiling, and as she stepped out from behind the counter, she bowed low. Soo-Lee begged to pour tea for their guest, and when her mother consented, the child was overjoyed.

Amanda was deeply touched by the gesture, for she guessed that tea-pouring was reserved only for special occasions. She and Soo-Lee's mother spoke, each in her own language, and were able to arrive at almost perfect understanding.

Finally, they lapsed into silence, and Amanda realized that she would not be able to question them without seeming rude. Soo-Lee served the tea with ritual ceremony in back of the store, while Amanda tried to imitate each motion. Watching her Amanda asked herself, How will Soo-Lee feel when she grows up? Will she be a rebel like I am, bursting to break away? Or will she continue with the old ways, like her ancestors?

As they exchanged smiles Amanda guessed that they were probably curious to know who she was.

"Soo-Lee," she ventured, "I'm going to tell you a little bit about myself, then, if you like, you can tell me a little bit about *you*."

Soo-Lee said nothing, but her eyes grew wide with anticipation.

Carefully Amanda explained that she worked for a newspaper. "I write about people in order to help them. Right now I'm writing about the people of Seattle." She didn't mention the immigrants, but encouraged Soo-Lee to talk about her family.

Soo-Lee glanced at her mother for an approving nod, then carefully began to unfold their trials with a kind of gentle innocence and detachment, like the unfurling of a tapestry upon which a story of hardship had been artfully stitched. Gradually Soo-Lee lost her shyness, explaining that her father now worked in a coal mine in Rosalyn, sending home his earnings each month so that her mother could quickly pay off the mortgage on the store. Yes, her parents wanted their children to have an education, but for the present they had to learn at home from Chinese books and from the elders, whose duty it was to keep alive their culture by passing it on to the younger generation.

While her mother excused herself to wait on customers, Soo-Lee recited the names and ages of her six brothers and sisters.

"My oldest sisters are sixteen and seventeen, but they don't live with us," she revealed matter-of-factly.

"They don't?" Amanda was surprised. It seemed odd that the family would not remain together, especially with their father away.

"They live at the Grand Union Hotel, not in Chinatown."

Amanda put down her teacup. She felt a certain uneasiness which prevented her from asking why they lived at a hotel.

"They send us money, too," Soo-Lee went on. Then she added proudly, "We're not poor, you know."

As soon as Soo-Lee's mother joined them again, Amanda decided the moment had come to risk their trust.

"I have one more question—I want to know how you feel about the new Chinese immigrants, if you welcome them, and what you think will become of them?"

She saw at once that she had gone too far. Soo-Lee's face suddenly went blank, as though she had heard nothing. Her mother's reaction was stranger still. With a sharp intake of breath, the woman turned and fled through the curtain as though she had understood.

And without a word, Soo-Lee rose and led Amanda politely to the door. Regretting immediately that she had caused them distress, Amanda turned in the doorway to apologize, but Soo-Lee had already disappeared. As Amanda walked away in frustration, she realized she *had* learned something—that silence could tell a story, too. But how do you help people who won't speak out?

Amanda returned to the Denny by streetcar, arriving so tired that her only desire was for a warm bath and bed. Convinced that she could never make the stairs, she headed for the elevator, where a middle-aged couple waited, holding the door for her.

"Aren't you the young lady who rode up in the carriage with us this morning?" the woman asked as they began a slow ascent on creaking cables.

Amanda smiled tentatively, not remembering them. The woman went on, nonetheless. "I'm Effie Clough and this is my husband, Cyrus. He's a partner with the Clough-Hartley Mill in Everett." She extended a gloved hand.

Amanda introduced herself, adding, "I'm a student."

"Oh, we already know that," said Cyrus Clough. "Entering the University of Washington this fall, am I correct?"

Amanda nodded, amused to think that the manager had been gossiping about her.

"Which steamer did you arrive on?" Mrs. Clough asked, drawing off her gloves.

"*The Puget Queen.*" The words were out before Amanda realized what she had said.

"Gracious! Wasn't that the dreadful boat that brought all those reporters? Why, you must have been the only woman aboard, poor child!"

Cyrus cleared his throat. "Well, Miss Lamar, as an educated young lady, what do you think of this Chinese business?"

"I think they have every right to be here," she replied, wondering if he suspected who she was.

"So do I," Cyrus agreed unexpectedly. "And the more the better."

The elevator vibrated to a halt and the doors opened.

"It was nice meeting you," said Amanda, stepping out. She really meant it, heartened to have found someone who felt as she did.

"We're on this floor, too," said Cyrus, as he and his wife followed her. "I don't admit to being a humanitarian," he went on, keeping pace with her down the corridor. "In business you can't afford to. But I say, let all the Chinamen come in. I'd be glad to put 'em to work in my mill. Why, I'd be the first to use Chinese labor in the entire lumber industry. You know what that would mean?"

Amanda slowed her steps. She glanced at him with sudden interest.

"It means that those Chinamen can save me enough money to build another mill! Why, I hear from friends in the construction business that those fellows can work twelve hours a day on a handful of rice and do all kinds of jobs that the white man wouldn't touch. Why, they don't have the good sense to be afraid. If one has an accident, there's a dozen more to take his place. So, goddammit, I say bring 'em on in!"

"Cyrus, don't curse," his wife pleaded, laying a hand on his arm.

"My apologies, Miss Lamar. But I know you'll forgive me for getting carried away. I've got a lot at stake here with these Chinamen. If I can put 'em into my mill, I can wipe out those damned—pardon me—ding-busted unions that are always crying to raise wages. They can call strikes all they please, but I won't have to budge an inch, 'cause I know that if the white boys walk out, the yellow will come in and work for one third what I have to pay those lazy white sons of—guns."

Cheap labor. Just like Tom had said. Suddenly it dawned on her. Cheap labor was actually a means of defeating the unions. Management wanted the Chinese, labor didn't. Excitedly she realized she had her story. She even had the headline: "BOSSES, THE REAL CULPRITS." But at that moment a vision of mutilated workers intruded in her thoughts, a disturbing reminder that the problem would not be easily resolved.

"I'm glad we're all in agreement," said Cyrus Clough amiably, and he handed her his card. "If you're ever up Everett way, stop by the mill and we'll give you a tour."

"I wish I could," Amanda replied, then bit her lip. She had almost slipped and told him that she would soon be off on a new assignment—far from Seattle and all its turmoil. In a way, it seemed too bad to have to leave just when things were getting interesting. "But who knows?" she added. "Maybe someday I *will* come up to see your mill."

When Amanda came down to the lobby the next morning, Tom Maynard was waiting.

"There you are," he said with pretended nonchalance. "It's about time."

"You found me! But how?" Amanda made no effort to conceal her delight in seeing Tom again. It was especially flattering to think that he had sought her out.

"It was easy," he lied. "I just picked the most unlikely place I could think of, and sure enough, my hunch was right." His tone became suddenly stern. "Why did you slip away from me yesterday?"

"It wasn't on purpose—didn't you see me go aboard the Chinese ship?"

"Good Lord, no! How did you manage that?"

"By pretending to be a nurse."

Tom shook his head in awe. "Why didn't *I* think of that?"

"I don't think you could have gotten away with it—for obvious reasons."

"What was it like?"

"I'll give you a tip." She glanced around, then lowered her voice. "There's yellow fever aboard."

"Yellow fever! Are you sure?"

"That's what I was told."

"So that's why the Chinese aren't coming ashore. Wonder why they haven't hoisted the quarantine flag?"

"Because they're trying to keep it quiet. What do you think we should do?"

"*I* think we should forget the whole thing and go on a picnic."

"Sounds wonderful, but don't you want to stay around the pier in case anything happens?"

"Today's Sunday—the immigration office is closed. And the gates to the pier are locked. Well, what do you say?"

"I'd love to."

"Good. We'll take the streetcar out to Lake Washington—there's a bandstand and boat rides, or we can just sprawl under the trees, or if we want to be alone, we can go into the woods . . ."

"And do what?"

"Pick berries," he answered innocently.

"Will there be any Indians?"

"Maybe. But only tame ones."

Lake Washington was a good distance from the heart of town. A single track carried them eastward through dense forest. They climbed hills, then descended into gulleys, while foliage brushed the windows. Though the streetcar was crowded with other picnickers, Amanda felt the intimacy of being alone with Tom, a willing captive of the heavy shadows which screened out the sun.

"This was a good idea of yours, Mr. Maynard," she said after they had been riding for some time in silence. "I like being off in the wilds."

"With me?" he asked, putting his arm over the back of the seat.

"*Especially* with you."

"Miss Lamar," he said, moving closer, "do you suppose we could call each other by our Christian names? I mean, now that we're friends, we don't have to go on being so formal."

"You're quite right. But if you don't mind, I'd really like to be called just plain 'Lamar.' "

"*Lamar?*"

"And I'll call you 'Maynard.' "

"But why?"

"Don't men always call each other by last name, like when they're on the same team?"

"Yes, men do. But not men and *women.*"

Amanda smiled. "Then we'll be different. I like it because it makes us more—equal."

"I never thought of it that way."

"Well? Are we agreed?"

"How will I ever learn to call you 'Lamar'?"

"You just did."

Tom's face crinkled into a wide grin and he took her hand in both of his. "I've never met anyone like you, Lamar."

Though the day was warm, his hands were cold. "That's nice to hear, Maynard," she said, her voice softening. "I might say the same about you."

It was almost midnight when the last streetcar brought them back to town from Lake Washington. Tom kissed Amanda good night outside the Denny, longing to be asked to her room, yet reluctantly thankful she wasn't that kind of girl. His expression conveyed suffering, for which she sympathized, knowing as he did that this was the only possible way the evening could end. He left her, promising to see her at the pier the next morning.

Not until she went inside did she notice that her dress was stained with wild blackberries and that several thistle burrs still clung to the hem. However, she did not expect to encounter anyone at that hour in the lobby of the Denny.

She was mistaken. Cyrus Clough was standing at the reception desk asking the night clerk for his key.

He brightened when he saw Amanda, greeting her with the familiarity of a long-time friend.

"Hello there!" he sang out, eyeing her boldly. "Out on the town?"

Amanda noticed his glazed look, and that his breath carried the vapor of whiskey.

"Out for a walk," she replied. Turning, she headed for the stairs, deciding not to get trapped with him in the elevator.

"Wait up!" He came after her, then lowered his voice. "In case you're wondering where Mrs. Clough is, I sent her home on the evening train. She's not a well woman, if you know what I mean." He winked.

"That's too bad," said Amanda.

"She's at that age . . ." He let his voice trail off, grinning like a schoolboy who had just said something naughty. "What I'm trying to say is that I'll be staying on until I see how this Chinese thing is to be settled. Which means that you and I are both here alone, so to speak."

Amanda feigned surprise. "Whatever gave you the idea that I was alone?" And while Cyrus Clough was left blinking, she bade him "Good evening," and went upstairs.

When Amanda returned to the waterfront the next morning, the gates to the pier were standing open—and the *George Elder* was gone.

Hurrying closer, she noticed that a barricade blocked a gaping hole which had been torn in the middle of the pier. Blackened timbers projecting from the rim bore ominous evidence that the pier had been damaged by an explosion. The blood began to pound in her ears as she tried to visualize what had happened to the immigrants. But there was no one to answer her questions, for the area was deserted and the steamship offices closed.

Suddenly she was struck by a disturbing thought. It was an odd coincidence that the situation would come to a climax the very day that Tom had taken her on a picnic. Could he have known that something was going to happen and wanted to prevent her from getting the story? Of course not. That didn't make sense, for then he would have cheated himself as well. But as the minutes passed, and he failed to show up as promised, her suspicions grew stronger. Tired of waiting, she crossed the street to the Green Parrot Saloon in search of her colleagues.

But the minute she stepped through the door, she spotted Tom, his foot resting on the brass rail. He turned at once, as if he felt her eyes, and waved her over eagerly without showing the least surprise that she would be there. Amanda walked toward him, her anger mounting, oblivious to the interested eyes which followed her.

"Explain, Maynard!"

Tom's smile turned to helpless bewilderment. His mouth moved soundlessly, at a loss to defend himself.

"So you wanted to spend a day at the lake! Thank you very much. Now maybe you'd like to tell me what went on while we were gone?"

"Wait a minute, Lamar, you've got it all wrong. I didn't know any more than you did—until now. Ask *him*."

Amanda turned. There was Officer Crowley from the *George Elder*. They stared at each other in confusion.

Tom quickly introduced them.

"We've already met," said Crowley, and murmured an awkward greeting.

Amanda looked at Tom questioningly.

"The Chinese are still here," he explained. "Only the ship had to be moved because somebody bombed the pier. But fortunately, no one was hurt."

Amanda felt her cheeks warm with embarrassment. "What a relief." But the next moment her suspicions returned. "How come you two are friends?"

"We only met an hour ago. I was following through on your tip about the yellow fever."

"I told you that in confidence."

"Naturally. I only wanted to find out if it was true."

"And did you?"

Tom scratched his ear. "Not quite. I tried to board the ship by passing myself off as a health official."

Amanda raised a brow. "What a clever, original idea. Did it work?"

He grinned sheepishly. "I wasn't as lucky as you were—I got caught. But all is not lost, the lieutenant here kindly consented to have a drink with me. I think he'd like to co-operate with us."

Amanda looked sharply at Crowley. "*Is* there yellow fever?"

"A touch perhaps," he replied evasively. "No cause for alarm. The cases are completely isolated."

"Then what's preventing the immigrants from coming ashore?"

"It has nothing to do with illness," he replied hastily. "They'll be released as soon as it's safe for them. Soon as tempers calm down." With quick nervous fingers, he reached into his pocket and took out several bills, which he dropped on the bar. "Let me pay for the refreshments."

Amanda stared. He had put down one hundred dollars.

"What are you doing?" asked Tom, pushing the money away.

"I insist," said Crowley.

Amanda raised a brow. "Is that a bribe?"

Crowley cleared his throat. "Bribe? It's just—good fellowship."

"So that we won't write anything about the yellow fever?"

"Well, I'd hate to see you cause a panic for no good reason."

Amanda snatched up the bills and tucked them into Crowley's jacket pocket. "Good-by, Lieutenant. Sorry you have to rush off."

Crowley's face darkened. "If you go through with this, you'll only be harming the immigrants, not us," he warned in a low voice. Then he turned and left.

Amanda sighed. "I think I'll have a glass of beer."

Tom signaled the bartender, then gave Amanda an anxious look. "Still angry?"

"No."

"I'm sorry, Lamar. But don't think I was going behind your back. I only wanted to get more information for *both* of us."

Amanda smiled coolly, deciding to forgive him. "That's all right. The important thing is to get the truth. Which I guess we have."

"But we still don't have a story."

"Then we'll just have to make one up. My theory is that the immigrants are going to be quietly spirited away to some remote place where there's no danger of risking an epidemic. So if we write about yellow fever, it won't matter. By the time it's in print, they'll be gone."

"Or maybe they'll be sent back to China. That would be worse for them. And it could bring an end to immigration."

"Is that what you're going to predict?"

"I don't know. I haven't decided."

"Poor people." Amanda shook her head. "They have no say-so about their own futures."

"Not like *us*," said Tom reaching for her hand.

That night he introduced her to stuffed oysters at the Merchant's

Café in Pioneer Square, a restaurant dominated by businessmen and cigar smoke, dark paneling and elk heads.

The dinner passed pleasantly, but Amanda caught Tom's worried expression several times and wondered what was troubling him. Toward the end of the evening he finally managed to tell her.

"Lamar," he announced suddenly, "I'm going back East tomorrow. But only for a short time."

"How wonderful," said Amanda, feeling a pang of disappointment. "How come you didn't mention it before?"

"I only decided this afternoon."

"What about your story?"

"That's the reason I'm going. I want to try placing it in an eastern paper."

"Instead of the local papers?"

"They turned me down before I even knew about the yellow fever."

"But why?"

"I'm afraid I didn't move fast enough. Too many other fellows got in ahead of me. So I say, to hell with them."

"That's too bad."

"But don't worry, I'll be back before you know it."

Amanda knew it was unreasonable to feel hurt, but she did. "I'll probably be gone by the time you get back."

"Gone? You can't!"

"Maynard, I'm only here on assignment. I have no reason to stay."

"But what about *us?*"

Amanda gave him a puzzled look.

"What did you think?" he said. "That we were just friends?"

"I don't know what we are. We haven't talked about it. I know of course that we would correspond, and perhaps visit back and forth . . ."

"Visit back and forth?" he repeated in a panicky voice. "There will be three thousand miles separating us!"

"Maybe more than that." She leaned across the table, eyes wide. "What if my next assignment takes me to Europe?"

Tom looked horrified. "How would I ever find you?"

"You can always write to me in care of the *World.*"

"The *World.*" His voice dropped in despair. "You're going to forget all about me."

"I'll try not to."

"There'll be other men in your life."

"There haven't been so far."

"Twenty years old and you haven't had a beau?"

"I was in a boarding school, remember?"

Tom groaned. "I can't leave. I'm not going after all."

"Don't be silly. You have a career to think of. And so do I."

"Damn our careers!" He pounded the table. Then he sighed heavily. "You're right. I'm being silly. But I'll go only on one condition—that we work out some way to be together. So don't leave town until I call you—promise?"

"That depends," said Amanda with a smile, "on how soon you call."

After dinner they strolled uptown arm in arm, while Tom bemoaned the fact that he lived at home with his parents, and therefore had no private place to entertain a young woman. And while Amanda was terribly curious to know him better, she was glad not to be put to any tests. She'd heard that even nice girls sometimes found that in certain circumstances they would have absolutely no resistance, a chance which she didn't trust herself to risk.

"What do you usually do for excitement?" she asked, half teasing, half serious.

"I go down to the Skid Road."

"What on earth is that?"

"It's a very disreputable section where ladies don't go unescorted. Want to see it?"

Amanda laughed. "Maynard, you are really old-fashioned. There's no part of town I'd shy away from—with or without an escort."

The Skid Road was south of Yesler Way, surprisingly close to the restaurant where they had eaten, a crowded six-block area of theaters, saloons, gambling houses and brothels. Lumberjacks, merchant seamen and stevedores mingled drunkenly with men in business suits, who looked out of place, while flamboyantly dressed individuals of every description wandered at ease.

"It wasn't always like this," he explained almost apologetically. "Not so many years ago the Skid Road was the route used by ox-teams to skid logs down to Yesler's Mill. It also marked the center of a strip of land my grandfather gave to Henry Yesler so that he could have a convenient place to build his mill. For a while it was even called Maynardtown!"

Amanda laughed appreciatively and begged to hear more. Tom was proud of his city, where he seemed to have such strong roots. She tried to see it through his eyes, to feel its pull.

"How did it get so disreputable?" she asked, using *his* word to describe it, for she actually found it alive, exhilarating.

"I guess because it was unrestricted. First came loggers, then entrepreneurs to take the loggers' wages. Now anybody comes who wants to have a ripping good time without losing his reputation. Anybody but ladies, that is."

They turned a corner to see looming before them a tall green building laced with fire escapes. It bore an odd, not very successful pretense at elegance. An oversized sign with large letters destroyed the attempt: "Grand Union Hotel."

Why did the name sound so familiar? Then she remembered. That was the hotel where Soo-Lee had said her sisters lived.

"What kind of place is this?" Amanda asked.

"It's not first class like the Denny, but it does have character. That's where the reporters stay."

Amanda sighed. She would have enjoyed staying there, too. "May we take a look?"

"If you like." Tom encircled her with his arm as they crossed the street.

Suddenly Amanda stopped short. There, only a few feet away, just stepping out of a carriage was Cyrus Clough. And on his arm was an attractive young Chinese girl. Together they went into the hotel.

"Never mind," said Amanda abruptly. "Let's just keep walking."

It was dismal camping on the pier in the rain. But Amanda had decided it was the only way to be sure that the Chinese would not be moved without her knowledge. Though it was still summer, the skies had grown heavy, the mountains had disappeared and even Puget Sound was lost in a vague mist. And like a huge gray whale, the *George Elder* heaved and fell with the tide, while its human cargo remained out of sight in its belly.

Amanda had been advised to go to the Arctic Outfitters on First Avenue to purchase her tent and buy rain clothing. By so doing, she had lost her identity—and sex—in an enveloping rain cloak and heavy rubber galoshes.

"You can cross a river in 'em and never wet your feet," the sales clerk had offered.

As Amanda maintained her solitary vigil, prepared to wait out the immigrants' release no matter how long it took, she again felt twinges of homesickness. It was easy to be independent when surrounded by friends, but to be suddenly alone was a different matter. She still felt disappointed by Tom's decision to leave, especially when he had seemed so taken with her. But then, she had probably assumed too much. After all, he wasn't as lucky as she was. He was still searching for something meaningful in life. It was best to put him out of her mind.

Amanda's persistence was quickly rewarded. At dawn on the second day she was awakened from a fitful sleep by the sounds of clanking chains, wheels grinding and loud clopping of hoofs. Peering out through the flap of her tent, she saw a strange assortment of conveyances pulling up. There were not only police wagons, but delivery wagons—Kristopherson Milk, McKinnon Coal, and Murphy Wine & Liquor. The immigrants were going to be moved!

The police unchained the gates and a long gray line of bent figures began filing down the gangplank. Wearing no protection against the elements other than the clothing with which they had come, the Chinese splatted through the rain with small rapid steps. Each carried a bundle of personal belongings, meager preparation for life in a new world.

Amanda hurriedly pulled on her galoshes and raincoat and crawled out of her tent. "Where are they going?" she asked the officer who had become her friend in order to relieve the monotony of guard duty.

"To Spokane," he said with smug satisfaction.

"To do what?"

"Work in the mines. Who else could they get?"

It was just as she had guessed—the immigrants were going to drop from sight and quickly be forgotten.

Each wagon departed the moment it was filled, a clever plan, Amanda observed, to avoid attracting undue attention.

Suddenly a face smiled at her from the shuffling line and Amanda recognized the Chinese boy who spoke English. Waving eagerly, she hurried to walk beside him.

"How are the men with yellow fever?" she asked in a rush, certain that at any moment she would be ordered to step aside.

"No more," he replied, shaking his head.

"You mean they're well again?"

"They die."

Amanda stared in dismay. "Do you know where you're going?" she asked suddenly.

"To America," he replied with a grin.

"Yes, but do you know what work you're going to do?"

"I find job," he said with youthful confidence. Then added, "In laundry."

Obviously, they had been told nothing. And now there was no more time, for the boy was climbing into the wagon.

"Good luck!" she called as the doors were slammed shut.

"Want to ride along?" the policeman asked. "We're taking them over to the train depot."

Amanda accepted eagerly.

At the depot the immigrants were herded into cattle cars for the long precarious trip across the Cascades to eastern Washington. She searched frantically for the boy again, determined to warn him what was in store, so that he in turn could alert the others. And perhaps when the time came, they could rebel. But the smiling face never again emerged. Had he been warned not to talk to her?

The immigration officials supervised the exodus. But when the last of the Chinese had passed through the turnstile, the officials called a halt, and immediately went into a huddle.

Amanda moved closer to hear what they were saying.

"A damn nuisance to be short by only *one*."

His partner agreed. "I don't even think it's worth a recount. Who cares about one goddam Chinaman? Let's just change our figures like we always do and save time."

Amanda's heartbeat quickened. Had the boy come to some harm because he had been seen speaking to her? Or had he learned of their destination and managed to slip away? She would never know.

The signal was finally given for the car doors to be closed.

When Amanda saw the fleeting looks of panic which crossed the faces of the captives as they headed toward the unknown, she wondered if they knew instinctively that they were going to be in bondage to people who didn't think of them as possessing rights, or even as human beings? Perhaps the men who had died of yellow fever were the lucky ones.

At that moment Amanda knew that it wasn't enough just to report what had happened; she had to *do* something. Most reporters would say that it wasn't their responsibility, but she didn't care what the others did. She would kick over the rocks and turn up the worms. She would be just like her friend, Emma Goldman.

Chapter Four

A BULKY ENVELOPE from the New York *World* awaited Amanda at the reception desk. This was it—clippings of her story.

Taking the stairs two at a time left her breathless. The minute she reached her room, she slit the envelope and eagerly unfolded the newspaper. Her eyes darted over the page for her headline, "BOSSES: THE REAL CULPRITS." But instead she saw: "CHINESE AND AMERICANS IN CONFLICT." Her name was on the article, sure enough, but as she read through in stunned disbelief, she discovered that her whole point concerning the labor issue had been deliberately edited out.

Gone were the mutilated mill hands, the encounter with Soo-Lee, Cyrus Clough's remarks about cheap labor, and worst of all, the yellow fever cover-up. All that remained was the factual reporting of events—the ship's arrival, the demonstrations, the bombing. The final stroke of irony was a small note from Joseph Pulitzer attached to the clipping, saying: "Congratulations on a fine job! Check enclosed."

She stared at the note as angry blood rushed to her cheeks. "Congratulations for nothing!" she said aloud, crumpling the article. But the next minute she smoothed it out again, deciding to save it as a reminder of what she felt must be the most disillusioning experience of her entire life. Being expelled from school had been nothing compared to this.

How she hoped that Emma had not seen that tepid article bearing her name. Yet she was sure that if she wrote to her explaining what had happened, she would understand completely. Emma had probably experienced the same thing—seeing her speeches distorted by the press, so that she appeared either as a villain or a fool.

Amanda stretched the task of packing to fill the rest of the morning, though it could have been accomplished in minutes. Her white lawn dress which the rain had shrunk, gaiters, khaki hiking suit and boots, and the green taffeta gown—just in case. Why did her body feel so weighted, like in a dream when it's impossible to move quickly? Tom hadn't called, as he had said he would. But that was to be expected. So with her assignment finished, there was no reason to linger. Yet, she dreaded the prospect of returning home after such a brief taste of freedom, especially as Mr. Pulitzer's note had said nothing about her next assignment, a fact which made her feel strangely apprehensive.

When she came down to the lobby to settle her bill, Amanda discovered an envelope addressed in her mother's handwriting. She opened it reluctantly, guessing she would find a duplicate clipping of her story. But instead, she found a more recent edition of the *World* with an article bearing the headline: "AN UNWELCOME CARGO —CHINESE AND YELLOW FEVER by Tom Maynard." A subheading read: "Bribery Attempt Revealed."

"I don't believe it!" Amanda gasped aloud.

"Beg pardon?" The desk clerk looked up.

"How *could* he?" Not expecting a reply, Amanda turned and headed back to her room.

Slamming the door, she forced herself to read every word. When she finished, she had to admit that given such skimpy information, Tom had skillfully managed to construct a very interesting story, which left her both hating and admiring him. Above all, it told her that his boyish innocence *was* façade. He was far more experienced than she was. In the margin her mother had written, "Who is Tom Maynard???"

That was a good question. But as Amanda grew calmer, she reasoned that she could hardly blame Tom for beating her out. Hadn't she advised him to "get away from home for a while"? Hadn't she told him to "please yourself first"? He was only doing what any other reporter would have done. Why, then, did she feel so used? Because I liked him, she admitted. And I thought he liked *me*. I was mistaken. It's over and that's that. Suddenly she realized that not only were she and Tom finished, but that she and the *World* were finished as well. Obviously there would be no more assignments. And even if there were, would she want to write for a paper that was interested only in exploitation? Clearly they didn't consider the labor issue to be half as newsworthy as yellow fever. Too bad for them. As far as she was concerned, the *World* had missed their chance.

She began to unpack.

When the telephone call came from Tom, Amanda hoped she could control her emotions.

"Guess what?" Tom's voice could hardly contain his excitement. "I've got an article in the *World,* too!"

"I know."

"When's yours going to be in?"

"It already was."

There was a moment of awkward silence.

"Lamar, is anything wrong?"

"My assignment is over, that's all."

"I don't understand. I thought you were on staff."

"I was on trial. Anyway, they paid me off."

"Not because of *me?*"

"No, it's my own fault, really. I should have realized they wanted something more sensational than what I had written."

"I don't know what to say—I'm shocked! Here I thought we would both be working for the same paper!"

"Maynard, you know damn well you went there to beat me out!"

"You're wrong! I went because you had inspired me to make something of myself—and because I wanted you to be proud of me."

"Well, actually, you did me a favor. You helped me to realize that the *World* isn't the paper I want to write for after all."

"It isn't?"

"I've decided to write about the labor issues here in the Northwest —all the stuff that the rest of the country doesn't seem to be interested in."

"Then—you're not coming back to New York?"

"That's right. And I'm not going home to Washington, D.C., either. I'm going to stay right here, just as you advised."

"You can't do that!" There was sudden desperation in Tom's voice. "I had this all planned out so that we could work together—*be* together. I wanted to surprise you!"

"Well, you did."

"Please. You've got to change your mind!"

"It's no use, Maynard. I've decided to work for a Seattle paper. My intuition tells me that the Northwest is sitting on a time bomb and I want to be here when it goes off."

"But how will I ever see you again?"

"Nobody's forcing you to stay there."

"You don't understand—I'm out of money. I have to earn my trip home."

"Then I guess there's no more to be said."

"But there is! Lamar, I want you to wait for me. I want us to have a future together."

"Don't tie yourself to a promise, Maynard. If and when you come back will be time enough to talk about it."

"I *will* be back. With you there how can I live anywhere else?"

After Tom had hung up, it dawned on her that he had intended to remain in New York all along. No doubt he needed to win the approval of his family and of the town which his grandfather had founded. He had to succeed in the eyes of the world. If he failed, she guessed he probably wouldn't come home at all. One thing was clear —he was driven by stronger forces than his need for *her*.

The following day she received a note from Joseph Pulitzer expressing the hope that when she returned to New York, she would drop by to discuss the possibility of future assignments.

"Don't let backwoods politics swallow up your talents," he warned. "If you want to amount to anything as a reporter, stick to the big issues."

It was just as she had thought—they weren't interested in the Northwest. But more than that, Pulitzer thought that she shouldn't be either. Amanda felt the pall of sudden doubt send her spirits plunging. In so many words he was telling her that she wouldn't make it if she remained in Seattle. Supposing he was right?

Amanda slowly tore up the letter she had started to write to her mother. Perhaps she shouldn't tell her just yet about her plans to stay. Perhaps she should reconsider. After all, wasn't a job with the *World* the chance she had always wanted? Wouldn't she be foolish to turn it down? Then too, Tom was there. Maybe it was destiny after all that she should accept.

A sharp knock on the door startled her from her thoughts.

"Visitor in the lobby!" the bellboy called.

Wondering who it could possibly be, Amanda hurried downstairs. A tall, pleasant, energetic woman came forward to greet her. Thick white hair suggested she might be in her early sixties, though her skin was smooth, her eyes lively. She shook Amanda's hand warmly.

"I'm Mary Kenworthy, a friend of Colonel Blethen's. He asked me to introduce myself and to find out how you were getting along."

"How nice of you!" said Amanda in surprise.

"The colonel thought you might enjoy a female companion to show you around town," she added.

"I'd love it. That's really very kind of both of you."

"Good. If you're free this evening, I'm having a small gathering at my house. It might be a chance to meet a few people."

As soon as Amanda accepted, Mary Kenworthy insisted that they begin their friendship on a first-name basis.

"I hate titles," she explained. "Miss always makes me feel like an old maid, and Mrs. leads everyone to believe that I have a husband somewhere. Which I don't, any more. May I call for you at seven?"

Before Amanda could say that she would be happy to come by streetcar, Mary was halfway across the lobby, her skirts billowing as she hurried along.

Mary Kenworthy lived in the woods near the university campus.

"I don't think of this place as just a home," she explained, showing Amanda around. "It's more a center of agitation. Against the 'interests,' you know."

Amanda nodded eagerly, encouraging Mary to continue, for it sounded as though they were very much of the same mind. But there were other guests to meet, both young and old, and so many bright sparks of conversation going on about the room that Amanda's head was soon whirling.

Amanda would have preferred to listen rather than talk, but everyone was curious when it was discovered that she was a reporter. And as the questions flew, Amanda had to admit that she had been inspired toward her profession by Emma Goldman. This, however, caused such a mixed reaction that she almost wished she had never mentioned the name.

"Goldman is misguided," Mary declared briskly. "She's been seduced by socialism. That may be all right for the East, but it will never work in Seattle. We're too independent."

Amanda felt a twinge of protest stir inside. These were harsh words to hear spoken of one's idol. But as the dissection of Emma was picked up by the other guests, Amanda's resentment gave way to curiosity, then fascination. What a strange breed these Northwesterners were!

"Did I tell you that I met your mother when I was on one of my lecture tours?" Mary asked abruptly.

Amanda shook her head, surprised that this piece of news had not come out earlier. But Mary was matter-of-fact, as though *everyone* knew Temperance Smith.

"Susan Anthony introduced us, so of course we talked of nothing but suffrage. Just try to interest Anthony in another subject!"

Everyone laughed.

"Still, we had an enjoyable lunch together, and for once I found myself in the presence of two invincible women with whom I was in total agreement."

There was laughter again from those who knew that Mary thrived on argument and seldom agreed with anyone wholeheartedly.

The debate moved on to politics, but the coming presidential election was disposed of quickly, as no one could decide which candidate was more poorly qualified, William Jennings Bryan or William McKinley. Of greater interest were local affairs.

"Here in Washington, we women are still fighting for the vote," she explained to Amanda. "We won it in '83, then lost it four years later. Now we're almost as badly off as the Chinese!"

Amanda was reminded of Cyrus Clough. Before she knew it, she found herself telling them about her encounters with Clough, of his interest in exploiting Chinese labor, *and* Chinese women. No one seemed surprised. But when they heard that the *World* had backed away from Amanda's story, they were incensed.

"That's what we're up against," said Mary heatedly. "To the rest of the country we don't exist. Well, we shall just have to fend for ourselves, as we've always done."

Looking from one to the other, Amanda could feel her excitement mount. Here were people willing to struggle upstream like a run of salmon, knowing they would be battered, but fighting on nonetheless

with an instinct to fulfill their destiny. In a rush she told them everything, but when she related her account of the mutilated millworkers, a strange silence fell. Everyone stared at her as though she
had stumbled onto a forbidden secret. Amanda glanced around anxiously, wondering what she had said wrong. There was a nervous
clearing of throats. Then Mary smilingly reached over to place her
left hand on Amanda's arm. It felt cold, rubbery. A sudden chill
seized her. It was not a human touch. It was not flesh and blood.

"That's all right, Amanda," said Mary in a quiet voice. "I don't
mind talking about it. In fact, when I first had the accident five years
ago, I talked about it a great deal, hoping to bring attention to the
plight of factory workers."

Amanda stared at the facsimile of a hand, a bit too smooth and
tight like scar tissue, but which at a glance looked real enough.

"Did it happen at a mill?"

"No, there aren't any women in the mills, thank heavens. It was in
a salmon cannery, which employs *only* women—twelve hours a day
for starvation wages. I was alone and in poor financial circumstances
at the time, so I took the job because it was the only one I could get.
There were no safety devices—still aren't. I lost my hand in one of
the machines."

"Oh, Mary! What a terrible, senseless thing!"

"Oddly enough, it was a turning point for me. As I was no longer
able to get another factory job, I was forced to become a social
reformist!" Mary paused to laugh. "So now I spend my time lectur-
ing and campaigning for change. Needless to say, I'm extremely un-
popular in some circles."

"Good for you!" said Amanda. "How can I help?"

"Are you serious? Don't you have to get back to your job in New
York?"

"Mary, even before I came here tonight I was debating whether or
not to stay. Now, after seeing what happened to you, I've made up
my mind. I want to do stories about what's going on in the factories
and mills."

"Do you think the *World* will actually print them?"

"I'm not going to be writing for the *World* any more. I've decided
to try a Seattle paper."

Spontaneously, everyone in the room came forward to shake her hand, congratulating her for the decision, as though they thought that her abandonment of a promising career with the *World* entailed a tremendous sacrifice.

"We're not used to outsiders getting involved in our problems," Mary explained. Then she added with a quick smile, "Of course you're not an outsider any longer. You're one of us."

Chapter Five

On August 10, 1896, the first edition of the Seattle *Times* came off the press bearing the masthead of Colonel Alden J. Blethen. With its birth, the old *Press-Times* ceased to exist. There had been virtually no publicity to herald the new paper, certainly not from its uneasy rival, the *Post-Intelligencer.* Amanda looked it over eagerly. The front page carried a story about Blethen himself with an accompanying sketch which made no attempt to flatter. The likeness appeared bushy-browed, rumpled and determined. Without offering apology for the abbreviated edition, he admitted it had been turned out in a small printing shop on Yesler Way, using what must have been the most primitive equipment. He promised that within a few days they would be moving to larger quarters on Second Avenue and Columbia Street, the center of the business district.

Good, Amanda thought. By the time he's settled, I'll have a story ready for him. But will Colonel Blethen be ready for *me?*

Mary Kenworthy eagerly showed Amanda the industrial area, pointing out oyster-packing plants, woolen mills, steam laundries, flour mills, tanneries, a dye works and finally the salmon cannery, where she drew her carriage to a stop. Painful memories clouded her face for a moment, then she resumed her usual brisk manner.

"Here's where my life changed," Mary said ironically, "which just goes to show there's no such thing as a bad experience."

Amanda nodded, wondering if she could ever be capable of such courage.

"Remember," Mary continued, "if they agree to a tour, you'll be seeing the plant under very controlled conditions. They'll show you only what they want you to see."

"I can't do it that way," said Amanda. "They mustn't know I'm a reporter. I've got to be able to talk to the women."

"That will be difficult," Mary admitted. "Maybe you'll have to sneak in—pretend to be one of them."

Amanda brightened. "Mary, you've just given me an idea! Why merely pretend to be a worker? Why not really *be* one?"

At the salmon cannery, Amanda found a half dozen women ahead of her in the hiring office. While she waited her turn, she listened to an Indian woman in front of her who was speaking to the interviewer in a native dialect. He seemed to understand her perfectly, responding in the same language.

"*Kah mika mitlite?*" he asked.

The woman's grin displayed two jagged teeth, as finely honed as steel tools. "*Konaway kah,*" she replied with a shrug.

"What are they saying?" Amanda whispered to a woman next to her.

"He's asking her where she lives, and she says 'everywhere.' It's a stupid question to ask an Indian," the woman complained with an impatient sigh. "It wastes time."

"I wonder how he learned the language?"

The woman squinted suspiciously. "Everybody knows Chinook."

Amanda was asked the same questions as the others. Did she have dropsy? Dyspepsia? Tuberculosis? St. Vitus's Dance? Dizzy spells? Fainting spells? Was she expectant?

He didn't ask if she had experience or request references. He didn't care to know where she was born, or how long she was going to stay. Nonetheless, she was hired, and so was everyone else. Instructions were brief. They were presented to the foreman, Mr. Hodges, who stated that wages were ten cents an hour, then marched to a rack where a row of stained smocks were hanging. Each woman took one without needing to be told.

Mr. Hodges recited an ominous list of warnings. "The machines are sharp enough to cut tin, so they'll slice through flesh as well." As he spoke, he eyed each woman through keen slits as though inspecting some new property or testing for vulnerability. Was he already selecting favorites? Or spotting troublemakers? Amanda kept her eyes down. All she could see were the brownish streaks of dried blood on her smock.

"And the steam from the boilers will burn your skin off. So pay attention. The company is not responsible for injuries caused by carelessness. Conversation is forbidden." He pointed at the Indian woman. *"Mesida! Klaghanie!"* he ordered, gesturing toward a side door. She hurried out.

"Why did you send her away?" Amanda asked.

"Indians work outside. They unload the fish."

"But why can't they work inside?"

Hodges tolerated the question only because it was apparent that he liked Amanda's looks. She felt his eyes appraising her.

"Would *you* like to work next to an Indian?" he asked.

All the women laughed.

Hodges turned abruptly and led the way through heavy double doors into the dim cavern where conversation was not only forbidden but was impossible because of the hissing and roaring of boilers.

Hodges' stubby finger directed Amanda to her place, which required that she stand in a puddle of cold water, while a water-filled flume sped the fish toward her. As she watched the salmon travel from station to station, she couldn't help thinking that the manner in which their shimmering silver bodies were reduced to an indistinguishable mass of pulp provided a grim parallel to the lives of the women themselves.

The speed at which the fish came slithering down the flume set the pace for each function. Arms and hands flew in a furious race which could never be won. Amanda saw that a second of hesitation would cause the fish to back up and the water to slop over onto the floor. So it was that most women found themselves, like Amanda, standing in vast puddles which accumulated faster than they could dry up.

Amanda was shown her job—to seize the salmon after it had been de-boned, and extract all the remaining slivers, a task requiring sharp eyesight and dexterity. Her only training was the few minutes allowed to observe her partner, who until now had apparently been doing the work of two persons. The woman's hands were purple and swollen from constant exposure to the icy water. Amanda watched her in amazement, certain that she could never acquire the same skill, for the woman's movements were almost too quick to be followed. She was the perfect machine. She didn't need to be oiled, nor did she require electricity in order to run. Her motions were automatic, exactly timed. It appeared she could go on forever.

All too soon the relentless finger of Mr. Hodges directed Amanda to begin her task. Everything went wrong.

The numbing coldness of the water slowed her fingers so that masses of pink flesh banked up against the sides of the flume while she struggled to keep ahead of the onslaught. Amanda's five-minute break came at last as a sharp tap on the shoulder sent her reeling from the room. Her legs were already stiff from standing in the freezing water, which had soaked through the soles of her shoes. Until she was outside she hadn't realized how deafening had been the constant pounding of the canning machines and the shrill hissing of steam from the boilers. Her head throbbed as she tried to blink away the spots dancing before her eyes.

"You'll get used to it."

Amanda jumped at the sound of Mr. Hodges' voice, unaware that he had followed her out. He grinned through blackened teeth and rolled some tobacco up in brown paper.

"Want to sit down?"

Amanda hesitated, but Hodges motioned insistently for her to follow him, as he led the way down a hall littered with packing boxes. At the end he opened the door to a windowless storage room furnished with a single couch.

"We've got soft jobs for them that wants them," he said winking. "So a smart girlie like yourself can make her life real easy." He took a step toward her, confident that she would not refuse him.

"How easy?" asked Amanda, stepping back.

"Well, now, them that labels cans don't work too hard. They get longer rests and more time for lunch. Sound good?"

"Do they get an increase in wages?"

Hodges' chuckle erupted into a dry cough. When he recovered his face twisted into a frown. "You're asking a lot of questions. Just tell me plain—yes or no?"

"I'll give you my answer at the end of the week."

Hodges put the cigarette to his lip, where it adhered, dangling while he spoke. "Why waste time?" he asked suspiciously. "You trying to stall me off?"

"Wouldn't it look odd if I were given an easy job on my very first day?"

"Nobody's gonna complain. I'm the foreman, remember?"

"I'll tell you Saturday."

Hodges flung his cigarette away impatiently and grabbed Amanda's arms, pinning them at her sides.

"I want an answer *now!*"

Amanda sniffed. "Mr. Hodges, did you eat garlic for breakfast?"

Hodges quickly stepped back. "Why, no." He put a self-conscious hand to his mouth. "I don't think so."

"You should try some chicle gum," advised Amanda, edging past him. "Especially before next Saturday."

At the sound of the noon whistle, the machinery ground into silence and the women raced to the wooden benches lining the walls to gulp their lunches. Instantly they became a row of dull eyes staring into space, their mouths working mechanically.

Amanda noticed that the three girls assigned to label cans were the only ones who didn't rush, but sauntered out of the room with a certain arrogance, as if they had all the time in the world.

Amanda sat next to her partner and introduced herself. For a moment it seemed that the woman wasn't going to acknowledge her at all. But finally she drew a long sigh and gave Amanda a weary sidelong glance.

"Annie Bleaker," she responded in a flat voice.

She was older than the others. Too old, Amanda thought, to be doing such demanding work. But beneath the worn, haggard look, a trace of beauty still remained, suggesting how attractive she must have been as a young girl.

"I'm glad to meet you. Is it Miss or Mrs.?"

"Mrs." She spat out her admission in disgust. "Although my husband left me a good number of years ago."

"I'm sorry."

"Well, you needn't be. It was all for the best." She glanced again at Amanda and volunteered, "I was one of the girls that Asa Mercer brought around the Horn in '66." There was a note of defensive pride in her voice.

"You're a Mercer Girl?" Amanda asked in awe. Even as a child she had heard the romantic story of Mercer's famous shipload of girls, who had been transported to the Northwest for the purpose of providing marriage partners for throngs of eligible bachelors.

"It was a great adventure while aboard ship," said Mrs. Bleaker. "But we had no say in the matter of selecting our husbands. When we arrived in Seattle, we were looked over and chosen. There was no courtship, no time to become acquainted. Most of the marriages took place within a week. They *had* to, I'm afraid, to preserve our morals." For the first time, Annie Bleaker managed a faint smile.

"You weren't pleased with your husband?"

"My feelings were of no importance," she said, shrugging. "Like the other fellows, he wasn't much interested in me as a person. One woman was as good as another, so long as she was strong and healthy. We were selected much as a mule might be—for our ability to haul a load."

"I wouldn't have stood for it! What happened to the other Mercer Girls?"

"A few were lucky. Those whose husbands made money. But most fared no better than me. Mr. Bleaker may have been a hard man, but at least I was never beaten. Why, some of those poor girls were so mistreated they were driven to the brothels down on the Sawdust—the Skid Road, that is. God only knows what's become of them."

As the week progressed, Annie Bleaker grew increasingly garrulous on the subject of her husband, but only compressed her lips whenever Amanda attempted to question her on safety hazards and the frequency of accidents.

"Whatever you do," Annie warned repeatedly, "don't suggest that machines be used to pick out the fishbones. Once those machines are put in, we'll all be out of a job."

"How long have you worked here?" Amanda finally asked.

"Eight, ten years," she answered vaguely. "I haven't kept count."

"Then you probably remember Mary Kenworthy."

Annie shook her head almost before Amanda's words were out.

"She lost her hand," Amanda prompted.

A shrill whistle terminated their conversation. But at closing time, Amanda made a point of walking with Annie to the streetcar. Quickly she returned to the subject of Mary's accident.

"Her hand got caught in the canning machine," Amanda reminded. "She told me it happened about five years ago."

Annie increased her pace, staring straight ahead. "It was her own fault," she said at last.

"How do you mean?"

Annie stopped suddenly and turned on Amanda in anger. "I don't talk to union people, is that clear?"

"But I'm not with the union," Amanda protested. "Whatever gave you that idea?"

"Well, Mary Kenworthy was union. And you seem to be a friend of hers."

"I barely know her. Was she trying to organize the cannery?"

"She hired on only to stir up trouble. She cost a lot of the girls their jobs. And she got what was coming to her."

Annie began walking again, faster than before. Amanda hurried to keep pace.

"What do you mean by that?"

"There *was* no accident, do you understand? This plant is as safe as can be."

"Are you saying it was deliberate?"

"She was warned, but she didn't listen."

"That's a crime! The cannery could be closed down!"

"Oh, it wasn't the bosses that did it. It was the girls. They put something into the machine to make it act up."

Amanda gasped. "And all because Mary was trying to organize a union?"

"We were scared of our jobs." Then she added quickly, "But mind, *I* had no part in it. I didn't approve one bit."

"No one was ever punished?"

"Nothing could be proved. The girls stuck together. Not one of them would talk."

"What about Mary? Did she know?"

"Of course. She knew what was going on. But the way I see it, she wanted that accident to happen. She wanted to be a martyr."

It was early Saturday morning when Annie ran a sharp splinter under her thumbnail. She quickly tied her handkerchief around her thumb so that she could continue working, but within moments the blood had soaked through. No one paid the least attention, neither to Annie's pain, nor to the drops of blood being carried along on the fish.

"Go for help! I'll take your place!" Amanda tried to make herself heard above the din.

But Annie turned on her screaming, "You're *not* taking my place! You just want me to lose my job!"

Astounded by her outburst, Amanda opened her mouth to protest, but Annie again lashed out. "You should have spotted that bone—that's *your* job! Hodges is going to hear about this!"

Suddenly Annie's flushed face paled and her eyes rolled back. Amanda reached out to catch her just as she crumpled to the floor. Hodges came on the run, his expression tight with irritation. Together, he and Amanda managed to carry Annie outside.

"Now get back to your place!" Hodges ordered. "The boss is here today."

"What about Mrs. Bleaker? You can't just leave her here on the floor!"

Annie began to moan. Her eyelids fluttered.

"Are you all right?" Amanda knelt beside her and tried to support her head.

"What's the matter with her, anyway?" Hodges demanded, angry at Amanda's defiance.

"She ran a bone under her nail."

He sighed in disgust. "That happens all the time. It's nothing to faint over."

"Can't you see she needs help? Look at the blood." Amanda loosened the handkerchief and gently removed it. The thumb had turned black. "You'd better get a doctor."

Furious, Hodges went into his office and slammed the door.

It was noon before the doctor arrived. He took one look at the thumb, then ordered Annie into his carriage.

"I'll have to remove the splinter in my office," he declared. "If it's not too late."

"If she misses the rest of the day," Hodges snapped, "she's out of a job."

The doctor peered over his spectacles in disdain. "This woman has more at stake than her job, sir."

Amanda watched in frustration as they drove away, realizing that she had no idea where Annie lived or how to locate her.

"Good riddance," Hodges grumbled. "She was too old anyway."

Then a slow smile spread over his face. "By the way, girlie, I hear a rumor that you came here to start a union. What do you say to that?"

"I say it's a lie."

"Even so, I'd hate to have the boss hear about it. Hope everybody keeps their mouth shut." He twitched slightly.

Amanda fixed her eyes on Hodges' nervous face, knowing what was coming.

"Looks like I'm the only one who can keep you out of trouble."

"Well, you needn't bother. I'm quitting."

"Quitting?" Hodges' smile faded. "We made a bargain. You can't get out of it that easy!"

"I didn't make any bargain. I said I would think over your offer and give you my answer on Saturday."

"You tricked me. You never meant to stay!"

"Now may I please have my wages?"

"I forgot to tell you. The first week is free training. So, it looks like you're out of luck, girlie."

"I don't think so, Mr. Hodges," said Amanda, swallowing the anger which welled up in her throat. "I think *you're* the one who's out of luck."

Chapter Six

COLONEL Blethen's office was situated behind a glass partition which faced the front entrance of the *Times*. His shirt sleeves were rolled up above the elbows, his tie was askew and his vest buttoned crookedly, so that there was an extra button at the top and a spare hole at the bottom. Like his clerks, he wore a green eyeshade, whose beak pointed down at a cluttered desk. But with the jangling of the bell above the door, his head snapped up. Seeing Amanda, he grinned broadly and without rising from his chair, motioned for her to come in.

"You've lost some weight," he observed, without bothering to offer a greeting. "Been sick?"

"Why, no," Amanda replied, somewhat startled. "I wasn't aware of losing any weight."

"Well, you have and it's not becoming. Hope you've been eating right."

His scolding was interrupted by the ringing of the telephone. He snatched up the receiver on the first ring and shouted for the party on the line to begin speaking. His conversation was curt and brief.

After hanging up, he said to Amanda, "Glad you had the sense to present yourself in person, instead of calling me up on that blasted thing. We would have shouted at each other in vain, for I'm convinced that the telephone's sole purpose is to scramble the English language so that it's completely unintelligible."

Without pausing for breath, Blethen leaped to his feet, insisting that Amanda have a tour of his new plant.

"I've got ten employees," he declared proudly. "Two men to run the presses, two to set type, and a pack of clerks, who are kept busy gathering the news and advertising, proofreading and all that. I, of course, put the whole mess together."

Opening the door to the pressroom, Blethen let escape the ear-splitting clamor of machinery.

For a moment Amanda felt as if she were back in the cannery. Giant cylinders were revolving at incredible speed carrying great rolls of paper which were feeding from spools like thread in a sewing machine. Blethen trotted ahead, trying to explain the process above the roar. Amanda shook her head in awe as she watched the printed sheets emerge from between the cylinders and smooth steel rolls, then the blades which severed the sheets and the final step which folded the pages. With a gesture of triumph, Blethen removed one of the papers from the stack and presented it to her. The ink was still wet and bore a mysterious chemical odor which belonged only to newsprint, and which seemed to speak of all that was immediate and urgent. The great events of the world rolled from those presses, matching the speed with which they occurred. As Amanda held the first edition of the day, whose print was fresh enough to blacken her fingers, she felt a tingle of excitement. At that moment she knew there could be no occupation more important, more exciting than newspaper work. She was only sorry to see there were no women working in the pressroom. I wouldn't mind being a pressman, Amanda thought. If I had a paper of my own, I'd try every single job.

When she returned with Blethen to his office, she had to confess that this was the first time she had ever been inside a newspaper plant.

"Well, you came to the right place," he stated immodestly. "We may be small at the moment, but we know what we're doing. I've kept on the boys who worked with the old *Press-Times,* and most of 'em are damn good. Till now they were never lucky enough to have a fella like me running the ship!"

Alden Blethen was the only man Amanda had ever met who could so openly compliment himself without appearing to be a braggart.

"But I'm sure you didn't come here merely for a tour," he said, and immediately busied himself at his desk.

"I've written an article."

"Yes," he drawled without glancing up. "What about?"

"About the women who work in the salmon cannery."

Blethen's head shot up. "Isn't that the place where Kenworthy lost a hand?"

Amanda nodded. "She was the one who inspired me to get a job there."

"A job?" Blethen tipped his chair back. "Good Lord. No wonder you look so poorly."

"A woman that I worked with had her thumb amputated. And you know what? She was a Mercer Girl!"

"A Mercer Girl?" Blethen leaned forward. "Now we're getting someplace. Tell me more."

Amanda handed him a large envelope. "It's all here for you to read."

Blethen snatched it from her eagerly. "Take a seat," he commanded, "and don't move till I've finished."

Amanda sat down slowly, on a chair so hard she was sure it was intended to discourage visitors from lingering.

Blethen adjusted his spectacles. "SALMON CANNERY: HOUSE OF SHAME," he read aloud. He glanced at her sharply. "That's a pretty strong head."

He then proceeded to mumble through the article, half aloud, but reading to himself, nodding now and then or raising his brows over a particular statement. When at last he was through, he brought down his fist, sending up a puff of dust from his desk.

"Sensational! This is just the kind of controversial stuff that could double our circulation overnight. And if you need the money, I'll pay now." Determinedly, Blethen reached into his back pocket and pulled out a roll of bills held by a rubber band. He chuckled. "All my assets are right here. It's the only way I can keep track of how much we're spending."

He counted out the bills, then scribbled a notation on a small scrap of paper, which he promptly buried in the disorder on his desk.

"Thirty-five dollars is what I pay. If you can keep it up, you should do well for yourself."

Before Amanda could thank him, he went on, "I like the Mercer Girl angle. That should win a lot of sympathy. In fact, I'd like to see you expand this thing into a series—to keep folks picking up the paper every day. We'll call it 'The Mercer Girls: What Are They Doing Today?' "

"Excuse me for disagreeing, but I think we should emphasize the labor issue—Mercer Girls mistreated by their bosses."

"Well, I'm not interested in crusading for factory workers. Factory workers don't read. And my job is to sell papers. Folks will be sympathetic to this Bleaker woman because by all rights she doesn't even belong in a factory. They'll be shocked."

"I see." Amanda started to get up. It was clear that Blethen was not going to give her the freedom she had hoped for after all.

"Where are you going?"

"I thought that as long as we're not in agreement, it would probably be best to . . ."

"How do you know what's best? Only *I* know that. It comes after years of experience. You're here to learn, aren't you? Well, I'm willing to teach you. You're a fortunate young lady, Miss Lamar. Stay with the *Times* and you'll go places."

Amanda sat down again.

"Now go find that Bleaker woman and get her to help you track down the other Mercer Girls. Bet you've got a dozen stories there. A dozen sensational adventures!"

The doctor was just emerging from his office when Amanda arrived. He seemed preoccupied, and when she stopped him, it took him a moment to recognize her.

"Where can I find Mrs. Bleaker?" she asked. "I'd like to pay her a visit."

The doctor's expression was grave as he stared at the bouquet of flowers that Amanda was holding. "I regret to tell you that Mrs. Bleaker has passed away."

"I can't believe it! How could that be?"

"She was doomed before I amputated. A fragment of fishbone had apparently traveled into her blood stream and right to the heart. It happens rarely and perhaps would not have happened at all if she had been given immediate treatment. But I fear I was not called in time."

Amanda's lips tightened in anger. "It was Hodges," she told him. "It was all his fault!"

The doctor sighed heavily. "I see many industrial accidents," he confided. "And almost always the fault lies with the management. Something should be done. But what?" He shrugged hopelessly, dismissing any possibility.

The following afternoon as the newsboys crowded around the loading dock to pick up their papers, Amanda watched nervously. She had followed her story along each step of the way, for Blethen had not only given it front-page prominence, but upon learning of Annie's fate, had decided to make it the lead story with: SALMON CANNERY: HOUSE OF DEATH. Both he and Amanda agreed that the word "shame" was no longer strong enough, that "death" was justified. Blethen was very excited by this new twist, for he felt that it lent even greater impact to the Mercer Girl disgrace. He couldn't resist gloating in anticipation of the *P.I.*'s reaction.

"Don't let 'em spirit you away," he cautioned. "They'll want Amanda Lamar for themselves!"

Amanda tried to smile, but she couldn't share his elation at benefiting from such a tragic development. "I only hope that the story will help the girls who are left at the cannery, who have no means to help themselves."

The paper was sold out within an hour. By evening everyone in town not only knew of Annie Bleaker, but of Amanda Lamar.

Inevitably her notoriety also came to the attention of the Denny Hotel. Much embarrassed to discover that they had been harboring a reporter, the manager placed a curt note under Amanda's door inviting her to leave.

Despite the fact that she hadn't the slightest idea where she would go, Amanda felt an exhilarating sense of relief to be departing the Denny and all its pretensions. But when Mary offered her a room, Amanda turned it down. She knew she didn't want to live in the woods, but in the very heart of the city. Suddenly she remembered.

The advertising carried in the *Times* for the Grand Union Hotel was straightforward: "Workingmen! Name your price, we furnish the room." That's the place for me, Amanda decided.

The lobby of the Grand Union appeared to be a congenial meeting place for a great variety of types. Theatrically dressed people mingled freely with those in working clothes, and the mixture of races was not likely to be seen in any other part of town.

Amanda particularly noticed several attractive Chinese girls, and wondered if any of them were the sisters of Soo-Lee. One looked familiar. She couldn't be sure, but she might have been the same girl she had seen with Cyrus Clough. Amanda felt vaguely uneasy. Then, when she was assigned a room on the third floor, she soon discovered that the entire floor was occupied only by women. This unconventional arrangement made it immediately obvious that something was going on. The housekeeper enlightened her.

"These ladies are actresses," she told Amanda testily, as if to correct the mistaken impression that anything was amiss. "They perform at the People's Theatre." Her tone implied that she was referring to a place of prestige.

Amanda decided it was probably wise not to mention to Colonel Blethen where she was living. No point in causing him unnecessary worry, or having her mother find out that the Grand Union might not be the most respectable place to stay. Mary Kenworthy's address would set everyone's mind at ease.

Looking about her room, Amanda pondered how to make it livable. Having grown used to a view of the Sound, she found facing the brick wall of the neighboring building depressing. The room definitely needed some scenic pictures of great panoramas, such as Yosemite and the Grand Canyon, or perhaps Indians on horseback against the sunset. A vase of flowers in the window, a bowl of fruit for the table, and a small cheerful lamp would add just the right homelike touches.

However, she was glad that Blethen had found a desk for her at the *Times,* where she could write her next story in the welcome company of colleagues. Immediately she began her search for other Mercer Girls, a task assisted by letters from the public volunteering information. Grudgingly she had to admit that Blethen knew how to capture readers.

She was only two days into her assignment when the *Times* received a letter stating that Mr. Hodges had been fired from the cannery. More surprising was the fact that the news came from the cannery owner, who absolved his plant of any blame in the death of Annie Bleaker, accusing the foreman of being at fault. Happy though she was to learn that Hodges was out, Amanda had the disquieting feeling that he had been sacrificed simply to save the cannery from a more thorough investigation and at the same time to boost its reputation in the eyes of the public. The following day Amanda received an anonymous note telling her that Hodges had just been hired as foreman at the oyster-packing plant.

Amanda flew into Blethen's office, her cheeks aflame. But Blethen merely shrugged.

"It's all political," he declared. "Did you think for one minute that your article was going to bring about some massive social reform? Ah, youth!"

"But it's not fair. Men like Hodges shouldn't ever work again!"

"Lamar, I'm going to talk plain. Do you know what incest is?"

"I think so," admitted Amanda, hardly able to believe her ears.

"Well, incest is the glue that holds the factories together. They all help each other. And the worker is their common enemy. Nothing's ever going to change that. Not the best story in the world. They've got power and unity on their side—two things that the workers haven't got. So don't fight a battle you're doomed to lose. Your article was a huge success. We sold a ton of papers, got a ton of letters and new subscriptions galore! Get my meaning? You're a success, Lamar. So take off the long face and buck up!"

It didn't take long for word to spread among the guests at the Grand Union that they had a celebrity in their midst. So it was that one afternoon, three of the actresses from the People's Theatre invited Amanda to join them for tea. She accepted eagerly. How strange it seemed after such a long time to be once again with girls her own age.

Bertha volunteered to have tea served in her room. She gave no surname, nor did Sally and Henrietta, explaining that it was an agreement among all the actresses to use only first names.

Amanda soon found herself answering more questions than she was able to ask, for the girls insisted on knowing how she came to write the cannery exposé. They confessed that everyone they knew felt very disturbed by Annie Bleaker's death.

"My mother was a Mercer Girl," Henrietta divulged matter-of-factly.

"She was? Do you think perhaps I might write about her?"

"Oh, she's been dead for years. Since I was a baby."

"I'm sorry. What about your father? Is he alive?"

Henrietta shrugged. "He disappeared. Same as Annie Bleaker's husband."

"The men must have been terrible drifters in those days," said Amanda.

"They still are. All men are drifters. And Seattle men are the worst, so don't lose your heart to any of them."

Henrietta's warning caused her friends to giggle, glancing at Amanda for her reaction. She thought immediately of Tom.

"I think you're right," she agreed.

Though Bertha's room had the same dismal view as Amanda's, she kept a gaily painted window shade drawn all the way down to the sill, even in the middle of the day. Oriental scatter rugs covered the bare floor, and hand-crocheted pillow covers, silk scarves and artificial flowers in Indian baskets brightened every corner. A fringed lampshade muted the glare of the bare electric light bulb. Dresser and tables were crowded with collections—animal miniatures and china figures of every description, as a child might have for a doll's house.

However, she took greatest pride in the trinkets which she claimed were gifts from theater patrons. "That's the nice thing about working for John Considine," she added. "We have special privileges."

"Is he your boss?" Amanda asked.

"And our *friend,*" Bertha emphasized. "After performances, we're allowed to bring customers to our rooms."

"But don't think this is a brothel," Henrietta cautioned. "If you were to do the same, you might be asked to leave."

"Why is that?" Amanda asked fascinated.

"Because you don't work for Mr. Considine. He has an arrangement with the hotel. When we bring customers to our rooms, it promotes business for the theater. Of course he gets a portion of our earnings, which is only fair."

"It sounds to me like you have *two* jobs."

"Not really," said Bertha, running to answer a tap at the door. "The more customers we bring to our rooms, the better parts we get to perform. So I see it all as being one job."

A bellboy wheeled in the tea, paying no attention to the conversation, which continued openly while he arranged the cups and saucers.

"What if you refused?"

They all laughed.

"How silly!" said Bertha. "Why, we can make five or six dollars a night."

"In addition to your pay as actresses?"

"Oh, we don't perform for wages, just for meals."

"But that's slave labor!" Amanda protested.

They laughed again, a little uncertainly. The bellboy blotted up some spilled tea with a napkin, then hurried from the room.

"We feel lucky," said Bertha, "not to be working in a factory, like Annie Bleaker."

"So if you're going to write about us," prompted Sally, "you be sure to put that Mr. Considine is a wonderful man." She paused, then added as an afterthought, "Because of him we have a nice place to live, plenty to eat and jobs."

"And say that the daughters of the Mercer Girls are a lot better off than their mothers," Henrietta added.

After Amanda returned to her room, she felt shaken and blue. She had thought herself very worldly until now. It was one thing to be exploited, it was another to be exploited and not know it.

"So you want to take on John Considine, is that it?" Blethen tipped his chair back and regarded Amanda with bright, expectant eyes. Though it was only seven in the morning, his sleeves were rolled up, as usual, held in place by bright yellow arm bands. And his forearms were smudged with newsprint.

"Those poor actresses are in a sweatshop as surely as if they were in a cannery," Amanda insisted, seeing that he expected her to sell him on the idea. "Why, they're modern-day slaves!"

"What happened to the Mercer Girls? Tired of 'em already?"

"Henrietta is a second-generation Mercer Girl. Which I think is even sadder."

"The fact remains, you're going after a very powerful gentleman—a gambler, an entrepreneur. He can make trouble."

"Are you telling me not to do it?"

"Hold your hat. I like the idea. High time somebody took him on. Just don't use your name on this story."

"You mean I should use a pen name?"

"Exactly. If you're going to make it a practice to stir up trouble, then we should invent a name that you'll be able to use from this day forward, no matter what you write."

"I don't want to be a coward and hide," said Amanda, imagining what Emma Goldman would say.

"Pshaw! You don't want to get yourself killed either. Besides, a pseudonym adds intrigue. The public will beat their brains out trying to guess who you are."

Amanda's eyes narrowed as she tried to visualize herself as a woman of mystery. This Blethen was beginning to make sense. Still, it was a funny feeling—to have the public guessing who she was when she wasn't even sure herself. It was like becoming a personality before she was entirely a person.

Blethen studied a crack in the ceiling. "A one-syllable name would be best. Something that would come to be identified with the kind of story you're known for, or your style." He shut his eyes for a moment, as if descending into some vast, hidden reservoir deep within his mind. He emerged with a cry, his eyes flew open and he stood.

"Firebrand!" he thundered. "That's what you are, by Jove, a regular firebrand!"

Amanda was startled. How did *he* know? That was exactly what she wanted to be.

When "SLAVERY ON THE THIRD FLOOR by Firebrand" appeared in print, Amanda was extremely grateful that she had bowed to the will of Colonel Blethen and taken a pen name. Despite the fact that she had mentioned John Considine only by implication, he brought an immediate lawsuit against the *Times,* claiming that his identity was obvious to all. Then he went on to state that as owner of the Grand Union, he had every right to conduct whatever business he wished on his own premises.

Amanda was shocked. Throughout her investigation, she had unearthed no evidence connecting him with the hotel, other than the third-floor arrangement. She was certain even the girls were unaware of this—until now, of course. It was an uncomfortable predicament. She had the uneasy feeling that it was only a matter of time until Considine would trace her to the third floor of his own hotel.

Blethen was undismayed by the lawsuit, which he confidently predicted would be thrown out of court.

"We'll just have to ride out the storm," he told her.

And a storm it was indeed. Almost as many letters supporting Considine poured into the *Times,* as those condemning him. It was apparent that he had hundreds of friends in high places, so numerous were his defenders. Amanda found the response disillusioning.

"You're the only reporter I've ever known who's daunted by success!" chided Blethen, shaking his head.

Still, Amanda read each letter, helping him select a balance of pro and con for publication. Among them she spotted a letter from the Clough-Hartley Mill in Everett. It praised John Considine as a man of enterprise and integrity, and denounced Firebrand for the "vicious attack." The letter was signed, "Cyrus Clough, President." Amanda smiled as she assigned it to the pile to be published. How satisfying it would be to respond by letting him know that he had been seen entering the Grand Union with a young lady.

"We can keep the story alive for weeks by printing a few letters every day," Blethen went on. "So the angrier, the better. Yes, we've lost a few subscriptions, but we've gained twice as many new readers, a number of which I suspect have been stolen from our worthy rival."

Blethen remained in fine spirits, reminding Amanda that a tough shell was the best protection against the wrath of the public.

"Folks don't have to love you for you to be a success," he emphasized. "In fact I'd say it's just the opposite."

John Considine's lawsuit was thrown out of court, exactly as Blethen had predicted. As always, he took victory in stride, eager to get on with the building of his newspaper.

But for Amanda the repercussions continued. She awoke one morning to find that every girl on the third floor had gone. Open doorways gaped onto the corridor like astonished empty mouths, left ajar in hasty exodus. She hurried the length of the hall, peering into vacant rooms for some sign of life. Bertha's room, like the others, was stripped of personal effects. In the strange silence Amanda saw that it was just as dismal as her own with the brick wall view and exposed light bulb. The housekeeper wept as she changed the linens, shunning Amanda as though she were contaminated.

Amanda turned away, ashamed to think that whatever had happened, *she* was responsible.

The following day a letter arrived at the *Times* addressed to Firebrand. It was from John Considine. She ripped open the envelope, gearing herself for the worst. Startled, she saw that he began, "Dear

Miss Lamar . . ." Uneasily she guessed that by taking the trouble to learn her true identity, he was letting her know that she hadn't escaped him.

He wrote: "Congratulations. You have made a name for yourself at the expense of my employees, young ladies who now find themselves without means of support. If your intent was to punish *me,* you have failed; it is they who are suffering. Think of this the next time you use your pen as a weapon. Let me also remind you that in the future, I intend to pursue any business I wish. That's because we have a system called free enterprise, which is the nemesis of agitators like yourself. Therefore, I advise you not to attempt reforms which interfere with the system, as it cannot be defeated."

Blethen shrugged off the incident with customary unconcern.

"You put a stop to prostitution at the Grand Union. Wasn't that the whole purpose?"

"I'm thinking about those poor girls with no place to go."

"That, young lady, is not your problem."

"I hate to go around uprooting people without offering them something in return."

"Your function was to bring an abuse into the open. Which you did. Now it's up to society."

"Aren't *we* society?"

"You fought the battle, so put down your sword. Those girls have youth in their favor, like you. They'll survive." With this, Blethen dismissed the subject.

"I know how you must feel," Mary Kenworthy sympathized, "but don't be discouraged. After all, Considine pronounced you an agitator, which I would take as a compliment. More tea?"

Amanda nodded. "I hate being at the mercy of a man like that. If the truth can't be told, then I might as well pack up and go home."

"What would that solve? Social change is a slow process. You don't have to shake the foundations with every article you write. There are other ways to make people aware of the problems, other ways to help the worker besides an open attack on management."

"How?"

Mary gave her a confident smile. "You'll think of something."

"I know I have people on my side. For every nasty letter I receive, there are two favorable ones."

"There you are! Before you know it, you'll have a following. That's very important."

"In fact, I brought one of the letters with me. Would you like to read it?" She handed Mary an envelope which had become crumpled from riding in her pocket. "I don't know what to make of it."

Mary began reading aloud. "Dear Firebrand: What a great relief to discover you're not a man!"

She paused while they both laughed. Then she continued. "When I first saw the name Firebrand, it didn't occur to me that the writer might actually be a fiery, passionate *woman*. But once I began to read, it was obvious that such depth of emotion could never spill from the pen of a male. Your words have helped me to create an image of beauty which I carry in my mind like a photograph. And if it seems presumptuous of me to *know* that you're beautiful, it's all due to what you have written. I could tell that you really *cared* about the hapless girls at the Grand Union. I can also tell that you are warm and sensitive. As I eagerly await future stories, I remain your sincere admirer, M.R."

Mary looked up, brows raised in amusement. "Well! That's quite a love letter."

"Is that what it is?" Amanda blushed. "I've never gotten one like that. At first I thought it might even be from another woman."

"Possibly. But I don't think so. A woman would be more open. She wouldn't sign her initials because she wouldn't be hiding. This person wishes to conceal his identity—maybe to spark your interest."

"Or because he's married!"

They laughed again, then Mary added seriously, "But the important thing this letter tells us is that being a *female* firebrand has its advantages. Readers don't often get a woman's point of view."

"What do you mean?"

"You attack your subject much more directly than a man would. You make no attempt to be subtle, in fact you are utterly unsparing. Why do you think this reader sees you as a 'fiery, passionate woman'? I think men must find your style intriguing and may be more easily won over. At least this mysterious M.R. was!"

Amanda smiled nervously. Until now, she wasn't aware that she even *had* a style. But as she thought about it later, she hoped that Mary was right. Using her womanhood as a kind of secret weapon would give her the freedom to tackle subjects that a man would never think of, and to be as daring as she pleased—or as Blethen would allow. Blethen. Now he was the only possible stumbling block to curbing her independence.

Chapter Seven

THE MINUTE Amanda saw the small neat house on First Hill with its "For Rent" sign hanging on the picket fence, she knew that she had to live there.

It was a real home, far more cheerful than a hotel room. And much more reasonable. Amanda felt that she could just about manage the rent—twenty dollars a month—as long as Colonel Blethen continued to pay her thirty-five dollars for every article she wrote.

The house was actually a three-room cottage, with parlor, bedroom and kitchen of diminutive dimensions. The plumbing was located in a lean-to at the back, but at least it was under the same roof. An encircling garden of newly planted fruit trees assured privacy. But best of all, there was a view of the Sound, for the house was situated halfway up the hill, only a short walk from downtown.

The furnishings were sparse, but adequate. The Lang smoke-burning range gave off enough heat to warm the entire cottage, almost too much in fact, for Amanda burned most of what she cooked. But it made no difference. This was a house, and with it came a heightened sense of independence.

She wrote to her mother in high spirits, trying not to sound like, "I told you so," while making it clear that she was doing just fine on her own.

"There is nothing to worry about," she wrote. "I'm not the same person I was when I left home three months ago. I've shed my girlhood and taken on responsibilities. I am regarded *seriously* by the people who read my articles. (Clippings enclosed, but don't be

alarmed by my forceful, candid tone. That's *Firebrand* speaking!)
Will be staying in Seattle at least through the winter. Hope you're not
still unhappy with me. I remain always, your loving daughter,
Manka. P.S. Your Col. Blethen values me highly—to the tune of $35
per article! If you ever run into any of my old schoolmates, I
wouldn't object a bit if you'd chance to divulge this 'confidential' information."

But despite Amanda's optimism, she gradually became aware that
she was no longer Blethen's only reporter. As the *Times* continued to
grow, stories poured in from around the state and beyond. The wors-
ening depression had uprooted entire communities, all of whom
seemed destined for Seattle to seek work.

"Newspapers always do well when business is in a slump,"
Blethen maintained confidently. "Newspapers and barbers."

Clusters of hungry reporters milled about in front of the *Times,*
hoping for an appointment with Blethen. And most of them were
eventually rewarded for their patience. Sooner or later, he saw everyone. For the lucky few there were assignments. Blethen never lowered his pay for a story from thirty-five dollars, even knowing he
could have paid less. He believed it was important to demonstrate his
stability.

"We've got a problem, Lamar," Blethen announced one day as he
sifted through the stack of submissions which overflowed the wire
basket on his desk. "Everybody's trying to imitate you. They all want
to be another Firebrand. Well, we don't need another one." He
removed his spectacles and massaged his eyes with slow deliberation.
"The truth is, we don't even need *one* Firebrand."

"You're letting me go?" Amanda stammered in disbelief.

"Not you, only Firebrand. I'm afraid she'll have to go into moth
balls for a while."

"You mean—I'll have to change?"

"Exactly. There's lots of folks out there who've been laid off from
their jobs. So there isn't much public sympathy for stories about dis-
contented workers. Most folks feel they're lucky to have jobs at all,
including the workers themselves. Look at our cannery story. The
minute Hodges was fired, everybody simmered down. But what did it
really accomplish? The women now wear gloves to keep their fingers
on, and galoshes to keep their feet dry. But do they have better pay
or shorter hours?"

"They would if they had a union. But they're afraid."

"That's my point. The owners know there are plenty of workers ready to take their places if they stir up trouble." Blethen's tone softened. "But when the good times come again, maybe they'll rise up. You gave 'em a germ of hope they won't forget."

Amanda swallowed the ache of disappointment which suddenly turned her throat dry. All she could picture was a procession of lost opportunities escaping over a fence like fleeing sheep.

Noting her distress, he said brightly, "You'll be pleased to know that Considine has just sold out."

"Because of my story?"

"Undoubtedly. He tried to keep the sale hushed up, but those things always leak out."

Amanda forced a smile. "Well, that's *some* comfort."

"Lamar, I'm damn sorry about all this, but a newspaper has to change with the times. We have to serve our public, just like politicians do. Right now folks want something in a lighter vein to take their minds off the depression." He paused. "I want to add a feature that will appeal to women. A feature that will be all yours."

Amanda raised her eyes from the floor, feeling a sudden spark of hope.

"Advice to the lovelorn! Now *that* should sell papers to beat the band!"

She stared, smile fading. "Are you serious?"

"Dead serious. Why not? You want to help women, don't you?"

"Well, yes. I want to help *everybody*. But I don't see how I can if I have to write something so—trivial."

Blethen's eyes narrowed. "Lamar, have you ever been in love?"

Amanda shifted uncomfortably. "That's a pretty personal question."

"Course it is. Have you?"

"No, never," she replied a bit too quickly. "Who has time? I think there are more important things to do in this world than fall in love."

"The majority wouldn't agree. And this paper is for the majority. Why, Seattle is filled with lonely people all trying to meet the right partner, or once they've met, trying to hang onto 'em. Well, what do you say?"

Amanda stood up. "I can't do it," she blurted. "I've never had a real beau and I have no idea how to find one. So you better let somebody else write it—somebody who's worldly and experienced. Not me." She turned and rushed for the door, blinded by sudden tears.

Walking home, Amanda felt ashamed of her outburst and resentful that Blethen had led her to betray herself. When he had asked her if she had ever been in love, he had hit a painful target. Of *course* it hurt. She was one of the lonely people that he spoke of. Worst of all, he had forced her to think of Tom just when she was beginning to get over him. Tom had written only once to say how much he missed her, but it was hard to believe him. The four-page letter she had written to him in reply had not yet been answered. She told herself she didn't care, but having no other friends her own age to occupy her time made it difficult to put him out of her mind.

Her new house now seemed very isolated. Instead of a cozy haven of privacy, it felt like a cramped box from which she could view the rest of the world passing by. The high ceilings never echoed with laughter, the floors never groaned under the tread of feet running and dancing. And the wood range never simmered with bubbling roasts and pies, for she cooked only the plainest fare, as one is inclined to do who lives alone.

It was late afternoon when she heard the front gate creak, an unfamiliar sound indeed. Puzzled, she went to the window. There was Colonel Blethen, all dressed up with top hat and walking stick. He leaned on the gate for a moment, catching his breath after the steep climb. Amanda dropped the curtain quickly before he should see her and tried to collect her thoughts. Should she pretend not to be at home? But it was too late, for at the very moment she heard his knock, the shrill whistle of the teakettle sang out from the kitchen.

When she opened the door, Blethen was holding his hat against his chest, the other hand behind his back. But as if fearing that the door might be closed in his face, he swept out a hand-picked bouquet of wild flowers.

"I came to smoke the peace pipe," he announced gruffly.

There was something pathetic in the way he stood on the doorstep, like a schoolboy hoping to avoid punishment. For the first time, she was struck with the thought that perhaps Blethen, too, was lonely. Why would he have thought of a lovelorn column, unless he himself had experienced some heartfelt loss?

She held the door open wider. "You're just in time for a cup of tea."

Amanda pulled the sheet from her typewriter and read it aloud with as much expression as possible.

"Dear Lovelorn: I am a young girl nineteen years old. I have been going out with a young man since July, who has asked me to be his wife. I promised I would, but about three weeks ago, the young man that I used to go with came back to me, and I like him much better, and I don't think I could ever love that other young man. Please give me your advice as to what I should do. Signed, Worried."

Amanda paused, changing to a sophisticated voice. "Dear Worried: Think before you flirt! You are far too immature to give your heart to *any* man. In fairness to all, take your time in making a decision. Meanwhile, keep the friendship of both young men, but remember, there is a price to pay for passion. Beware of lingering kisses. They can quickly get out of hand. Good luck."

Blethen choked slightly. "That's pretty blunt language."

"It isn't *me* speaking," Amanda hastened to explain. "It's Beatrice Fairfax."

"Good Lord! Another pen name?"

"I thought I'd better not use my real name, for if anyone were to discover I was only seventeen . . ." She stopped short.

"Seventeen? Heaven help us!"

Amanda flushed. Damn! It had just slipped out. But despite Blethen's comment, he didn't appear at all surprised.

"Anyway," she continued, "what do you think of my new name?"

"I like it. But you don't sound like a Beatrice. You sound like . . ." He searched for the word, then his cheeks rounded into a broad grin. "You still sound like a Firebrand!"

"Then I guess that's the real me," she said, feeling pleased. "I'm not in moth balls after all."

"But watch your step," he cautioned, trying to be serious. "We can't be too risqué."

Her eyes grew wide. "Colonel Blethen, I only want to help everybody forget the depression—just like you said."

The column was an immediate success, far exceeding Blethen's expectations, for Beatrice Fairfax quickly captured the greatest share of the mail. The first rash of what Amanda termed "silly problems" soon gave way to an uninhibited stream of confidences. It was apparent that her straightforward advice was encouraging readers to divulge the most intimate details of their personal lives, which often made her feel like a doctor.

Who am I to be giving advice to others? she asked herself. But no one else asked that question. They were grateful that someone—*anyone* was willing to help.

As the secret confessions flowed in, Amanda had to admit that Blethen had been right in saying the town was filled with lonely people. What he had failed to realize was that most of them came from the industrial neighborhoods. When she showed him each day's pile of letters, he was happy to admit that workers *did* buy newspapers.

Amanda, however, was happy for a far different reason—the chance to reach the working class. She had often thought of Mary's mystifying comment, "There are other ways to help the worker besides an open attack on management." At the time Amanda hadn't the slightest idea what she meant. Now it was clear. Beatrice Fairfax was in a perfect position to accomplish what Firebrand could not. In helping the worker to solve love and marital problems, Beatrice would give them the confidence to solve *all* their problems. Or so she hoped.

In the process, Amanda was learning a great deal about the lives of her readers. Loneliness was the by-product of factory existence, thriving on the fact that certain industries hired only men, others only women. In addition, long hours and low wages unfailingly conspired to keep the sexes segregated, for there was little spare time or funds available for recreation. Most workers were too exhausted at the end of the day to engage in social activity, even if they had the means to do so. Which left only Sundays. For this reason, if for no other, the churches were well attended. Many expressed belief that the church was the single respectable place where a formal introduction was not required. When Beatrice assured them there was nothing wrong in a chance meeting on a streetcar to and from work, she received a dozen requests from male readers wanting to meet her, and two proposals of marriage. On another occasion when she suggested that union parties and picnics provided excellent opportunities for meeting those whose interests most closely matched their own, she received seven photographs from hopeful suitors wishing to know if *she* would be attending any of the functions she mentioned.

At times she was amused, at other times disturbed by the undercurrent of desperation which she had learned to detect. And though she searched her mail for the initials of her one-time admirer, M.R., he never wrote to Beatrice. It was obvious that he had been attracted only to Firebrand. It was also obvious that he needed no advice in the love department.

Although not every letter could be printed, Amanda felt obliged to write personal answers to each one, bearing in mind that Beatrice was a real woman to the reader, for whom it had been necessary to create a personality and a past. Beatrice was raven-haired with violet eyes and a pale complexion from years spent working in a factory. However, she was by no means tubercular, but pleasingly well formed and energetic. Alas, Beatrice had known tragedy. As a girl, many years ago, she had met a young man at a union picnic, had married him and lived happily—for a while. But one day the young man was killed in an industrial accident. As a heartbroken widow, Beatrice resolved to work for better factory conditions, and by her dedication managed to rise in the union to a position of importance. Now at the age of forty, she had reached the ranks of the middle class, yet never forgetting the class from which she came. Beatrice didn't mind revealing these details about her life whenever a reader asked, though of course she had to decline if they requested a photo, or offered a proposal of marriage.

"I think we should set up a marriage bureau," Amanda suggested to Blethen, "and arrange introductions." She gave him a sly glance.

"God help us!" was his answer.

Then a curious thing happened. Amanda noticed the content of her mail was shifting to more complex issues. Letters became less concerned with husbands or lovers, and more centered on problems at work. With growing fascination, she saw a seldom discussed subject begin to emerge—adultery. As with Hodges at the cannery, Amanda discovered that many bosses took advantage of their female employees, treating them as personal possessions, especially the younger, prettier ones, by forcing them to trade sexual favors for special privileges. These women often turned greedy, doing all in their power to maintain their positions, making life miserable for their less "fortunate" sisters. Amanda was especially shocked to learn that abortions and children born out of wedlock were commonplace, but as these incidents were always hushed up, there was no public awareness that such conditions existed. And when a woman died as the result of an abortion, this, too, was covered up to protect the reputation of the man involved.

Male workers also had their share of complaints, the most common being favoritism shown those who were willing to pay the foreman under the table. But as no one could be trusted, even those willing to play the game could never feel secure. Workers were often relieved of a week's wages while walking home on payday, by gangs collaborating with the boss. Amanda soon accumulated impressive evidence that the entire working class were victims of a system which cared nothing for them. She gathered the most shocking examples to show to Blethen.

"What am I supposed to do with these?" he asked.

"I want permission to do some investigating."

Dutifully Blethen read the letters and listened to her argument. Then with great patience he told her, "Don't take the burden of the world's problems on your own shoulders. If Beatrice doesn't have all the answers, let her impart a few words of comfort. Then forget it. Nobody can expect more than that."

"I don't think these problems can be solved by comforting words. People know that Beatrice worked in a factory herself—they expect her to stand up for them."

"Good God, you've let that woman take over your life!"

Ignoring him, Amanda plunged ahead. "Beatrice should be able to tell a worker to walk off the job, if necessary. Or form a delegation and go straight down to Olympia. Or sign up with the union. And if there isn't a union, then start one. Take up petitions . . ."

"Whoa, there! In short you want the *Times* to become the voice of the working class, is that it?"

"If it only could, that would be perfect!"

"Well, it's not going to happen. I'm willing to lean a little; however, I'm not going to change the policy of my newspaper. But I'll tell you what. You can print all those letters to let the public know what's going on. And when you write your answers, you can tell your workers where to go for help. Just don't advise taking action on labor problems. That's not Beatrice's job."

Amanda leaned across his desk, fists planted in the disorder.

"There must be more to journalism than consoling people. And there must be more than just reporting. I want to change things!"

"Only the boss can do that," Blethen replied solemnly. His fierce brows relaxed and he reached across to pat Amanda's determined fist. "Now why don't you run over to Frederick and Nelson and buy yourself a hat?"

Amanda looked at him suspiciously. "Why? What's wrong with the one I've got?"

"Nothing whatsoever," he declared cheerfully. "It was just a figure of speech. I meant that I'd like to see you do something for yourself for a change. You're too young to be so serious. Relax and have some fun." He dug into his pocket and counted out two one-dollar bills. "Here's an advance on your wages. Go ahead, take the afternoon off."

As Amanda walked up Second Avenue toward Pike, she stared at the displays in the shop windows without really seeing them. What she saw was her own reflection moving beside her—bright anxious eyes looked back and a tight expression around the mouth was just a bit too determined. It was a mouth which had forgotten how to smile.

What's happened to you, Manka? she demanded sternly. What are you doing to yourself?

She stopped at the entrance of Frederick and Nelson, for it suddenly dawned on her that when Blethen had told her to go buy a hat, he probably meant "go meet a fellow!"

He had guessed that her dedication to work was inspired in part by a lack of social life. And even though she had become quite good at suggesting to her readers all the various ways they might meet members of the opposite sex, she hadn't learned how to follow her own advice.

Nevertheless, she went into the store and looked around, trying to summon up enough enthusiasm to buy something. The sign read: "Correct Apparel for Women," but the clothing appeared to be more sturdy than stylish, reminding her of school uniforms. She found nothing which didn't look as though it would last a lifetime. She wandered by racks of goatskin suits lined with squirrel which advertised: "No passing shower will cause serious damage," until she reached the blouse department. It was there she saw at last one item which struck her fancy—a green crepe de chine blouse cut flatteringly low. It was totally impractical, being out of season and thus reduced in price, but Amanda knew it would turn heads. It was designed for a redhead—for *her*. She needed no further reason to justify the purchase.

You tromp around like a tomboy, always in a damn raincoat, she scolded herself. No wonder you don't meet anybody.

Impulsively she handed the clerk the money which Blethen had advanced her, plus a dollar that she had already had. It was a shameful extravagance, but it lifted her spirits immediately. It was a good feeling to know that she could be womanly and desirable whenever she wished. It was even better to be able to make a decision without having to ask someone else.

As she left the store with her package, she thought how pleasant life would be if every decision could be hers and hers alone. Unless of course the right man came along. If that happened, *he* would have to make the decision to marry her, and she needed only to accept. For even Beatrice knew there was no decision at all when it came to falling in love. It just happened.

Chapter Eight

T HE winter of '97 passed so swiftly that Amanda could scarcely believe how long she had been gone from home. Memories of school and her former life were fading. A letter from Tom had arrived at Christmas. It sounded optimistic, but vague. However, he did say how much he missed her and that he hoped she was waiting for him. Little did he suspect that she was waiting, not by choice, but by lack of opportunity. Amanda had met a few young men through Mary Kenworthy, but no one who made her feel like wearing her green crepe de chine blouse. She determinedly accepted every invitation she received to attend parties or the theater, yet she still felt a certain emptiness which no amount of socializing could fill.

A heavy snowfall in January buried Seattle up to the tips of the picket fences, and with it came temperatures cold enough to freeze all the small fresh-water lakes. On occasion Amanda had joined a group to go skating on Green Lake. But just when she had grown proficient at skating backward with one leg extended, the ice began to melt. With the coming of spring, heavy skies lifted and moved away to reveal that the Cascades and the Olympics were still there, sharp and silver-crusted against the horizon, while the solitary peak of Mount Tacoma floated above all else. Barren patches of logged-off land came alive with pussy willows, Scotch broom and other strange forms of abundant new growth, all made possible by a constant precipitation. But the innocent mantle of nature never lulled her into complacency. For always in the background the mills and factories hovered like ominous shadows reminding her that for those who worked there, spring never brought hope or change.

"Advice to the Lovelorn" was now called "Beatrice Fairfax Listens," a compromise to which Amanda had agreed only when she saw that Blethen could not be swayed to allow Beatrice to take a bolder stand. Although the new format allowed even the most incriminating letters to find their way into print, the replies were restrained. Beatrice was clearly listening and little more. Blethen was pleased because the column sold papers as never before, which he claimed proved that folks were content simply to tell their troubles, never mind the answer. But Amanda knew better. If they were content, it was because they hadn't yet been stirred to revolt.

As the column grew, so did Beatrice. She was now a staff of three, whom Blethen had hired to help with the mail, and to learn Beatrice's style in case Amanda ever got sick. But Amanda stayed well, for Beatrice had become a vital link to a world that needed changing. And although she didn't speak out as strongly as Amanda would have wished, she was still her best friend and inseparable companion.

But the relationship was not to last. It was early in July of 1897 when news flashed around the world that two Indians and a white man had staggered out of the Yukon wilderness, each bearing a gunny sack bulging with gold. But of even greater significance was their claim that hundreds of other lucky prospectors, like themselves, at that very moment were hauling away as much gold as they could carry, and yet they had barely scratched the surface. The press jumped to pronounce it the most fantastic strike ever made, which caused the public to wait breathlessly for the evidence to reach civilization. The S.S. *Portland* had already departed Skagway, heading for Seattle, supposedly with an incredible cargo of gold shared among sixty-eight exultant miners. It would be a twenty-one-day wait until the truth of the rumor could be confirmed.

The *Times* carried the story briefly, for no more than a brief account was available, on the second page. With his characteristic skepticism Blethen reminded the reader that there had been gold strikes before. They always caused a great stir, but more often than not, the vein would run out almost before the stampede could begin. He didn't care to play it up, like the *P.I.* was doing, until he had something more substantial to go on. But as the days passed, no one could escape the excitement, which began with a sudden influx of people into town. Hotels and rooming houses filled to capacity, while on the outskirts, villages of canvas poked up between stumps like an army camp on the edge of a battlefield.

But most significant of all, letters to Beatrice Fairfax began to drop off. At first Amanda was alarmed, then it dawned on her what had happened. People could think of nothing but gold. Entrepreneurs, ready to take a gamble, had already opened up outfitting stores in anticipation of the rush. Hope alone had dispelled the specter of depression, for even the jobless somehow scraped together enough to purchase prospecting supplies. And no wonder. The prospector was the only worker who enjoyed total freedom. He depended on no one, had no hours to keep, no boss to tell him what to do. Best of all, he had a chance to become very rich in the shortest possible time. The discovery of gold had given the worker the hope that even Beatrice Fairfax had been unable to provide.

As soon as Amanda saw the potential, she couldn't contain her excitement.

"The *Portland* will be here on July 17," she reminded Blethen eagerly. "Will you let me cover it?"

"When she gets here is time enough to decide. Let's see how much gold she's actually carrying—if any."

"But even if there isn't an ounce aboard, it's still news. How can we ignore it?"

"I'd rather you were worrying about how to pep up your column. Once Beatrice shows an interest in gold, it's good-by to your readers. Why, they'll be walking off their jobs to catch the next steamer heading north!"

"I know! Won't it be wonderful? If Beatrice supports the gold rush, the factories will empty out. And management will be down on their knees begging them to come back! What do you say?"

"I say that Beatrice is going to look like a foolish, irresponsible young girl—not a mature woman of forty," he replied grumpily.

"But if we could scoop the *P.I.* when the *Portland* docks, look how many papers we'd sell!"

Blethen gave her a bushy scowl. "Maybe. But it won't be easy. Every reporter from here to San Francisco will be stampeding down to the waterfront, just like they did for the Chinese."

"Then I'll board the ship *before* she docks. Maybe at Everett."

"If you can do that, I say go ahead and cover the damn thing. But remember, if Beatrice loses all her readers, she's out of a job."

On the morning of July 16, Amanda was in a fishing boat plowing through the rough water of Everett's congested harbor on her way to meet the *Portland*. From all directions various small craft, schooners and tugs joined them to form an armada outward bound at full throttle. The excited voices of fishermen calling from boat to boat in Scandinavian accents carried over the Sound, until at last the bow of the *Portland* could be seen slicing through the morning mist.

As soon as Amanda's boat signaled the *Portland* that they were approaching with a passenger, the ship gave a massive shudder, cutting her engines. When they drew alongside, a rope ladder was lowered. Amanda realized it was meant for her.

"Their gangplank won't reach," the fisherman explained. "Think you can make it?"

Amanda nodded firmly, determined to conceal the panic she felt at the prospect of dangling in mid-air high above the water. As there were more than enough willing hands to help her grasp hold, she clutched the rope and began the dizzying climb, not daring to look down.

Midway up the ladder she imagined that among the voices cheering her efforts, someone was wildly calling "Lamar!" There were only two people who called her that—Colonel Blethen and Tom Maynard. She looked up with a start to see Tom looking down, his arms extended to help her over the railing.

"Maynard!" she gasped. "Is it really you?"

Joyfully he lifted her over, then spun her around. Only when he stopped to catch his breath did she notice that he looked like a miner himself, with his hair grown long and wearing mackinaw trousers and shirt.

"Thank God you're here!" he said, as though *she* was the one who had been away.

Then he stepped back, suddenly shy, and gave her a long look. She could see that he wanted to kiss her, but was too self-conscious to do it in front of so many curious faces.

"I don't believe it," he kept repeating. "I just don't believe it!"

"Me either," she said. And they laughed together in sheer amazement, both at a loss for words.

Much as she was glad to see Tom, she didn't feel quite the same as she had last year. The passage of time had somehow taken the edge off that elusive excitement she had experienced when they first met. Now he looked like a pleasant, attractive young man whom she didn't really know. And the chore of getting acquainted all over again left her pondering where to begin. She couldn't think clearly enough to ask any of the obvious questions. Instead she said, "Don't tell me that *you* have a sackful of gold, too?"

"If only it were true! No, I'm afraid I'm the poorest man aboard. Such is the lot of a lowly reporter."

Then abruptly he turned serious and glanced away. Amanda sensed his discomfort.

"How did you like New York?" she asked.

Tom smiled ironically. "The truth is, I got tired of struggling, and the *World* got tired of *me,* so home I came. The reason I didn't call . . ."

"You don't have to explain. I understand."

"It wasn't because I didn't want to see you . . ."

"I know. You had to see your family, get settled, figure out what to do next. It takes time."

Tom sighed in relief. "That's about it. The folks were very disappointed, naturally. I probably wouldn't have come back at all if I hadn't run low on funds. I didn't want to face them—or you. It was a miserable experience."

"Maynard, you never have to worry about facing me. When I didn't hear from you, I guessed that things weren't going too well. It's nothing to be ashamed of." She squeezed his hand. "So cheer up and tell me what you're doing here."

"I've had one piece of good luck—an old family friend took pity on me. Do you know Erastus Brainerd, publisher of the *P.I.?*"

"I've heard of him, but we've never met."

"He took me on staff, which was very decent of him considering the depression and all."

"I always thought the *P.I.* was quite a conservative paper."

"It is. But Brainerd is a fine fellow who can sniff out a story before it happens. He had actually sent me to the Yukon to do a story on prospecting, when by a quirk of timing, I found myself in Skagway right at the moment of the big strike. So I decided to sail home with the miners." He stopped abruptly. "What about you?"

"I'm with the *Times*."

"Oh no! We're rivals again!"

Their conversation was suspended as the jubilant miners crowded around, eager to show off their fortunes.

Once the ship was underway again, the captain appeared to confirm the incredible news. "We're carrying a ton all told. And a couple of these boys are worth more than a hundred thousand dollars apiece! Nobody has less than five thousand." Then he added, as if he hoped to be quoted, "It's the discovery of the century."

Amanda turned to Tom puzzled. "If you're here to cover the story, how come it hasn't been in the *P.I.* yet?"

"Mr. Brainerd wanted to hold it to build suspense. We're getting out a special edition to coincide with the docking of the ship."

Although Amanda felt a sudden letdown, she wired her story anyway, warning Blethen of the *P.I.*'s special edition so that he would understand why the *Times* had been scooped.

When the *Portland* docked in Seattle at noon, Amanda stood next to Tom at the railing, as if in a strange re-enactment of history. It was almost exactly one year ago that *The Puget Queen* had brought them to Seattle. Only this time, the crowds on the pier were welcoming, exultant.

She turned to Tom with a smile. "Congratulations, Maynard. I see them waving newspapers down there, so I guess your special edition was timed just right."

"The credit goes to Mr. Brainerd. Anyway, I'm sorry."

"Don't be silly. All's fair."

Suddenly Tom took her by the shoulders. "You're a peach, Lamar. You've done more to restore my confidence in this one day than anyone else was able to do over the whole past year."

Taken by surprise, Amanda laughed self-consciously. "What did I do?"

"You've made me feel that we're *more* than friends—that you *did* wait for me. I hope it's true."

Amanda smiled, feeling a bit sad. Tom hadn't changed; only she had changed.

A brass band struck up a lively march as the miners spilled down the gangplank. The crowd cheered them, and they in turn cheered the crowd, making the most of their sudden fame.

Tom and Amanda followed. Suddenly Tom stopped. "Wait!

That's not my headline!" He pointed to a newspaper being held aloft. Bold four-inch letters proclaimed: "GOLD! GOLD! GOLD! GOLD!"

"No wonder," said Amanda. "That's the *Times!*"

Tom's jaw dropped. "Then it's *your* headline!"

"It is, isn't it?" she said excitedly.

"But *how?*"

"Knowing Blethen, I'm sure the headline was all ready to go. Besides, I told him we were docking at eleven, not twelve—just to make sure we'd be first."

"That's what *I* should have done."

"As soon as you told me that Mr. Brainerd was holding his special edition until noon, I figured we had a chance to beat you out."

Tom stared at her in amazement. "You've learned a lot this past year."

"I've just learned how reporters survive, that's all. *You* taught me that."

No one was happier than Colonel Blethen. The gold discovery story not only scooped his rival, but sold papers as never before. Nonetheless, within a week he was already growing nervous trying to get wind of other events, even more spectacular, if possible, to keep all his new converts.

"We're going places, Lamar," he announced. "Together."

It was clear that he not only considered Amanda the key player on his team, but wanted to be quite certain that she understood where her loyalties belonged.

"Don't get carried away by any big offers from New York," he cautioned. "Remember who gave you your chance. Old Joe Pulitzer didn't know a good thing when he had it. So let him stew. Show him you don't need the *World.*"

"I hadn't given it a thought," Amanda admitted, amused to see Blethen being so childishly possessive.

"I'm increasing you to fifty dollars per article, not a penny less," he went on, lacing his fingers over his paunch. His eyes twinkled in anticipation of Amanda's joy.

"Fifty dollars? That's a lot!"

"If you didn't deserve it, you wouldn't get it."

However, Blethen's keen and experienced nose failed to pick up the scent of anything to equal the gold rush. Even the ongoing battle for right of way between the Great Northern, the Northern Pacific and the Oregon Improvement Company could muster little interest, despite his insistence that the issue always be given front-page coverage. The railroad squabbles had faded into insignificance for all but the powers involved.

Amanda was disturbed to see how quickly he turned his back on the gold rush once he had had the glory of scooping every paper in the country. It didn't matter to him that when the gold aboard the *Portland* was actually weighed, it weighed more than *two* tons; that was yesterday's news.

"Send me to the Yukon," Amanda pleaded. "They're leaving the factories in droves! We can't let all those good stories go to waste!"

"Pshaw! The gold will run out, if it hasn't already, and everybody will be right back where they started—maybe worse off. It doesn't deserve any more publicity than we've already given it, or the whole economy will collapse. What if the factories have to close down for lack of help? What then? Do you want to see this town disappear off the map? Do you want to see the *Times* fold up?"

However, the gold rush continued to flourish without Blethen's support. Even as his readership declined, he stubbornly maintained that it was all a flash in the pan.

Finally, with the greatest reluctance, Blethen was forced to send Beatrice Fairfax on an extended vacation and Amanda was approached with a new assignment—editor of the homemaking department.

"It's a step up," he said unconvincingly. "Main thing is to keep you on the payroll till something big comes along."

Amanda turned to the chore halfheartedly. The women's page consisted of fashion notes, society news, recipes and serialized love stories, which left little chance to sneak in any ideas of substance. Though she agreed to give it a try, the job soon proved to be even more dismal than she had anticipated. Most of the copy which crossed her desk seemed either demeaning or quaintly outdated. None of it had anything to do with what was really happening in the world. Inevitably one day as she was sifting through submissions, she found one particular item which was so annoying that she knew she could go no further. Under the heading, "Jewel Don'ts," it advised: "Don't wear your rings all the time. If worn constantly, they deaden the expression of the hand. The slightest pressure pushes back impulse. This is the chief evil of modern dressing."

Amanda stared at it for a moment, not sure if she was going to laugh hysterically or throw up. But it went on: "Don't, if your past has been densely populated, and your heart sentimental, make an emotional junkshop of your hand with unrelated souvenirs."

That did it. There was no way she could be sympathetic to *that* audience. Calmly she swept every piece of copy off her desk and into the wastepaper basket. She stood up, dusted her hands, gathered her belongings and walked out the door.

Chapter Nine

ERASTUS Brainerd's office at the *P.I.* was not behind glass in full view of the front door, like Colonel Blethen's; it was private and difficult to locate through a maze of corridors on the second floor. Amanda thought it was almost too neat, too tastefully furnished for what she had come to expect of a newspaperman. What would he be like?

She smiled at Tom slyly. "How do I look?" she asked, trying to catch her reflection in the glass doors of the bookcase.

"Good enough to kiss," he replied with a sigh.

"And here I am hoping to look clever and efficient! Oh well, he probably won't hire me anyway. But you were a good sport to let me talk you into this."

"You could talk me into *anything*," said Tom. "Now don't worry. He'll love you." He squeezed her hand reassuringly. "You don't mind if I dash off and leave you on your own, do you? I'm on deadline."

Amanda sat in a leather chair and glanced about skeptically. It was evident that Erastus Brainerd wasn't as hard-working as Blethen. She knew before he appeared that he would not have his sleeves rolled up, but would be wearing a jacket. He would be stuffy and polite, with an air of superiority. She was only partially right.

Brainerd entered his office with a brisk step. He *was* wearing a jacket. But other than that, he was far different from what Amanda had expected. Tom hadn't mentioned that he was young, perhaps no more than thirty, and attractive. His manner was easy and he greeted her cordially.

"It's about time we met!" he said, clasping her hand. "Tom speaks of you so often and so highly I feel as if we're already friends."

"He speaks a good deal about you, too," said Amanda politely, which wasn't exactly true, but what else could she say? From behind her smile, she studied his face. There was a kind of handsome emptiness about him—too-perfect white teeth, with that not-a-hair-out-of-place look. She found herself searching for nonexistent blemishes, aware of her own imagined imperfections. He was a striking contrast to Tom, who dashed about like a disheveled professor, not caring about his appearance.

"Does Tom think me quite a tyrant?" Brainerd wanted to know.

His smile was genuine, even a bit shy. Amanda could not help saying what he wanted to hear. "He thinks the world of you."

"He does?" Brainerd said in pleased surprise. "That's awfully good to hear."

This will be easy, she thought, relaxing.

"Has he told you anything about the *P.I.?*"

"Only how much he enjoys working here. I'm afraid I'm not as familiar with the paper as I should be, but I do like seeing all your gold rush articles printed in gold ink. Your coverage is wonderful!"

Brainerd's gray eyes lit up. She had obviously touched upon his favorite subject. "I hope everyone feels as you do, because I've got a hunch that the gold rush can put Seattle on the map. In fact, I'm going to see that it does."

Amanda smiled, thinking how Mr. Brainerd's views were the direct opposite of Blethen's. Beginning to feel quite comfortable, she dared to cross her legs. He glanced at her ankles, but didn't attempt to flirt.

"I want people, not just in this country, but all over the world, to look upon our city as the fastest and *only* route to the north. And when they return from the gold fields with their fortunes, I want them to settle here, build their futures here. Now this may sound like a farfetched dream, but I know it can become a reality." He paused to apologize for his exuberance. "You see? I can't even *talk* about the gold rush without getting carried away!"

Amanda thought he looked rather flushed, and wondered if it was really the gold rush that excited him, or *her*. "I know just how you feel," she said. "I think it's the best thing that could happen. You know why? Because it's going to benefit the whole working class."

"Inevitably," said Brainerd, pleased to find that Amanda had an opinion. "There'll be plenty of new jobs for everyone."

"Oh, I'm not talking about new jobs—I'm saying that maybe now the worker will be more appreciated. When their employers see them all running off to prospect, they'll wish they had treated them better."

Brainerd looked at Amanda with keen interest, as though he was seeing beyond her obvious physical appeal. "I hadn't thought of it that way," he admitted. "Do you believe people are going north because they're unhappy with their jobs?"

"The way I see it, if they had better pay, safe conditions and decent hours, they might not be so anxious to escape."

"That's quite an order to fill!"

"I know. It's farfetched—just like *your* dream. But it *can* come true."

Brainerd smiled consolingly, touched by her innocence. "I hope we both live to see it happen. Some day in the future."

Amanda stood up, compelling Brainerd to stand also. "Except that it won't just happen by itself. That's something we have to work for. *Fight* for."

"Do you have a fighting spirit, Miss Lamar?"

"When I see things that need changing, there's no stopping me!"

Brainerd didn't laugh. He reflected for a moment, then came around from behind his desk. "Are you happy at the *Times?*"

"I *was*. And I have the greatest respect for Colonel Blethen . . ." She glanced away, reluctant to continue.

"Never mind. The fact is, you're here and you'd like a job. Am I right?"

"I only came to *see*," she replied quickly.

"Of course. But I could use another reporter. The only thing I must tell you is that we're a conservative paper—and Republican. Workingmen don't read the *P.I.* However, that shouldn't prevent you from covering the gold rush for us, if you'd like."

"Me? Cover the gold rush? What about Tom?"

"There's plenty of news to keep both of you busy, don't worry."

"You don't find me too radical?"

"You know how to think. And that's more important to me than your politics."

I've impressed him, she thought, feeling flattered. I'm sure he's not just taken with my figure, but with *me*.

"What happens to me when the gold rush is over?" she asked, trying not to get her hopes too high.

"It will never be over. Once Seattle has grown and changed, it can't ever go back to what it was before."

He spoke with such conviction that Amanda felt a shiver of excitement.

"I'm sure you'll see some of your ideas come to fruition," he continued. "Perhaps in time you can find a way to convince management that improved working conditions will increase productivity. I'd like to see both sides profit."

"Management's already profiting. And I don't think they're going to do anything for their employees unless they're forced to. Unless the employees themselves stand up for their rights."

Brainerd ran his fingers through perfectly groomed hair, rumpling it, but not caring. "Amanda? May I call you Amanda?"

"Please do." She waited apprehensively, wondering if he was going to edge up.

"You like the newspaper business, don't you?"

"I love it."

"Can you tell me why?"

"Because a newspaper can do a lot. If it wants to. If I had a paper of my own, I wouldn't be afraid to take chances. But that's me. You probably don't agree."

"Don't be so sure. I like what you have to say. And do you know something? I think you *should* have your own paper someday. I haven't met many young people your age who feel the way you do."

I wonder how old he thinks I am? At least he's not trying to flirt. "You're young, too," she ventured. "How do *you* feel?"

Brainerd smiled, slightly embarrassed at being caught off guard.

"I may not be as adventurous as you are, but that doesn't mean my mind is closed to new ideas. I'd like to have you here. And even though I can't give you completely free rein, I promise I'll never assign you to 'household hints' or 'how to make a perfect peach pudding.'"

Amanda felt her face redden. He knew what she had been doing at the *Times*. Suddenly she had a pang of guilt. "I'm afraid Colonel Blethen doesn't know I came to see you."

"Listen, Amanda, I can give you the chance to make your mark here. Blethen will understand. It's not being ungrateful to want to move ahead."

Amanda hesitated in confusion. "May I give you my answer later? I want to talk to him first."

"Of course. I'd do the same thing."

His handshake was firm, persuasive, hoping that she'd return. Despite her dilemma, she left feeling relieved and encouraged. He had made no advances, but most important he was willing to give her a chance.

"So you're off to the gold fields, is that it?" Blethen demanded gruffly.

Amanda knew from his tone of reprimand that he was not going to be as magnanimous as she had thought. "I haven't given Mr. Brainerd my answer yet," she replied carefully. "I want you to know that it isn't just the chance to cover the gold rush that's influencing me, but the chance to move ahead."

"Eighteen years old and already you think you're not moving up fast enough. Typical youth! Can hardly wait to trade security for adventure."

"Colonel Blethen, please don't think I'm ungrateful. I *wanted* to stay with the *Times,* but I don't want to do the women's page."

"Tell me this, Lamar. What do you think Brainerd's going to have you doing once this gold rush is over? I'll bet my bottom dollar it'll be fashion and food!"

"The gold rush isn't going to be over."

"So *that's* what he told you. I'm not surprised."

"If you could offer me anything else, I wouldn't leave."

"Well, I can't. So go have your fling. You'll be back."

"Then you don't mind?"

"Of course I mind," he answered tartly. "But I'm not going to force the truth upon you. Maybe this will be a good lesson for you."

"What do you mean?"

Blethen raised his brow. "It'll teach you not to fall for flattery. If I know Mr. Goodlooks, he probably told you he thought you should have a newspaper of your own!"

Amanda opened her mouth to deny it, then changed her mind.

"As a matter of fact, he did," she admitted. "But I paid no attention. That didn't sway me in the least."

"Well, well," he replied in amusement. He waved his arm toward the door. "Then go if you must, but beware of any man who builds his paper on the expectation of a gold rush. He shouldn't be called Brainerd, 'cause *brainless* is what he is."

On her first day at the *P.I.* Brainerd informed Amanda that he wanted her to cover the gold rush from Seattle, not from the Yukon.

"You'll be of greater value here, working closely with me," he emphasized. "We'll let Tom go back up north."

Amanda received the news with a sinking feeling as she remembered Blethen's prediction. Of course Brainerd hadn't actually *said* that she would go to the Yukon, she had just assumed it. Now she'd have to worry that he had designs on her after all, a possibility she dared not convey to Tom, who was deeply disappointed.

"I thought for sure we were going together," he moaned. "Now we'll be separated again."

"It's not the end of the world," she replied gamely.

"I'm sorry I introduced you."

"It was *my* idea, remember? So I have nobody to blame but myself."

"Look, if we can't be together, let's at least trade places. I know you had your heart set on going to the Yukon, so *you* can go and I'll stay here."

"Thanks, Maynard. But I have a feeling that Mr. Brainerd would rather send a man than a woman."

Once Tom had booked passage on the next voyage north, Amanda noticed a remarkable change of mood. He actually seemed eager to be off. When she commented on it, he confided that he was going to try his luck in the gold fields.

"I figure as long as I'm there, I might as well go prospecting. Well, what do you think?"

"I'm filled with envy! Are you going to do it just for fun or seriously?"

"Can't you guess?"

"You don't seem like the type who cares about getting rich."

"That's true, but a man's got to have some means of his own, so that he doesn't have to depend on his family. I may want to settle down, have a home—someday."

"I thought you didn't want to settle down?"

Tom looked at her intently. "A man can change his mind," he said.

Amanda nodded, suddenly aware that he was doing it for her. "Won't it be expensive buying all the provisions and equipment?" she asked, anxious to change the subject.

"I figure it'll come to $140, but that's everything—groceries, clothing, tools."

Amanda let out a low whistle. "That's a big investment." She paused. "I've got some money saved. Maybe I could put in half the amount."

"You want to be equal partners?"

"What's wrong with that?"

"Nothing. It's just that most girls wouldn't want to. They'd expect to be taken care of."

"I bet they'd like to be equal partners if they were given a chance."

Tom's eyes were unusually bright when he took off his glasses. Unmindful that they were equal partners, he kissed her possessively, then warned, "Don't forget that you belong to me and no one else!"

During the remaining days before Tom's departure, Amanda helped him make his purchases, using the opportunity to interview the would-be prospectors who stood with her in long lines.

For blocks the downtown sidewalks were piled high with sacks of flour, corn meal, oatmeal, rice and sugar, like sandbags in preparation for a flood. The flood did indeed come. Wagons and wheelbarrows clogged the streets as unquestioning buyers carted away their goods in staggering proportions.

As Amanda observed, she became uneasy. She hoped that those who had left their jobs would not be disappointed, for it seemed that rumors of gold nuggets the size of birds' eggs had bedazzled the vision of everyone she talked to.

"People are spending their life savings," she reported to Brainerd worriedly. "But so far it looks like only the outfitters are getting rich."

"You have to have one before the other," he replied. "When all these prospectors return with gold, it shall balance out, I guarantee."

Amanda didn't mention her fears to Tom, so as not to dampen his spirits. But it bothered her that no one spoke of failure. It was as though the possibility didn't even exist.

On the morning that he was to sail, Amanda arrived at the pier early to record some impressions of the departing stampeders, as everyone now called them. There was singing, laughter and so much good humor on display that the most confirmed skeptic would have found it difficult not to become infected with gold fever, which one old sourdough described to her as "a contagious disease whose only known cure is a long sea voyage to Alaska."

Encouraged by their sheer enthusiasm, Amanda began to feel that perhaps the venture was going to turn out all right after all.

As she moved through the crowd searching for Tom, she was suddenly startled to come upon Bertha, her old friend from the Grand Union.

"Bertha! Do you remember me?"

Bertha stared for a moment, then a flicker of recognition crossed her eyes. She didn't smile. "You're Firebrand," she said, "the one who got us kicked out."

"Oh, Bertha, I never meant to! I was after John Considine, not you . . ."

"Never you mind," she interrupted with an upward tilt of the chin. "We all found other work."

"I'm glad," said Amanda. But she saw from Bertha's painted face that she had not changed professions. "Are you going prospecting?"

"Yes," she replied with a hard laugh. "I suppose you could call it that." Shifting her pack, Bertha turned and disappeared into the crowd.

Amanda gazed after her sadly. It was just as she had feared. Her exposé had been a failure. The girls were no better off than before; perhaps even worse.

"Lamar! Over here!"

She turned to see Tom struggling toward her with an enormous pack, the perspiration shining on his forehead. "I never thought a hundred pounds could feel so heavy," he gasped, lowering his burden to the ground.

"Hope you don't sink," said Amanda, trying to joke. She noticed that the steamer was riding very low and that the number of passengers seemed to exceed its capacity. The steamship companies were going to make fortunes, just like the outfitters.

Proudly Tom showed her his canvas pouch, on which he had sewed his initials in red yarn. "When I come back, this will be full to bursting!" he vowed.

A hollow blast from the steamer was the signal for a wild stampede up the gangplank. He looked at her with a kind of desperation. "I must be crazy to leave you—so much can happen when people are separated for such a long time."

"We were apart for almost a year and survived," she reminded him. But immediately she thought, *did* we survive?

"I'll be thinking of you every moment," he went on in a husky voice, "longing for the day I can make you my own."

"Don't lose your eyeglasses," she cautioned, not knowing what else to say.

He pulled them off impatiently and wrapped her in his arms.

"I don't know how I can wait," he whispered. "There's nothing wrong in giving yourself to someone you love."

She didn't reply. Did I say I loved him?

"I have to have you the minute I get back. Don't disappoint me."

Another warning blast sounded. This time it was sustained and urgent.

She was glad. For his closeness made her feel a warmth in her cheeks and a strange tingling inside.

"Better hurry, Cheechako, or the ship will sail without you."

"Cheechako? Is that what you think I am—a tenderfoot?" he asked, crushed.

"I don't mean as a man," she said quickly. "I mean as a prospector!"

He closed his eyes in relief and gave her a hard, lingering kiss, as if to prove his manhood, until shouts from the deck made him aware that the gangplank was about to be pulled up.

Lifting his pack, he turned away abruptly. He didn't look at her again until he was aboard and there was no possibility of changing his mind.

As the steamer churned away from the pier, Tom remained at the bow waving tirelessly until she could no longer distinguish him from all the others. When she finally looked around, there were only a few stragglers left on the pier. It was quiet now, except for the soft sobs of a woman carrying a sleeping child. Amanda started for the gates, walking briskly.

The next morning Brainerd called Amanda into his office and shut the door.

"I know you were disappointed not to be going up north, but I had a reason for keeping you behind." He smiled mysteriously.

Amanda smiled back, but she could feel herself tense.

"I've been appointed head of a publicity committee for the Chamber of Commerce. Which means that from now on I'll have to divide my time between two jobs." He paused, watching her reaction. "So I'll need you here more than ever; in fact I'll be depending on your help."

"I'll be glad to do anything I can," she assured him, suddenly relieved. "I love responsibility."

"I know, Amanda. That's why I hired you." He, too, looked relieved. "I'm launching a massive campaign to promote Seattle," he went on, "but first I have to think up a slogan, something that will tie us in with the gold rush. So if you get any ideas, I'll be glad to hear them."

"How about—'Seattle: The Gateway to the Yukon'?" she offered, then frowned and shook her head. "No, that's not grand enough. Let's make it—'The Gateway to *Alaska!*'"

"Gateway to Alaska! By Jove, I think we've got it. Amanda, you're ingenious!"

"I have lots of ideas," she volunteered immodestly.

"Let's hear them."

"Well, now that all the mills are emptying out, how about if I write an article urging women to apply for men's jobs? This way they can learn new skills and make better wages."

Brainerd's smile of expectation faded. "Amanda, let me explain something. We've got to look beyond the local problems. Our mission is to bring the world to Seattle. Nothing else is important."

Amanda felt her spirits collapse. He was sincere and well-meaning, but so shortsighted. Just like Joseph Pulitzer.

"I don't want to dampen your enthusiasm, Amanda, but you can't always be a firebrand."

I know, she thought. That's what Blethen used to say.

"Try to be patient," he urged. "Your time will come."

The steamers arrived and departed, always fully booked for the northbound voyage. As the rush gained momentum, even the skeptics became lulled into believing that an endless supply of gold did exist. No one seemed to notice—or worry—that as time went on, the arriving vessels carried more passengers and less gold. Amanda first became aware of it when she tried to interview a passenger who refused to give his name, saying only that all the good claims had been taken, that the whole venture had been misrepresented.

"The hardships are beyond belief," he told her bitterly. Amanda did believe him, for his hollow-eyed look betrayed an ominous side to the adventure, a side which had not been told.

After that she observed that only the victorious talked to reporters; the defeated skulked away, ashamed to have failed when failure was deemed impossible.

When she told Brainerd of her discovery, he suggested that perhaps these were only a few isolated cases.

"Tom hasn't sent us any discouraging reports," he reminded her. "At any rate, let's wait till he gets home before we print anything alarming." But when he noticed Amanda's concerned look, he hastened to add, "Naturally we won't distort the truth."

Tom's stories arrived with the bi-weekly steamer. They gave no hint of disillusionment, but continued to paint an optimistic picture of the opportunities to grow wealthy. And with each article, there was always a letter for Amanda. Or rather, a love poem. As the poems became bolder and more passionate, she sensed that Tom was trying to force her into a situation she wasn't ready to face. And much as he had a certain appeal, the truth was, he didn't fill her with overpowering desire. When the time approached for his return, she found herself wishing there was some way to postpone the inevitable.

On the day of his arrival, she met the steamer, but in her anxiety, she had forgotten all about their investment. So when Tom came down the gangplank with a poke of gold slung over his shoulder, Amanda was stunned.

"But why did you keep it a secret?"

"I wanted to surprise you!" Tom laughed with abandon and thrust the canvas pouch into her hands. "Hold it!" he urged. "Half is yours—three thousand dollars for you, three thousand for me!"

Amanda shook her head in wonderment, feeling the weight of the pouch.

"What's the matter? Aren't you happy?"

She looked at him hard. Her fears that he was becoming too serious had been for nothing. The passion which his poetry had expressed had found a new object of love—gold.

"Haven't you forgotten something?" she asked quietly.

Tom's face clouded in distress as he drew her into his arms. "Lamar, you weren't out of my mind for a single minute! This gold is nothing. In fact, there's so much to be had up there that it loses all meaning."

Amanda drew back.

"What is it? Don't you want to kiss me?"

"You seem changed."

"Changed? How?" he asked with a puzzled laugh.

"You don't sound like your poems. You talk faster and you don't look at me. I feel like an outsider to the world you've just come from."

Tom blinked uncomprehendingly. "Don't you know that all my efforts were for *us?*"

Amanda shrugged.

Tom held her at arm's length. "I *do* see you. And you look more beautiful than ever. I love everything about you—the way your hair is waved to catch the light, the glow in your cheeks. And a most becoming green blouse. Is it new?"

"I bought it a long time ago. But this is the first time I've worn it."

"You were saving it for me?"

She nodded.

"Then if we care for each other, how have I made you unhappy?"

"It's the way you talk about the gold. It frightens me somehow to think that it can be acquired so easily. I was under the impression that it was running out."

"Who told you that?"

"A few have come back disappointed, I'm afraid. More than a few."

"Then it's their own fault," he declared. "So I wouldn't say anything to alarm Brainerd. His whole career is at stake."

"I already have. He wants to know what it's really like up there. He's willing to print the truth."

"The truth is in your hands—six thousand dollars' worth!"

"That's what bothers me. There's something—wrong about getting all this money for doing nothing. It's not real to me."

"I admit I got it more easily than most. Want to know my secret? I traded my goods to a prospector who wanted to stay on another year in exchange for part of his gold. He offered me one third of what he had already dug."

"That makes a big difference. You made it sound like the gold was just lying around, waiting to be picked up."

"I may have exaggerated—just a little. But next time I might not be so lucky—I might have to *work* for it!"

"What do you mean—next time?"

"Naturally I'm going back."

"But why, Maynard? You've got three thousand dollars!"

"Remember when I told you that I wanted to prospect so that I'd have enough money to be independent and have my own home? A home means—a wife."

"You want to get married?"

"What did you think? That I merely wanted to rob your virtue?"

Amanda blushed. "It sounded that way in your poems."

"I was courting you, Lamar. That's how it's done. You say those things so a girl knows how you feel about her, to show that you're a man. I thought any girl of twenty-one would know that."

"I'm not twenty-one. I'm eighteen."

Tom groaned. "Why didn't you tell me?"

"Would it have made any difference?"

"Not in the way I care for you, but in the way I think of you. You're far too young to be on your own—to be working."

"Well, I am. So please don't tell Mr. Brainerd."

"Then the sooner we marry, the better. That way you won't have to work any more."

"It's not work, it's my career."

"That's fine for spinsters. But I want to take care of you. It's a husband's duty."

"I can't give up journalism—I'm just getting started."

"Is that more important than me?"

Amanda hesitated. "Maynard, I don't know how I feel about you. So I can't make a decision. I need more time to think about it."

"Then you don't love me."

"I don't know how it's supposed to feel, so how can I say for certain?" she asked, feeling miserable. "Oh, Maynard, please don't insist on an answer now. Let's wait until you're home for good before I tell you."

"I know why you're putting me off. You're afraid the gold will corrupt me, is that it?" he asked stiffly.

"I don't know what I'm afraid of. I only know that I don't want to make a mistake."

"I won't go if you don't want me to."

"Maynard, it isn't what *I* want; *you* have to be certain, too. I think you should do whatever you feel is right."

"I need you up there, Tom," said Brainerd persuasively. "Don't you realize as a reporter how you can capitalize on your own good fortune? Why, that's a story in itself. Poor one day, rich the next—just the kind of luck people want to read about."

Amanda looked from one to the other, but said nothing.

Tom scratched his ear. "Of course not everybody can expect to have the same experience I had."

"It doesn't matter," said Brainerd. "The important thing is to inspire people to keep going. Seattle needs this gold rush—desperately." He turned to Amanda. "What do *you* think, Amanda? Do you agree?"

"I think people need to have hope that their lives will be better. If the gold rush can give them that, then I'd agree."

"Exactly," said Brainerd. "Hope. Well, Tom? Can I talk you into going back, or do I have to give the job to someone else?"

Tom gave Amanda a quick glance. She could see in his eyes that he wanted to go, even at the risk of losing her. The burden suddenly lifted and she nodded encouragingly. "I'd go if *I* had the chance," she said.

After Tom had gone, Amanda deposited her money in the Dexter Horton Bank and breathed easier. It was slowly beginning to sink in that she now had the means to change her life. She could use her fortune to go around the world, or buy a house—or start a business. A business. Now *that* was true independence! To be like Colonel Blethen or Erastus Brainerd. Set policies, give orders, answer to no one!

What began as daydreaming soon became preoccupation, leaving her with a restless stirring inside that wouldn't go away. And almost without realizing it, she began to nurture an idea which Brainerd himself had once implanted—in the most casual way, of course—to have her own paper. When that day came, she was certain that all her problems would be over.

Just as the gold rush had diverted public attention from the depression, an event occurred in February of 1898 which abruptly diverted public attention from the gold rush. The U.S. battleship *Maine* was sunk by the Spanish in Havana harbor, and America was headed toward war.

Brainerd immediately wired Tom in Skagway to return home in preparation for going to Cuba to cover the war as a correspondent. He then waited patiently, knowing that Tom would receive the message only by a relay system which all reporters used when they were off in the gold fields. But weeks passed and no answer arrived. In fact, no more articles arrived.

Everyone at the *P.I.* grew uneasy, knowing that Tom had already been gone far longer than planned. Amanda refused to believe those who suggested that he was hiding out like a number of miners who had conveniently dropped from sight, fearing conscription into the Army. After all, Tom was adventurous. If anything, he'd *want* to go to Cuba and have the chance to prove himself. But despite her mounting anxiety over his safety, she grimly faced the fact that this was wartime and that it was the duty of all to volunteer.

"I'll go to Cuba," she told Brainerd. "Tom is probably in some remote place beyond reach, so I don't think we should wait any longer."

Brainerd said he appreciated her offer, but that he had someone else in mind to go. The mission was too dangerous for a woman, he explained.

"Why is my life more valuable than a man's?" she asked. But Brainerd couldn't answer.

Another wire was sent to Tom. And again the days dragged by without reply. By now Brainerd was seriously concerned, admitting at last to the possibility that something had happened to Tom.

Meanwhile, Amanda had been meeting each steamer to question the passengers for news, on the chance of finding someone who could offer a clue.

An answer came suddenly when a grizzled prospector came swinging down the gangplank waving a copy of the Dyea *Trail*. Its headline sent a wave of anxiety through the waiting crowd: "SEPULCHRE OF ICE AND SNOW. An Awful Avalanche Buries a Great Host of People."

The joy of relatives and friends became immediately subdued as word of the disaster traveled, then turned to fear when loved ones failed to materialize among the passengers.

"I was a witness," the prospector boasted loudly, "a witness to the calamity." Yet, he couldn't recall a single detail. And he had never heard of Tom Maynard.

With her throat dry and heart pumping furiously, Amanda bought his paper and rushed back to the office.

Together she and Brainerd scanned the article to see if casualties were listed, but it stated that the victims had been buried so deep that the exact number was not even known. The most discouraging detail was that it had occurred at White Pass, where Tom had planned to cross. The paper went on to quote a witness who claimed that death for all had been instantaneous.

"I'm not satisfied," Brainerd announced angrily. "I will not accept the word of some demented miner whose wits have been dimmed by too much whiskey. We've got to be sure."

"We'll never be sure without going to see for ourselves. This time, I think it should be me."

"Amanda, I know how you feel," he began patiently.

"You *don't* know how I feel. I encouraged Tom to go. In fact, he wouldn't have gone if I'd asked him not to. So in a way, I'm responsible."

"I didn't realize you were—that close."

"He's asked me to marry him."

Brainerd reacted as though he'd been struck. "Are you?" But before she could reply, he laughed sharply. "What a foolish question! Why wouldn't you? I should have guessed."

"I haven't given him my answer. I told him I wanted to wait till he came home."

Brainerd turned slowly toward the window. "Do you love him? No, don't answer. I have no right to ask. I'm sorry."

Amanda saw the tension in his back as he gripped the window sill. And suddenly she couldn't think clearly, for her heart seemed to be beating inside her brain. He had always been the perfect gentleman, never attempting to flirt, though he had ample opportunity. Yet, he was far from aloof. He seemed to want her close by at all times, and he never failed to ask her opinion, listen to what she had to say, all the while observing her intently. She wondered nervously whether her openness and sometimes teasing manner had given him reason to believe that his affection for her might be returned?

"That's all right," she assured him, then waited in embarrassment for him to speak. But he remained at the window in silence without turning around.

"*Will* you let me go to search for Tom?" she asked finally.

Brainerd's shoulders slumped. "Of course."

Amanda took a deep breath. "There's something else you should know—I'm going to tell the truth. No matter what I find out."

He revolved toward her slowly. She saw that his expression was calm, betraying no emotion.

"I'd expect you to," he replied, his gaze steady.

"It may ruin your publicity campaign."

"To hell with the campaign."

"Thank you," she whispered. She felt the tears close behind her smile. "I never doubted that would be your answer."

Chapter Ten

SKAGWAY. Home of the cruel wind. Situated at the head of the Lynn Canal in a fjord-like valley, the stampede town was where it all began and ended. A thriving tent and shack city with a constant population of ten thousand, Skagway proudly proclaimed itself "the roughest place on earth."

For Amanda and the other wide-eyed cheechakos arriving for the first time, Skagway was primitive and chaotic, the last outpost of civilization. The permeating fragrance of virgin spruce, which had traveled alongside the steamer all the way up the inland passage, upon reaching Skagway became muddied with animal dung, oilskin, sweat, burning coal and the rotten-egg smell of tideflats. Amanda imagined that this was very much like Seattle might have been twenty years ago, when horses and unwashed bodies labored together to log off the great forests. Or even as the West might have been in her mother's day.

But for the seasoned sourdough—the experienced miner—awaiting the next southbound steamer after spending a year in the wilds, Skagway was an exciting metropolis, where all that was worth having was available. It mattered not that most of the stores, banks, outfitters, packers, information agencies, saloons, restaurants, hotels and dance halls had walls of timber and canvas roofs. It was the city.

Amanda's first impression was one of disorder and confusion. The dock was piled high with luggage and equipment which had been dumped off the steamer with little regard as to the convenience of the passengers. But the task of locating one's gear was only the first of many obstacles waiting to catch the stampeders by surprise. For they had to be wary of those who would part them from their savings before they could even set out for the gold fields. Makeshift stores had been set up by enterprising merchants right down on the mudflats, so as to catch the trade the minute the passengers stepped off the boat. Amanda noticed that many items not to be had in Seattle were in great demand, among them Indian-made salmon-skin boots lined with fur, carved ivory good-luck charms and bear meat.

But that was only the beginning. Needing to find a place to stay, Amanda joined the flow of traffic—dog teams, pack horses and wagons—which jammed the rutted streets. Although it was still early spring, the weather had warmed, breeding favorable conditions for the multiplication of flies and mosquitoes, an annoyance from which there was no escape. She saw at once from the grim faces trudging past her that reality had set in. The twenty-one-day voyage on an overcrowded steamer had been a minor discomfort compared with what awaited them in Skagway and beyond. In broad daylight she observed pickpockets operating apparently without fear of the law—if there was a law. Certainly there was no evidence of enforcement.

If only Erastus Brainerd could see this, she thought. Would he still in good conscience be able to promote so perilous a venture? The joy and optimism which prevailed in Seattle was now replaced by a ruthless determination to see it through, perhaps because it was too late, too costly to turn back. She saw many of her companions from the boat setting out at once, without pausing for so much as an hour's rest, sensing the urgency to reach the gold fields before all the claims would be taken.

Amanda, too, hurried as though every minute was vital to her mission. Supposing Tom was lying injured someplace? Every time she caught sight of someone with eyeglasses and curly hair, her hopes would soar, thinking it was *him,* expecting that at any moment he would come bounding toward her. Other times from out of the crowd she would hear his familiar cry, always slightly frantic, always startling her at an unexpected moment. But although every voice she heard seemed to be shouting her name, Tom was never there when she turned around, but only total strangers calling to someone else.

At last Amanda found herself before an "information agency" housed in a mud dugout, which offered to reveal for a fee the name of the only decent hotel in town. Too tired to argue, she paid what they asked and followed directions to the end of the street, where she was amazed to discover a two-story building surrounded by formal gardens, complete with ponds and ornamental bridges.

The Pullen House, the agency had told her, was named for its owner, "Ma" Pullen, a sturdy widow with four children who had landed in the hotel business by necessity. Amanda thought Ma looked as if she had endured every hardship which the wilderness could inflict. Yet, her establishment was a haven of sorts, where the pendulum swung slowly and where Ma took her time scrutinizing each guest.

Amanda's smile of greeting was not returned, for Ma's feelings lay sealed beneath a tough, weather-beaten armor of dry wrinkles, like the hide of an ancient Indian.

"*Klahowya?*" asked Ma, planting herself behind a counter which served as both registration desk and bar.

"Pardon?"

"I asked how you was." Ma's eyes narrowed scornfully, indicating that Amanda had failed the test. "You come to dig?"

"I'm here to find out about the avalanche."

"Which one?"

"You mean—there was more than one?"

"There's always avalanches in the spring."

"My God! Have any lives been lost?" Amanda asked fearfully.

"How should I know?" Ma laughed without smiling. "You hafta ask witnesses."

Amanda sighed, seeing the futility of questioning her.

"Are ya staying or not?"

"Yes," said Amanda wearily. "How much will it be?"

Ma took a moment to size up Amanda's mackinaw outfit, which seemed to meet with her approval. "I'll charge you the stampeder's rate," she decided at last. Then added, "Dance hall girls pay more. But if you take any gents up to your room, the price doubles."

Amanda agreed to the terms and signed the register. It appeared from the date at the top of the page that Pullen House had accommodated very few guests over the past months. Which wasn't surprising, she thought, considering the exorbitant prices.

Suddenly she took another look. There among the signatures was a name scrawled in haste which might have been—Tom Maynard? She held the book to the light. Although she had never seen his handwriting, she could recognize the careless abandon, the impatient hurried manner of getting on to more important matters. It *was* Tom!

"That's who I'm looking for!" Amanda cried excitedly. She pointed to the name. "See right here? March first!"

"Oh, Mr. Maynard," she nodded matter-of-factly. "He used to come and go a lot."

"Used to? He hasn't been here since the first of March?"

"Nope," said Ma. "He went back up the trail," and she pushed a packet of Mail Pouch Tobacco across the counter. "Have a chew."

Amanda declined, then asked all in one breath, "*Back* up the trail? He went more than once? Which trail? White Pass?"

Ma helped herself to a plug of tobacco, which she rolled around in her mouth with slow deliberation. When at last she spoke, her voice sounded far away. "He went back up the trail and never come down."

"Oh, my God, then it's true!" Amanda covered her face in despair.

"Here one day and gone the next," continued Ma chewing thoughtfully. "Should've quit while he was ahead."

Amanda looked up sharply. "What do you mean by ahead?"

"Nothing."

"Had he found a lot of gold?"

"Hard to say." Ma's voice was vague as she gazed at the ceiling.

Amanda had to resist the temptation to shake her by the shoulders. "I've got to know what happened to him," she pleaded. "I won't leave until I know! Please help me!"

Ma let a stream of brown juice fly into the spittoon. "I got four fellas in Room 20 that's settin' out for White Pass tomorrow. They know the trail, so why doncha join up with 'em? They can show you where the avalanche was."

Amanda's pack horse was almost as stubborn as Ma Pullen. No sooner had she hired him on the basis of his docile, trusting manner, than he showed surprising agility in a sudden sprint for freedom. Realizing it was useless to try to get her money back, Amanda saw no recourse but to pursue him. After a wild chase through the streets, she finally caught up with the animal to find that it had taken three men to subdue him. After thanking them, she took the horse aside for a serious talk, letting him know who was in charge. However, as she led him back to the hotel with a firm hand, she had the uneasy feeling that he sensed the rigors of the journey ahead. She wondered if he had ever crossed White Pass before.

Suddenly the beast came to a halt in the middle of the street and would go no farther. Ironically, he chose to stop directly in front of a lopsided tent upon which was posted a sign: "Recruiting Office. United States Army. Physical Examinations $5.00."

Amanda's attempts to prod him on caused a curious group to gather, eager to see how a woman would handle the situation.

"Gone broke? Claim run out? Don't despair. Join the Army and win a free trip to Cuba!" a resonant voice sang out.

Amanda looked up to see the first smiling face she had encountered in Skagway. It belonged to a rangy and rumpled gentleman, dressed outlandishly in a vested suit with tails, who was dancing a jig in front of the tent. He seemed to know how to coax a hesitant face out of the crowd, for a short line of men had formed to await their turn.

He winked at Amanda, but kept right on with his jig.

"He's fulla beans," a gravelly voice complained to whoever would listen. "Anybody falls for that's a sucker."

Amanda glanced over at the disgruntled prospector and couldn't help asking why he would say such a thing.

"I got took myself," he admitted. "He's got a phony doctor in there and when your clothes come off, one of his cronies cleans out your pockets."

"He's not with the Army then?"

"Hell no!"

The con man winked at Amanda again and this time doffed his hat.

"Ah, a feast for the eyes! How's about a cake of soap? It's special, just for the young lady."

The prospector nudged Amanda. "Don't do it," he warned. "That's his oldest trick. That's how he come to be called 'Soapy.' "

But Amanda was fascinated at the audacity of anyone who would openly break the law without fear of punishment. Here was the perfect opportunity to lead him on, then write about him. Perhaps her efforts would eventually land him in jail.

"This soap is wrapped in a five-dollar bill," Soapy went on, holding it up for all to see. "But I'm going to let the lovely lady have it for only two American dollars! That's right, a mere two dollars. Incredible? No, siree. If she likes the soap, she'll come back to buy more."

When Amanda handed over her money, several other cheechakos also wanted to buy the soap. One of them even asked if he could buy *two* bars. But Soapy insisted only one to a customer. However, as Amanda turned away she heard him reluctantly agree to make an exception.

She could see at once that the five-dollar bill was counterfeit, and a poor imitation at that. Was the need to believe, the need to win such a powerful, blinding force that the stampeder could no longer perceive the world of reality? What had become of hard work and common sense? Amanda felt suddenly ashamed of her part in encouraging people to leave the only security they knew for such a hazardous venture. If only she could warn all the others before they left home. For those who had reached Skagway, it was already too late.

The following morning at dawn Amanda set out in the company of the four sourdoughs, as arranged by Ma Pullen. The presence of a female was welcomed, not for any romantic inclinations, she was relieved to learn, but for a more practical consideration—someone to do the cooking.

The sourdoughs were familiar with the trail from years of prospecting, and told Amanda that the site of the avalanche was a five-day trek, almost to the summit of White Pass.

There was no conversation on the climb, and Amanda knew her trail mates only by nickname: Pinky, Slim Jim, Packer Jack and Digger. On impulse she gave her nickname, too—Firebrand—which they accepted without showing the least curiosity as to how she came by such a name. Amanda quickly learned that a person's background went unquestioned. But God help those who violated the moral code —a man's claim and his cache of goods were sacred. For those caught stealing, punishment was swift. A "fall" into a ravine apparently ended the career of many a thief, for on the first day out, Amanda glanced into a crevice to see a body sprawled on the rocks far below. The matter received scant attention from passing climbers. No one needed to ask what had happened. They knew.

On the second day the trail narrowed and steepened. Those descending had to squeeze aside to allow the climbers to struggle past.

The overloaded pack animals stumbled on the loose rocks and balked at crossing canyons and rivers. Amanda led her horse with patience, but she noticed that her companions were not so kind. They seemed to feel that only constant beatings and cursing would inspire their animals to move on.

By the third day they were above the fragrant spruce forests, and bleak treeless ridges crowded the horizon. Chilling winds blew down the canyons, and at times threatened to sweep the climbers from the trail. The horses clung in fear to the narrow ledges which they were forced to travel. Amanda couldn't blame them. They had reached dizzying heights, yet still had worse to come. A wet snow began to fall that night, but no one considered waiting for the weather to clear. They pressed on with renewed determination, as though each new obstacle existed only to be challenged.

But on the fourth day, the frantic compulsion to push ahead was gruesomely demonstrated when they began to come across the carcasses and rotting cadavers of horses. At first there were only a few, but as the day wore on, they appeared in ever increasing numbers until they were beyond counting. Amanda was horrified to learn they had been starved and beaten to death in a vain effort to hurry them over the pass. But worse than the overwhelming spectacle of carnage, was the thought of the suffering beasts, the terrible waste of life. It was hard to believe that many of these desperate stampeders had once been farmers whose livelihood had depended on the very animal they could now so cruelly destroy. But Amanda found no sympathy in her companions. The horses were not only lazy and stubborn, they said, but deserving of ill treatment, for they would push their masters over a ledge if they got the chance. If they died, they died for spite. It was the stampeders one should pity, for without a pack animal, it was almost impossible to get their load over the pass.

"We call this Dead Horse Trail," said Digger. "It's the place whar you either turn back or push on. For every dead beast thar's a man that didn't make it."

When they camped that night, even the damp snowfall failed to overcome the stench of decomposing flesh. A few feet from where Amanda had pitched her tent lay one pathetic carcass which had been crushed by the weight of a piano. Her companions, however, found this a hilarious sight. They cheered the optimistic fellow who had tried to carry with him a token of civilization. In fact, Packer

Jack was bound to see if the piano still worked. Though most of the keys were broken, he managed to pick out a feeble tune with one finger, sending his friends into spasms of laughter. In the middle of the night, as she tried to sleep, Amanda could still hear an occasional mournful note. She wasn't sure if it was the wind or some small animal depressing a key, but the futility of the sound filled her with sadness.

On the fifth day they came upon a crowded campsite of tents encircling a ravine.

"Thar's your avalanche," announced Slim Jim, pointing toward the gaping hole.

Amanda's heart thumped painfully as she hurried ahead of the others to peer over the edge. Was it the high altitude or anxiety which made her feel fit to burst? As she paused to gulp the thin air, Slim Jim caught up with her to caution against going too close. Yet all she could see was what appeared to be a vast snow field, which could have been mistaken for solid ground were it not for the craters and pockets where the surface was melting.

"Don't walk on it," he warned. "It's filled with air."

How peaceful, how innocent it looked. Sadly she glanced across the ravine to the encampment. "What are they doing there?" she asked. "Have they come to dig out the bodies?"

Slim Jim laughed sharply. "Nope. They're just waitin' for the thaw. Waitin' for the bodies to appear by theirselves."

"But why?"

Slim Jim looked at Amanda as though the answer was obvious. "For gold. What else? And if they don't find gold, they'll take the gear. And the grub. Hell, why not?"

Amanda gazed hopelessly over the snow field, trying to make herself accept the fact that the chance of survival didn't exist. Not after so many weeks in which no effort had been made to reach the victims.

A few of the prospectors who were keeping the grim vigil straggled over to see what the newcomers were up to, scowling suspiciously at the prospect of sharing their bounty with any late arrivals. But as soon as she assured them that she was only interested in identifying a friend, they welcomed her to join them. One old-timer volunteered the information that the snow was sinking at the rate of two or three feet a day. He cheerfully predicted that the bodies would emerge within a week.

But that night another heavy snow fell, and by morning the surface of the field was smoothed over and several feet higher. At that point, some disgusted stampeders, impatient with waiting, trekked on. Digger held out his hand to Amanda, indicating that they, too, were on their way.

"Good luck, Firebrand. Hope you find your man."

"Look us up when you get to the Yukon," said Pinky, who still didn't understand that Amanda's mission was to trace her missing friend, not dig for gold.

Packer Jack's practical eye appraised Amanda's gear. "If you want to get rid of any grub, we'll be glad to take it off your hands."

"I'd better not," she said. "I don't know how long I'll be here. "

"Don't wait too long," advised Slim Jim. "If the rivers get too swelled up, your horse can't cross."

Then they were off, hurrying up the trail, still cursing and kicking their animals. Amanda turned away.

That night the old-timer invited her to join the others around the campfire. But no sooner did she seat herself than she noticed that one of the prospectors was dipping his pipe into a canvas pouch which looked disturbingly familiar.

"May I see that, please?" she asked in sudden apprehension.

He handed it across with a grin. "Help yourself!"

She turned it over slowly. And there, just as she had feared, were the hastily sewn initials in red yarn—T.M.

"Where did you get this?" Her voice was trembling.

"Found it," he answered readily. "Hangin' on that tree yonder."

"When?"

"Right after the snow slide. I been here since the day it come down."

Amanda felt her stomach drop. "You saw it happen?"

"Not with my own eyes. But I heerd the rumble and come along right after. Found all kinds of stuff scattered around. But the men was gone. Not a body in sight." He paused to chuckle. "How that pouch landed up in a tree I'll never know! Too bad it wasn't fulla gold!"

The others laughed with him, shaking their heads.

But Amanda could only stare at the pouch as it gradually blurred before her eyes with the sudden release of pent-up emotion. As soon as the prospectors noticed her tears, they fell silent. She could feel again the weight of the gold when Tom had handed her the pouch; she could see his face shining with excitement. It had meant so much to him. More than his own life.

Slowly she forced herself to explain her mission, drawing a reluctant conclusion that the discarded pouch seemed to be final proof that Tom had perished.

"You can keep it, ma'am," offered the prospector, moved by her story. "I'll find something else for my tobacco."

"Thank you," she replied. "I would like it as I have nothing to remember him by." But her own words spurred a fresh flow of tears.

"There weren't any gold in it, I swear," declared the prospector, raising his hand. " 'Twas empty, 'cepting for a fake five-dollar bill."

Amanda looked up. "Soapy!" she gasped aloud. So Tom had met him, too!

"You know Soapy Smith?" asked the prospector in surprise.

When Amanda told about her encounter with him, everyone knew exactly who he was and each had a woeful tale to relate.

"That Soapy Smith is as slippery a character as you'll ever meet up with!" the old-timer confirmed, shaking a fist.

Amanda remembered Ma Pullen's strange comment that Tom should have quit while he was ahead. Did she know something?

"Watch your step, young lady," the prospector warned, seeming to read her mind. "Soapy is bad apples."

It wasn't difficult to learn that the Packhorse Saloon in Skagway was Soapy Smith's unofficial headquarters. The same day she returned to town, Amanda found him there, holding court with his hangers-on, the less talented who evidently hoped that some of the Soapy magic might rub off.

He didn't notice Amanda at first, engaged as he was in dispensing advice to an audience of eager young Swedes.

"So you want to know how to detect gold? I'll let you in on a secret." He lowered his voice. "You can tell by the taste of the water! I happen to have a sample right here in this bottle. Carry it with you, and when you test a stream, if it tastes like the water in this bottle, then get your pan and sluice box ready. You're in business! That will be ten dollars, please. Ten dollars *apiece*."

Smiling, Soapy tapped his forefinger on the table to indicate the time had come for them to put down their money.

"Dumb Swedes!" muttered a skeptic. "They deserve to git took."

Amanda observed that along with contempt for Swedes, there was a certain admiration for Soapy. All enjoyed the hoax, as long as it was not at their own expense.

"Well," said Amanda in a loud voice, "I don't need any bottled water to tell me how to find gold. I just came back with a trunkload!"

Everyone turned in her direction. Soapy's face brightened.

"Well, if it isn't the lovely young lady who bought the soap! Struck it rich, eh?" Soapy rose from his chair and sauntered over. "This calls for a celebration! Bartender, bring champagne for the lucky lady!" Bowing to Amanda, he kissed her hand. "Jefferson Randolph Smith, at your service!"

Amanda introduced herself, then dropped her voice. "That bottled water isn't a bad way to find gold, but I've got a better way that works every time."

"You do?" Soapy's eyes widened. "What is it?"

"Well, I can't go giving away my secrets for nothing, now can I?" Soapy smiled slyly. "How much will it cost me?"

"How can I place a value on a secret that opens the door to wealth?"

Soapy leaned closer. "Look, maybe you and me should team up and split the profits. What do you say?"

Amanda's eyes narrowed. "Why should I?"

"Because I've got schemes for making money that I'd be willing to share with you," Soapy confided from the corner of his mouth.

Amanda considered for a moment. "Fifty-fifty?"

"Fifty-fifty," he agreed, then asked slyly, "Sealed with a kiss?"

"With a handshake," said Amanda.

Soapy squeezed her hand, and at the same time pulled her closer. He moistened his lips. "Now about that trunkload of gold . . ."

"Answer one question, then I'll tell you how I found it. Did you ever meet a Tom Maynard?"

"No," replied Soapy, dropping her hand.

"That's too bad," said Amanda, "because he cheated me out of some gold. If I ever find him, I'm going to get even."

Soapy smiled tentatively, his eyes unsure. "Well, I'll let you know if I run across him."

She would have to be patient. Soapy wasn't ready to trust her.

"Now it's my turn," he reminded.

Amanda glanced about as if to make sure no one was listening. "There's only one sure way to detect gold. By looking at the way the trees are bending. They always point *away* from a vein, not toward it. That's how a lot of folks get fooled."

"That right?" said Soapy with wide-eyed interest.

Amanda nodded solemnly. He seemed to be taken in—or was he? Anyway, I'll be gone before he can test my theory, she thought. I'll be far away and safe.

"I hear you teamed up with Mr. Smith," Ma Pullen announced the minute Amanda came downstairs.

"Why, yes." She hesitated, surprised that the news had traveled so fast. "What do you think of him?"

"I'm here to serve folks, not to judge 'em," said Ma self-righteously. "See that sign there that says 'No Credit'? Well, if I feel like it, I'll break my own rule. I'll give credit to any miner whose luck is on the ebb. And that goes for Mr. Jefferson Randolph Smith."

"I'm glad to hear somebody has a kind word for him," said Amanda.

"You bet! Nobody gits took by him that don't deserve to." Ma went on at length, confiding all the details of Soapy's better side, the soft spot in his heart for widows, small boys and stray dogs.

"Why, he thinks nothing of giving my boys a gold nugget, just for running an errand. A good man is Mr. Smith—if you don't double-cross him."

The unexpected warning made Amanda feel strangely uneasy. Was it just her imagination, or did there seem to be a keen and meaningful look in Ma's eye which hadn't been there before?

Suddenly, Amanda was conscious of a rustle of skirts on the stairs, then abrupt silence. She glanced up. There was her friend Bertha again, this time elegantly dressed, her hand resting lightly on the banister. She looked down on Amanda with smug disdain, then continued to descend. At first Amanda thought she was going to speak, but it was soon apparent that Bertha still harbored ill feelings from their days at the Grand Union, for she swept past without a word, content in her display of finery to show she had gotten even with Firebrand at last.

Amanda sent a wire to Erastus Brainerd with the sad news that she had proof of Tom's death and that she would be leaving for home soon. She didn't tell him about Soapy Smith or her efforts to trace the events leading up to Tom's decision to go back up the trail. It would be time enough when she actually had her story on Soapy, and with luck, enough evidence to put him behind bars.

But Soapy was not as gullible as she had at first supposed. Try as she would, it was impossible to lead him into a trap. Reluctantly, Amanda realized she could do no more.

She purchased a ticket on the next southbound steamer due to arrive that night and depart two days later, then walked back to the hotel. A half block away, she stopped short. Soapy was going up the steps of Pullen House. She hesitated outside, then on impulse decided to go in the back way.

From the kitchen she could hear Soapy and Ma conversing in low tones. She crept behind the door to listen.

"You're sure then?" Soapy's voice was intense, threatening.

"Sure as can be. When Miss Bertha saw her in the lobby, she acted real cool like. But later, when she got me alone, she was fit to go through the ceiling. 'I'm not staying under the same roof with any two-faced reporters!' she said. 'That woman's real name is Firebrand, and Firebrand brings bad luck!'"

"I'll be damned—Firebrand!"

"Looks like you two got to be real good friends," said Ma with ill-concealed jealousy. "I reckon her shape caught yer eye."

"Nothing of the sort and we're not friends," he snapped. "I figured she was a reporter when she mentioned that smart aleck Maynard. So I just played her along."

"Well, now you know for sure, thanks to me. So how about my nugget?"

"Not so fast. Your job isn't finished yet. I can't let her go blabbing to all the papers about me!"

"Let 'er blab. It wasn't *yer* fault her fella got caught in an avalanche."

"What'ya mean it wasn't my fault? Who took all his gold in a card game? Me! Who conned him into going back up the trail? Me again!

Hell, if Firebrand gets wind of *that,* there'll be a big hullabaloo. And next thing you know, I'll be run outa town."

"Well, it's pretty late for regrets. That's what you get for mixing with reporters in the first place."

"That Maynard was on to me, Ma. He was all set to do a big story, so I had to think fast. That's why I sent him off on a wild goose chase to a phony gold field. Why, he wanted that gold so bad he'd still be wandering around in the middle of nowhere, if mother nature hadn't dumped a ton of snow on him!"

"What do you aim to do about Firebrand?"

"What do *you* think? Keep your eye on her, Ma. And the nugget is yours."

There was a long silence. Too long. Amanda began to back away. Why did the floor have to creak so? She reached the door at last, turned and ran. No one came after her.

Amanda waited for Soapy at the Packhorse. He arrived acting as nonchalant as ever.

"We're going to Dyea," he announced without bothering to greet her.

Amanda looked at him quickly, heart pounding. *"We?"*

"Yep." He smiled broadly. "There's a gold field right out of town that nobody knows about but me. You don't even have to cross Chilkoot Pass."

"You never mentioned it before."

"I didn't know you well enough before. But now I want to let you in on it—I need you to help me figure out which way the trees are bent and all that—seeing as how that's your specialty."

"You could do that yourself. All you have to do is dig in the opposite direction."

"Still, I want you along," Soapy insisted, continuing to smile, "to bring me good luck."

"All right," Amanda agreed. "Long as we split half and half." She hoped her voice sounded normal, but in her own ears it seemed forced, shaky.

A steamer whistle sounded in the distance. The other saloon patrons tipped up their glasses and began to drift out. The arrival of the steamer from Seattle always meant new faces, opportunity for business, and news from the outside world. For Amanda it meant her only chance to escape.

"Do we have time to watch the boat come in?" she asked.

"Sure," he said with a shrug. "It's too late to go to Dyea today anyway. So we'll go first thing tomorrow."

Amanda's heart was thundering. The steamer wasn't scheduled to depart until the day *after*.

"I can't tomorrow," she said, trying to sound casual. "I need time to get ready."

Soapy gave her a suspicious glance. "The next day then. But no later. Time's running out."

The following morning, Amanda went directly to the telegraph office. There was an urgency now that didn't exist before—to wire her story immediately, rather than wait until she was aboard the steamer. This way, if anything happened to her . . . but she couldn't think of that.

Just as she was about to enter the office, the door was flung open and out came the old prospector who had found Tom's pouch. His face was flushed with anger, his hair flying in all directions.

"Don't go in there!" he warned fiercely. "They cheated me outa ten dollars!"

Before Amanda could question him, he seized her by the arm and steered her down the street until they reached the Packhorse Saloon.

"Let's have ourselves a whiskey—on me. And I'll tell you why you don't wanna send no telegrams outa *this* town!"

Amanda pulled back. "Let's go someplace else. Soapy's in there."

"Ding-busted, I know that! He's just the snake in the grass I wanna see!"

"Well, I don't!" Amanda turned away quickly and started off in the opposite direction.

The prospector hurried to catch up with her. "Soapy and that telegrapher are in cahoots," he panted. "Afore I went up the mountain Soapy took ten dollars off me so's to send messages home to my family while I was gone. Now come to find out I gotta pay *another* ten dollars in order to git the re-plies!" As he related the story, he grew even angrier, and pulling off his hat, he punched the crown repeatedly with his fist. "I'm a danged fool, that's what I am! Betcha Soapy never sent no message in the first place! Betcha them re-plies are as fake as his five-dollar bills!"

Amanda slowed her pace. No wonder they hadn't heard from Tom for all those weeks before the avalanche—his reports must have been intercepted. And of course hers would be, too.

"Thanks for warning me," she told the prospector gratefully. "You came along just in time."

Amanda didn't check out of Pullen House.

"I'm going to Dyea with Mr. Smith," she told Ma, observing her reaction, "and I don't know how long I'll be gone. So save my room for me."

"Enjoy your trip," said Ma, her mouth twitching slightly. "If you want to leave yer valuables, I'll look after 'em for you."

Amanda smiled. "I'm afraid I don't have any, only some gear, which I won't be needing."

As she walked out of Pullen House for the last time, she carried only her mackinaw and a small pack. When she turned to wave from the doorway, she saw the distress on Ma's face. For a moment it seemed that Ma was going to warn her not to go, but instead, she looked away quickly, unable to meet Amanda's eye, pretending to be busy.

Amanda forced herself to stroll toward the dock, trying not to look as if she were in a hurry. As the steamer would leave with the tide in the evening, her only hope was to be allowed to board early.

The captain remembered Amanda from her voyage north. He greeted her enthusiastically, saying that it was good to see a pretty face once again. She knew then she would have no trouble boarding ahead of time.

"There is a certain gentleman I don't wish to see," Amanda explained. "So I'd appreciate it if my name could be left off the passenger list until we're underway."

"I understand," he nodded, grinning. "If anybody asks, I've never laid eyes on you."

Amanda took a last look at Skagway, home of the cruel wind, and went into her cabin.

The Seattle skyline was a welcome sight. Amanda remained on deck as they steamed into the harbor, watching the city grow closer.

Home at last. A June sun burned her cheeks, while the salt spray cooled them. It seemed she had been gone far longer than two months. She knew that she had changed, at least inside. The world appeared less overwhelming than it once had, and she was swept by a great sense of being part of it.

As she came down the gangplank, she saw a bright splotch of color coming toward her. It was Erastus Brainerd with an armful of roses.

"Erastus!" Amanda waved excitedly, surprised that he would have taken the time to meet her.

"Welcome home, Amanda." He thrust the roses into her arms.

Amanda flushed, embarrassed by the flowers and by the fact that she had inadvertently called him by his first name.

"I'm sorry about—everything," he said haltingly. "I hope you don't think it wrong of me to come bringing flowers, but I didn't want you to have a sad homecoming. I felt you'd been through enough."

"Flowers are never wrong," she assured him, feeling a sudden lump in her throat.

Three weeks at sea had given her endless hours to think about Tom, about the strangeness of life and especially about the future. The soothing, timeless motion of the waves had gradually restored her hope. One phase had ended, but another was beginning.

As soon as they reached the office, Amanda sat quietly by the window and opened the paper to read her story, "A SCOUNDREL RULES SKAGWAY." Her account ran word for word, just as she had wired it from the steamer. She breathed a sigh of relief. Erastus had changed nothing.

"I'm standing behind you, Amanda. You've shown us the dark side of the gold rush, the side none of us knew about. Or didn't *want* to know. We were too late to save Tom, but if your story can save others, then it was worth the journey."

I'll soon be taking another journey, she thought. You don't know about it yet, but it was you who gave me the inspiration. Surely you haven't forgotten telling me that someday I should have a newspaper of my own? Well, you did. Though it was probably said in jest. After all, my share of the gold rush money is still collecting interest in the Dexter Horton Bank. If I use it to buy the land now, then when the time is right, I'll build my paper. What could be a more fitting memorial to Tom, who made it all possible? But don't worry, Erastus, I won't be leaving you yet. In fact, I'll enjoy working even more than before, because now I have a purpose. I have something to look forward to.

"What about the Gold Rush Committee? And all your hard work?" she asked.

"I resigned. It was my own choice."

"That must have been a difficult decision."

"On the contrary, it was the easiest one I've ever had to make. Unfortunately, I was a bit too late."

"What do you mean?"

"While you were gone, a lot of newcomers have been pouring into the city—not bound for the gold fields, but to grab the jobs of those who left. Which is too bad for anybody who returns from the Yukon empty-handed, because his old job might not be waiting."

"Then the gold rush was all for nothing!"

"Not quite." Erastus smiled faintly. "It got people to face reality. Myself included. I don't want this paper ever again to be indifferent or neutral on any questions involving public interests." He paused. "So in spite of what's happened, I hope you're not too disillusioned to stay. The *P.I.* needs a Firebrand. And so do I."

Amanda gazed into space, thinking, You may have me now, but someday I'll be your competition.

"The letters we've been getting on your story have been mostly from men," he went on as if trying to spark her interest. "And some of them, I don't mind telling you, are quite smitten. There was one in particular I saved to show you—from a bashful fellow who signed initials only, but what he wrote will turn your ears pink!"

Amanda snapped back to reality. "Was it from M.R.?" she asked eagerly.

"Why, yes. Do you know him?"

"He's written before—several times. But I don't take him seriously. May I see it?"

Erastus sighed and began to search his desk. His resigned expression told her that he realized his cause was hopeless. He was probably wondering, how can I compete with the romantic appeal of an anonymous admirer?

A week later a brief news bulletin was received from Skagway.

Jefferson Randolph Smith, having shot a man in an argument, was pursued and slain, the victim of vigilante justice. The incident had occurred right after Amanda's story had been syndicated in newspapers throughout the country. And like the life of Soapy Smith, the great stampede was over.

PART TWO

The Lumber Struggle

1904–1917

Chapter Eleven

AMANDA leaned close to the steaming window, and strained to penetrate the blackness rushing by outside the train. It was stifling and crowded, with every seat taken, but when she raised the window for a breath of fresh air, a damp wind tore through the car, depositing soot from the engine. She closed it quickly and sank back to finish her letter, reading over what she had already written, wondering if Emma would lose faith in her.

October 9, 1904

Dear Emma:

Forgive my scribble, but it's the middle of the night and I find myself on a very bumpy train heading for Aberdeen (ho-hum, you're saying. Anyway, it's a four-hour ride southwest of Seattle) to cover a fire that's raging out of control. But I'm sure that fire can be nothing compared to the one raging inside *me!* While others envy my "exciting" job, I race from one assignment to the next—just for the money. No, that's not true—also for the experience. Erastus is pleased of course to have such a hard worker, knowing nothing of my ambitions. Yes, I'm afraid that my poor newspaper is still unborn, though I comfort myself by visiting my property at least once a week. I can already visualize the building, though not an inch of ground has been turned. The money is *so* hard to save! Sometimes I think that I'll never be able to do it alone."

Amanda paused to stare into the night, hoping she didn't sound too whiny. She missed having someone to share the struggle with.

But men shied away, not understanding her dedication to work. Once they found they couldn't seduce her, they were gone. Erastus of course was always there, keeping a gentlemanly distance, waiting for some sign of encouragement. But much as she was fond of him, her emotions told her that when you start as friends, you can never end as lovers. He was hardly to be pitied, however, for as an eligible bachelor, he had more than his share of opportunities; as an unmarried woman, she wasn't so fortunate.

Amanda resumed her letter, hurrying to finish.

"I regret very much not keeping in closer touch, for which I blame myself entirely. However, this doesn't mean I don't think of you and hope that you're having better luck with your goals than I am. Back to the fire. I'm sure it won't merit a single line in any eastern paper, but here it's big news—Aberdeen is a mill town, so if the whole town goes up, it could seriously cripple the lumber business. As you well know, I've been wanting to investigate lumber for a long time, but so far it's been impossible to get any co-operation. And though Erastus sympathizes with my efforts, he feels that the industry is too big and powerful ever to open its doors to a reporter. But maybe this fire will give me an excuse to worm my way in. I desperately need one truly sensational story that will get lots of attention and—who knows?—some backing to launch my paper . . ."

Amanda looked up. The conductor had come into the car to announce that they would be terminating in Cosmopolis, a few miles east of their destination, because the Aberdeen station had already burned to the ground. Anxious relatives, coming to search for loved ones, pressed to the window to view in fearful silence the inflamed sky, growing brighter as they approached. Amanda was always amazed to see how news often managed to travel even before it could be printed. She wondered if the day would come when newspapers would be obsolete and all news would be disseminated by word of mouth?

An old logger sitting across the aisle finally broke the silence. When she had interviewed him earlier, she had learned that although he was now retired and living elsewhere, he was on his way back to find his son, also a logger.

"I know he's safe," he kept insisting. "He can look after himself. We *all* can," he added meaningfully, including himself in the closely knit fraternity of timbermen. Amanda recognized the characteristic pride and independence which made it so difficult for millworkers to admit to any problems within the industry which they couldn't resolve themselves. She guessed it was the myth of strength which they had to live up to. They stuck together—another factor which could hamper an investigation.

An eager young *Times* reporter, fresh out of college, sat opposite Amanda throughout the trip, listening wide-eyed as she solicited opinions as to the cause of the fire. So in awe was he to be in the presence of Firebrand that he forgot to take notes, and toward the end of the journey, timidly asked for her help.

With an understanding smile, she handed him her notebook. "If you can read my terrible scribbling, you're welcome to copy it."

As she watched him feverishly take down each interview word for word, she thought to herself: You poor boy, you're never going to make a reporter. Shall I do you the kindness of telling you now? Or let you find out for yourself? When your boss, Colonel Blethen, sees a very familiar line of questioning in your article, he's going to know that somewhere along the way you encountered Firebrand.

She decided to say nothing, but when the boy at last handed back her notes, she couldn't help but offer a word of advice.

"Don't be afraid to plunge in—to march right up to people, look them in the eye and ask your question, politely but without apology."

The boy nodded eagerly, then wrote it down.

Amanda sighed. Times were changing. It seemed that most young people hoped to get ahead with the least amount of effort. They didn't care to think or to work, which was far different from the days when *she* was starting out eight years ago. Had it really been that long? Yet, in some ways Amanda felt much older than twenty-five. Not so much because of all she had achieved, but because of what she had *failed* to achieve. Her paper was still in the future, and so was someone to share it with. Love. That seemed the most elusive dream of all.

When at last the train slowed to a stop, Amanda was as eager as the others to reach the platform and a breath of fresh air. But the minute they stepped outside, they were hit with a blast of heat. Bewildered passengers milling about on the platform held handkerchiefs to their faces in a vain effort to protect their throats from the choking sting of smoke. Ashes sifted down like snowflakes, carpeting the ground and muffling the sound of each footstep. A cascade of live cinders suddenly descended, scattering the crowd in all directions. In the eerie orange glow, everyone seemed to be desperately searching for a familiar face.

From the far end of the platform, Amanda could see the flaming sky reflected in the Chehalis River. But when she reached the wooden swing bridge, she soon realized it would be futile to cross. Even from a distance of two or three miles, it was apparent that little remained of the town of Aberdeen.

Refugees straggled across the bridge, carrying whatever possessions they had been able to salvage. Among them were six men bearing a burden which at first looked like a coffin. But as they came closer, Amanda saw that it was a piano. With a sudden pang, she remembered the broken piano lying in the snow on Dead Horse Trail so many years ago, and it struck her that in a time of crisis the objects most likely to be saved were those which assured a continuation of civilization, not the useful everyday articles.

As soon as they had crossed the bridge, the men put down their burden and paused to rest. Amanda noticed her young friend from the *Times* bounding toward them.

"Hello, I'm a reporter. May I ask why you chose to save this piano?" Amanda heard him ask all in one breath.

"I own the Humboldt Saloon—or I *did* own it," one of them replied. "Big Fred Hewett's the name."

"Wait, let me get this down!" said the reporter, fumbling for paper and pencil.

"We couldn't move the bar, but I figured we could save the piano," Big Fred explained. "It came around the Horn ten years ago without a scratch, so how could I leave it behind? It brought me years of good luck and a fine business. It will again."

His friends nodded in agreement.

The reporter thanked him profusely and hurried off. As soon as he had gone, Amanda stepped in.

"Mr. Hewett, I'm with the *P.I.* and I'd like your opinion as to how this fire got started?"

Big Fred seemed flattered that she knew who he was. "I don't want to get anybody into trouble," he began, "but I *know* who did it. Union fellas."

"*Union?*"

"The millworkers union."

"I didn't know they had one," said Amanda in surprise.

"They do, but they haven't had much luck. They got kicked out of Slade."

"Slade, did you say?"

"That's right. The manager told them that any more union men seen prowling around would be shot on sight. So the fellas decided to burn the place down. I heard them bragging about it right in my saloon!"

"Where can I find them?" Amanda asked hurriedly.

"Oh, they must be a hundred miles away by now. If I was them, I woulda caught the first train outa town."

"That's all right. I'll find out for sure!"

"Wait! Better steer clear of Aberdeen till the fire's out," he advised. "The police set up a barricade so's nobody can go back. Anyways," he added, "one of my boys is coming along with a barrel of beer. Soon as he gets here, we'll be in business again. So you're welcome to wait with us."

"Thanks, I will." Amanda opened her notebook and began to record their conversation.

Big Fred turned to one of his friends, who had been helping to carry the piano. "Play us a tune, Roscoe. Something lively."

As soon as Roscoe began to play, the refugees flocked around, eager for some cheer. A few started to sing along, then one by one, they all joined in.

But their display of undefeated spirit was not appreciated by everyone. Amanda turned at the sound of heavy boots marching down the boardwalk to see a grim-looking contingent of barrel-chested men heading toward them from the direction of Cosmopolis. And at the same moment, the boy from the Humboldt appeared, rolling a keg across the bridge.

"Take your goddam piano and go back where you come from! We don't want no Aberdeeners here!" a voice warned from the crowd.

"Keep playing, Roscoe," Big Fred ordered. "Tap the keg! Everybody's thirsty!"

Suddenly a giant of a man stepped forward. Amanda saw that he wielded a brutal-looking ax with as much ease as if he were handling a fishing pole.

"Git back across that bridge!" he thundered.

Heads turned in his direction, but no one moved.

"Why, if it isn't Jumbo Reilly," drawled Big Fred. "Didn't I toss you out of my saloon once?"

Jumbo Reilly's laughter rolled out like tumbling logs. "Nobody bounces Jumbo!" he scorned.

"Play on, Roscoe," urged Big Fred.

Though half the size of Jumbo, he clearly felt he had the power to match his opponent. However, the onlookers were less certain.

"Watch his ax," one of them cautioned.

Roscoe played, but very gently, keeping an eye on Jumbo as the giant strode toward him.

"He's all bluff," Big Fred assured. "Pass around the beer. Tonight it's on the house!"

Suddenly, without warning, Jumbo lunged forward, and raising his ax high over his head, brought it down full force, splitting the barrel in two. Beer gushed from the wound and was quickly absorbed by the ashes.

"Why, you son of a bitch," growled Big Fred. "Only a coward would strike an unarmed barrel!"

"Call me a coward, will you?" Jumbo bared his teeth.

The refugees scattered in haste, certain that Big Fred was about to be sacrificed. But instead, Jumbo tramped over to the piano.

"Do you know 'Mother o' Mine'?" he asked Roscoe menacingly.

Roscoe nodded, swallowing with difficulty.

"Then play it!"

Roscoe began timidly, his fingers trembling.

"Louder!"

But instead of playing loud, he played fast. It was the fastest "Mother o' Mine" that anyone had ever heard.

"Enough!"

However, Roscoe was unable to stop quickly enough to suit Jumbo. Enraged, Jumbo swung his ax, bringing it down with all his strength right in the center of the piano. With the sickening scream of ripping timber, the music died. And Roscoe collapsed in a faint.

Jumbo dusted his hands with satisfaction, as if awed by his own strength. "Never felled a piano before," he admitted modestly.

"You'll pay for this!" Big Fred's voice quavered with helpless anger. "That piano came around the Horn!"

"Well, it couldn't play 'Mother o' Mine' worth a damn," Jumbo snarled. "So now you know what I think of your piano. And that goes for all you Aberdeeners. The first one of you that sets foot in town gets *this!*" And he waved his ax in the air.

Having issued the warning, Jumbo turned and led his followers back up the boardwalk toward the bright lights of Cosmopolis, leaving the refugees huddled on the riverbank.

It was almost four in the morning when Amanda checked into Simpson House, the only hotel in Cosmopolis, to catch a few hours' sleep. She immediately placed a call to Erastus, guessing correctly that he would be anxiously awaiting her report.

"You mean to say union organizers set the fire?" he asked incredulously.

"That's the rumor. I'll try to verify it."

"I don't like the sound of all this. And I don't like the idea of so much violence going on. God knows what's going to happen next. Maybe I should come down."

"Erastus, you worry too much. Go home and go to bed. I'll call you again later."

"Don't call. Just try to get the first train home."

Amanda hung up without arguing. "I might as well be married to him," she complained aloud.

Later that morning when Amanda awoke, she saw that the flurry of ashes had been replaced by a gentle drizzle. From the window of her room, she could look across the river toward Aberdeen where the smoke had cleared to reveal blackened chimneys projecting from the rubble. The fire was out. She dressed and hurried downstairs.

When she stepped outside, the air was cool, carrying only a slight aroma of burned wood. Amanda turned her face upward. The mist felt wonderfully refreshing. There were no carriages in sight, so she quickened her pace for the long walk into Aberdeen.

Though it was early in the day, the saloons were doing a brisk business, with the sounds of voices and laughter spilling into the street.

Suddenly she stopped short as a pair of saloon doors swung out in her path sending a logger flying past her into the gutter. Right behind him came the challenger, his face dark with anger, ready to fight.

"Get up on your feet!" he commanded, his body tensing into a half crouch.

Amanda stared as he raised a muscular left arm. But his right arm clung uselessly to his side—severed at the elbow. She looked again at the face. It was the millworker she had met on the Portland dock, the one who had been battered by the police!

"Gus Johnson!" she gasped, remembering his name instantly.

Gus Johnson's head pivoted toward her, his startled expression groping for recognition.

"Portland—eight years ago," she prompted. "Remember when you tried to keep us from getting on *The Puget Queen?* And the police came and dragged you away? Well, I'm the reporter you spoke to!"

"Christ Almighty!" he whispered in amazement. "I don't believe it!" Forgetting his opponent, he gripped Amanda's hand with his thumb and forefinger, his strength undiminished by the ordeals of the last eight years. "Would you be willing to join me for a drink?"

"Could we make it a cup of coffee? I haven't had breakfast yet."

"C'mon!" He seized her by the elbow and led her across the street to Simpson's Café.

"I always wondered what became of you," Amanda said. "I've wanted desperately to do something for the millworkers and for everyone in the logging industry, but I've never been able to break down the barrier."

"And you never will," said Gus. "They're stubborn as mules." He hurried ahead to open the door.

"They? But you're one of them, aren't you?"

"Not any more. We never did get our pensions, so if it hadn't been for the union, I'd be a bum. Nobody wants to hire a man with one arm."

"The union helped you? How?"

Gus gave her a sly grin, casting his eyes about the café to see if anyone was listening.

"I'm one of 'em," he confided in a low voice. "I'm a paid organizer for the United Mill Workers and Loggers of America."

"Then *you* must know who started the fire!"

Before answering, he led the way to a table at the back. Only when they were seated did he reply, his voice dropping even lower. "You can print this and give me credit." He paused. "I did it."

"You—set the fire?"

"Me and a few of the boys," he admitted modestly. "We gave 'em warning, but when they threatened our lives, we had no choice. So we taught the bastards a lesson." He caught himself. "Don't print *that* word—I shouldn't have said that in front of a lady."

"Don't you know that you've given management an excuse to ban unions completely?"

Johnson blinked. "Hell, I didn't want to burn down the whole town. We were only after Slade."

"Well, I think you made a serious mistake—killing and injuring innocent people!"

"Nobody died that I know of," he murmured lamely. "From what I hear, everybody got out."

"But you've destroyed a city, put people out of work! I'm surprised you didn't leave town. Aren't you afraid?"

"Of what?" asked Johnson defensively. "If the folks here in Cosmopolis knew it was me that set the fire, I'd be a hero."

"A hero? Don't these people depend on the lumber industry for their livelihood?"

"Sure they do. But this here is a company town. Owned by Simpson's Lumber. They don't mind seeing their competition eliminated."

"Simpson's! Now I'm beginning to understand. To think that one company, one *man* has so much power . . ."

The waitress set down two cups of coffee, then waited expectantly for their order.

Amanda stared into her cup, thinking of the eight years wasted in concern for the fate of Gus Johnson and his fellow workers. How could one who had suffered ever be able to inflict suffering on others?

Johnson waved off the waitress and leaned across the table. "I know that you think what we did was wrong, but sometimes that's the only way to get where you want to go."

How much he sounded like Emma, who always believed that the end justified the means.

"What are you going to do now?" she asked.

"I'm going to find John Looney and teach him a lesson."

"John Looney?"

"He's the fella I was about to fight when you came along. He works for me," Johnson added with a note of pride. "I'm teaching him how to be a good, strong union man, so he'll never get pushed around."

"In other words, you're showing him how to be violent."

One corner of Johnson's mouth curled upward. He looked Amanda in the eye. "If it comes to that, yes."

Amanda sighed heavily. "I always believed that unions could benefit the worker. Now I wonder."

"They can!" Johnson declared vehemently, pounding his mangled fist on the table till the cups rattled in their saucers. "Without the unions, the worker is doomed! Trouble is, most of 'em are too dumb to know it!"

"Not dumb, *scared*. It used to be they had only their bosses to fear, now it seems they've got you as well. What do you expect them to do?"

"Look here, little lady, if you really want to help them, then print *our* side of the story. With your help, we won't have to hurt anybody." He leaned closer. "You still with that New York paper?"

"No, I'm with the *P.I.* now."

Johnson's eyes narrowed. "The *P.I.*—what did you say your name was again?"

"I'm Firebrand."

"Well, I'll be danged! Now that's a piece of luck! You've got my permission to write down everything I told you."

"If I do, I won't mention your name."

"Hell, I don't care. Write me in. I'm not scared."

"I know. That's why I won't. The last thing I want to do is to help you become a martyr."

As Amanda walked among the ruins, she tried to visualize what Aberdeen must have looked like. Only the charred skeletons of a few dozen structures remained standing.

It was a lonely experience, shared with a number of dazed townspeople who prowled the rubble hoping to find that some treasured item had miraculously been spared. She watched them kick at the dead coals and stomp the occasional spiral of smoke which continued to rise from the ashes. But no one spoke or looked at one another, each keeping his losses private. Amanda also felt a sense of loss. After talking to Gus, some of her idealism was vanishing. How could a pro-union paper, such as hers would be, ever survive in a climate of violence?

Turning toward the river where the mills had been located, Amanda wondered which charred ghost was Slade's, and if its owners would be there looking about for some evidence of arson. But only a lone young man roamed through the ruins, wearing the tin pants, calked boots and the lived-in BVD's of a logger. She watched him for a while with curiosity, for it seemed strange to find a logger examining the spectacle of destruction with such keen interest. Now and then he would crouch down for a closer look, then take off his battered hat to scratch his head. He had blond hair, neatly trimmed, and handsome features. But he was so absorbed in his exploration, that Amanda ventured quite close before attracting his attention.

"Good morning," she smiled when he finally looked up. "Are you finding anything interesting?"

He straightened up, looking guilty. "You can see for yourself, ma'am, there's nothing here but charcoal." He turned over a piece of blackened timber with the toe of his boot. "It's a mess."

"I guess Aberdeen will have to build with brick next time."

"Maybe. But nothing can beat good solid wood construction. Wood can last a hundred years—if it's treated properly."

"You must be in the logging business."

"That's right. Always have been and always will be." He looked at her curiously. "Are you from out of town?"

"Yes, from Seattle."

"Thought so," he nodded. "Could tell by the way you talk."

"You mean—I have an accent?"

"I mean Seattle folks talk faster. Down here we take our time, think about what we're going to say next."

"I always thought loggers were quick to take offense and quick to insult their enemies," she shot back with a smile.

"Oh-oh! Sounds like you've been going into the wrong saloons!"

They both laughed.

"I hope you didn't lose your home."

"Not me. I'm from Cosmopolis. And proud of it."

"Well, I hear it's a company town, so I wouldn't think you'd have much to be proud of."

"I always thought reporters were supposed to ask questions, not give opinions."

"How did you know I was a reporter?"

"Oh, word gets around."

"All right, then. I'm here to investigate the fire. How do you think it got started?"

The logger's mouth curved into a slow grin. "It wasn't me that set it. Who do *you* think did it?"

"I don't know. Maybe it was the Simpson Lumber Company."

The logger raised a brow. "Do you have any evidence?"

"I'm not saying they *set* the fire, but they might have supported those who did. After all, Slade was their competition. Anyway, I'd like to talk to this Simpson. Do you happen to work there?"

"Sure do." He smiled. "Everybody does."

"Then maybe you can help me. What kind of man is he?"

"Don't ask for the old man. He has a younger partner who's very open-minded and fair. Name's Mark Reed. He's the fellow to see."

"Reed? Thanks for the tip. I'll do that."

"Good luck."

As Amanda walked away, she had a strong feeling that if she turned around, he would still be watching her.

The Simpson Lumber Company dominated the south shore of the Chehalis River just east of Cosmopolis. Wreathed in clouds of steam from its busy smokestacks, the vast complex of buildings sprawled over a wild landscape of driftwood, stumps and railroad tracks. Chutes and pipes and water-filled flumes projected from the buildings in every direction, like the spidery appendages of a giant log-consuming insect. The sounds of groaning steam engines and howling saws furiously split the air as the afternoon fog swept across the harbor and mudflats with a dampening gloom. Logs came in; lumber went out, as freight cars and schooners arrived and departed. Amanda waded through sawdust and chips to reach the main entrance.

The reception area was cramped, poorly lit and unheated. But it was alive with the day and night activity of an industrial empire. It was more frantic and overwhelming than a newspaper plant.

Amanda gave her name to a secretary, then waited while she checked to see if Mr. Reed was available. He will surely be too busy, thought Amanda. The logger meant well, but he had probably never entered the front door himself. She was surprised when the secretary returned almost immediately to show her the way to Mr. Reed's office.

"You came," said Reed, rising to greet her. "What a pleasant surprise!"

"*You're* Mark Reed?" asked Amanda in dismay.

It was the logger! Only he was no longer wearing the tin pants and boots of his profession, but flannel knickers and a black turtle-neck sweater.

"Oh dear, I said all the wrong things, didn't I?" She smiled in embarrassment.

"Don't give it a thought." He came around from behind his desk and pulled up a chair for her. "Please, make yourself at home."

As he took her arm, she noticed that his hand was knotted and calloused, unlike the hand of an executive. She also noticed that he had the trim, yet solid build of an athlete.

"I never thought I could feel at home in a lumber company," she confessed, "but I do."

"I knew you would," he declared confidently. "This is *my* home—this mill and all the miles of timber behind us."

She smiled again, wondering why he was being so charming when she had behaved so foolishly.

"Now then, what can I do for you?" he asked.

"Since I already gave away my reason for coming here, I feel a bit awkward questioning you."

Reed drew up another chair and sat down, gazing at Amanda closely, his blue eyes reflecting amusement. "I owe you an apology, Miss Lamar, or shall I say—Firebrand? I led you here on purpose."

"What do you mean?"

Instead of answering, Reed got up and went to the bookcase behind his desk. Pulling a large scrapbook from the shelf, he brought it around, then drew his chair closer to Amanda's, so that they could examine it together.

"Go ahead," he urged. "Open it."

Amanda turned to the first page. There, neatly pasted in columns, was her salmon cannery article, the first she had ever written for the *Times*.

She looked up in amazement. "What is this?"

"Keep turning! Your whole career is there. I don't think I've missed a single story."

Suddenly it dawned on her. "You're—M.R.!"

He smiled. "Disappointed?"

"I'm too shocked to feel *anything!*" She hesitated shyly. "Are *you* disappointed?"

"How could I be? I gave myself a chance to sneak a look before I invited you here. That's why I was prowling around in the ruins."

"Spying on me?"

"Shamelessly, I'm afraid. Making sure you were the person I hoped you'd be."

"But I was being so smug, so silly. I feel terribly embarrassed."

"That's not how I saw you. I thought you were beautiful. You *are* beautiful."

Amanda shook her head in disbelief. "This must be a dream. I've wondered about you for so long, trying to picture how you looked. There were times when I didn't *want* to know you, afraid to spoil the mystery. You're going to laugh at this, but for a while I even thought you must be a misshapen dwarf who dared not show himself!"

"And if I had been?" asked Mark, teasing.

"It wouldn't have mattered," she answered seriously. "Your letters were so—full of feeling, that I thought I wouldn't care even if you were ugly or old."

"Then you're not angry with me for being such a coward?"

Amanda shrugged, not knowing what to say. "You were playing a game."

"It wasn't a game," he protested quickly. "Well, it may have started out that way, but you soon became very important to me. Yes, it's true."

"Yet you made no attempt to meet me?"

Mark laughed, reddening slightly. "I guess I was afraid, too. After all, you knew how I felt about you, but I had no way of knowing what you thought of me. For all I knew, you were annoyed by my attentions, or even worse, perhaps you were tearing up the letters without ever reading them. It was easier, safer not to know the truth."

"Then you suffered needlessly."

"But I didn't suffer. I enjoyed having an ideal, even if she existed only in my imagination. You filled a great emptiness in my life."

"You settled for an ideal, instead of a real flesh and blood woman? You should have written to Beatrice Fairfax! *She* would have told you what to do."

Mark's eyes narrowed. "*You* weren't Beatrice Fairfax, were you?"

"Of course. Who else?"

He shook his head. "I must admit I never bothered to read the column. But that's only because I didn't know you wrote it."

"Well, I don't suppose a man in your position needs advice on affairs of the heart."

"Don't be too sure. I'm probably more in need than the next fellow. I've always been too involved with the mill to take time to court anyone. Besides, loggers are a shy lot, you know."

Amanda felt swallowed by his gaze. Despite his words, she couldn't detect a trace of shyness.

"Is it too late to get some free advice?" he asked.

"That depends. What would you like to know?" Stay calm, Manka. It's only a flirtation. He has dozens of girl friends and you know it.

"I'd like you to tell me how to win over a fiery, delectable red-head."

Amanda felt her cheeks bloom crimson. How heavenly it was to be a redhead!

"Well, Mr. M.R., much as redheads love to hear flattery, they still prefer a man of honesty."

"Then I shall have to prove myself. What would you have me do?"

"Let me investigate Simpson's."

Mark looked abashed. "I didn't think we were talking business."

"That's why I came, remember?"

"No, you came because *I* brought you here."

"But you knew my motive."

"I thought that once we met things would be—different."

"They *are* different. I came here with a preconceived notion that mill owners were all rather crude and pompous. I was wrong."

"You must have met someone who filled that description."

"I did. Cyrus Clough. Do you know him?"

"Of the Clough-Hartley Mill in Everett? Well, no wonder. I hope you're not equating Simpson's with *them!*"

"I don't know them and I'm making no judgments."

"In that case, I *want* you to investigate us. In fact, I welcome it. I think you'll be pleasantly surprised."

"I'm warning you—I'll be ruthless as always."

"I expect you to be. A clean slate from Firebrand should absolve Simpson's once and for all. I'm at your disposal."

Amanda relaxed. "When can we begin?"

"How about at dinner tonight?"

On her way back to the hotel, Amanda's head pounded with thoughts. One minute she was furious with herself for allowing Mark to sway her emotions, the next minute she rationalized her decision to trust him. But not for a single moment could she stop thinking about him. Unconsciously she began to compare him with the other men she had known. Mark had the good humor of a Tom Maynard, yet he knew exactly where he was going. He was not a dreamer or an adventurer as Tom had been. He was dedicated to his work. In that respect, he was a good deal like Erastus. Any similarity ended there. Whereas Mark was no handsomer than Erastus, he had the distracting ability to fill her with desire. He possessed the kind of attraction which Erastus, unfortunately, lacked. Erastus was too proper, too careful. Always a gentleman. Mark gave the impression of not being proper at all. He seemed to exude just the right amount of mischief— or was it wickedness? Suddenly Amanda realized that all her observations about him had already been revealed in the letters he had written to Firebrand. Of course she had saved them, just as he had saved all her columns. Mark was not really a stranger at all. He claimed he had no time to court anyone, but hadn't he been courting Firebrand all these years? Hadn't he known they were destined to meet?

As she changed her clothes, she thought of Erastus, rather nostalgically, much as she used to think of Tom after he had died. Now they both belonged to the past. Smiling to herself, she remembered how she had once asked Erastus teasingly if he ever visited the girls in the Skid Road hotels, a question which had embarrassed him so much that the truth was obvious, even though he laughed it off without answering. She was sorry she had asked, for after that she always felt envious to think he enjoyed the opportunity for physical release whenever he wished, while she did not. She worried that her passions would be cooled by the passing years and that she would have to become reconciled to an honorable spinsterhood. But that was before this special afternoon. Before Mark Reed. Now her life was going to change.

Chapter Twelve

 W E'LL have dinner at home," Mark announced when he came to call for Amanda. "I only live a short distance."

Amanda didn't mind walking, but Mark's idea of a short distance was almost a mile. Still, she was flattered that he would invite her to his home on such brief acquaintance, and wondered what he had told his parents about her.

The house was raised on stilts above the mudflats, only a hundred yards or so behind the Simpson mill. It was a tall Victorian, new and freshly painted. A rowboat was tied to the veranda railing, its anchor protruding from the mud.

"That's how I get back and forth to the mill at high tide," he told her matter-of-factly.

"Where does Mr. Simpson live?" she asked.

"Oh, he's way up on top of the hill, hidden in a grove of trees." He laughed indulgently. "Mr. Simpson likes to view his domain from above, but as you can see, I prefer to be right in the middle of it all. I don't think I could fall asleep at night if I couldn't hear the whining and screaming of saws."

The house was comfortably furnished, but far from traditional. Instead of the usual Morris chairs and rockers, there were hand-hewn benches and settees of original design, such as one might find in a wood carver's chalet in Switzerland. Even the library table was uniquely carved. The walls were adorned with animal skins and framed maps showing timber regions of the Northwest. But there were no family portraits. As Amanda looked at each object with curiosity and fascination, it gradually dawned on her that Mark lived alone. There was no evidence of anyone else's interests but his own.

"You don't live with your parents?" she finally asked.

"I haven't in years," he admitted cheerfully. "The folks live in Tacoma. Father's a retired banker, and he's never gotten over the fact that I chose lumbering over the banking business. He felt that my college education was a waste, because I studied forestry instead of finance."

He waved his arm toward an archway opening into another parlor. "Go ahead, take a look. I've got ten rooms to rattle around in."

"That's a lot, for one person."

"It's not really the number of rooms that's important to me, but the space. If I had my way, I'd have just one gigantic room, but unfortunately, they don't design houses that way."

"Well, I like it the way it is. Did you build it yourself?"

"Only the finishing. And a logger friend of mine made the furniture. I told him what I wanted, so he carved each piece by hand. Took him a whole winter."

"I've never been in a house which showed so much individuality. It feels like more than just a place to live. It has your personality everywhere I look."

"Glad you like it," said Mark, beaming. "Not many people do. The folks around here think I'm a bit eccentric. Even Mr. Simpson worries about me. He'd really like to mold me to his own specifications."

Although Mark laughed about it, Amanda noted that each time he mentioned Simpson, he spoke with fondness and respect, always careful to call him *Mister* Simpson, even though they were partners.

"Does Miss Lamar live alone?" Mark asked.

"Yes, she does. And Miss Lamar would like you to call her Manka. That's my nickname, for special friends." Amanda suddenly felt shy and unreasonably nervous.

"Manka," he repeated, as if testing it. "Mank and Mark—sounds like a vaudeville team."

Amanda laughed, a bit too eagerly. She hadn't thought of herself as Manka since she had lived at home. But hearing it again from *his* lips filled her with warmth and a feeling of well-being.

Suddenly urgent footsteps came padding down the hallway.

Amanda looked up questioningly as a rotund Chinese man wearing an apron all the way to his toes appeared in the doorway.

"Dinner ready, Sam?" asked Mark.

Sam nodded, scowling, then scurried back down the hall before Mark could introduce him.

"Don't mind Sam Wing," he explained. "The reason he's so surly is because he worked for too many years as a cook in a logging camp. God help the poor cook if the butter is rancid, or he runs out of sugar. Loggers, I'm afraid, have little patience when it comes to their food. I think I rescued Sam just in time!"

They sat down to a meal of thick venison steaks and champagne. Amanda was served a logger's portion, which covered her entire plate.

"Eat every bit," Mark warned, "or Sam will be insulted."

Amanda did not need to be urged, and Mark seemed pleased to see that she had a good appetite.

"I was going to have salmon," he told her when they had finished, "but then I remembered your article on the salmon cannery and decided you probably wouldn't be able to stomach the sight!"

Amanda shook her head in amazement to think how much Mark had figured out about her. She could no longer resist asking why he had kept the scrapbook.

"I got the idea when I was in college and all my friends were collecting postcards of nude women. So I decided to be different and have a chronology of Firebrand." He laughed without embarrassment.

Amanda laughed with him. "A poor substitute, I should think!"

"Not at all," he hastened to assure her. "Even though I had no idea what you looked like, I could create you in my imagination—just from the sound of your writing."

"You could? How did I look?"

Mark tipped back his chair and fixed his eyes on the chandelier.

"Oh, petite with raven hair and green eyes, like some exotic half-breed."

"So that's the type of woman you like."

"Not necessarily. Tall redheads with brown eyes are fine, too."

He was teasing, thank goodness.

"At first I never expected to meet you," he went on. "But some-how I continued with the scrapbook long after my friends had outgrown their postcards—or by marriage were forced to get rid of them. I didn't intend it to be a lifetime project, I just got caught up in it and finally became so taken with you that I didn't want to stop."

"You know, Mark, it's a funny feeling to realize that eight whole years can be contained in a few pages. Every one of those articles is a piece of my life, yet sometimes I think it doesn't add up to much after all. I ask myself, what does it mean?"

"Isn't it enough to be Firebrand? It's enough for *me*." He reached across the table for her hand.

"I'd rather be known for what I do than for who I am."

"Well, it seems to me you're doing far more than most women."

Don't you understand? she wanted to say. I need to be free. Free to love, to have a husband and children—all the normal things that every woman wants. Is it wrong to also want a newspaper that will give a voice to those who can't speak for themselves? These are the things I really want out of life. All things I can't put into words. Not yet.

When they had finished dinner and returned to the parlor, Mark put a ragtime cylinder on the Edison and cranked it up. Sam followed with a hurricane lamp and served the coffee.

"I've got electricity," said Mark, "if you prefer."

"No, I like the soft glow of a lamp. I think the electric light is best suited for factories, not the home."

Mark sat next to her on the settee. "What is your house like?"

"It's just a very ordinary little cottage, right in the heart of the city —close to work, like yours. It has only three rooms, but sometimes when I'm alone it seems almost too big. Isn't that strange?"

"Not at all. It has nothing to do with size, it has to do with being lonely."

"Oh, I'm not lonely," Amanda corrected him hastily. "I'm far too busy. Why, some days I hardly have a moment to myself."

Mark nodded slowly. "Here, have one of Sam's fortune cookies."

"Are there really fortunes inside?"

"Of course." He pointed to the one he wanted her to take. "Try this one."

Amanda took it with some skepticism. Sam didn't strike her as the type who would bother with fortunes. But when she broke open the cookie, out fell a thin slip of paper. It said: "A tall blond man will enter your life."

She smiled. "What a coincidence! Now read yours."

With a straight face, Mark broke his cookie and read aloud: "A beautiful redhead will return your love." He reached for her hand. "That's the best fortune I've ever had."

Amanda felt the color rise to her cheeks. She was glad they were not sitting beneath the glaze of an electric light bulb.

"Sam is a very perceptive gentleman," she said.

The tune on the Edison whined to a finish.

"I'm glad you came, Manka. Maybe if I hadn't kept that scrapbook, none of this would be happening."

"Then you don't think it was only the fire that brought me here?"

"Whatever it was," he declared dramatically, "I believe that you've ridden in on the tide of fate." Suddenly he stood up. "Good God, the tide! I forgot."

"What about it?"

Mark rushed to the window. "It's high tide. How am I going to get you back to the hotel?"

"I thought you had a rowboat?"

"I told Sam he could use it to go home. He won't be back till morning." Mark turned around and shrugged apologetically. "I'm afraid you're stuck."

Amanda got up slowly and joined him at the window. It was true, the boardwalk had disappeared. They were surrounded by water.

"Well, I'll just have to make the best of it," said Amanda, gazing out. The lights from the mill danced in the water, plumes of smoke sailed from the stacks against the night sky, while the grinding and screaming of gang saws continued relentlessly, drowning the sound of her heartbeat.

"You'll grow used to it," Mark assured, his lips whispering against her ear. "After a while you won't even hear it any more, it will be only a throbbing rhythm in the background." He turned her to face him. "It will lull you to sleep and you'll forget everything."

When he kissed her at last, she could feel the tide of passion begin to rise, leaving her with no will to resist. It was the feeling she had been waiting her whole life to experience. To be, just once, weak and helpless. To think of nothing but the moment. To give herself totally.

Was it wrong? her eyes must have questioned, for Mark asked gently, "Have you ever known a man before?"

"No," she said.

"I knew it." He tenderly stroked her hair, moved by her obvious willingness to submit to him. He seemed almost reluctant when he said, "I'm happy that I'm to be first, but sad to be taking from you that which can never be returned."

"If what you feel for me is love, then it *can* be returned."

His arm encircled her waist as he led her toward the stairs. No words were spoken as they ascended, but Amanda felt that each step was carrying her away from the longing and loneliness that was reality, toward the world which lived in her fantasies.

She embraced him without fear, and it was just the way she had always dreamed it would be. How easily the gentle explosion of his passion transformed her body with the healing flow of love. Only one man could exist for her now. Only Mark Reed.

The following morning Amanda telephoned Erastus as soon as she returned to her hotel.

Erastus answered his phone on the first ring. "Where have you been?" he demanded in a worried voice. "Is everything all right?"

"Of course," she assured lightly. "And it's a good thing I stayed, because I've picked up some incredible information." Amanda spoke rapidly, taking advantage of the hotel manager's momentary absence. She told Erastus about her encounter with Gus Johnson, but she passed over Mark Reed.

"Good work! You can write it up on the way home. Just tell me which train you'll be on and I'll meet you."

"Oh, I'm not leaving yet. This investigation will probably take a few more days. A very helpful gentleman named Mr. Reed has promised to take me out to a logging camp today, so that I can see firsthand what goes on."

Amanda could feel Erastus' puzzlement. "What has that got to do with the fire?"

"I hope a great deal. Mr. Reed is a partner in the Simpson Lumber Company and I just have a feeling that they're behind the fire—that they might have put Gus Johnson and his crew up to it."

There was silence at the other end.

"Erastus? Are you there?"

"I'm trying to figure out why you would have such a strange suspicion."

"It's obvious—Simpson's wouldn't dare be directly involved, yet they stand to benefit enormously from putting their competition out of business. On the other hand, the union people have it in for Slade. Johnson told me himself he wanted to take credit for setting the fire. He thinks the publicity will bring him sympathy. But I think he's endangering himself and jeopardizing the efforts of the union. So if I could find evidence to show that Simpson's is behind it, the whole picture changes."

"Amanda, I appreciate what you're trying to do, but I think your chances of getting evidence on Simpson's are very remote."

"Erastus, listen to me. You know how long I've wanted to do an investigation like this—it's the perfect opportunity. Especially with Mr. Reed being so co-operative."

"Co-operative? I'd be very suspicious."

Amanda's reassuring laugh did not carry enough conviction to dispel his doubts. Erastus released a heavy sigh. "Darling, I can't help feeling uneasy about the whole thing, though I can't give you a good reason. I know you're not holding anything back . . ." He let his voice trail off, which only emphasized his misgivings.

"Such a fuss! I'm in absolutely no danger—really. Erastus, I have to go."

"Then be careful," he cautioned. "Don't let any trees fall on you!"

Amanda hung up slowly, nudged by guilt. He rarely used a term of endearment, yet today he had called her darling. Should she tell him that she had fallen in love? Or did he already sense it?

When Amanda arrived at the mill, Mark was on the dock supervising the transportation of a load of cut board onto the deck of a waiting schooner. Once again he was wearing loggers' clothing. Observing him for a few minutes, she noticed that he wasn't content merely to shout orders to his employees, but involved himself in each step of the operation. Seeing where he was needed, he leaped up to help secure a load of boards in a wire sling beneath a pulley-wheeled traveler, then signaled to the winch operator to send the cargo down the cable to the deck of the schooner. He was not only familiar with every phase, but he was quicker and more agile than those he was supervising. Yet, he didn't berate them or show impatience.

As soon as he spotted Amanda he waved, but continued with the task until he was satisfied that everyone understood what had to be done. At last he hurried over, stopping several times along the way to pick up nails scattered in the sawdust.

"Sorry you had to wait," he apologized breathlessly, "but we've got an order for forty-five thousand board feet down in San Francisco. The shipment's got to leave this afternoon."

"Are you sure you have time to take me out to the logging camp?" she asked, feeling a sudden letdown. He sounded so businesslike and impersonal.

"I have to go anyway. It's part of my job. If we hurry, we'll be in time for lunch. That is, if you don't mind eating in the mess hall with the boys."

Stepping back, he inspected her with lowered lids, his eyes traveling her body furtively so that no one would notice.

"We're going to be tramping through the woods, so you better wear a pair of my boots. Otherwise, you look fine," he said meaningfully. "Very fine indeed."

She smiled self-consciously, her fears subsiding. He wanted her as much as last night, only he dared not show it in public.

Mark drove her out to the camp in a lumber wagon, a distance of ten miles. It was a slow trip, for the wheels consisted of thick slices of wood rimmed with heavy metal bands, and the trail was no more than two parallel ruts. The early morning fog was beginning to burn off, and the air was sharp with the mingling scents of hemlock, pine and Douglas fir.

"I love the mill, but out here is where I thrive." Mark inhaled deeply, as though the air itself infused him with strength. "Out here in the forest. It's pure, it's raw. It waits for us to come to take it. And we do. But carefully, because we know it won't be here forever. This is our last stronghold. Our backs are to the sea."

There was an urgency in his tone, and as he turned to her, Amanda sensed that he was speaking of more than the forest.

"I always worry," he said, "thinking how easily a single spark can start a fire."

Have *I* started a fire? she wanted to ask.

"It bothers me to think that these vast stands of timber will disappear, that *I* might be the one to cause it." He covered her hand with his, but looked straight ahead again.

"If you really love the forest, then how will you destroy it?"

"By wanting too much, taking too much." His hand tightened on hers. Then in the same tone he said, "I'm aching for you, Manka, at this very moment."

She searched his eyes anxiously. "You don't sound happy about it. Do you—regret last night?"

The reins slackened in his hand, the wheels ground even more slowly. "If I seem too serious, it's because I'm in awe—you are in every sense the Firebrand I had dreamed of, too good to be true. And now, to have you here with me in the forest is the ultimate fantasy."

Conflicting emotions crowded her mind. Would she have to compete with the forest, this overpowering phenomenon of nature? Perhaps he expected too much. And the worst thought of all, what if she discovered that Simpson's had been involved in the fire? What would she do then?

"I think you're having a romance with the forest," she said, giving him a sidelong glance.

"I think you're right," he admitted with an amused smile. "Do you know when it started? Way back when I was in high school—it was one summer when I heard there was an opening for a whistle punk with a logging crew."

"A whistle punk! Somehow the title doesn't fit you!"

They both laughed.

"Seriously, it's a very essential job. The punk signals the engineer of the donkey engine by means of a long wire attached to a whistle on the donkey when it's time to haul in a log. It may be the most menial job on the crew, but it's not without danger. The boy I replaced had been killed when a steel cable snapped and broke his back. So I had to step lively!" He smiled in reminiscence, as though death was of little consequence.

"Did the danger appeal to you?"

"In a way, yes. But it was more than that. It was a challenge to survive. Most important of all, it was as far from banking as I could possibly get!"

"Good for you. That shows you have a mind of your own, that you don't need to conform."

"What about you?" he asked. "Have you always been a Firebrand?"

"Always. For as long as I can remember. But I've paid the price." At Mark's urging, she told him about her family and her ill-fated experience at Cedar Ridge, but took pains to credit her mother as the inspiration for all her ambitions. "Even at a distance we manage to stay close. In fact, we may be closer now than we've ever been. She doesn't feel the need to advise me any more, and has gotten over her disappointment that I never went to college."

"The best thing in the world is to be independent," Mark agreed. "Far as I'm concerned, I learned more in the woods than I ever did in school."

"Then why did you go?"

"Mr. Simpson wanted me to. He said it wasn't enough just to work as a logger, I had to get an education. He wouldn't have taken me in as a partner otherwise."

Amanda suddenly realized that Mark was Simpson's protégé.

"Is he grooming you to take over the business?"

"I already have. At least I do all the work. But I don't mind. I prefer it that way. Besides, he's not in very good health. Having me to run things puts his mind at rest." He paused, then added fondly, "He's a wonderful man."

"I'd like to meet him."

"Can't." Mark shook his head firmly. "He seldom comes down to the mill and he doesn't like visitors. Not even attractive ones. You'll just have to be content to interview *me!*"

"I don't mind that," said Amanda smiling. "I like the fact that you've come up from the bottom. A story like yours will give encouragement to others."

The logging camp consisted of a bunkhouse, mess hall, the bosses' shanty, a barracks to house the Chinese cooks and a corral for oxen and horses.

"This is one of our smallest camps," Mark explained as they rode into the forest clearing. "We have only a hundred men here, but at other sites we've got as many as a thousand, with shacks for the families of those who are married." Then he added, "But there aren't many families. Most loggers never marry."

Amanda smiled at this despite a sinking feeling that Mark included himself in the statement.

As they pulled up in front of the mess hall, Amanda could smell the decisive flavors of plain, solid fare. Two of the cooks came out to see what he had brought, both looking as surly as Sam Wing. Mark greeted them by name and helped to unload the sacks of flour and sugar and cartons of eggs.

"I've also brought coal oil, some extra lamps and parts for the broken stove," he explained, handing down each item.

Suddenly the sound of voices and the grinding of wheels could be heard echoing through the woods.

"We better go inside before the stampede," said Mark, leading the way.

The mess hall accommodated three long plank tables covered with oilcloth and lined with benches. Tin plates, cups and soup bowls were set upside down at each place. The kitchen, with four stoves, dominated the far end of the room, and a wide array of utensils hung from the beams. Two young boys scurried back and forth, barely able to transport the huge steaming caldrons to each table.

"Loggers like to find their food already in front of them when they sit down," said Mark with a grin. "And that includes me."

A moment later the floodgate opened to the ravenous herd and the floor resounded to the tread of heavy calked boots.

Most of the loggers waved their hats at Mark in familiar salute, calling him by his first name. Needless to say, the unexpected presence of a woman did not go unheeded. Even the serious business of eating suffered from occasional distraction as the curious loggers turned to steal glances in Amanda's direction.

"Are you going to tell them I'm a reporter?" she whispered.

Mark shook his head. "Not necessary. It's better they just think you're the lady in my life." He smiled. "Which you are."

I'm part of his life! she thought, staring hard at her plate. She was beginning to feel a warming tingle flow through her body, just as she had the night before. Was it visible? she wondered, not daring to look at Mark. It was enough to be sitting next to him so closely that the grease from his canvas pants brushed her skirt. It was unbearable joy and agony. She ate automatically, helping herself to a small portion of each dish that was passed, for to make a decision was impossible. A parade of roast ox, smoked fish, hash, stew, boiled greens, sausages, thick sliced bread, homemade mustard, pickled herring, blackberry pie and coffee blurred before her eyes.

At last she had to refuse to take another bite. "Now you'll have to put me to work," she told him. "I feel that if I were to roll off a log into a pond, I'd sink right to the bottom!"

The loggers devoured their food in strict silence, scraping their plates, then taking second portions. Throughout the meal, the cooks hovered anxiously, sending the boys to fetch additional servings, alert to any hint of dissatisfaction. But today there were no complaints.

"I had no idea that loggers ate so well," said Amanda when they went outside.

"They do at Simpson's," said Mark with emphasis. "You can see for yourself that our men are happy and well taken care of. Mainly, I want to convince you that anybody who loves their work—who loves *trees*—doesn't go around setting fires."

"Mark, I never believed for a minute that *you* were responsible!"

"I know. But all the same you feel better seeing firsthand how well our men are treated, don't you?"

"This is the first time I was ever glad to be wrong."

"Wrong perhaps. But human, warm and loving. Oh, Manka, I'll never forget last night as long as I live! The only way I can keep from seizing you in my arms this very minute is to go and chop down a hundred trees!"

Amanda ached to cry out: Forget the trees, take *me* instead! But she didn't yet have the courage. She dared not make a move that would risk spoiling their perfect union.

They rode with the crew out to the logging site on the empty flatcar of a horse-drawn tramway. A mile or so into the forest, they descended into a vast basin where the equipment had been set up. A steam-powered donkey engine huffed in readiness to reel in the logs which had been felled that morning. A dozen fallers separated by pairs to resume work on the trees which they had abandoned at the sound of the lunch whistle. Mark noticed that one of them was limping and stopped to ask him what had happened.

"Landed wrong when I jumped off my springboard," the faller shrugged, dismissing his injury.

"Then I don't want you back up there," said Mark. "Go help the peelers instead, and when you get back to camp, ask the boss for some liniment."

Mark surveyed his crew, frowning. Then he said half aloud, "I don't have any extra men to send up. I'll have to go myself."

"Way up there?" Amanda's eyes traveled up the gargantuan trunk of a Douglas fir to the springboard scaffolds high off the ground. The teeth of a ten-foot crosscut saw protruded from a deep gouge which penetrated almost to the core of the trunk.

"That's nothing," he shrugged. "The undercut's already been made."

"It looks awfully precarious."

"More for you, Manka, than for me. When we holler 'timber' you better look sharp for widow-makers—those are the loose limbs that fly out of control as the tree begins to fall. But don't worry, I'll figure out where I want her to land, so I can make sure you're safely out of range."

Amanda watched intrigued as Mark backed off about two hundred feet from the base of the tree, selected a spot and planted a stake in the ground.

"That's where it's going to fall," he predicted. Then he turned to consult his partner, who nodded in agreement. "Stay where you are," he warned her, "until it's down."

Gripping his ax, Mark drove it deep into the trunk above his head. This enabled him to cling to the handle in order to boost himself up to the first springboard, then on to the next, repeating the procedure until he was well over twenty feet aboveground. His partner ascended in the same manner. Both positioned themselves firmly on their own scaffolds, and immediately set to work, sawing in steady rhythm, deepening the cut. At a certain point they stopped abruptly, abandoning the saw for their axes, and moved their springboards to the opposite side of the tree.

"Now they're ready to back-cut her!" said a high excited voice.

Amanda glanced down to see a thin boy about fourteen years old standing next to her. He rested a broom on one shoulder and carried a pail of grease in the other hand.

Amanda felt that he wasn't talking to her so much as expressing aloud his obvious involvement in the drama above.

"What do you do?" Amanda asked the boy.

"I'm the skid greaser," he declared with pride, keeping his eyes on Mark and his partner. "I run down the hill between the oxen and the logs and swab them skids with bear grease so's they'll be nice and slick."

Amanda glanced up the hill where a trail of embedded logs snaked through the forest like railroad ties, and realized that she was looking upon an actual skid road. A skid road that bore little resemblance to its modern-day namesake in Seattle.

"Do you like the work?" she asked him.

He shrugged, his eyes still riveted to the fallers. "I'd rather be a high climber. But Mr. Reed says I gotta be able to do every other job first. So it's going to be a long time."

"Well, you're young," said Amanda. "You have plenty of time."

The boy looked at her, surprised by her ignorance. "I wouldn't say so. You can be killed quick as I can wink my eye. Why, only yesterday one of our river pigs fell off a log and drowned. Nobody even saw him fall. Just heard the splash."

"A river pig?"

"They're like cowboys. They drive the logs down the river—break up jams, go after strays and that kind of thing."

"Oh, like a cattle drive."

"That's it," said the boy, grinning. "The logs are branded, too, just like cattle. Anyways, I want to move up to fill his job. A river pig gets good pay 'cause he's wet all the time."

"You better learn to swim," advised Amanda.

The boy laughed and turned his attention back to the tree. But Amanda was troubled by his words. Though he talked like a little old man, he seemed very young to be doing such dangerous work—or any work at all. Shouldn't he be in school? Even as these thoughts drifted through her mind, she heard Mark shout "Timber!" and, looking up, she saw him fling his ax into the underbrush, and take a single flying leap from his springboard to the ground, clearing the tree just as it began to topple.

Amanda stared in awe as the mammoth fir rushed to earth with a great swish, the upper end of its trunk driving the stake which Mark had planted straight into the ground. The forest floor trembled on impact, limbs and dust exploding into the air, showering the clearing with debris. But fortunately, no one succumbed to the widow-makers.

"Hot damn!" The skid greaser's face shone with admiration.

Mark picked himself up and ambled around the uprooted base to shake hands with his partner. Then he inspected the cut, examining the torn fibers with a critical eye.

Amanda hurried over. "Oh, Mark, you were wonderful! That was a sight I'll never forget!"

"Glad you enjoyed it." He encircled her with his arm. "But it could have been cleaner. We wasted some feet unnecessarily."

"But you weren't off your mark by even an inch!"

"We can't afford to be off. Can't afford to have accidents."

Without pausing to rest, Mark bounded away to another chore, and Amanda was left in the wake of his exhilaration.

The afternoon fled as Amanda followed one performance after another with rapt attention. No matter which job he tackled, Mark excelled, gathering momentum as the day progressed. Amanda talked to a few of the loggers when she found the chance, though none approached her or volunteered information.

At last she couldn't resist asking one of them what he thought of Mark's amazing ability. The logger chuckled. "We call him Paul Bunyan. That about sums it up."

Amanda nodded appreciatively. "But it's such dangerous work. Why do you do it?"

The logger reflected, scratching his head. "I like the woods," he finally responded. "You can be a man out here. You're on your own."

"Do you have a union?" she asked.

He looked at her, mystified. Then his weathered face cracked into a grin. "If a union fella showed up around camp, we'd show him the butt end of our ax!"

"You don't feel you need any protection?"

"Protection? From what?"

"There seems to be a lot of accidents."

"Well, that's the nature of the work. You can't log without risk. It's no job for a weak belly. That's the way we like it."

In the late afternoon as they rode back to town, Mark recounted the day's labor with the exuberance of an athlete who had just broken a record. Amanda listened eagerly, trying to share his enthusiasm, longing to be part of the world which he found so fulfilling. Yet, she was bothered by the casual acceptance of accidents, and wondered how Simpson's safety record compared with its competitors.

Mark paused finally to give her an anxious glance. "Why so quiet, Manka? Am I talking too much?"

"Mark," she began slowly, "I once saw some workers from Slade whose hands and arms had been mangled by machines. I've always wondered if all mills were hazardous?"

"You mean—Simpson's? I'll give you an example—we've never had a union man set foot in our mill. Why? Because there's never been a complaint to investigate. Our boys are loyal. They don't want anybody from the outside telling them how to live their lives." He paused. "Hope that will put your mind at ease."

Amanda nodded quickly.

"Anyway," he went on, "if those Slade workers had respect for their mill, they wouldn't parade their injuries, stirring up trouble. But Slade doesn't give a hoot for their men." He thought for a moment, as if reconsidering. "Of course there's always an element of danger. But we have the most up-to-date equipment and we don't have to compete with *anyone*."

He watched approvingly as Amanda opened her notebook and began to write.

"Nothing compares to bringing down a tree. Think of it—a puny man toppling a mighty giant!" Then he added almost to himself, "And when the trees are gone, which will happen in my lifetime, I'll feel like Alexander, with no more worlds to conquer."

Amanda listened uneasily. The idea of conquering obviously excited him. "What will we do then?" she asked.

"I guess wood will go out of fashion and some new material will be discovered to take its place."

"Take its place?" she repeated in dismay. "Impossible. That will never happen. You mustn't let it happen."

He smiled at her concern. She knew that he failed to detect her *real* fear.

"Too many lumbermen subscribe to the 'cut and run' policy. Once they log off the land, they abandon it rather than pay the taxes. So the government is stuck with acres of stumps that it can't afford to reclaim. But we don't operate that way. Our policy is to keep the land we clear and pay the taxes. All our competitors think we're crazy. But who's to say? The day may come when land itself will be worth something, even without timber."

Amanda quoted him word for word.

"I'm glad you're writing that down, Manka. I want people to know what Simpson's stands for."

They reached Cosmopolis at dusk. As Mark pulled up to Simpson House, he reached for Amanda's hand, his eyes ablaze with desire. "Think you could stand to spend another evening with a timber beast?" he asked, confident of her answer. "If you want to change, I'll be waiting right here."

Amanda found herself rushing to wash and dress. There was no time to think clearly, for her mind was numb with the joy of anticipation. How pleasant it was to abandon all reason, to be giddy and irresponsible! And just for once, to have someone else making the decisions.

It didn't take her more than fifteen minutes, but when she came downstairs and hurried outside, Mark was gone.

"Miss Lamar!" the manager called, running after her. "Mr. Reed said to tell you he had to leave. There's been an accident."

"My God! Where?"

"Out at camp. He went to help bring back the bodies."

Amanda stared down the street. Mark's wagon wasn't even in sight. "Where can I hire another wagon?"

"Can't. Mr. Reed said for you to wait here."

"You don't understand. I'm a reporter—I *have* to go!"

The manager shrugged. "I only know that's the way we do things— we just wait. Then when the bodies come down, we go over to the mill to see if we know who they are."

"You talk as if this happens all the time?"

"Most every day," he admitted readily.

Amanda suddenly felt sick. "I'm going to wait at the mill."

The manager shook his head in disapproval. "It won't be a sight for female eyes," he warned.

As Amanda hurried through the gathering darkness, she tried to reason that Mark must have been terribly upset. Still, she puzzled over his decision to leave without her. Didn't he realize that she would want to be with him, and that as a reporter she had a job to do?

Great shafts of light spilled into the mill yard illuminating a knot of people huddled at the entrance. They didn't notice Amanda approaching, as one man was holding their attention, gesturing wildly and shouting to be heard above the relentless scream of saws. She strained to understand what he was saying, for he spoke with a heavy Scandinavian accent.

"I saw the whole thing! Happened just at quitting time. Thank the good Lord all three were killed instantly."

A distraught woman was sobbing softly, comforted by a friend who kept a protective arm around her shoulders, as if to shield her from the truth. When the friend spotted Amanda, he immediately included her into the group without questioning who she was or why she was there.

"One of them was her son," explained the friend.

The witness turned to Amanda excitedly, eager to relate the incident again. "It all came about when a hunter took sick way back up in the hills. Well, the only way they could get him to a doctor was to float him down the flume in a boat—just like a log. So down he comes a mile a minute, and remember, that flume runs along a trestle thirty feet off the ground!" He paused to shake his head solemnly. "Well, as luck would have it, the flume tender was on the catwalk when he saw that boat coming at him like lightning! And sure enough, it was coming so fast the hunter couldn't make the turn. He flew right off and hit the flume tender. And down they fell, striking this woman's son, who was on the ground below. One accident, three victims."

"Why did he have to be standing underneath?" the woman wailed.

"He died doing his job," reminded the witness in a comforting voice. "Running down the road swabbing the skids. Passed under the flume at the wrong moment. Just doing his job."

"Oh no! Not the skid greaser!" Amanda gasped.

"You knew him?" cried the woman.

"I only met him today when I visited the camp. He was a fine boy who loved his work, who wasn't afraid of danger. You should be proud of him."

Praise from a stranger seemed to give the mother great comfort, for she stopped weeping and blew her nose. At that moment Amanda decided to reveal that she was a reporter.

"You're from a newspaper in Seattle?" the woman repeated several times in awed disbelief.

"Yes, and I'm going to write about your son. I'll tell the whole story."

She grasped Amanda's hand. "Will you say he's a logger? And put his name, Edvin Svenson?"

"Of course," Amanda promised, writing it down.

The woman turned to her friends, her voice rising. "My son will be known in Seattle!"

The door behind them opened suddenly, and Amanda turned to see a man about sixty, bundled in an overcoat, loom in the doorway. Her first impression of him was one of deep jowls and wild white hair standing on end.

"What's going on out here?" he demanded, tapping his cane impatiently.

He was answered by a murmured greeting, "Good evening, Mr. Simpson," followed by respectful silence.

Although Mr. Simpson hardly looked like the benign benefactor Mark had portrayed, Amanda approached him with a confident smile.

"Are you one of those gossip mongers?" he asked, fixing his eyes on her.

"I didn't know that the press had treated you badly," she replied politely. "I know *I* haven't."

"Who are you with?" he snapped.

"The *P.I.*"

Simpson gave a sarcastic laugh, which resulted in a short, violent fit of coughing. "Well, I shouldn't think subscribers to the *P.I.* would care to read about loggers," he rasped.

"Our readers are entitled to *all* the news."

He brought down his cane with a thud. "I better not see the name of Sol Simpson in print," he warned. "I never give interviews."

"I'm not asking for one."

Simpson turned to the group and waved his cane threateningly. "And that goes for the rest of you as well. No relatives of Simpson employees should be talking to the press." He gave Amanda a sharp look. "We don't need any publicity. We get along fine without it."

Amanda almost told him that she was a friend of Mark's, but suddenly thought better of it. Such an admission might only get Mark into trouble.

"I'm sorry you feel that way," she replied instead. "So far I've been very impressed with what I've seen."

"That so? Well, I've never met a reporter yet who could find anything good to say." He peered at her closely. "What impresses you so much?"

"Mainly the company spirit—the loyalty and enthusiasm . . . ."

"Step inside!" he commanded abruptly.

As soon as the door was closed behind them, Sol Simpson was seized with another coughing spell. "It's the night air," he wheezed, catching his breath at last.

"May I fetch you some water?"

"Young woman, if there's one thing I can't stand, it's being waited on. I fend for myself." He stood proudly, trying not to lean on his cane. "And I expect my employees to do the same."

Amanda wrote down his statement, which appeared to give him great satisfaction.

"Now what else impresses you about my company?"

"You have the latest equipment, good food—things which benefit the employees. But I do have a few questions. I'd particularly like to know what safety measures are taken to protect the lives of the loggers? And are they covered by insurance?"

He stared at Amanda in stunned silence. Then unpredictably he exploded in laughter. Again his outburst resulted in a convulsive coughing spell, and as before, he recovered quickly, impatient with his affliction.

"I see you know nothing about this business. A man becomes a logger because he wants to be free. If he wanted to be protected, he wouldn't be a logger. And another thing. When a man comes to us for a job, we don't ask questions. We don't care about his past, if he's running away, or in disgrace, or the black sheep of his family. When he's ready to go, he can go as he pleases. He can take his pay however he wants—by the day or let it lay. We operate the way *he* wants to operate." Simpson paused to gasp for breath, then continued, his voice weakening. "A man has a right to live as he wishes. And to die as he wishes."

With this final statement, he clamped his lips together, marched to the door, holding his cane off the ground, and went out.

It was almost midnight when the wagons came down the trail, their lanterns bobbing through the darkness. The number of those keeping vigil had swelled to fifty or so, as the loggers drifted over from the saloons. Amanda observed an eerie absence of emotion as the hum of conversation broke the stillness. But when the wagons rolled into the lumber yard, everyone surged forward, silent now as the terrible moment arrived.

Mark climbed down from the first wagon, his exuberance gone, and turned a haggard face to the waiting crowd.

"I've brought the boys down," he explained wearily. "Is anyone here to claim Svenson or Merkle?"

A path was cleared for the relatives. Amanda watched Edvin's mother and her friends form a slow procession to the wagon. Mark spoke a few words of sympathy, without apology or expression of regret. Throughout the ordeal of waiting, Amanda had noticed that no one sought to lay blame for the accident; it was simply accepted.

Mark peered over the crowd. "Are Merkle's people here?" he asked.

"He's got no kin," a voice volunteered.

Mark nodded, showing no surprise. Then he announced, "The man who was in the flume has not been identified. So if anyone wants to help me out, come on up and take a look."

Everyone obligingly moved forward, leaving Amanda standing alone. Mark spotted her and hurried over.

"Manka! What are you doing here?" He took her by the shoulders.

"Waiting for you."

"Manka, this isn't a story for Firebrand. What happened today was nobody's fault. It wasn't caused by a defective machine, or a slave-driving boss, or by any kind of carelessness. It was an act of God—as unpreventable as an earthquake or volcano. My dearest Manka, I hope you won't change your opinion of Simpson's merely because of one tragic event. You won't, will you?"

Amanda saw the tiny lines of exhaustion around his eyes and mouth.

"No one blames you, Mark," she replied. "And no one blames Simpson's. I haven't heard a word of criticism from any of these people. I'm satisfied with what you've told me, and with what I've seen. That's the way I'm going to write it."

"Thank you," he said with emotion. "I must be the luckiest man in the world to have a woman like you at my side. Wait for me, I won't be long."

Amanda shook her head firmly. "You're worn out, Mark, and so am I."

"At least let me walk you back to the hotel."

"Absolutely not. Do you want to fall asleep on your scaffold tomorrow?"

"Then I won't go to work at all," he said. "I'll save the day for you."

The following morning the Grays Harbor *News* carried a terse report of the deaths. "A man and two loggers lost their lives on Tuesday, October 11, in an unfortunate accident out at the flume ten miles from Cosmopolis." No names or details were given.

"A man and two loggers," Amanda repeated aloud. What a peculiar distinction.

The week somehow escaped despite Amanda's feverish efforts to stretch each hour and day. Time became a cruel master who refused to slow his pace, yet was kind enough to give her a love which grew more perfect each time she and Mark were together. Her story also grew. But not in the direction she had originally intended. The logger was emerging as a romantic idealized symbol of independence; Simpson's as a benevolent patriarch.

Finally, in order to steal an extra day, Mark insisted he be allowed to help write the article. Well, not write it exactly, but advise. That is, if Amanda wanted him to.

So they set to work, thinking first of the right title. Amanda decided that Mark's suggestion was best—"THE GREEN GOLD RUSH," to stress the value of timberland. She also liked his idea for openly admitting that what had begun as an investigation of fire and possible arson had resulted in the surprising discovery that at least one major company cared about the land and about its men.

"I think you're prejudiced," she teased.

"Of course," he agreed.

"Don't you think I should interview Slade's owners, too?"

"They're not here. I heard they went East right after the fire to try to raise funds to rebuild, poor fellows."

"Very convenient. Maybe they want to avoid investigation."

"It's possible. But I hope you'll give them the benefit of the doubt." Seeing her surprise, he added, "When you say something negative about one mill, it reflects on *all* mills."

The night before she was to leave, Mark could talk of nothing except how dismal it would be without her.

"Can't you stay?" he begged unreasonably. "How can you make me go back to living with a damn scrapbook?"

Amanda laughed and cried at his illogical pleas for remaining together. But as he didn't ask her to marry him, she didn't know what he expected her to do.

"What about my job? What happens to Firebrand?"

Mark drew her close to him. "The warmth of your body is the only Firebrand I'll ever need. Give up your job and stay here with me."

"But the Firebrand you love *is* the Firebrand in your scrapbook. It's me! How can I give up part of myself?"

"Isn't my love enough? Isn't it what you said you'd always dreamed about?"

"Yes, but . . ."

"Darling, listen, I've kept you at my side every minute this entire week, hoping you'd learn to love the forests as much as I do. A man wants a woman who understands what's important to him."

"Mark, I *do* understand, I want to be part of it!"

"Then leave the *P.I.* You told me yourself you were tired of working for someone else."

"Yes, that's true. But I didn't tell you why. I've had a reason for staying at the *P.I.* all this time." She waited excitedly for him to ask what it was, but he just looked at her, mystified. "I'm going to start my own newspaper."

For a moment Mark stared blankly. Then in a slow voice he repeated, "Your own newspaper?"

"I already have the property to build on. Of course it won't be for a while yet, I've got to save a lot more money. But I've planned it all in my mind." She stopped. "Why are you looking at me that way?"

"I just don't see you doing such a—masculine job. You're far too beautiful to be a newspaper publisher!"

Amanda couldn't help but laugh at his horrified expression. "Thank you for the compliment, but I don't agree. Firebrand *should* have her own paper." Her tone softened. "My independence is as important to me as the forest is to *you*."

"More important than love?"

"Why must I choose? I want both!"

Mark shook his head in bewilderment. Amanda knew the moment she had spoken that he would misinterpret.

She hurried to assure him, "But you would come first, naturally. So if I *did* agree to stay here, I'd simply divide my time . . ."

Again she had said the wrong thing. Mark released her slowly, as though she had become suddenly a stranger.

"Of course I could always have my paper *here,* it doesn't have to be in Seattle . . ."

But her words were lost. He had already turned away.

On the trip home Amanda reviewed every moment they had spent together, trying to restore some semblance of logic to what had happened. If he really loved her, why would her plans for a paper give him second thoughts about their relationship? Then she remembered his remark, "most loggers don't marry," and felt a sudden anxiety. She also remembered what Sol Simpson had told her—a man becomes a logger because he wants to be free. At that moment she realized she had forgotten to tell Mark about her encounter with Simpson, and wondered how it could ever have slipped her mind?

Chapter Thirteen

I CAN'T believe you wrote this!" Erastus looked up from the copy on his desk uncomprehendingly. "This isn't Firebrand speaking. What on earth are you thinking of?"

"I wrote it the way I saw it," said Amanda. "If you're disappointed that I didn't dig up all kinds of terrible things, I've got to be honest, they're just not there."

"Amanda, if I didn't know you, I'd think this reporter was on somebody's payroll. The entire article is written from Simpson's point of view!"

"Well, I didn't take a bribe," she snapped, hurt by the jab, "nor was I offered one. And I'm getting damn tired of having to answer to you for everything I write!"

Erastus was on his feet in an instant, his face paling with remorse. "I don't know what got into me." He reached to take her hand, but Amanda turned away. "Darling, don't be angry. I'm only upset because you stayed away so long and because you called only once. I was worried, but now I see that I had no reason to be, for you seem to have found your assignment quite pleasant."

Amanda looked at him quickly. Again he had called her "darling." And why the sudden concern? But there was no indication in his eyes that he knew anything at all beyond what he had read in her article.

"I don't want to fight about it," she said wearily. "We haven't gone to press, so you can pull the story if you don't like it."

"I'd never do that. I just want to know what happened down there that changed you so. Didn't you talk to any loggers?"

"Of course I talked to loggers," she replied defensively. "I found them loyal and proud, men who loved their work. Go see for yourself!"

Erastus picked up her copy. "You've enshrined Edvin Svenson as a young hero who died pursuing the work he loved, but don't you realize he was a victim of child labor? Probably forced to support his family?" He paused, but when Amanda said nothing, he continued. "What amazes me most is how you've completely reversed your position on the unions, as if they were solely responsible for that fire."

"I had no choice. Gus Johnson admitted that he set it."

"I realize that. What he did was a terrible thing. But the Firebrand *I* know would have seen the issue from more than one side. She would have recognized that labor is having a bitter struggle, and understood why men are sometimes driven to desperate acts."

Amanda forced a smile to mask the sting. "You've become very open-minded, Erastus."

"Because of *you*. So don't change, Amanda, for both our sakes."

"If you don't agree with what I've written, I wish you wouldn't run it. This is *your* paper and I'm not a child who has to be indulged."

Erastus looked at her with tender sadness. "Amanda, I'd risk this damn paper for you any day."

"Don't. If it were *my* paper, I wouldn't risk it for anybody."

He turned to the window and stared out. "Sometimes I get the feeling that I'm holding you back." He paused. "Perhaps I've come to depend on you too much." He turned to her again. "I've never even given you a vacation."

Amanda looked at him warily.

"Why don't you take some time out to think about Amanda? About what she believes and where she wants to go?" He added quickly, "At full pay, of course."

Free time to do as she pleased? The thought was both exciting and a bit frightening. "For how long?" she asked.

"For as long as you like. Three months, six months. Whatever you need. There may be something you've always wanted to do, but didn't have time for. Now's your chance."

My paper! If only I could get it going. But the next moment she found herself thinking of Mark. Free time would also give her the chance to be with him.

"Maybe *we* can spend some time together," Erastus suggested hopefully. "I could use a vacation myself. Here we've been quarreling like an old married couple, and for what? For nothing more important than a lumber story!" Then quite unexpectedly, he slipped an arm around her waist and tipped her face up to meet his lips.

Taken by surprise, she allowed him to kiss her, though she stiffened instinctively. It was a chaste kiss, which left her unable to respond. Her only thought was that it was a kiss intended for a virgin, the kind reserved only for the woman he might someday wish to marry. Couldn't he feel how rigid her body had become, that she felt no desire? But no, for her restraint was exactly what he expected, and he seemed to admire her all the more for living up to his ideal.

When Amanda reached home, she paced for hours before summoning the courage to telephone Mark. Three days had passed since her return, and still there had been no word from him. Was he angry? Hurt? Or, God forbid, undecided about his feelings for her? Their parting had been strained, it was true, but surely by now he would have had time to reconsider his demands that she give up everything for him. Unable to bear the agony of suspense a moment longer, she impulsively placed the call, then waited while her heart beat ten times for each ring. At last he answered. And to her enormous relief, the tone of his voice told her that he was overjoyed to hear from her, admitting that he, too, had been in torment since she left. Before she could tell him about her vacation, he said he had a surprise—he was coming to Seattle.

"I couldn't tell you until I knew for certain, but Mr. Simpson just agreed to let me sign up for a new forestry course being offered at the university twice a week. Of course he doesn't know that I'm taking it mainly as an excuse for us to be together!"

"How wonderful! But if you're going to class, when will I have a chance to see you?"

"Why, in the evenings. Naturally I'll have to stay over. It's too long a trip to go back and forth the same day."

"Then maybe I can find you a room close by."

"I was hoping I could stay with *you*," said Mark. "That is, if you don't care what the neighbors think."

"Heavens, no. It wouldn't bother *me,* only . . ." She hesitated, trying to think why she should object. It wasn't as though they hadn't already been intimate, yet for some reason, she was disturbed by his suggestion.

"Look, Manka, I understand. You don't want everybody to see me coming in and out with a suitcase, am I right?"

"I know it sounds silly, but I hate petty gossip." She forced a laugh. "Lord knows I get enough criticism just from my articles!"

"Then reserve me a room at a boardinghouse," he said, without taking the slightest offense.

He arrived the following Tuesday on the noon train. Amanda met him at the station. He swept her into his arms and kissed her lingeringly, not caring who was looking. Then with his usual exuberance, he was in a rush to be off.

"My first class is at one o'clock, so I'll have to hurry. Where can I catch the streetcar?"

"Don't worry, I've hired a carriage. Where's your suitcase?"

"Didn't bring one. Everything I need is jammed in here," he said lightheartedly, indicating his briefcase. "By the way, I got a thrill seeing your article in print, Manka, especially knowing I had a hand in it."

"I'm glad," Amanda murmured, averting her eyes.

"Mr. Simpson was very grateful—says he's changed his opinion of reporters." Then he added with a grin, "I've already entered it in my scrapbook."

It took almost an hour to reach the campus.

"Wait for me?" he asked, jumping down from the carriage.

Amanda smiled. "I have nothing else to do."

The chimes in the bell tower of Denny Hall struck the hour. Mark waved over his shoulder, as he hurried off. Amanda watched him until he was lost among the students running to class. A minute later the grounds were deserted, and the quiet of a long afternoon had settled.

All of a sudden Amanda was engulfed by a wave of unbearable loneliness. It was somehow depressing to find herself with three hours in which to wander aimlessly, an outsider to yet another activity in Mark's life. She couldn't help feeling jealous of that vast stone building with its sweeping staircase which presided so serenely over the broad empty slopes. With its tower visible for miles, Denny Hall was so far the university's only structure. But the logged-off land stretching away in all directions was an optimistic sign that provision had been made for expansion. Soon there would be other buildings. Instead of a few dozen classrooms, there would be hundreds, and the hundreds of students now enrolled would grow to thousands. Amanda sighed. This was Mark's world, but she wasn't part of it.

Leaving the carriage, she began to walk, following the curve of a new path leading to nowhere. A grove of glossy-leafed madrona trees with roan-colored trunks of shredded bark had survived the logger's ax. They seemed to be waiting for the grass to grow around them, for students to sprawl in their shade on spring afternoons. Everything in sight seemed to speak of the future. But what of my future? Amanda wondered. I had a chance to do a big story and I threw it away. I might be launching my paper, but instead, here I am hopelessly in love with a man who wants me to give it up.

"Amanda!"

She revolved slowly at the sound of a familiar voice.

"Over here!" Mary Kenworthy waved from a distance.

"Mary!" Amanda felt a surge of joy.

Mary's stride was as energetic as ever. She gave Amanda a quick hearty embrace.

"How did you ever recognize me from such a distance?"

"Well, there still aren't many tall redheads around. I knew it had to be you."

"Oh, Mary, I feel terrible not to have called you in so long."

"No apologies necessary," she said briskly. "You're busy and so am I. Besides, I expect time goes more quickly for me than it does for you."

"Are you on your way somewhere?" Amanda asked.

"Just to the library in Denny. What about you?"

"Nowhere in particular."

"Then come with me. We can talk on the way."

Linking arms, they began to stroll.

"I suppose you're all involved in the election," said Amanda. "Do you think Roosevelt will win another term?"

"Without a doubt," declared Mary firmly. "But let's not talk about politics. I want to know what you've been up to. Is Erastus behaving himself these days?" she asked with a twinkle.

"Actually I'm on vacation."

"You haven't been fired, have you?"

"What makes you ask that?"

"I'm going to be honest with you. When I read your lumber story the other day, I thought to myself, 'Either the *P.I.* has changed its policy, or Firebrand has changed hers.' Which is it?"

"What do you mean?" asked Amanda defensively. "I spent a whole week tramping around in the woods, going through logging camps. I gathered all my information firsthand. So I'd like to know why everyone's so upset."

"Is Erastus upset?"

"He was furious. Oh, Mary, I did a stupid thing. I lost my whole perspective."

"Do you know why?"

Amanda hesitated, undecided as to whether she should tell Mary about Mark or confide her plans for the paper.

"*Something* must have happened," Mary prodded gently.

"I fell in love."

"Is that all?"

"I fell in love with a lumberman."

Mary let out a sharp whistle. "Say no more. I see the whole picture. You're in love with old Simpson."

Amanda had to laugh in spite of herself. "Not with Simpson, with Mark Reed, his partner. He's young and handsome and—just about perfect. Not like most lumbermen," she hastened to add.

"Well, I guess that's the end of Firebrand," said Mary with a sigh.

Amanda flushed in momentary anger. Mary's frank humor often hurt, for it was invariably too close to the truth to be really amusing. Amanda's thoughts flew back to all the incidents that her article had failed to disclose—mainly, the hostility she had seen between Jumbo Reilly and Big Fred Hewett, which clearly indicated a struggle for power between the mills and even between the towns that they supported. Then there was the subject of accidents. Except for reporting the tragedy of young Edvin Svenson, her story had said nothing about the high fatality rate.

"The end of Firebrand? You're wrong, Mary. She's only just beginning. She's going to have her own newspaper."

"Hallelujah! It's high time!"

"I already have the land on Denny Hill, but I still have to put up a building and buy—or rent a printing press. It's overwhelming and it's taking forever, but nothing's going to stop me, Mary, not even Mark Reed."

"That's our girl," said Mary encouragingly. "Now what kind of paper is it going to be?"

"The only kind it *could* be—for the working class reader. It will have all the features of any big city paper, but with the emphasis on union news, government decisions affecting the worker and all that."

Until now, Amanda had never described her objectives aloud, only in a letter to Emma. But talking about her paper made its reality seem suddenly closer.

"Good. Now, if you want my advice, I'd do that lumber story over again—right from scratch. Only this time fly into the buzzards' nest with your talons out. Then, when you've captured your prey, launch your paper at once—even if you have to borrow somebody else's press. The important thing is timing. Ask Blethen."

Amanda nodded eagerly. "You're right. I've got to do it again— pick up the missing pieces." Her face clouded. "Only . . ."

"Don't worry. The innocent can't ever be hurt by the truth. They can only be helped."

"You're right." Amanda gave Mary an impulsive hug. "I'm so glad we talked!"

"One last word?"

"Please!"

"Be careful of Mark Reed."

"What do you mean?"

"Loving someone *too* much can be dangerous."

Amanda smiled indulgently. "I'll follow all your advice, but on that I make no promises."

That night at dinner Mark talked animatedly about his class. Though he ate with relish, he made no comment about the food; nor did he seem to notice the pains Amanda had taken with the meal and table setting. He didn't care that the radishes had been sculptured into roses and the carrots curled, for he popped them into his mouth without really seeing them. He did, however, notice the centerpiece of dried flowers and greenery, which he removed from the table without asking. But Amanda didn't mind, for she realized that he saw the arrangement as an obstruction to their conversation.

At last he put down his fork and gazed at her with a quizzical smile. "You've braided your hair."

"I always wear it like this," she replied, startled into a laugh.

"Only in the daytime," he reminded her almost reproachfully, "not at night."

Amanda could feel the glow from the candles suddenly hot on her cheeks. He *did* notice the small details after all. "I guess I forgot. I'm afraid my mind was elsewhere."

"There must be another man in your life," he said with a frown.

"That's not true!" she denied vehemently. Then she felt foolish, seeing that he was teasing her.

"In that case, take out the pins; I like to see that beautiful red hair falling down over your shoulders."

Amanda did as she was told, eyes downcast in sudden embarrassment. Knowing that he was watching her loosen her hair made her feel as vulnerable as if she had been removing her clothes. God, I must be crazy! she told herself. Gone were her intentions of telling him that she was going to do another lumber story, or her resolution to send him to a boardinghouse. The evening was beginning and the moment for love fast approaching. All serious matters would have to be banished for another time.

"You aren't going to send me away, are you?" he asked plaintively.

She looked him in the eye. "You know very well I'm not. You knew it when you left home. That's why you were discreet enough *not* to bring a suitcase."

At dawn Amanda was awakened by the creaking of floor boards to see Mark, fully dressed, tiptoeing toward the door.

"Are you leaving?" she asked, sitting bolt upright, the sheet clutched to her breast.

"Shhh!" he whispered, a finger to his lips, although there was no one to hear them. "I'm just taking a run down to the water."

"At this hour?"

"If I can find a boat, I might go for a row."

"When will you be back?" she asked in an uncertain voice.

"Before you know it!" he promised, and went out.

As soon as Amanda heard the front door close, she crept to the window. Mark had stopped before the gate, and with his head thrown back and arms stretched to the sky, he seemed to be gulping great breaths of air. Then, after a moment, he vaulted the fence and was off down the hill, loping like a deer through the forest.

Amanda wondered if he found her small cottage stifling. She crawled back into bed and lay wide awake until she heard the front door open again two hours later.

At breakfast Mark noticed that Amanda was unusually quiet. "You're not worried about what the neighbors will think, are you?"

"I'm not worried about them, only about myself. I guess I can't stand having a vacation. It's given me the blues."

Mark's knowing smile seemed to say, "Oh, is that all?" for he passed over her comment lightly as if he thought she was probably approaching that time of the month.

"It's *more* than the blues," she said in a rush. "I have a guilty conscience." And before she could falter and change her mind, she told him how ashamed she felt about neglecting so many crucial issues in her story, and that she had no choice but to do a more thorough investigation. Unburdened at last, she waited calmly to receive the hurt or anger he was bound to express. But instead, he listened with detachment, like a priest hearing confession, then insisted that he understood perfectly her reason for feeling upset.

"I think you *should* do another story, Manka, to satisfy yourself. Much as I hate to see the industry torn apart, thank God, Simpson's has nothing to fear! You'll find we can stand up under any criticism."

"Oh, Mark, I don't want to do anything to hurt you, believe me!"

"You won't." He smiled confidently. "But before you begin, I have a suggestion. Why not take the forestry class with me? It'll be great background for you. What do you say?"

It was a tempting idea, but was it really essential to writing the story?

Before she could venture an argument, Mark added, "We can study together." Then with a mischievous grin, he said, "You'll be the only girl in the class."

Suddenly she realized that he was doing this for *her,* showing that he accepted her ambitions and still wanted her to be part of his life. "I will!" she said. "I'll do it!"

"You'll learn a lot. Conservation and management are the latest thing. You know, Manka, when the day comes for me to take the reins at Simpson's, I've got plans to make some tremendous changes.

I want to learn how to grow trees, not just chop them down. I want to know how to combat the timber pirates. And in the future, I want to build my own ships, a whole fleet—just to transport Simpson lumber. I've always seen the logic of linking shipbuilding with logging, but Mr. Simpson is content with the way things are. He's getting old and he likes to go slow."

"With that terrible cough I should think he would want to retire." The words were out before Amanda realized what she had said.

"How did you know he had a cough?"

"I met him the night of the accident—briefly."

Mark looked suddenly concerned. "Funny, you never mentioned it before."

"I didn't think of it before. I didn't think it was important."

Mark shrugged and abruptly changed the subject.

Amanda never thought she would enjoy being in school again. But she found herself devoting every spare minute to studying, eager to absorb as much about the subject as possible. Yet, the more she learned, the more she realized how much there was to know. And in her determination to keep pace with Mark, it was easy to forget that she was supposed to be preparing for a lumber investigation.

When she wrote to her mother that she was in college, she received an immediate telephone call. Temperance was thrilled.

"You mean—they'll let you into the university without a secondary school diploma?"

"They made an exception when I told them I was Firebrand."

"Well, I'm very glad you decided to go to college of your own accord, not because I had nagged you! But what about your job?"

"Erastus has been wonderful, he's agreed to let me take off as much time as I need."

"He must think a good deal of you." She waited in expectant silence for a moment, then added, "He'd better watch out. Doesn't he know that being the only young lady in class, you'll probably receive plenty of invitations to go out?"

Amanda smiled to herself. Now was the time to tell her about Mark. "Mama, I didn't take the course to meet a man—because I've already found one."

"You have?" Her voice went up an octave.

"His name is Mark Reed. He's in lumber. And, Mama, he's the most perfect fellow you could ever hope to meet."

"Oh, Manka, that's such good news! Is it serious then?"

"Well, he hasn't proposed yet, but he's the one who persuaded me to study forestry. I'm sure he'd like to have a wife who understands the business."

"Darling, I couldn't be happier. He sounds levelheaded and so do you. To tell the truth, I'm relieved to hear that you've gotten away from reporting. You were so enslaved to your job that you had no time for a personal life. Now you can make up for lost years."

After Amanda hung up, she felt strangely touched to think that her mother had been worrying about her. But of course she would. Temperance, too, knew the cruel isolation of being a woman alone, having married late and been widowed early. It was sad to think that her mother—and all single women—were expected to remain pure, denying the existence of their own passions. It was no wonder mothers prayed their daughters would marry.

However, she felt uncomfortable imagining what her mother would think if she knew *her* daughter had been too impatient to hold out for marriage, that she was too much a Firebrand. Fortunately, she thought, I'll soon have a ring on my finger and Mother can breathe a sigh of relief.

Chapter Fourteen

THE winter and spring of 1905 passed memorably, but far too fast. There were weeks when Amanda never gave a thought to the *P.I.*, for her vacation had evolved into a leave of absence. Luckily Erastus approved of her reason for studying forestry, so in anticipation of a new lumber story, he continued to pay her a modest stipend so that she could survive without working. Of course she had mentioned nothing about her romantic involvement with Mark. And until Mark actually proposed, there was no reason to say anything.

Though not yet engaged, Amanda had begun to feel as if they were already married. Most of the time Mark checked into the boardinghouse for the sake of appearance. But as he and Amanda were together constantly, it mattered little that he rented a room just for sleeping. He arrived every Tuesday morning, left on Wednesday, arrived again on Friday, and returned home on Saturday. Amanda counted, not the days, but the hours which stretched between his departures and arrivals. She hated Sundays, Mondays and Thursdays because Mark was never there, yet she consoled herself by anticipating their next time together.

Attending class was a stimulating experience, but she sometimes paused to wonder whether it would have been so without Mark to share it with her. Their relationship seemed close to ideal, but still she worried. Whenever she would mention her paper, even in the most casual way, Mark would always change the subject. Although he never attempted to discourage her plans, he showed no interest in them, either. There was one other slight flaw, which Amanda almost hesitated to consider a problem—he wasn't jealous.

One Friday evening when Erastus dropped by unexpectedly, Mark showed not the slightest sign of annoyance.

Erastus stood on the doorstep, a bouquet of roses frozen in his hand, while Amanda, in great embarrassment, attempted to explain Mark's presence.

"We're studying, but you're welcome to come in," she murmured, feeling the cool hurt in his gaze.

But as Erastus fumbled for a graceful excuse to leave, Mark called out from the parlor, "Tell him he must stay for a brandy!"

Erastus did stay—reluctantly—and even managed to recover his composure sufficiently to pass a pleasant conversation. Sitting between them, Amanda felt uncomfortably on display. But Mark seemed undaunted, not regarding Erastus as competition. Amanda could see immediately, however, that Erastus knew his attempt to court her was doomed. But he left the roses anyway, and accepted two brandies. Then he consulted his pocket watch, as though it measured the weeks, not hours.

Winding it, he asked Amanda, "When would you like to come back?"

"Soon," she replied slowly. "The quarter is almost over."

Erastus nodded. He mentioned nothing about the lumber story.

After he left, she hastened to explain to Mark what their relationship had been. But he shrugged it off without comment, apparently not bothered by Erastus' intentions. How Amanda envied his self-confidence, for she knew that had their situations been reversed, she would have been sick with jealousy just knowing there had been another woman in Mark's life.

However, he did say a short time later, "I hate to see flowers in a house. They belong outside, alive and growing."

One day Amanda gazed out the kitchen window to find the backyard depressingly strewn with dead fruit. Summer was over. And so was the last quarter of her class. Only the final examination remained. Mark would be attending the fall quarter without her, while she returned to work. Of course she could still see him on the evenings when he was in town, but somehow it wouldn't be quite the same.

Mark had not been happy to learn that she was serious about going back to her job. Even when she patiently explained that she was committed to the *P.I.* for another lumber story, and that she felt indebted to her boss for his generosity, Mark seemed disturbed.

"Are you sure that's what you really want?" he asked several times. But aside from this, he made no attempt to influence her.

No, it wasn't what she wanted. But it had to be done.

"I'm working for our future," she told him, hoping that he would now finally propose. He looked at her questioningly. "To get my paper started. *Our* paper," she corrected. "I was hoping we could do it together—as partners."

"Me? In the newspaper business?"

"You only have to be involved as much or as little as you want to, and if you like, I in turn can help you run the mill."

Mark looked at her with obvious disappointment. "Being a lumberman is a full-time job," he said. And the subject was closed.

Amanda had felt well prepared for the exam, certain that she would earn a high grade and that Mark would be proud of her. But when she met him at the station, he was tight-lipped and gloomy. With immediate foreboding, she insisted that he tell her what was wrong, even though he said he preferred to wait until after the exam.

"I'm not coming back," he finally admitted in a faltering voice. "Mr. Simpson thinks I'm spending too much time away from the business."

"But that's not fair!" she gasped. "Haven't you told him about us?"

"That's the *last* thing I'd tell him. If he thought for a minute that I was seeing a woman, I'm certain he would have put a stop to my taking the class long ago."

"Seeing a woman? What a strange way of putting it."

"You know what I mean—that's how *he* would see it. He's all business."

"So you can't have a personal life, is that it?" she demanded, blinking back angry tears.

"Nothing that drastic," he said with a forced laugh. But he had no words to console her.

Amanda went to the examination with a hollow ache in the pit of her stomach. And when she finished, she had no idea how she had done. Later, however, when she and Mark compared notes, she was amazed to discover that she had answered every question correctly, even though it had seemed at the time that her brain was barely functioning. I'm alive after all, she thought, with some degree of relief.

"This should prove to Simpson that I haven't stood in your way," she told Mark, "and that I can even be an asset to you."

There was pain in his smile. He nodded, but all he said was, "I don't want to stay at the boardinghouse tonight."

Later, when they made love, Amanda sensed it was for the last time. By prolonging his passion, not wanting it to end, Mark seemed to be telling her that it *was* ending. Afterward she had an intuitive flash that he was expressing the only way he could some terrible frustration which raged within him.

The next morning he was drawn and sober. As they rode on the streetcar to the station she knew that he was not going to say anything about their future, for had he intended to give her hope, he would have done so by now.

On the platform his embrace was distant, resigned.

"When will you come back?" she asked, clinging.

"I don't know," he replied with an empty shrug. "Mr. Simpson has—plans."

"I see." She waited for him to continue.

"I'm sorry, Manka. I didn't know it was going to turn out this way."

"I understand, really I do." Even as she insisted, trying to remain reasonable and calm, she understood nothing. She was no longer a rational woman, she had become an abandoned woman filled with fear. Why didn't he at least tell her that he loved her, as she had told him?

She returned home in despair. But exactly four hours later, he called.

They both laughed and cried, then laughed again and tried to joke, but it was no use. At last they fell silent. Amanda knew that the situation was no better.

"You know, Manka, being a logger, I'd rather *do* than *say*. So I hope that all the times we've been together have spoken my feelings about you. And no matter what happens, remember that I'll be thinking of you."

"You still don't say that you love me."

"I can't hurt you that way."

"If you don't say it, I will be hurt even more."

Mark sighed deeply. Amanda could feel his torment.

"I know you said once that most loggers don't marry. Well, if that's what bothers you, I just want you to know it's all right. I don't mind continuing as we are. I feel as though we're married already!" She tried to laugh. "Anyway, at least we can be together again when I come down to do my lumber story."

"Don't come—not now," he pleaded.

"What do you mean—don't come?" she asked, stunned. "You don't want me to do the story?"

"Amanda, please don't think that! It's just that Mr. Simpson . . ."

"I'm tired of hearing about Mr. Simpson!" she flung back in sudden anger. "I knew he owned the town, but I didn't know he owned you!" And hung up. Only then did she realize he had called her Amanda.

He didn't call back.

The next morning Amanda walked down to the *P.I.*, entered Erastus' office quietly, then waited until he looked up. His face brightened, as it always did when he saw her.

"Amanda! At last!" He jumped up and hurried around from behind his desk to greet her with a hug. "I was just thinking about you."

"I'm ready to work," she said briskly. Last night's tears had been replaced by an overwhelming need to plunge into her task immediately.

Erastus nodded in sympathetic understanding—almost as though he sensed how she had been suffering.

"I was hoping that would be your decision," he said, his voice unusually gentle. "I think it's very courageous the way you've pulled yourself together. I was so afraid that you might do something rash."

"Rash?" She gave a short puzzled laugh. "Whatever are you talking about?"

He blinked rapidly. "You—don't know? About Mark Reed?"

"Oh, God! Has something happened to him?"

Erastus looked pained. "It's there—in this morning's edition." He gestured toward his desk. "I'm sorry, Amanda, I thought he'd have the decency to tell you."

Amanda picked up the paper, her eyes rushing to a one-paragraph item at the bottom of page one. "SIMPSON-REED BETROTHAL."

For a moment she wanted to laugh, for it seemed to be a ridiculous misprint. Then she began to read: "Mr. and Mrs. Sol Simpson announced today the engagement of their only daughter, Irene Marjorie, to Mark Reed, junior partner in the Simpson Lumber Company. An April wedding is planned."

The terse, numbing statement held Amanda's eyes. Then the words began to blur, the paper slipped from her fingers, and her mind went mercifully blank.

Dr. Fiset diagnosed Amanda's condition as "nervous collapse brought on by a severe emotional strain," for which he prescribed plenty of rest, brisk walks in the fresh air and a diet of meat and dairy products to build up her strength. It was almost the same as the program prescribed for tuberculosis patients, except that the latter were required to simply breathe cold air, not exercise in it.

Amanda suspected immediately that the renowned physician had ordered this tedious regimen because he was at a loss to know the remedy for a broken heart.

Unknown to Amanda, Erastus had called her mother with the alarming news of her daughter's illness. Temperance came at once and stayed, following Dr. Fiset's recovery program as faithfully as if she were a patient herself, so that Amanda would not feel alone. It was her first visit to Seattle and an emotional reunion for both of them. But Amanda could not help feeling pangs of guilt to think how she had always resisted her mother's pleas to make a trip home. It seemed too much like a sentimental pilgrimage back into a period of her life which had no relationship to the present and which could only result in disappointment. Nor did it ease her guilt to see that her mother was aging. There were thin tired lines around her mouth, and her auburn hair was now muted by a silver haze. Still, despite the subtle etchings of time, her fading beauty belied the fact that she had reached her middle fifties, for she bore no visible mark of struggle or suffering, though she had known both.

Temperance's cheerful optimism only made Amanda feel increasingly inadequate. The fall of 1905 passed like purgatory without promise of salvation. Each day was endless and empty, made worse by a continuous trickle of letters from well-wishers. Amanda began to feel ashamed of her sickness, for there was no visible malfunction to justify her being treated as an invalid.

She discouraged visitors, with the exception of Erastus, and a few old friends, such as Colonel Blethen and Mary Kenworthy. For much as she hated being a recluse, she hated even more being pitied. Yet, she hadn't the slightest idea how to go about promoting her own recovery, or returning to a normal life.

Temperance stayed on until after the New Year. But a backlog of court cases awaited her in Washington, D.C., and reluctantly she set the date for her departure. However, the day before she planned to leave turned out to be unseasonably mild, which gave her a sudden idea.

"We'll have a picnic!" she announced brightly. "The sunshine will do us both good. Where would you like to go?"

Amanda felt doubtful at first, but as she thought about it, a faint smile crept over her face. "I'll surprise you," Amanda said. A stirring of excitement inside began to dispel the gloom, and she saw her mood reflected in her mother's expression of relief.

When the Seattle Street Railway deposited them at the foot of Denny Hill, they carried the picnic basket between them as they started up the steep incline.

"When I first came here, there was nothing on this hill but a hotel," Amanda explained as they climbed. Suddenly she noticed that her mother seemed short of breath.

"Are you tired?" she asked anxiously.

Temperance clasped her throat. "I'm still not used to these terrible hills!"

"That's all right, we can rest for a minute."

"Is it much farther?"

"All the way to the top. Think you can make it?"

Temperance nodded vigorously, but every few feet she would pause to smell the fragrance of fresh timber and marvel at the amount of construction going on.

"But where are the gardens, the landscaping?" she wanted to know. "I see nothing but stumps."

Amanda smiled, thinking how that had been her first impression, too. "This is the forest. The land has to be cleared before you can build."

At the summit, they stopped before a freshly logged plot, which like the others, bore the stubble of sawed-off trees. "There," she said pointing, "is our picnic ground—my little patch of earth."

"Yours? You own this land?"

"I own it, but the gold rush bought it. I had great plans at one time to build my own newspaper right here on this spot." She gazed wistfully into the distance. "I wanted to have the only factory in Seattle with a view of the mountains from every window."

"Your own newspaper? How exciting! Why did you change your mind?"

"I didn't. It's just that—certain events got in the way. I tried to share my dream with Mark, but he didn't approve. I realize now that he wanted a woman whose life revolved around him. He tried to destroy the very qualities which had attracted me to him in the first place. He wanted a Firebrand, all right—but only in the bedroom."

Temperance turned pale, then quickly recovered. "We don't need to talk about it," she said firmly. "The past must be forgotten. Let's talk about your paper. Is there anything now that's standing in your way?"

"Only me. And a little more money."

"Could you get a bank loan?"

"As a single woman, I doubt it." Amanda's face clouded as she thought of Mark again. "Married women are spared those problems."

Temperance took the tablecloth from the basket and spread it over a stump. "Married women have other problems." She took out the leftover turkey and a half loaf of bread. "Would you like to come home for a while, Manka?" she asked without looking up.

"Don't call me Manka any more, please. And don't feel that I need to be looked after. I'll be fine."

"I know you will, darling."

"This is my home, Mama."

"I know."

"And even though I've been abandoned, I must learn to live with it."

Temperance nodded encouragingly, heartened by this glimmer of rationality. "Yes, you're right. It will be hard at first, but with each day the task becomes easier. The past recedes more swiftly than you think. Then one day the pain will be gone and only the pleasant part of the memory will remain. At that point you'll feel that even if the situation could be changed, and you had another chance, you wouldn't go back. The desire will no longer be there."

Amanda listened with intense curiosity, sensing that her mother was speaking from experience.

"Have you ever suffered as I have, Mama?"

"More than you can imagine. But it all happened long before you were born."

"And the pain is gone?"

"It was gone by the time I married your father."

Suddenly Amanda remembered. Once as a child she had been looking through the family album and had come across a photograph of a handsome dark-skinned man, which she had found underneath a photograph of someone else. She had immediately demanded to know who the attractive mysterious stranger was and where did he live? Temperance had told her that his name was Hyde Calloway, a very successful lawyer who lived in San Francisco. But the most intriguing part of the story was that he was half-Choctaw, and had worked with Temperance when she rode the circuit throughout the Indian Territory. More curious than ever, Amanda had insisted on knowing if her mother had been in love with Mr. Calloway. But Temperance had admitted only to a deep and trusting friendship, nothing more. Amanda had objected by asking, "If he was such a great friend, why do you cover him up?" Temperance had had no answer.

Amanda reminded her mother of the incident.

"Good Lord, Amanda, how did you ever remember that? Why, you were only eight years old!" Temperance shook her head in amazement.

"Then you *were* in love with Hyde Calloway?"

"Yes, I was. I didn't want to lie to you, but I was afraid you were too young to understand, that you would think I didn't care for your father. The truth is, I loved two men. I had to decide between them. I've never had a court case that gave me such agony."

"Then you felt you made the right decision?"

"Heavens, yes," she answered a bit too quickly. "Once I had made up my mind, I never looked back. You can do it, too, Amanda. And someday, when you least expect it, love will come again."

At the end of January 1906 Amanda returned to the *P.I.* Erastus made a great fuss over her, as did all the other employees—the very thing she didn't want. However well intentioned the welcome, it only reminded her of happiness lost, followed by a bleak and wasted period in her life. She was treated as gingerly as a fragile piece of china. Was it just her imagination, or did it seem that the subjects of love, marriage and lumber had been banished from the paper and even from conversation?

Amanda struggled to find her place again, despite the reluctance of Erastus to allow her to tackle the lumber story. It was too soon, he told her. Wait awhile longer. In fact, he hesitated to assign her anything controversial. He rejected in horror her idea of visiting the insane asylum at Fort Steilacoom in order to observe the treatment of lunatics. Amanda saw in his refusal the fear that she might end up as a patient herself. Yet, the subject of illness in the mind held a certain fascination. She knew that she had come dangerously close to such an illness, that it was important to try to understand it. But unfortunately, like sex, it was not a fit topic for discussion. It was certainly not something people wanted to read about, said Erastus.

Amanda came to realize that no one would consider her completely recovered or treat her in a normal manner until she resumed some sort of social life. So when she received an invitation from Horace and Elizabeth Cayton to attend a party at their home on the evening of April 17, she talked herself into accepting. And though she feared it would be an ordeal, she liked the Caytons too much to refuse.

The Horace Cayton residence was the showplace of Denny Hill. It was larger, grander and had a better view than its neighbors. And it was as conservative and traditional as its owners. The Victorian mansion, oriental garden and livery stable on a sprawling acre of hillside reflected the taste of hard-earned reward. Above all, it proved that in 1906 in Seattle you no longer had to be white to succeed.

Amanda had gotten along well with Horace when he first came to work at the *P.I.* She appreciated his eagerness to learn, his early struggle. She didn't even mind when Erastus had sent Cayton to Buffalo instead of her, to cover the murder trial of Leon Czolgosz, President McKinley's assassin. Ten years older than Amanda, Cayton had felt that time was running out. Besides, he had a family to support. However, Amanda soon observed that he was driven not so much to become the best reporter in the world, but to gain a foothold in society. Once he had achieved this objective, reporting no longer interested him. His ambition was to own. By 1902 he owned property, by 1903 he had built his home and now in 1906 he had his own newspaper, the *Weekly Republican*. In his first editorial he made it clear what kind of newspaper it was going to be. "Let the Negroes come to the Northwest like I did—strong enough to win their dignity, courageous enough to demand their rights, intelligent enough to find a proper place in polite society." He never spoke of Negroes again.

Amanda twisted the bell handle, and at the same moment felt a sudden gust release a strand of hair from her pompadour. Serves me right, she thought, for attempting a new hair style on such a windy evening.

The minute the Filipino houseboy opened the door, Amanda could hear the loud buzz of conversation and laughter from the drawing room, with Horace's deep resonant voice predominating.

"I won't have it. Mr. Thomson is going to have to deal with *me*. Somebody has to put a stop to his harebrained schemes!"

Amanda smiled as she paused before the hall mirror for a quick repair, her nervousness vanishing. Horace would be holding the spotlight. Good. How much better it might have been for all had he become an opera singer instead of a newspaperman. However, he willingly relinquished center stage the moment Amanda entered the room. She took a deep breath.

"Hello, Horace. I'm sorry to be late."

"Ah, Miss Amanda!" His bass voice rose an octave and his eyes brightened. "We were beginning to worry. But no matter. You look lovely as always—green certainly does become you."

As he came forward to greet her, Amanda noticed that he was putting on weight, looking a bit too comfortable for a man who had worked his way up. His prematurely gray hair and mustache contrasted sharply with a youthful coffee complexion that could almost pass for Caucasian.

At the same moment Elizabeth Cayton hurried over from the opposite side of the room, arms outstretched. "It's so good to see you, Amanda."

Slender, darker than her husband, Elizabeth spoke just above a whisper. Though she seemed aloof to those who didn't know her well, she was open and friendly with Amanda.

"We've missed you," she added in a soothing voice.

Amanda nodded, feeling a sudden lump in her throat. As Elizabeth hugged her, she heard Horace telling the others, "I think you all know our charming guest better as Miss Firebrand, the young lady who has made the *P.I.* such lively reading!" He chuckled in a low register. "Though heaven knows I don't agree with its policy. But I try to be broad-minded and keep myself open to new ideas." He spoke as though he had forgotten that he, too, had once worked for the *P.I.*

"Don't worry about all the new faces," said Elizabeth in a whisper. "I'll introduce you, a few at a time."

"Now don't you two go off into some corner to discuss politics," said Horace. He turned to his guests to explain. "Miss Amanda and Mrs. Cayton are both the daughters of United States senators, so naturally they have a good deal in common. Every time we get together, seems they end up talking about what's wrong with the government!" Then he added with wry humor, "My wife's father was the first *colored* senator, a claim which I'm afraid Miss Amanda is unable to match."

Everyone laughed, as they always did whenever Horace made this remark.

"By the way," said Horace, glancing about, "we don't seem to have the pleasure of Mr. Brainerd's company tonight." He looked directly at Amanda. "Where could he be?"

"He telephoned just as I was ready to leave, asking me to extend his regrets."

"I hope he's not ill?"

"No. Just working late, as usual. He feels guilty even taking out time to go to a party."

"That's a shame," Elizabeth murmured. "Can't you use your influence to persuade him to ease up?"

"I'm afraid no one can influence him in that respect. He's married to the *P.I.*"

"Well," said Horace in a booming voice, "he should be married to *you!*"

There was an awkward moment of silence until Amanda began to laugh, then she was joined by the others. "It's just as well he's not, or I should feel like a widow!"

"Mr. Brainerd is a foolish fellow," declared Horace stoutly.

Amanda was relieved to find that she could still laugh. And though no one could possibly have known the real reason for her long retreat, it was inevitable that someone would inadvertently touch a sensitive chord.

Elizabeth squeezed Amanda's hand, confiding, "Listen to him talk! My husband has learned all of Mr. Brainerd's bad habits—he devotes every minute to his paper, too, so that I feel just like a widow myself!"

"But at least I entertain. Why, a man's got to mingle. Mingle and socialize. Without friends, where are you? Nowhere." Horace paused. "I can tell you what it's like. I remember."

Horace was only partially right. At least he had a wife with whom to share his success. One could survive without friends if one had a partner. But did he know what it was to be entirely alone? Amanda wondered if even having your own newspaper could take the place of another human being.

"Come, join our discussion," Horace invited, drawing Amanda into the circle where he had been presiding. "I need someone to take my side."

"Why, Horace, don't you know by now that I'm bound to take the opposite view?" Amanda teased.

Horace shook his head firmly. "Not this time you won't. We're talking about the leveling of Denny Hill, that's what. Surely you don't approve?" Before she could answer he rushed on, working himself up. "People's rights are at stake, that's why Firebrand should take up the cause!"

"Regrading the hill will put people to work," Amanda reminded. "So whose rights are being violated?"

"Mine are. Mine and everybody else who lives on Denny Hill. This is valuable real estate up here. Too valuable to carve up and dump in the Sound. Why, you own a lot up here yourself!"

"That's true, but I don't feel that I stand to lose it. Nor will you. You'll still have your house. All that will be missing are a few tons of dirt underneath."

"Miss Amanda, I paid good money for this magnificent view. I refuse to be lowered!"

One of the listeners cleared his throat. "I think that the leveling of Denny Hill will be a boon to the future of this city. It will open us up to expand northward to Lake Union and beyond." Then he added with a smile, "After all, Horace, we've got six other hills."

"Easy for you to say, Olmstead. But if you lived here instead of on Capitol Hill, you'd feel differently. Just remember this, if they cut down Denny, what's to prevent them from cutting down all the others? Think about that!"

"Then you're going to oppose the project?" Amanda asked.

"Certainly am. Wait till you see my editorial this week. I'm asking for Thomson's recall. Why, he's the most irresponsible city engineer we've ever had." Cayton took out his handkerchief and dabbed his forehead. "Taki," he called to the houseboy, "bring over the champagne!"

"Supposing they go ahead with the regrade," suggested Amanda. "What then?"

"I intend to stay put. They can cut around me if they like, but they can't cut underneath. I already checked with the Department of Engineering."

Everyone stared in disbelief.

"Then you'll be left maybe several hundred feet up in the air!" Amanda shook her head in bewilderment. "How will you get up and down? What about your horses and carriage? And the water pipes?"

"I'll pay extra, if necessary, to have pipes brought up. As for my horses, they can stay below. Of course I'll have stairs built for me and my family. It will be inconvenient, yes. But worth it."

"Are you sure?" asked Amanda.

Horace sighed heavily. "No, I'm not sure. But I've made up my mind. You know, when we first came to Seattle, we lived down in Coon Hollow with all the other Negroes. It was crowded, dismal and swampy. I vowed that if I ever got out, I'd never live below ground again. I wanted to be on top of the hill. That's where I am." He paused. "And that's where I'm going to stay."

After the party that night, Amanda lay awake thinking of all the problems that Horace was going to create for himself and his family, simply because he insisted on seeing the world as he wanted it to be,

216

not as it was. In a way, she had done the same thing with Mark. She had viewed the lumber industry through *his* eyes, her life through *him*. Like Horace, she had rejected the future. Yet, the future was all she had. Realizing this at last, she knew it was time to move forward.

Chapter Fifteen

Wᴴᴇɴ the train pulled into the new Aberdeen station, Amanda felt that she was arriving for the first time. In a sense she was. Memories of ashes and rubble faded as she beheld the sight of gleaming two- and three-story buildings, which had been constructed entirely of brick, stone, cement and mortar. Wood was used only for trim and for sidewalks. On the surface, Aberdeen hardly resembled a mill town.

As she walked up Heron Street, Amanda tried to imagine the fire-ravaged scene which had greeted her less than two years ago. But there was nothing to remind her of that fateful day, for the place where she and Mark had first met was buried forever beneath the foundations of some new structure. Looking about calmly, she was grateful that she could think of Mark without pain, just as her mother had predicted.

Mark had already been married a month now—it was April 18, an easy date to remember, as it coincided with the day of the San Francisco earthquake. How ironic, she had thought, that the details of the wedding had been lost to the back pages, overshadowed by tragedy. She had vowed that it would stay in the back pages of her mind as well. And so it had.

At the end of the street the recently completed Aberdeen Hotel reposed invitingly on the banks of the Wishkah River. Amanda checked in.

But beneath the deceptive façade, she soon discovered that the underpinnings shook with the impatient thunder of calked boots. Mill hands and loggers, restless from layoffs due to the fire, roamed the streets looking for an excuse to brawl and the chance to get back at an unfair world. The saloons which depended upon their patronage were taking no chances—the loggers were welcome, but not their chief weapon, for signs were posted warning: "No Calked Boots Allowed."

Amanda thought immediately of Big Fred Hewett, a likely source of information, and wondered if his saloon had ever been rebuilt. Her search was quickly rewarded when she came upon the new Humboldt halfway down F Street.

Though it was only the middle of the afternoon, the dim smoky Humboldt, pungent with the odor of beer and fresh sawdust, was doing a lively business. Having parked their boots by the door, the loggers crowded the bar, resting stockinged feet on the brass rail. As daylight poured in through swinging doors, heads pivoted in Amanda's direction.

"Oh, oh, it's one of them W.C.T.U.s!" a voice bellowed.

Uncertain laughter trailed into silence, as they waited for the lecture which was sure to come.

Amanda's eyes swept past the questioning faces for Big Fred's familiar smile to confirm that she was a friend, not a member of the Women's Christian Temperance Union. But instead of Big Fred, Roscoe the piano-player was presiding as bartender. Unfortunately, he didn't remember Amanda at all. Nor could she blame him, recalling the terror with which he had played "Mother o' Mine" at the command of Jumbo Reilly. But when she reminded him of the incident, and asked to see Big Fred, his wary smile trembled and fear again danced in his eyes.

"Big Fred ain't here—he's gone to jail!" Roscoe blurted.

"For what?" asked Amanda.

The loggers shuffled uneasily, on guard against a probing female outsider. Amanda could see from their warning frowns that they were prepared to escort her to the door.

"I'm his friend," she assured hastily. "Maybe I can help him."

"They say he killed Jumbo Reilly," Roscoe volunteered.

"My God! Did he?"

"If you're really his friend, it don't matter if'n he did, or if'n he didn't," growled one of the loggers, sauntering toward her. "Jumbo's gone whar he belongs. Got that?"

"How did it happen?" she asked.

With a sudden violent gesture, the logger pulled down his suspenders and ripped open his shirt, exposing a barrel chest riddled with small holes.

Amanda stared, wondering if they had been made by some strange kind of bullet.

"I got the lumberjack smallpox!" he howled, and was immediately joined by his friends in a rumble of laughter.

"Jumbo did a fandango on my chest with his boots on, so some of the boys here gave him the same treatment!"

"That's how he died?"

"Hell, no! Jumbo was found floating down the Wishkah. But Big Fred got blamed 'cause everybody knew there was a fight here the same night he was found dead. And they knew that him and Big Fred had a feud goin'. But who really kilt Jumbo, nobody knows."

The Aberdeen jail was as cramped and gloomy as if it had been standing for a hundred years. It even smelled musty, though it was brand new, and when Amanda entered she felt instantly a sense of hopelessness.

Big Fred almost cried with relief when he saw Amanda, certain that she had been sent by the *P.I.* to investigate the charges against him.

"I'm innocent!" he proclaimed in desperation. But when Amanda questioned him, he couldn't give the slightest clue as to who really killed Jumbo Reilly.

"I'll do my best," Amanda consoled, "to help find his killer. But I can't promise I'll succeed. After all, I'm a stranger here—you were my only contact."

Big Fred's shoulders slumped in despair. "Something terrible's happening," he muttered. "It's like an army of termites gnawing at the trees. Someday everybody's going to wake up and instead of finding a forest, all that's gonna be left is a big pile of sawdust." He held his head in chunky hands, as though the weight was too much to bear.

"That's why I'm here," said Amanda anxiously. "To find out what's going on. I wish I knew where to begin!"

Big Fred lifted his head slowly. "Go see my friend, Billy Gohl. He's an agent for the Seamen's Union and his office is on Heron

Street, right over the Grand Saloon. Now there's a fella who knows loggers. He hangs around town to recruit them to go to sea whenever they get fed up with logging. He can help you more than I can."

"A union man?" she asked excitedly. "Good! Has he come to see you?"

"Not yet," said Big Fred gloomily, "but I keep hoping. I know he's busy, but maybe you can tell him that a visit would sure cheer me up."

Billy Gohl's office was almost as cramped and stale-smelling as the jail. Amanda recognized the familiar odor from her treks into the forest—that of decayed matter which lies under dead logs. All the accouterments of the timber trade hung from nails on the wall—axes, saws, mallets, cant hooks, peavey heads and climbing irons. To make the recruits feel at home? she wondered. There was nothing reminiscent of ships, however.

An unkempt figure, back to the door, hunched over a massive desk, whose many cubicles were stuffed with papers so crumpled they looked like pigeon's nests. At the sound of footsteps behind him, he rolled back his chair and spun around, his body tensed, as if expecting attack.

Bottle-green eyes stared coolly from a youthful face, ruddy with clouds of red freckles. A battered hat flattened his red hair and curled his ears away from his head. With pouty defiant lips, Billy Gohl looked like the kind of boy who always sat at the back of the class, nor did it appear that his schooldays were far behind him.

Amanda quickly introduced herself as a friend of Big Fred's, but said nothing about being a reporter.

Billy listened without getting up or removing his hat, while she explained that she wished to find out who really killed Jumbo, so that Fred Hewett might be cleared.

When Billy spoke at last, his lips barely moved and his voice sounded like it was coming from inside a hollow log. "The UMWL killed Jumbo," he said matter-of-factly.

"The United Mill Workers and Loggers?"

"They wanted Jumbo to join, but he wouldn't. He worked for Simpson's. And Simpson's men don't join unions."

"But why did they pick Jumbo?"

"Some of his fingers had got in the way of a saw, so the union figured he was ripe to complain. They was all set to march right into Simpson's, but Jumbo was stubborn. He didn't want nobody callin' him a cripple, or tellin' him what to do. So he beat up on the union boys. And that was his big mistake." Billy's faraway voice broke into a dry laugh.

"When you say union, do you mean—Gus Johnson?" Amanda asked, feeling a pulse beat of excitement against her throat.

Billy spun his chair in one complete revolution, then sprang to his feet in a crouching position. His gray underwear clung to the taut muscles of his arms. He looked as if he would burst out of his suspenders and the baggy trousers that they held.

"How come you know Gus?" demanded Billy, hoarse-voiced.

"I used to work in a factory," said Amanda quickly. "I got to know a lot of union organizers. Well, everyone knows Gus Johnson, don't they?"

Billy slowly relaxed and straightened up. "Yeah," he drawled. "Guess so."

He began to pace about the room, his shoelaces straying from untied boots. The tongues lolled to the side, flapping with each step.

"He still runs the show," mumbled Billy, as though talking to himself, "from wherever he is. Damn!" He threw down his hat, stomped it beyond recognition, then jammed it down on his ears again so that they stuck out more than ever.

"Where do you think Gus might be?" Amanda asked.

Billy's lips stretched like thick rubber bands revealing large yellow horse teeth. "If I knew, I'd turn him in and collect the re-ward!"

"Somebody must be in contact with him—if he's still running the show like you say."

Billy's grin shriveled. "Sure. But nobody talks. So if the law can't catch him, you can't neither."

"He's been hiding a long time. He'll have to come out sooner or later."

Billy shook his head. "He don't need to. He's got an army behind him—and every last one of 'em is minus a piece of flesh. And that army's gonna keep growing, 'cause all you need to join is to be missing part of your body. And when they start to march, you'll see the war begin!" There was a shade of envy in his voice.

"What are we going to do about Big Fred?"

"Do?" repeated Billy with a blank stare.

"We can't just let him languish in prison for a crime he didn't commit. Can't you come forward and tell the police what you know?"

"And have Gus Johnson send his boys after me?" Billy's red freckles brightened in anger.

"But I thought Big Fred was your friend!"

"That crazy galoot?" His voice rose. "Where did you ever get a dumb fool idea like that?"

"He told me so. He was hoping you'd come to visit him."

"If I had a friend," said Billy contemptuously, "it wouldn't be him. Getting throwed in jail for nothing is plain stupid."

Amanda thought long and hard before taking the next step. To become involved in a murder case seemed to have little to do with her lumber investigation, but on the other hand, Jumbo's murder was no ordinary case. Didn't it represent the basic conflict between union and mill? Somehow, she had the feeling that if the murder could be solved, a lot of other questions would be answered as well. There was one problem. She would have to question everyone who knew Jumbo—including the man he had worked for, Mark.

Am I ready to face him? she asked herself. Going to the mill meant entering *his* territory, where every whiff of pine-scented air carried his smell. But the hardest part would be to see him again, knowing that he belonged to someone else. Pull yourself together, she demanded sternly. Get it over with quickly. Besides, how will you ever know if you're cured of him unless you actually meet? Deciding to go at once before she could lose courage and change her mind, she hired a bicycle, tucked up her skirts and rode across the bridge to Cosmopolis. But when she reached the far shore, she noticed that the streets were strangely empty of vehicles or pedestrians, and a solemn Sunday quiet had settled over the town. In fact, all the stores along Main Street were closed—including the saloons.

With growing uneasiness, Amanda pedaled toward Simpson's. She could see even from a distance that the gates to the mill were shut and the lumber yard deserted. But as she drew near, she spotted something hanging on the gate which made her heart do a peculiar turn. It was an enormous black wreath. A vision sprang to mind of a tree crashing down on Mark as he tried to leap out of its path. She dropped her bicycle and approached with leaden steps. A small card in the center of the wreath stated: "Closed in memory of Sol Simpson." Her heart quieted. It wasn't finished after all.

As she paused to stare at the silent buildings, it crossed her mind that this was probably the first and only day in the history of the mill when there would be no smoke billowing from the stacks, nor sound of screaming saws echoing across the tideflats. How neatly Mark had planned his life, how perfectly it was working out for him.

The ache returned as Amanda mounted her bicycle and rode back through deserted streets. Trailing behind her the distant strains of "Blessed Be the Tie That Binds," drifted down from the First Presbyterian Church. An odd selection, she thought, for a funeral. Or perhaps not so odd after all.

When she reached the hotel, Amanda was surprised to discover a hand-delivered letter in her mailbox. Puzzled, she immediately slit it open and glanced at the signature. It was signed "Gus." In excited anticipation, she hurried to the privacy of her room.

Without salutation, he had written: "For the true picture, go to the Slade Mill. After that, check a few saloons. You'll find out who your friends are—and your enemies." She crumpled it. Damn him! There was no explanation, nothing to go on. Only hints.

Helplessly Amanda gazed through lace curtains at the sluggish Wishkah, then across the rowboat landing to a long warehouse with blank windows. Are you there, Gus Johnson? Watching me from your hiding place at this very moment? With an involuntary shiver, she stepped back.

When she returned to the lobby to ask the clerk if he remembered who had delivered the letter, he reflected for a moment while the soft swish of the ceiling fan measured time. At last he recalled that the messenger had been a young man with close-cropped brown hair. But he could give no further description, for the man had been in a great hurry.

Billy Gohl was loitering outside the entrance to the Slade Mill, distributing flyers to the workers arriving for the morning shift. By the time Amanda saw him it was too late to turn around. He had already seen her.

"Going inside?" he asked with a sly grin that seemed to say no secrets were safe from him.

"Yes, I am."

Billy nodded. "Never know what you might find out. Mind carrying in a few flyers?" He thrust some into her hand before she could answer.

They said: "Sick of your job? Need big pay? Go to sea! Contact Mr. Billy Gohl, Agent. Seamen's Union—39 Heron Street, one flight up."

"Why don't you take them in yourself?"

"I ain't allowed past the gate."

"Well, I don't want to get kicked out any more than you do," said Amanda, handing them back.

"Suit yourself," Billy replied amiably, then added, "Good luck in there, and look sharp."

Amanda was halfway across the lumber yard when one of the workers fell in step beside her. She glanced at him with immediate suspicion. His features were nondescript, but beneath his cap she saw that he had short brown hair. He didn't look at her, but stared straight ahead when he spoke.

"Name's John Looney," he said in a monotone. "I was told to show you around."

So this was the man who had delivered the note from Gus.

"Your name's very familiar." Amanda stopped suddenly. "Now I know who you are! Gus Johnson once told me that he was going to fight John Looney to teach him a lesson. He said he wanted to make him a good strong union man. Was that you?"

He smiled in reply.

"Is Gus in town?"

"Can't say."

At the entrance, Looney showed his UMWL badge, explaining that his guest wished a tour of the mill. The guard waved them past. Amanda was surprised to see that union organizers were allowed to come and go as they pleased.

Setting a brisk pace, Looney led Amanda along a catwalk from which a breaking-down saw operation could be viewed. It was the first step, he told her, in reducing a log to manageable proportions. Giant loops of saw-toothed spinning steel carved the log as easily as if it were a piece of roast beef. Eye-stinging dust rose to envelop them. Like the sawyers below, Amanda kept her eyes half-closed, her mouth and nose covered by a handkerchief. Her eardrums throbbed with a piercing screech that even in the brief time it took to pass through was barely tolerable. She found herself hurrying, and had almost reached the exit when suddenly she felt the planking of the catwalk give way beneath her feet.

"Watch yourself!" shouted Looney. But his warning was lost.

Instinctively she grasped onto the broken railing, her fragile link to safety, and clung with both hands. The railing swayed like an uprooted tree, dangling her in space, while a rush of air from the giant blades chilled her legs. Oh, God, it's going to go! But even if it held, her arms felt as if they'd be wrenched from their sockets. Hold on! With eyes squeezed shut, she could still see the bared teeth of whirling steel only inches below. She was slipping, the blades almost grazing her now. A moment, perhaps, was all that remained. Let it be quick, she prayed! Her body was already numb to the unimaginable pain ahead. Shoot me! Why can't somebody shoot me? As she clung to the last second of consciousness, her only thought was, I'm going to die without Mark, die without my paper! It isn't fair . . .

When she opened her eyes, Amanda was lying on the sawdust, while curious faces breathed down. Aware of the throbbing silence, she turned her head from side to side, mystified to be alive after having experienced the shock of dying. Calmly she wondered if her legs had been severed, and if the extremities she felt were only ghosts.

Looney's face pushed through the others as he laid a damp rag across her forehead.

"You'll be fine," he assured her, but his color was waxen.

"This man saved your life," a stranger volunteered, pointing to Looney. "He grabbed you just in time."

Amanda moved her lips to thank him, but she couldn't hear her own voice. At any rate, he didn't wait for her thanks, but stood up abruptly and walked away.

The shock came later—nightmares, chills and sweat. Amanda endured it alone in her hotel room where she remained for a day and a half, telling no one of her experience. There were moments when she felt fearful and depressed, other times when her spirits rose with a sense of exhilaration at having survived. But each time she relived the scene in her mind, she asked herself, *was* it an accident? After all, the mill was new, there was no reason for the catwalk to have collapsed. Yet, Gus's note had clearly told her, "You'll find out who your friends are—and your enemies." Did she dare pursue his advice to check the saloons? Even as she considered the danger, she knew she had no choice. Having been lucky enough to survive one close call, she had to believe that destiny meant her to press on.

Leaving the hotel that afternoon, she had taken only a few steps when John Looney again appeared at her side, his sudden presence filling her with apprehension.

"You hurried away before I could thank you for saving my life. Do you have any idea why it happened?"

"They want you out of the way," he replied tensely. "Maybe they want me out of the way, too."

"Who's 'they'?"

"Slade."

"Slade is actually willing to commit murder? Are they so afraid I'll find something out?"

"If they are, they've got reason. So be careful."

"I don't know how to be careful," said Amanda. "I'm not sure it's possible for me."

"I'm going to leave you now, but one last word—watch the Wishkah River. On almost any day you can see the corpses of loggers floating by. Murdered loggers."

Amanda gasped. "Wait, don't go!"

"Have to. Don't forget to check the saloons along the riverfront."

"What am I checking for?" she called after him. But he was already crossing the street.

Amanda hurried down to the boat landing and gazed at the river, heart pounding. Then she remembered—hadn't Jumbo's body also been found floating down the Wishkah? But the current seemed to be carrying only stray timber and seaweed. When an hour had passed, she began to wonder if there was a conspiracy to put her off the track. She turned away, angry with herself for believing such an implausible story and for having lost valuable time.

Slowly she walked by the waterfront saloons debating whether or not further investigation would also prove futile. One last try, she decided. If she were to take a job as a barmaid . . .

The proprietor of the Lone Jack Saloon admitted that a number of girls were employed evenings to "entertain the customers," as he put it. Yet, he seemed reluctant to hire Amanda. He told her bluntly that he didn't think she'd be the type for that kind of work.

"Not that you don't have the looks," he added, appraising her with a candid eye. "You just seem too much—like a lady. This is a rough crowd we get in here. There's fights and what not."

"What would I have to do?"

"Oh, this isn't a brothel. Nothing like that."

"Then—what?"

He cleared his throat. "Well, we all know that these boys can get pretty out of hand when they're 'blowin' 'er in.' Celebrating," he explained upon seeing her questioning expression. "So if a fella's having too much to drink, for his own good I like my girls to pour a few drops of chloral hydrate into his glass, so's he'll pass out instead of causing trouble. All you have to do is to escort him to one of the rooms upstairs to sleep it off."

"And the wages?"

"You get a percentage of whatever you take. Once they fall asleep, it's easy."

"You mean—pick their pockets?"

"If you don't, somebody else will. They expect it. Don't worry. When they come into town after weeks out in camp, they've got a month's wages to blow and that's exactly what they aim to do."

"But what right do you have to rob them?"

"Look, they're not married, they don't have families or homes. To them, money is only for a good time." He paused. "But like I say, you might not want to hobnob with this kind of fella."

"I need the job," she told him. "I don't mind giving it a try."

The proprietor smiled skeptically. "What do you have to lose, eh? You can start tonight."

Amanda found her job at the Lone Jack far different from the proprietor's description. It wasn't easy to drug a logger's drink. They were neither gullible nor eager to part with their hard-earned wages. Most of them refused to drink from a glass, preferring instead to buy a bottle, which they opened themselves, then guarded hawkishly from that moment on.

The young logger who had singled out Amanda to keep him company throughout the evening, drank slowly, as if knowing how the night was destined to end. Amanda was touched by his rambling personal history, and while he unburdened himself of lonely memories, she resolved to return the money to him which she would be forced to take. However, his only address was the Slade Lumber Camp, twenty miles up the river.

"It's a rotten place," he admitted, his speech beginning to slur. "It stinks. We hafta sleep on the floor without blankets—even in winter. And the bunkhouses are crawling with vermin. And there's worms in the food. Know something else? They never wash the dishes cause they're nailed to the table—they just hose them down with cold water. So if you don't get hit by a tree, you die from throwing up your guts. It stinks."

Amanda made a mental note. "Won't you tell me your name?" she pleaded, having asked him before and been refused.

"Nope," he replied stubbornly. "I'm nobody. Just a son-of-a-bitch logger."

The proprietor gave Amanda a sharp look—a signal to take the boy upstairs. The logger turned his head at last, allowing Amanda just enough time to pour the chloral hydrate into his bottle, which was almost finished.

"Drink up," said Amanda. "The next one's on the house."

As soon as he had drained the last drop, she led the way upstairs.

"She's going upstairs with nobody," he boasted to those within earshot, and stumbled ahead, flailing his arms for balance.

A dingy corridor divided the rooms on the second floor. Uncertainly Amanda passed one closed door after another until she was suddenly stopped by the sound of a muffled cry, then scuffling and a dull thud. She sucked in her breath. The logger also stopped. In the dim light she could see from his startled expression that he had sobered instantly.

"Let me outa here!" he rasped, his voice choked with fear, and turning, he ran back down the stairs as if pursued.

Frantically Amanda tried to open the door behind which the sounds had come, but it was locked. She rattled the knob and beat her fists against it, and although she could hear labored breathing on the other side, there was no response.

Footsteps pounded the stairs as the proprietor raced up to find out what had happened.

"Something's wrong in there!" Amanda cried. "You'll have to break down the door—it's locked from the inside!"

"Get away from that door!" he ordered furiously. "What the hell do you think you're doing?"

Amanda recoiled, stunned. "But someone's been hurt! They cried out!"

"Mind your goddam business! Now, get outa here! You're fired!"

Amanda did not wait for a second warning. She quickly descended the stairs into a din of laughter and the tinny melody from an out-of-tune piano, all of which seemed to conspire to drown out the sounds from above. The young logger was not to be seen, but the doors through which he had exited were still swinging.

Outside she looked in all directions, but it appeared he had fled. He *knew* what was going on upstairs. He could tell her everything—if only he could be found.

Convinced that he must be hiding nearby, and that he would soon pass out from the chloral hydrate dosage, Amanda began to search. He wouldn't go far, she reasoned, for he was in his stocking feet, having left his boots still parked by the door.

Staying close to the building, she slipped around to the back where she could hear the water lapping at the pilings under the saloon. An outside staircase led to the second floor, which projected out over the water. Was it worth the risk to go back up to find out what was happening, or should she wait under the stairs to see if anyone came down?

As she debated her move, there was a sound overhead—like an object being dragged along the corridor. Holding her breath, she stepped into the safety of the shadows and glanced upward. At that instant a trap door above suddenly opened and a heavily weighted gunny sack came plunging down, passing only a few feet from where she crouched, and into the river. There was a splash, then silence.

The police lieutenant tapped his pencil in boredom as Amanda related her experience at the Lone Jack. When she had finished, he continued to concentrate full attention on the pencil, addressing his remarks to it rather than to her.

"There's nothing we can do," he admitted finally.

"But I know that someone was murdered, and the owner of the Lone Jack was in on it!"

"Madam," he said wearily, "there's something you should know about loggers. They're always in trouble. They have no roots and they're not very bright. If we investigated every case involving a logger, we wouldn't have time to keep law and order."

"Aren't they entitled to the same rights as any other citizen?" she demanded, aghast.

The lieutenant shook his head. "They're not like us. They don't go to church or belong to the Knights Templars or the Masons. They don't play in the band or march in the Fourth of July parade. They don't have wives or children, and they don't patronize the local businesses. Their territory is the woods, the mills, the saloons and the brothels. Besides, they're impossible to protect. They live beyond the law. So we leave 'em alone. If a logger disappears or has a fatal mishap, we look at it this way—that's one less to make trouble."

"I can't believe it! If it weren't for loggers, Aberdeen wouldn't even exist!"

"They're transient," he insisted. "They don't come here intending to stay, so we don't feel obligated to treat them like regular settlers."

Amanda stood up, breathless with anger. "Then you refuse to drag the river? Or question the owner of the Lone Jack?"

"We'll talk to him," he agreed reluctantly, "to get his side of the story. But we can't be bothered dragging the river. Sure, there's always a body or two floating by—mostly river pigs who fall in somewheres upstream. But the current carries them right on down to the sea. So what's the point of fishing 'em out?"

Amanda leaned close to the bars and fixed Big Fred with a calculating stare. "This isn't a social call, Mr. Hewett, so don't waste my time by giving me wrong answers. If you ever expect to get out of here, you'd better tell me everything you know." She dropped her voice. "Did you kill Jumbo Reilly?"

Startled by the blunt question, Big Fred was thrown off guard. "I never killed anybody, I swear!" he stammered. "I just got myself into a mess."

"I should think so!" she said with contempt. "I found out all about you and the other so-called saloonkeepers."

Big Fred recoiled in fear. "It wasn't my fault," he said hoarsely. "It was the mills! Slade, Jones, Weatherwax, Bay City—they all came to me at one time or another to get me to 'make a deal' with them. I held off as long as I could." He paused to watch Amanda take down his words.

"Don't put my name in the paper," he pleaded nervously.

"I won't. Go on!"

"I thought after the fire things might change, and they wouldn't bother me any more. But right off nobody would sell me any lumber to rebuild unless I agreed to co-operate. So I had to. Same as every other saloonkeeper in town."

"Co-operate?"

"Robbing loggers of their wages is a big operation. The mills split fifty-fifty with the saloons. That's how they recoup a good portion of their payroll. It's up to the logger to be on his mettle—to outwit the game. He knows it goes on, but he doesn't report it to the police. In fact, I think the police are in on it, too." He shook his head dismally.

"So that's why you're not getting anyplace."

"Well, I'm not leaving town till I do. What about Jumbo? And the bodies in the river?"

"I was never mixed up in any killings. Nothing like that ever went on at the Humboldt."

"Then what in God's name are you doing in jail?"

"Taking the rap." Big Fred's lip curled bitterly. "Seems I wasn't collecting enough off the loggers to suit Slade—that was the mill I had a deal with. They decided I was keeping the big money for myself. I figure they killed Jumbo just so I'd be blamed—to teach me a lesson!"

Amanda sank back on the hard chair and stared into space. Was it logical to conclude that they—or any mill—would engage in the murder of loggers? It was incredible enough to think that they would coerce the saloons into robbing them, but if she was to suggest they were involved in grand scale murder, there would have to be hard evidence. Could it be that Big Fred was accusing the mills only to save himself? After all, Billy Gohl had called him a crazy galoot. And Billy seemed to know what he was talking about.

Walking back to her hotel from the jail, Amanda realized that she had reached a dead end. With the police unwilling to investigate, she would have to return home, her exposé incomplete. If this had happened a year ago, she thought sadly, she would have had Mark's support. But now? Her footsteps slowed as she debated. If Simpson's was innocent of any criminal activities, Mark would have no reason to turn her down. If they were guilty—this was the time to find out. Her temples throbbed as she tried to make up her mind. But without realizing it, her legs were already carrying her toward the bridge to

Cosmopolis. Which proved that the decision to go was not a matter of logic, but of pure emotion—born of an overwhelming need to see Mark one more time. To know how he really felt about her. To discover, perhaps, that he was suffering just as she was—that his marriage had been a terrible mistake. When she walked through the gates into the lumber yard, the warming tide of happy memories washed over her, so that for a brief moment it seemed that her life had stood still all this time, that nothing had really changed.

The reception room was bright with fresh yellow paint. Sturdy plants reposed on pedestals and the walls were hung with the framed maps of timber regions which had once hung in Mark's parlor. With a pang Amanda noticed that his hand-hewn benches and settee had also found their way into the waiting room for strangers to sit upon.

A plain young woman came around from behind the desk to greet her. She wore her hair so severely pulled back that her eyes slanted upward, but her smile was open and pleasant. Amanda stared. She was wearing a black dress with gray stripes. Then she knew. This was Mark's wife, in mourning for her father.

"Are you Mrs. Reed?" she asked slowly.

"Why, yes," she replied in surprise. "Have we met?"

"No, we haven't. I'm a newspaper reporter."

Mrs. Reed looked puzzled, but continued to smile politely. "What can I do for you?"

"I'm a friend of your husband's. Would you tell him that Amanda Lamar is here?"

"Is that *Mrs.* Lamar?" she asked, twisting her fingers nervously while taking in every detail of Amanda's appearance.

"No—*Miss.*"

There was an instant of hesitation. "You're certain it isn't something *I* can help you with?"

"That's kind of you, but I'm afraid not."

Mrs. Reed blinked rapidly, collecting her thoughts. "Please sit down." She turned abruptly and fled down the hall.

Amanda glanced at the settee, where she had once sat so close to Mark, and remained standing.

From a distance, Mrs. Reed's voice carried over the partitions. "There's a very strange redheaded woman who says she knows you . . ." Her words were cut off by the slamming of a door.

Amanda froze. Much as she wanted to run away, she forced herself to wait.

However, after only a few moments she could hear Mrs. Reed's brisk step returning. She appeared, wearing an expression of relief.

"Mr. Reed is so sorry, but he's very busy and won't be able to see you. Perhaps another time."

"Tell him I doubt there'll be another time." She started for the door, then turned around. "Tell Mark that if he changes his mind, he knows where to find me." Amanda opened the door and went out.

Chapter Sixteen

AMANDA was staring out the window of her office when the phone rang. She answered distractedly, not caring who it was, her thoughts at a distance.

"I liked your article," said a hollow voice.

Amanda snapped back to reality. "Who is this?" she asked, recognizing the voice, but wanting to be sure.

"Billy," he said, matter-of-factly. "You put my name in five places —I counted 'em. I was in more than anybody else. And everything you said about me was good. So thanks for the free publicity. When will I be in again?"

"Why, I don't know," she replied, startled.

"Soon, I hope," said Billy. Then he added, "But you forgot one thing. You didn't give me credit for warning you before your accident. Don't you remember?"

Amanda gasped. She had forgotten completely. Now his words came back—he had wished her luck and told her to look sharp. "I didn't take it as a warning," she admitted.

"Well, it was," he said. And Billy Gohl hung up.

Amanda pondered his call with growing apprehension. Billy didn't act the least bit surprised to have learned that she was Firebrand. And the more she thought about his warning, the more she had the uneasy feeling that he was teasing her, laughing at her. He knew too much. She left for Aberdeen that night.

When she arrived at the Seamen's Union office on Heron Street, the building was boarded up. That told her all she needed to know.

The Aberdeen chief of police listened to Amanda's story with polite skepticism.

"I have no proof," she admitted, "just a strong intuition that Mr. Gohl is up to something. I find it very odd that he would suddenly be out of business, which leads me to believe that he may have left town."

"That's not a crime."

"Not unless he's running away. In fact, I feel so sure, that I'd be willing to call in Pinkerton's. But I think you'll agree it would be better if we didn't have to."

As soon as she mentioned Pinkerton's, the chief suddenly saw the logic of her argument, and grudgingly consented to assign two officers to the case. Within an hour they found Billy Gohl, armed with a gun, sneaking down the back stairs of the Lone Jack Saloon to a waiting launch. Seeing Amanda and the police, he doffed his hat with a grin, tossed his gun into the river and gave himself up without resistance.

On September 12, 1906, Billy got his wish. His name appeared again in the *P.I.* And this time, he was mentioned in sixteen places, enough to satisfy any killer's craving for attention.

When his trial began, Amanda returned to Aberdeen to appear as a witness, accompanied by Erastus. But when the train pulled in, she was astounded to see a welcoming banner strung across the platform proclaiming "Firebrand Day," and a crowd of jubilant well-wishers eager for a glimpse of Aberdeen's heroine.

"You'd think I'd survived the Battle of Bull Run!" she whispered to Erastus.

As the trial progressed, the details of Billy's story unrolled slowly, like a mildewed carpet, each segment exposing a more rotten patch than the preceding, until at last it lay totally open, decayed beyond saving.

Not only did he confess to Jumbo Reilly's murder—which resulted in freedom for Big Fred—but to the murders of 110 other loggers. Billy was precise in the figure, for he had kept a running tally.

"Sure I'm a crimp," he boasted. "Best there ever was. I persuaded thousands of men to go to sea—thanks to my friends at the mills." He grinned slyly, casting his bottle-green gaze around the hushed courtroom. "After all, without crews, the ships don't move, and if the ships don't move, neither does lumber."

But he saved the best for last when he described how he would singlehandedly bludgeon to death any logger who dared resist conscription, robbing him first, then dropping the body through saloon trap doors into the river.

At this point, the mill owners rushed forth to plead innocent. Billy Gohl acted alone, they claimed, when he masterminded 110 murders. But Amanda wrote in her notebook that Billy *did* have collaborators —greed and corruption. Throughout the trial she kept her eye on the door, fearing that at any moment Mark would appear to join those who felt the need to absolve themselves. He never came.

As expected, Billy was found guilty. But his eccentric behavior and the bizarre nature of his crimes convinced the judge that he should be committed to the insane asylum at Steilacoom, and Billy was taken away, whistling. Amanda felt a great wave of relief. It was over. She was free to go home. To forget about Aberdeen. And forests and lumber.

As she hurried from the courtroom, the clerk handed her a note. Even before opening it, she knew it would be from Mark. She read it at once in the crowded corridor, yet she felt alone and far removed from the present.

"Dear Manka:

I realize I have no right to expect your forgiveness, nor even your willingness to read this. But I can't remain silent when I know how much I'm indebted to you for your bravery in going after the truth. I think Firebrand has proved to the world that the *real* crime in this scandal is the low esteem in which loggers are held by the very men who employ them. While I deplore the bad name which the mills have earned, I'm encouraged to believe that total honesty will make things right again. If only human error could as easily be erased! I know I've lost your love, but I hope I haven't lost your friendship. I will do *anything* to heal the wounds. You must have your paper, Manka. Don't wait any longer. I'll take comfort in knowing that Firebrand will always be there to speak out, because if she doesn't, who will?

Loving you always,
M.R."

As Amanda stared at the words, fear and indecision seemed to melt away. *He* believed in her! Nothing else mattered.

"I *won't* wait any longer," she answered aloud.

Who needs to build a plant? If I can't afford it right this minute, then I'll build it when I can. And the money will come from advertising. So for now I'll only need to take on a reporter and someone experienced in layout who'll be willing to share the risk with me until I can pay them. I'll farm out the typesetting and printing to a small press, just like Colonel Blethen did when he started the *Times*. Then I'll be in business!

In her dreams, Amanda's newspaper had been created long ago. But putting it together, making it a reality, was another matter. Having run off a sample paper, she carried it from store to store, trying to sell skeptical owners on the advantages of advertising with the Seattle *Union Record*—that was the name she had finally decided upon. However, she quickly discovered that those companies which catered to workers were easiest to sell. And on October 1, 1906, the first to commit themselves to buy space was the Grand Union Hotel.

Exhausted by the effort required to perform two jobs at the same time, Amanda was glad to accept an invitation to Mary Kenworthy's party in mid-October. She enjoyed the evening immensely, but refrained from discussing her paper. The following morning she had planned to give Erastus notice, then the whole world could be told.

She returned home from the party later than usual and in good spirits, only to discover that her street had been roped off. Pushing through a silent gathering of neighbors, she was shocked to see that the spot where her house had stood was now a gaping hole. All that remained was a blackened pile of kindling and the twisted facsimile of a stove, half melted.

"Lucky you weren't home," the policeman told her. "It was a bomb."

Staring in horror, she remembered that she had left the lights burning, as she always did when she expected to be out for the evening, so that she wouldn't have to return to a dark house. With a chill she realized that whoever had set the bomb had assumed she was inside.

Why feel surprised? Her lumber story had captured nation-wide attention. Even Joseph Pulitzer had taken notice, sending her a telegram of congratulation, berating himself for not hiring her years ago when he had had the chance.

Erastus was so shaken by the bombing that Amanda had first to calm him down before breaking the news about her decision to leave.

"I'm getting you a bodyguard," he announced, raising a hand against her protest. "No argument."

"I can't give up my freedom, Erastus," she replied firmly. "I don't want to live in fear. I'll take my chances, same as always." She took a deep breath. "Besides, I have something to tell you."

Not hearing her words, he asked, "Where are you staying?"

"At the Washington, but . . ."

"I won't have you living in a hotel. I can see that I'm going to have to take care of you myself."

"Take care of me?"

"Amanda, listen. I'm going to say something I should have said years ago. I want to marry you." He paused. "Please don't shake your head. At least think it over!"

"It's too late, Erastus. We've been friends for too long. There was a time when I might have said yes, when I was very lonely. But that wouldn't have been fair to either of us. I'm very fond of you and always will be. Let's stay as we are—friends."

"Impossible. You *know* I feel more than friendship . . ."

"Then it's just as well that I'm leaving."

"What did you say?"

"I'm giving notice. Resigning."

"But why?"

"It's not because of how you feel about me, it's because I'm going to start my own paper."

"You can't start a paper—just like that!"

"I already have." She tapped her forehead. "It's all up here. I have only to put it in motion."

"You don't have any idea what you're getting yourself into. I wouldn't advise it."

"Then you must have changed your mind. Don't you remember telling me the very first time we met that I should have a paper of my own?"

"I can't imagine saying such a thing, but I'm sure if I did, it was just a figure of speech."

"Well, I took it to heart."

"Now be reasonable. This is no time to strike out on your own. You're in danger! Tell you what, I'll announce your resignation if you like, but I won't really let you go."

"You have to. Because I'm really going."

"At least wait until this bomb thing blows over!" He was pleading now.

"While I live like Gus Johnson? Writing from some secret hiding place?" Amanda shook her head. "That's not for me."

"I'll see to it that whoever set that bomb is caught and punished!"

"What would that prove? Eliminating an anonymous somebody doesn't eliminate those who've hired him. I have enemies, Erastus, enemies who I have chosen very carefully over the years. They haven't chosen *me*. So how can I be rid of them? Not by hiding. I've made them part of my life. But if I show them I can't be intimidated, I'll survive. That's why it's even more urgent to start my paper now—to be visible and strong."

Erastus pressed his lips together in a tight smile. "I should know better than to argue." He stood up briskly. "At any rate, I don't feel much like working. Come on, I'm taking you over to the Rainier Club. I've got a table waiting for us and a bottle of champagne."

In answer to her questioning expression he added, "That's where I was planning we would celebrate—just in case you agreed to marry me. So I see no reason to cancel. This is *your* day, Amanda. And it *is* cause for celebration."

"Then you don't think me selfish and ungrateful?"

"You left Colonel Blethen to come to me. Now you're leaving me, as I knew you would someday, to move ahead. And while I admire your courage, I also feel that in a small way I've helped you prepare for this step. So I want to share the moment with you—as a friend."

Amanda smiled in relief, but her eyes filled, nonetheless.

Amanda was cleaning out her desk when the Great Northern called. Where did she wish to have her shipment of lumber delivered? Puzzled, she told them there had been a mistake—she hadn't ordered any lumber. (To herself she thought, is somebody sending me a bomb?) But they insisted it was clearly marked. It had been shipped up by rail from the Simpson Lumber Company.

Mark's note arrived separately. "To help make your dreams come true" was all it said.

Amanda's property no longer offered the commanding panorama of the Sound, the Olympics, the Cascades and Mount Tacoma, which, much to that city's dismay, had been renamed Mount Rainier. For Denny Hill no longer existed. Despite Horace Cayton's petitions and protests, the regrade project had continued on schedule. Five million cubic yards of earth were sluiced down onto the tideflats, reducing the grade to a maximum of 5 percent. The view from Amanda's land consisted of huge mounds of dirt waiting to be washed away, interspersed with a few uprooted houses perched on blocks while new foundations were being built. Most private homes, however, had either fallen to the wrecker's ball or had been moved to a more desirable location. Few home owners wanted to find themselves next door to factories or commercial buildings—the inevitable fate of those who chose to remain in the area.

However, Amanda didn't mind the idea of living in an industrial environment. The Denny Regrade, as it was called, provided the ideal site for a newspaper. *And* house. As soon as she discovered that Mark had sent more than enough surplus lumber to replace her cottage, she was inspired with the unique idea of building it actually attached to the plant. This way, not only would her house and newspaper share a common wall, but the lumber saved would allow for the construction of a second story. She would have space and privacy, yet visually the two buildings would appear in harmony as a single structure. The best part, of course, was the convenience of living as close to work as she could possibly be. So, over the protests of the architect, the plans were drawn up. Knowing that construction would begin only when the regrade was finished, Amanda went each day to watch the project steam ahead.

Progress on the regrade was monitored by an army of engineers and awe-struck citizens, the latter having found that idle hours couldn't be better spent than in watching the gradual disappearance of a mountain. But of even greater concern and fascination for them was the handful of eccentrics who had elected to hold out, of which Horace Cayton was the most notable.

Viewed from below, his Victorian mansion now resembled a grotesque sculpture, precariously balanced on a finger of earth which looked far too fragile to support it. It had not been feasible to have pipes brought up, so water had to be hauled by a pulley from the tank below, a task which kept the servants busy most of the time. Flimsy wooden stairs, no wider than a ladder, provided the only access. When the Caytons came down, they had to do so backward, as the stairway was far too steep to descend in the usual fashion. Because of this, there was always a cluster of hecklers gathered below to greet Horace each morning when he left for his office, an invasion of privacy which infuriated him. And quite often there were reporters from rival newspapers eager to print his irate comments. A "No Trespassing" sign, posted at the foot of the steps, became the butt of cartoonists' satire, for no one would have made such a foolhardy climb, even if they had been invited. Already someone had scrawled on the sign: "Mount Cayton."

Sadly, Amanda observed Horace placing himself and his family in a position of ridicule and harassment, which had transformed him into a bitter, ranting oddity. Even old friends would no longer visit, either fearing that the spindle of earth would collapse, or feeling a lack of respect for his unreasonable stand. Worse yet, his newspaper, *The Republican,* began to alienate its readers, having become a platform for stern lectures on personal freedom. Amanda was one of the few who supported Horace's argument, though she tried in vain to persuade him that he had gone too far.

One day she happened to be passing just as he was coming down, and she paused to watch his labored descent. With a pang she could see why cartoonists had chosen to portray him as a cockroach, for he looked just like one, with his rounded body hunched into shiny black coattails, inching his way down the cliff.

At the bottom he stopped to catch his breath and consult with a pair of worried engineers who were trying to explain that the earth was shifting. But Horace would have none of it, insisting it was all a trick to capture his hill. The minute he spotted Amanda, he left the engineers in mid-conversation and hurried over.

"Haven't seen *you* in quite a spell," he said gruffly. "Hope you're not here to talk some 'sense' into me!"

"Not at all," said Amanda lightly. "I'm just saying hello."

"That's a relief," said Horace, still glowering. Then he added, "Elizabeth is upstairs."

Amanda glanced up. "I'll visit another time—looks like it's going to rain."

"You're not afraid of a little climb, are you? Look at *me*—I'm older than you and I do it every day! Why, even when it rains the water drains off beautifully. You won't find any mud puddles up *there!* We're high and dry." Horace forced a chuckle. "Bet you're sorry you let them lower down that nice piece of land you had."

"I still have it, Horace. I'm building a newspaper on it."

"Your own newspaper? How did you manage that?" he asked with ill-concealed annoyance.

"I haven't managed it yet," she admitted. "I still have to find a press that I can afford, not to mention all the other equipment."

"You need a press, do you?" Horace suddenly brightened. "Well, I just so happen to have one that I'm most anxious to be rid of. And I can let you have it at a rock-bottom price."

"What wonderful luck! Are you buying a new one?"

"I'm closing up shop," he declared unblinkingly.

"I don't understand."

"I'm bankrupt, Miss Amanda. Thanks to the Denny Regrade."

"Horace, that's terrible. You can't lose your paper!"

"To tell the truth, I've gotten fed up. I've lost most of my advertisers, but when my subscribers let me down, I said that's it. The old American spirit of independence is laughed at these days, so I made up my mind to go into another line of business." His mustache curled into a sly grin. "I've been asked to teach a journalism course at the university."

"I'm glad," said Amanda, greatly relieved. "You'll be good at that."

"Elizabeth says I talk too much, so I figured I might as well be paid for it. I'm going to entitle my course 'The Pitfalls of Publishing.'"

He was still chuckling as he hurried off to climb into his carriage.

"How much is the press?" she called after him.

"Don't worry about it," she heard him answer in the distance. "I'll get it down to bedrock—just like Denny Hill."

As the *Union Record* began to take shape, Amanda's room at the Hotel Washington took on the appearance of a newspaper publisher's office. But what looked like chaos to the casual viewer was progress to Amanda, who was rushing toward a self-imposed deadline for her first edition. With construction underway and the equipment guaranteed, it was amazing how every other piece fell into place as well, including the fortuitous discovery of two eager assistants fresh out of school. Amanda remembered when she had met

Colonel Blethen how impressed she had been to learn that he had made his fortune buying up bankrupt newspapers. And now, here she was, buying out Horace Cayton, though whether she would make a fortune or not remained to be seen. And if not, what did it matter? The important thing, once begun, was to *stay* in business. Success was bound to follow.

Erastus kept in close touch, still reluctant to accept the fact that they were going their separate ways after such a long association. He continued to warn her that the running of a newspaper was an enormous responsibility for a woman. Especially a woman alone. And although she dared not admit it to him, she knew he was right. She needed a partner. Unfortunately, he couldn't be it—he wanted a wife.

One morning, after Amanda had spent a particularly restless night wondering how she was ever going to manage alone, she was awakened by an urgent knocking. Dressing hastily, she admitted the hotel manager, who came in and shut the door, after first checking the hall in both directions to make certain he hadn't been followed.

"There's a very disreputable-looking man in the lobby asking for you," he whispered. "I can't seem to get rid of him. Says he's a friend from Alaska."

Amanda's heart began thumping. "I don't know anyone from Alaska," she said, her thoughts racing back through time.

"He says he wants to surprise you—that you think he's been dead all these years."

"Oh, my God," said Amanda, her throat closing. "Soapy Smith! You didn't tell him I'm here, did you?"

"I didn't tell him anything. Shall I call the police?"

"Yes, as quickly as possible! Can you make the call without his knowledge?"

"I don't see how. The phone is right in the lobby. I'll have to go next door."

"Then hurry, don't waste time!"

As the manager started for the door, there came a sudden knock. They both froze, waiting. But the knock was not repeated, nor did a voice call out. Instead, the knob began to turn ever so slowly.

Amanda's only thought was that she was trapped—three floors up —with no chance of escape, no means to defend herself. The perfect target for a madman. Not since her brush with death at the mill had she felt that numbing sense of impending doom.

The door, however, was locked, the manager having done so himself after entering. The knob turned futilely, then a muffled voice broke the silence.

"Lamar! Open up! It's me!"

Lamar! Amanda stared at the door in shock. She knew the voice. But how was it possible? She rushed to open it, then stopped dead. For an instant she feared she had been mistaken. The man standing before her looked like a sourdough out of the past, with mackinaw, full beard and shoulder-length hair. But there was no mistaking the bright, humorous eyes, still smiling through thick glasses.

"Maynard!" she gasped. "It *is* you!" And flew to embrace him.

"DOC MAYNARD KIN BACK FROM THE DEAD!" Amanda typed. Then underneath, *"P.I.* Reporter Suffered Memory Loss."

She looked up to find Tom watching her, and smiled.

"I still can't believe you have your own paper!" He shook his head in amazement.

"And I still can't believe you're really here—after nine whole years!"

"I know we haven't had much chance to talk yet, with all the fuss and confusion, but there's something I've got to say. Not for the paper," he added quickly. "It's about us. I was so afraid to come back, thinking that you had found someone else." He waited in uncertainty. "You haven't, have you?"

Amanda glanced away. "No, there's no one."

Tom hesitated, sensing her reluctance to talk. "I guess it's too soon to discuss—anything."

"A little," she admitted.

In some respects it seemed that she and Tom had never been apart. In other ways, it was almost as though they were together for the first time, shyly becoming acquainted all over again.

"Can I see what you're writing?" he asked. "Or do I have to wait till it's in print?"

"I'll read it aloud and you can tell me if I have everything," she replied, winding the sheet out of her typewriter.

" 'Tom Maynard, grandson of Seattle's founder, sailed off to the Yukon in 1897 as a young *P.I.* reporter on assignment to cover the gold rush, and was never heard from again until the morning of November 8, 1906, when he walked into the lobby of the Hotel Washington. The presumed victim of an avalanche that had swept at least sixty men from the treacherous Dead Horse Trail, Maynard was eulogized at a memorial service held in Seattle a few months after the tragedy.'"

Amanda glanced up to catch Tom's reaction. "It was a lovely funeral. Too bad you couldn't have been there."

"Now that's damn flattering!"

They both laughed. "Read on," he urged.

"'While friends and relatives grieved, the "deceased" was off on a new adventure, not however, of his own choosing. Although Maynard had survived the ordeal of being buried alive, he suffered such a severe lapse of memory that he had no idea who he was, where he came from, or why he was there. His life became a blank. All he had ever accomplished, all he had ever loved, no longer existed. His spirit had fled, leaving only a bewildered young man, a stranger even to himself . . .'"

"God Almighty!" he interrupted. "How did you know? You've captured it exactly. I felt like I was just born, because without memory, there's no past."

"I was only guessing, trying to imagine how it was."

"It was a vast emptiness. Very, very lonely."

Not much different from an unhappy love affair, she thought.

"Read the rest," said Tom.

"'Even at the terrifying moment when the snow came roaring down the mountain, he had thought that the tree might well be his salvation, as indeed it was. But only because an air pocket had formed around the trunk, allowing him to breathe while he struggled up through the branches to the surface.'" She glanced up. "That's where your pouch was found hanging. If only I'd had the brains to figure out what had happened!"

"You couldn't have. It was sheer luck. Anyway, by the time you got there, I was on a boat underway for Nome. How? I don't know. I got dizzy coming down the mountain, and when I came to I was at sea. One minute I had my whole life ahead of me and a wonderful future—with you. The next minute I had nothing. No one to love, no one to miss."

"Don't think about it any more."

"I have to. That's part of the story."

"At least your memory came back. How long did it take?"

"I don't really know. A year—maybe more. At any rate, it didn't come back all at once, but gradually, a glimpse at a time. Until finally I was able to piece together what had happened."

"How was it in Nome?"

"In a way, prospecting there was easier than in the Yukon. It was too far north to attract the average stampeder, so gold nuggets could often be picked up right off the beach. But by that point, gold didn't hold much fascination for me." A note of bitterness crept into his voice.

"There must have been some good times," she suggested quickly. "Didn't you ever meet any women?"

"There was one," he admitted with a certain reluctance. "She was a prospector, too. I was desperate for companionship. I didn't make any friends because I was afraid someone would ask where I was from and I wouldn't know what to answer. But she never asked me anything."

"Did you love her?"

"Love? I only know that when I saw this woman, I felt a terrible longing. Maybe it was for you. I wanted her—if only to remind myself that I was still a human being, capable of feelings."

"That was good," said Amanda gently. "You kept your sanity."

"We lived together. And were happy—for as long as it lasted. But when my memory began to come back, I became very confused, not knowing whether to stay or leave. Finally I decided it would be better for everyone if I simply let the world go on thinking I was dead. I couldn't bear the agony of coming home to find you married."

Amanda's thoughts had drifted. She was picturing Mark on his wedding day, taking the arm of his bride, while she watched helplessly from the sidelines, invisible to all. Her interlude with Mark, however brief, had really been another lifetime—complete with a beginning, middle and end. A short, separate life within the span of a greater lifetime, just like Tom had experienced.

"What became of her?"

"The woman?" He smiled ironically. "No sooner did I decide to remain with her, than she ran off with someone else."

Amanda nodded sympathetically.

"That's life," said Tom.

"You should have kept a diary."

"I did," he remembered suddenly. "Want to see it?"

Amanda had not expected the weighty bulging journal which Tom set before her. She opened it with curiosity, but the minute she began turning the pages, she realized that what he had written was far more than a simple account of daily life in the Arctic. It was a man's personal struggle with his own sanity, his search for some meaning to his life. In a kind of bitter irony it was the definitive story of the gold rush, a tragedy of greed and disillusionment, of hope and enlightenment, of a generation forced to grow up. It cried out to be rushed into print, and she knew at once that it must be published without further delay.

She looked up excitedly. "Do you realize what you have here?"

Tom managed a modest smile. "A good story, I hope."

"A good story for the *Union Record!* I'll serialize it!"

"Do you really think it belongs in a union paper?"

"Listen, Maynard, the gold rush affected *everyone*—the workers most of all. This is a story of you and me—of people!"

"Then use it. You know I wouldn't refuse you. Just think," he marveled again, "your own paper! I'm so proud of you."

"How would you like to be part of it?" she asked suddenly.

"You mean—work for you as a reporter?"

"Work *with* me, as a partner. What do you say?"

"I don't know," he answered slowly. "I'll have to think about it."

"I *need* a partner," she added. "Don't worry about Erastus. Much as I'm sure he'd like to have you back, I know he'll give you his blessing. Of course he's still in a state of shock that I'm striking out on my own, but he'll get over it."

Tom studied Amanda intently. "I've often thought of you and Brainerd. I know you've worked together for a long time. What I wonder is—I mean, was there ever . . . ?" His question hung in the air unfinished. "Well, that's none of my business, is it?"

"Was there ever anything between us? Nothing more than friendship."

"There's been no one, then?"

"I didn't say that. There was someone. But it's all over, Maynard."

"It's good to hear you calling me 'Maynard' again. It's like a reassuring echo from the past telling me that everything is all right. Is it?"

"I wouldn't ask you to be my partner if I didn't think so."

Tom's anxious eyes seemed to relax, his expression softened. He took her hand. "Lamar, if you want me to work with you, I will. Whatever you want is what I want. I'd do anything to turn back the years, to have things the way they were."

"We're not children any more, Maynard, with our whole lives ahead of us. We've been through too much. I don't want to build on the memory of how it used to be, but on the future. So let's not look back. Let's take each day as it comes. For now, let's build a news-paper—together."

Chapter Seventeen

AMANDA opened her eyes to the steady rhythmic vibration of machinery drumming against the bedroom wall. Its muffled throb was the most reassuring sound in the world—the pulse beat of her soul. It told her that another edition of the *Union Record* had gone to press, permitting her to relax, though briefly, until next time. The welcome moment of rising was always one of unbounded anticipation, with each day promising to be different from the one before, and yet never quite as exciting as the one to follow.

Unwilling to lose a minute, she threw back the bedclothes and reached for her dressing gown. The bracing sting of dry October air stirred the curtains and chilled the floor. Nevertheless, she hurried out into the hall, too impatient to bother with slippers, and was halfway down the stairs when a familiar knock reminded her that she had promised Tom she'd be ready early today.

"Coming!" Damn! She could see him through the curtains in the door. *He's going to surprise me with a gift, and here I am, not even dressed.*

"Happy anniversary!" he greeted.

It was exactly five years ago on October 15, 1907, that the *Union Record* opened its doors. She would never forget the thrill of that first moment, when she had led the way inside, followed by ten eager employees, and went directly to inspect the giant presses. Though secondhand, they were a magnificent sight—oiled, inked and ready to roll, while two pressmen stood nervously by, waiting for the signal to set them into motion. They came to life with a roar, just as she knew they would, and immediately began to devour the column of paper with neat precision, drawing applause from a staff who did not have to be told that they were witnessing a historic occasion.

Tom thrust a small package tied with silver ribbon into her hand.

"Is that for me?" she asked, knowing of course that it was.

Tom smiled, pleased that she was surprised. As he leaned forward to kiss her, she turned her head slightly, so that his lips grazed her cheek.

"Come on in, I was just about to make coffee."

"Aren't you going to open it?"

"Of course," she said, tearing off the wrapping. "I never dreamed you'd get me anything."

"Why not? It's your special day."

"We're partners, Maynard. So it's your special day, too. I think I owe *you* a present for putting up with me all this time."

"Being close to you is enough for me."

Amanda gave him a helpless smile. He still loved her, still held out hope. She wanted to return his love, but it hadn't worked out. He had remained a boy, immature enough to think they could turn back the clock and start their lives again from the point where they had left off.

She opened the box almost fearfully, hoping it wouldn't be something expensive. It was. The black velvet mold wore an exquisite necklace of carved ivory and green jade.

"It's lovely!" she gasped. "I've never seen anything like it." She threw her arms around Tom and gave him a hasty kiss.

"It was made by Alaskan Indians," he offered, beaming.

"Here, fasten it for me. I'm going to wear it to work. It will go perfectly with my green suit."

Tom secured the clasp, then kissed her on the neck. Amanda turned to the mirror hanging over the sideboard and viewed herself with critical narrowed eyes. Not bad for thirty-three. But how will I look at forty? Is my neck getting crepy? she wondered, leaning closer. That was the unfortunate thing about jewelry. It drew attention to the very parts of the body which were the first to age.

"It's made for you," said Tom admiringly.

"It feels so heavy," she said, then added quickly, "but I love it." Her words were sincere, yet why did she feel vaguely disturbed? Perhaps it was because he needed to please her, to give her something which she had never had before, while she could never give him what he wanted in return.

The façade of the *Union Record* building displayed a banner announcing: "Fifth Anniversary Open House—October 15, 1912—Public Welcome." And though the doors weren't open yet, when Amanda and Tom arrived she was delighted to find a small crowd waiting outside the entrance. She greeted them enthusiastically, promising that each visitor would receive a free copy of the special anniversary edition and a piece of cake.

Inside, the entire plant was decorated with paper streamers and balloons of every color, which the employees had done on their own as a surprise.

Amanda squeezed Tom's arm. "Isn't this fun?" she asked.

"They love you," said Tom. "And they should."

"They love both of us," she reminded. "They work for you as well as for me."

Tom smiled indulgently, but his shrug told her that he knew it wasn't true. They may have been partners, but Amanda was the guiding light. It had been a satisfactory arrangement, however, for Tom had instinctively gravitated to the background. He had shown a surprising aptitude for administrative duties, so as time went on, it was only natural that he would end up running the plant, while Amanda remained as the idea person, the vital entity who sparked controversy among her readers and inspired the respect of her employees. She credited Tom's easygoing manner with making the situation work, a blessing for both of them.

Like every other morning, Amanda's desk was covered with telephone messages, mail, advertising and copy proofs. But today, in the midst of the litter, reposed a large basket of flowers and several packages, addressed to her personally.

She smiled when she saw the flowers, knowing who they were from before she even looked at the card. It said simply: "To Amanda, Happy Fifth Anniversary, Fondly, Erastus." Next she opened a cardboard tube containing a calendar for 1913 which featured an illustration of the *Times* building. The card read: "From my house to yours—may you enjoy fifty more years of success, Aff., A. Blethen." Amanda laughed aloud, shaking her head. She held it up for Tom to see through the glass partition which separated their offices. He laughed also and shook his head. It had taken him a long time to get used to the idea of having a glass-enclosed office situated right in the center of the building. He called it a display case, declaring that it made him feel like a rare gem. But he didn't complain, knowing that Amanda favored such an arrangement. She firmly believed that privacy had no place at a newspaper.

Last of all she opened a modest-looking packet from Cosmopolis. It contained an envelope of Western Hemlock seeds with planting instructions. There was no card. This was the fifth year that she had received a seed packet from Mark, but each time one arrived, she would feel a pull from the past, a dim nostalgic longing which she knew she would never get over.

Her thoughts were disrupted by Tom, rapping on the glass. When she looked up, he motioned for her to show him what was in the package.

"Another tree," he mouthed when she held it up for him to see; shrugging, he turned away.

Mark had never visited the *Union Record* to see what his lumber had built. But if he ever did, she knew he would be pleased to discover that it shared a common wall with her house. He would appreciate her need to feel the presses pulsating against her bed, just as he found comfort in hearing the screaming of saws when he fell asleep each night.

By nine o'clock a hundred visitors had taken advantage of the invitation to see how a newspaper worked. They toured the plant, received their souvenir copies of the paper, and lined up to shake Amanda's hand.

When it was time to cut the cake, she made a speech telling them that the *Union Record* was proud of its employees and grateful to its readers.

"Together we've built an outstanding weekly newspaper," she reminded them, "the only one of its kind in the Pacific Northwest. We have some employees who've been with us long enough to remember that we were obliged to crank out our first edition—four whole pages —in a small printing shop on Yesler Way, the same shop in which my distinguished colleague, Colonel Blethen, started the *Times* over sixteen years ago. We've now grown to eight pages. And who knows where we'll go from here? With our population close to 250,000, perhaps someday we, too, will become a daily."

When the applause had subsided, she added that the *Record*

wouldn't be where it was today were it not for Tom's hard work. Then she introduced each employee, knowing everyone by name, and commented on their accomplishments. She saved for last a young woman whom she was proud to say had just been hired as a *pressman*. Visitors and employees alike greeted the announcement with laughter, certain that it had been intended as a joke. But Amanda quickly assured them that the girl was just as qualified for the job as any man, and she hoped that the other papers in town would take note.

Later Tom whispered to Amanda, "I hope you made the right decision."

"About what?"

"About putting a girl in the pressroom. I noticed our head pressman is wearing a very sour expression."

"He'll survive," said Amanda with a smile. "My only regret is that I've never had time to learn the job myself."

At noon the invited guests began arriving for the luncheon. Hurriedly Amanda showed Tom the guest list. He recited the names aloud in a bewildered voice, "Reggie Thomson? May Hutton—from Spokane? Judge Green! Abigail Duniway from Portland—*the* Abigail Duniway? Dr. McCulloch, Walter Sutherland—my gosh! Mary Kenworthy, Erastus . . ." He skimmed over the others, then looked up. "You mean to say you've gathered the city engineer, a women's leader, a famous writer and all those other professionals together just to meet our employees? Come on, Lamar!"

"And they've all accepted. Oh yes, and one more whose name isn't on the list—George Cotterill."

"The mayor? Good God!" Tom began to laugh. "You really think he'll come?"

"Of course. He already told me he would."

"You've met him?"

"Only by phone. I called him up to introduce myself and congratulate him on winning the election. He said that someday he'd like a tour of the plant, so I said he should come to our party. And he said he'd be delighted."

"Well, what else could he say? He was probably just being polite."

"I don't think so. He said he'd look forward to meeting me."

"Naturally. Everybody wants to meet Firebrand, don't they?"

Tom pretended to tease, but his remarks sometimes hurt. Amanda made no reply.

George Cotterill was a fit and youthful forty-seven, and didn't mind telling his age. He still spoke with a slight British accent, even though he had come to Seattle from England many years ago. However, he had not entered politics as an unknown, for he had worked under Reginald Thomson as assistant city engineer, helping to formulate the plans for reconstructing Seattle's water supply system and the topography of part of Puget Sound. He was modest about his accomplishments, preferring to talk about the future. At the luncheon he made it a point to speak to each *Record* employee, showing great interest in what everyone had to say.

"Looks like Cotterill's already campaigning for re-election!" Tom whispered, nudging Amanda. She only laughed.

After lunch, as everyone was milling about still sipping champagne, Erastus took Amanda aside. "George seems to be quite taken with you," he remarked.

"Mayor Cotterill? Why, we've hardly spoken."

Erastus smiled. "Give him time. He asked me earlier if you were married."

Amanda felt her cheeks flare. "I'll bet his wife would be happy to hear that." She took a quick sip. "You should have told him yes!"

"Somehow, I don't think it would make any difference."

Amanda swallowed and stared into her glass. When she glanced up, Erastus had drifted off and George Cotterill was making his way over.

"Don't I get a personal tour?" he asked, smiling.

"I'd be glad to take you through," said Amanda, "if I can persuade my partner to entertain our guests while we're absent."

"I'm sure he wouldn't refuse you."

However, when Amanda began to look about, Tom was nowhere to be found. She turned to Cotterill apologetically. "I'm afraid we'll have to make it another time. Mr. Maynard seems to have disappeared."

"A pity," he said in disappointment. "But at least I have an excuse to pay you another visit."

When the last guest had departed, Amanda hurried next door, wondering if Tom was waiting for her at home. A young man who looked vaguely familiar was standing at the gate. The minute he saw her, his hand shot out.

"Howdy, Miss Lamar! You don't remember me, do you?"

Amanda blinked for a moment. "I'm trying to place you."

"Clarance Ballard's the name. We rode down to the Aberdeen fire together back in '04. I was the *Times* reporter—and still am. You let me copy your notes."

"Now I remember."

"I've really gone places, thanks to you," he gushed. "Sure appreciated the helping hand."

"Well, don't forget to extend *your* hand to a fellow reporter on the way up," she reminded him, thinking to herself that he seemed just as inept as the first time they met, and wondering why Blethen had kept him on.

"Anything in particular you'd like to say about your achievements?" he asked, reading from a list of prepared questions.

"We fought for suffrage—and won. We campaigned for the eight-hour day for women, for workmen's compensation and a minimum wage. Also, I believe we're the first press in the Northwest to put a woman into a man's job. Our immediate concern is the workers' right to strike, and our ongoing goal is to promote safe and decent working conditions for every man and woman in this city. Anything else you'd like to know?"

"Do you support Woodrow Wilson for President?"

Amanda laughed. "Yes. For obvious reasons."

The reasons were not obvious, however, to Clarance Ballard, so Amanda explained that Wilson seemed to favor labor, and quoted from a recent speech in which he had said: ". . . The conservation of human life and energy lies even nearer to our interest than the preservation from waste of our material resources."

"How do you feel about the Industrial Workers of the World?"

"There's nothing wrong with a world-wide labor union. But their success remains to be seen. At any rate, the *Union Record* has never denied the Wobblies a chance to speak. Now, if you'll excuse me, I have a meeting with my partner."

"I don't think so, Miss Lamar. I just saw him leave and get into a taxi."

"You did? When?"

"Right before you came. I tried to interview him, but he said he didn't have time."

"Interview him?"

"I wanted to know if it's true that he frequents John Considine's gambling houses? Maybe you can tell me."

Amanda stared aghast. "Where did you hear that?"

"It was a tip from Mr. Considine himself," he admitted readily. "Do you have any comment?"

"Only that it's a lie!" she replied, and turning away in anger, hurried up the steps.

An hour later Tom arrived on her doorstep carrying an enormous bird cage.

"What on earth . . . !"

"Another present," he said, grinning broadly. "Lovebirds."

Amanda gave him a bewildered smile. "Lovebirds? How nice." She approached them cautiously. "But you already gave me a present."

"They're really for both of us, only I thought you should look after them. The big one's Caesar, the small one's Cleo. Colorful, aren't they?"

"I didn't know you liked birds."

"I didn't know I did, either. I just bought them on impulse. They reminded me of us."

How could she mention the Considine incident to him *now?*

"Well, what do you think?"

"They're very exotic-looking," she said, frowning. "I hope they get along."

"The man who sold them to me guaranteed they'd be faithful to each other till death," he replied confidently.

Amanda smiled, but the sight of the caged birds made her feel unexplainably sad.

"Dinner tonight?" he asked.

"This is Wednesday. Had you forgotten?"

"Damn! I swear it's always Wednesday! Don't you think the presses could roll without you just this once?"

"Of course they could. But I don't want them to. Can't we make it tomorrow?"

"I guess so." Tom shrugged in disappointment. "It's just that tonight is the Stampeder's Club dinner. I wanted you to come and hear my speech."

"I'm sorry, Maynard. But why don't you drop over afterwards for a brandy?"

"Just you and me?" he asked hopefully.

"For brandy only," she emphasized.

It was midnight when Amanda finally decided she couldn't stay awake another minute and went upstairs to bed. She was glad that Tom hadn't shown up after all. But no sooner had she dozed off, than she was awakened by the sound of his uneven step on the front porch. Still half asleep, she struggled into her dressing gown and hurried downstairs.

When she opened the door, he tottered for a moment, squinting at the light.

"Did I wake you up?" he asked thickly.

"It's all right," she sighed. "How was your speech?"

"Brilliant, as always," he replied, steadying himself as he marched past her, heading for the parlor. "Kept them on the edge of their seats for an hour and a half."

"What on earth did you say all that time?"

"Oh, I told them about the avalanche and how I survived it."

"Haven't you given that speech before?"

"Well, sure. I give it every year—for the benefit of the new members. They *ask* me to give it." Tom took off his collar, dropping his collar buttons on the floor. "Matter of fact, I think they're going to ask me to run for President again. Which I'll probably win."

"Wonderful," said Amanda sleepily.

"Where are Caesar and what's-her-name?"

"I put them in the dining room by the window so that they have a view."

As she watched Tom fumbling with his jacket, the throb of the press could be heard through the wall.

"Damn press!" he grumbled. "I don't know how you can sleep with that thing vibrating the whole house."

"I like it," she murmured. "I like to know that while I'm sleeping, the papers are rolling out."

"If I lived here, I'd take the back bedroom, as far away from that wall as I could get."

"Maynard, I'm tired. If you want to stay over, you're welcome to the back bedroom."

"You think I'm drunk, don't you?" Tom sat down heavily. "Well, I am. That's why you don't want to sleep with me."

"Go to bed, Maynard. Or you're going to hate yourself in the morning."

When Tom came down to breakfast, he found Amanda reading the paper. She didn't look up.

He sat down sheepishly. "God, but I must have been drunk last night! How did I end up in the spare room?"

She wasn't listening. "Maynard, there's something in the *Times* about you." She tossed the copy across the table. "It says you can be found more often at John Considine's gambling establishments than you can at your desk!"

"Does it mention which ones?"

"It's not true, is it?"

"Aw, come on! I may have gone once or twice after a club meeting just for a few hands of poker. But I certainly don't sneak off in the middle of the afternoon."

"Then it *is* true! How *could* you? Don't you know that Considine tipped off the *Times* himself?"

"So what? It's not the end of the world," he said with a laugh.

"He's opposed to everything we stand for! He must be getting a good laugh out of this!"

"Are you still brooding over that dispute you had with him so many years ago? That's all in the past."

"So's the gold rush! Didn't you do enough gambling for ten years? Do you still think you're going to strike it rich?"

"Thank God you're surrounded by factories and don't have any neighbors to hear you yelling," said Tom, digging at his grapefruit.

Amanda pushed back her chair and stood up. "Personally, I don't care what you do. But for the sake of the paper, I'm asking you not to go there any more. Don't undermine all we've worked for. This may come as a surprise to you, but there are people out there who'd like nothing better than to see us fail. I'm not going to let that happen."

Early in June Amanda felt that she needed a vacation. It would have been fun to go camping out at Alki Point or canoeing down the

Duwamish River, but in the end, she decided to spend her vacation at home. However, the thought of doing nothing was out of the question, so she hired a young Norwegian girl, Else, to come in for a week to help her with the house-cleaning.

She and Else laundered draperies, washed windows, then hung the summer curtains. Amanda loved the whole ritual, especially putting up screens, so that the windows could be opened wide to the balmy breezes blowing off the Sound, and the fragrance of blossoms. The smell of coal smoke also blew in, each year a little stronger than the year before, but it was tolerable, if only for the pleasure of being able to enjoy bright and airy rooms for three months. There was, however, one small mishap while the screens were being put up. Cleo somehow managed to open the door of the cage and fly out. For hours she sidestepped along the tops of the mirrors and picture frames but could not be coaxed back to her perch, though Caesar waited patiently, too timid to follow her. Later, forgetting that Cleo was loose, Else had opened a window. The next thing they knew, Cleo had taken wing, and though they whistled and called for her to return, they saw it was hopeless. She had become only a flash of yellow, green and blue, growing smaller as she soared over the chimneys and smokestacks. Amanda watched until she disappeared. Though she knew Tom would be unhappy when he found out what had happened, she was glad that Cleo had won her freedom.

When Amanda returned to work, she was pleasantly surprised to discover that Tom had thrived in her absence. Proudly he showed her the editorial which he had turned out, having made her promise not to pick up a paper during her vacation. She quickly read the issue she had missed, relieved to see that he had taken a firm hand in defense of the *Record*'s position on strikes and boycotts. In recent years a growing number of industrialists had begun to criticize the paper sharply for urging workers to "insurrection," as they put it. But Tom had steadfastly declared in his editorial that they would continue to encourage the working force to become aware of their rights and demand them. Therefore, they would support any strikes or boycotts that might result.

"I couldn't have said it better," she complimented. "I wish I could talk you into doing more of these." She glanced at Tom hopefully. But he shrugged off the praise with a laugh.

"That's your domain, Lamar. I'm an administrator."

"I hope by choice," she ventured. "I'd hate to think you felt stifled in some boring job, when you'd much prefer a more active role."

"Have I complained?"

She thought for a moment. "I guess not, but I know there are things we don't agree on, that you would like to do differently."

"No partners can ever agree 100 percent."

"I mean—I don't want to hold you back from something else you might want to do."

Tom looked at her oddly. "Like—a different job?"

"Sort of."

"Are you trying to get rid of me?"

"Oh, Maynard, it's nothing like that. It's just that you seem to do so much better when I'm not around."

"That's a queer thing to say."

"I want us to be honest with each other. I want you to tell me the things that you would change if you could."

"And will you do the same?"

"I don't need to. I have everything my way already. That's the problem."

"Well, I don't know of any problem," said Tom sharply. "Are you looking for one?"

Before she could answer, he turned abruptly and walked back into his office.

Now it was Amanda's turn to wish they didn't have glass partitions. It was painful to watch Tom hunched over his desk, frowning into a mound of paperwork, pausing now and then to remove his glasses and rub his eyes. She noticed with a pang that his curly hair was thinning. At thirty-nine he no longer looked like a boy. Yet, he only wanted life to go on as it was, even if it meant settling for an existence that had to be far from satisfying.

Amanda felt very much alone that summer. The glass wall which separated her from Tom might well have been a desert stretching for a thousand miles. He no longer wished to be consulted on policy, he said. Amanda should use her own judgment. When she told him that she planned to introduce a new feature disseminating union news and employment opportunities in the Chinook jargon for the benefit of the Siwash, he only smiled and shrugged. He had no suggestions. He neither agreed nor disagreed.

In early August, Mayor Cotterill invited Amanda to a special luncheon at city hall for Seattle business leaders, surprising her with a plaque honoring her efforts on behalf of the Siwash. Amanda could hardly believe this unexpected good fortune. Having the mayor's endorsement would give the *Union Record* a strong boost.

"I'm so grateful, George," she told him later in private. "You won't mind if I publicize the fact that we have your support?"

"Rest assured, I'd consider it a favor," he said, then added, "We're allies, Amanda. I hope I made that clear to everyone."

"I'm glad. I need allies more than ever."

"By the way, I noticed that Mr. Maynard didn't come. I hope nothing's wrong."

"You mean he didn't send his regrets?"

"Not a word."

"Then it was probably my fault. He must have thought I would respond for him. At any rate, he couldn't come because this is the day we go to press and one of us has to be there."

"I understand. A dedicated, hard-working chap like that is only to be admired."

When Amanda rose to leave, he walked her to the door and kissed her hand. "And I admire you, as well," he said.

Amanda accepted his flattery graciously. It was obvious that he found her attractive, but it was also obvious that he saw the *Union Record* as a powerful and important voice for his own office. She would never have to worry about his attentions—she had the upper hand.

Tom learned of Cotterill's position the following morning when Amanda showed him her front-page story. He read it with a grin.

"That gay blade Cotterill seems to know which side his bread is buttered on," he commented, tossing the paper aside.

"Why do you say that?"

"Look at all the free publicity we're giving him—letting the whole world know what a liberal mayor we have! No wonder he gave us an award."

"So what? We're allies. We can help each other."

Tom snatched up the paper again. "You quote him right here, 'Rest assured, I'd consider it a favor.' You see? We're doing him a favor. Now he owes *us!*"

In mid-August Amanda gave more than usual coverage to Potlatch Days, reminding readers that the annual celebration was originally inspired by the Indian tradition of gift-giving. It was also the time for union parades and picnics, a chance for the workers to demonstrate their solidarity. With so much additional advertising and announcements, the special Potlatch edition of the *Record* ran to sixteen pages—at no increase in price.

At Amanda's insistence, Tom looked it over before going to press, then nodded his approval.

"I'm glad we're not running anything for the Wobblies," he told her. "I thought for certain they'd try to worm their way in."

"But they *are* in," she replied. "They bought a four-page supplement." She handed it to him.

"God damn! I wish you'd said something before."

"I didn't think you were interested. What's wrong?"

"A *lot*. You should see them operate—night after night this maniac leader of theirs—this Carl Gerhardt—has been taking to his soap box down on the Skid Road to preach the virtues of socialism, while the police just stand by and do nothing!"

"So that's where you spend your time."

"I haven't been gambling," he said defensively. "I just go with the boys for refreshments after the Stampeder's Club closes. Anyway, the Wobblies are all over town, not just on the Skid Road. I even saw them in front of the *Times* building one night. Blethen was madder than hell, and I don't blame him."

"Well, I may not agree with everything they stand for, but they have a right to speak."

"To preach anarchy and revolution?"

"Maynard, they've been around for years. Why all the excitement?"

"Obviously you don't consider them a threat, but if you could see that Gerhardt with a crazed look in his eye stirring up all the loggers and migrants and every other down-and-outer imaginable, you'd think twice about free speech!"

"Sorry, I don't agree. When it comes to the basic freedoms, there's no compromise."

"Well, if I had any say-so around here, I'd take this supplement and stuff it down Gerhardt's throat."

Amanda laughed. "That, I'm sure, would be most interesting."

The supplement remained, but Amanda's Potlatch editorial was scrapped. She made no objection, however, when Tom announced that he intended to write one of his own—"to balance opinion," he said—for it was obvious that he needed to assert himself as a partner and decision-maker. As she expected, he used the opportunity to attack the Industrial Workers of the World, warning that their goal was to undermine America. He urged the working force not merely to ignore them, but to run them out of town.

Amanda thought he had gone too far by inviting violence at a time when organized labor was finally beginning to make progress. But Tom declared he hadn't gone far enough.

A week later, when Amanda was invited to Spokane, by women's leader May Hutton, to speak at a journalism conference, she almost declined in fear of what Tom might do while she was gone. He had taken such an unreasonable stand that it seemed he had left himself no possibility of backing down. Because of this, the *Record* was at a crossroads, torn between two directions. Even as she was becoming more keenly aware of her expanding obligations as a publisher, Tom's viewpoint continued to grow narrower. Supposing they canceled each other out? Nevertheless, she decided that the conference was too important to pass up. Mrs. Hutton piqued her interest when she told her that social reformist Anna Louise Strong had also been invited to speak. She had noticed Anna Strong's name in the news with increasing frequency, for she was not only a novelist, poet and playwright, but was active in children's welfare, leading the fight against child labor.

It proved to be a stimulating meeting and Amanda was thankful that she had made the decision to attend. In fact, she wouldn't have given Tom a thought the whole time had she not received a phone call from George Cotterill on her fourth day away from home.

"I don't mean to alarm you," he began, "but your partner came to see me yesterday. He was quite upset."

Amanda felt her stomach drop. Even before hearing the details, she immediately regretted having left Tom on his own. "What's he done now?" she asked.

"He was in a rather belligerent mood. He stormed into my office, demanding that I issue an injunction to prevent the Wobblies from speaking in public. At first I thought he couldn't be serious, that it was some kind of joke, and tried to laugh it off. But that only infuriated him. He challenged me to support him on the basis of *my* friendship with *you!* Can you imagine? He said, 'If you really care for Miss Lamar, you'll back us up.' He acted as though you were in on it, too. But of course I knew better. Then he babbled on saying something about how I owed him a favor. I honestly don't know what he was talking about."

"Oh, George, I could die! Had he been drinking?"

"As far as I could tell, he was quite sober. At any rate, I had to have him removed forcibly from my office. So I thought I'd better let you know in case there's a row when you get back."

"Believe me, I've never known him to do such a thing. George, I'm so sorry!"

"Don't apologize for him, Amanda. The way I see it, he must be jealous of our friendship. The poor chap probably feels left out."

"Yes, left out," she repeated slowly. "I'm sure you're right."

"I don't give it a second thought. I'm certain he could kick himself for having caused a scene. When you get home you can assure him that I'm not angry and have forgotten the whole thing."

At the end of the week when Amanda returned to Seattle, Tom acted as though nothing had happened. She waited for him to say something, and when he didn't, she asked him if all had gone well in her absence.

"Extremely well," he replied emphatically.

But in his eyes she read the hurt and fury which had banished the easy smile, the carefree laugh she was so used to. Now his jaw was tight, his movements quick and tense. He tossed her the paper.

"You'll see from my editorial that Cotterill has shown his true colors. But I took care of him. I've demanded that he be recalled."

"You've what?" Amanda asked in a faint voice. As she took the paper from him, she felt as if the blood were slowly draining from her body. He had written: "Anarchy, the grizzly hydra-headed serpent which Seattle has been forced to nourish in its midst by a naturalized chief executive for eighteen months, shall be plucked from this city only when our upstart mayor with his plastered-down hair and his treacly English manners is recalled from office . . ."

Too numb to speak, Amanda dropped the paper without reading further, and walked back to her desk. She picked up the phone and asked central for the *P.I.*

"Erastus?" Her voice quavered. "I need your help."

"I know," he replied soothingly. "I've been expecting your call. You want me to run a retraction on Tom's editorial?"

"You saw it?"

"I'm afraid by now everybody in town has seen it."

"Write it for me, Erastus. You know what to say. I'm too upset to think clearly." She paused to swallow the tears. "He's going to destroy us! What shall I do?"

"Buy him out," he replied without hesitation. "Get rid of him."

While Erastus urged her to remain calm, she could see Tom smiling quizzically through the glass, shaking his head, not understanding why she wouldn't back him up.

Chapter Eighteen

I<small>T WAS</small> a warm July day in 1914 when Anna Louise Strong stepped through the door of the *Union Record* for the first time. Heads turned in curiosity. A wiry athletic woman with stylishly bobbed hair, intense black eyes and suntanned complexion, she wore khaki knickers and knee-high boots. Several loops of brightly woven climbing rope hung over her shoulder with crampons dangling. She glanced about perplexed, like a hiker who had strayed up the wrong trail.

Amanda looked up from her desk. "Anna Louise—you're here!"

"I seem to be, don't I?" she said, breaking into a wide grin.

"I thought you were going to call me when you got in so that I could pick you up?"

"The train was early," she explained cheerfully, "so I decided to stretch my legs and look over the town."

Amanda smiled at her climbing rope. "I see you came prepared."

"I never travel without hiking gear—just in case. Actually, I intend to scale Mount Rainier. Care to join me?"

"I'm afraid I'm not very experienced, but I'm sure you'll have no trouble getting a party together. Anyway, I'm awfully glad you could come."

"It was good of you to ask me." She glanced about. "Looks like your paper's going full steam."

"I used to know everybody's name, but now I've got so many new employees that it no longer seems like a family. Sometimes I think we're getting too big."

"Nonsense. You're only suffering pangs of success."

Amanda laughed. "Come on, I live right next door. Let's get you settled first, then I'll show you around."

Anna Louise immediately made herself at home. "I don't want any fuss," she stated. "I'm used to looking after myself." She hung up her rope on the hall tree.

It was good to have someone to talk to. Amanda had to admit it had been lonely since Tom left, for despite their differences, she had grown used to him. Her only regret was that they hadn't parted on better terms. Tom had been bitterly opposed to dissolving their partnership, begging for a second chance one minute, making irresponsible accusations the next. But in the end he accepted the inevitable, telling Amanda that he had decided to leave Seattle for good. He claimed that the happiest years of his life had been spent in Alaska, so he had made up his mind to give it another try. He insisted that gold could still be found, that there was a fortune to be made for those willing to stick it out. She watched him leave with a trace of sadness, wondering if he would ever find what he was searching for. Now the *Union Record* was hers alone.

Anna Louise lit a cigarette and wandered restlessly from room to room, as if trying to absorb the feeling of a new environment. Watching her, Amanda was struck by the thought that many of her friends were now younger than she was. Anna Louise appeared to be still in her twenties, while Amanda was already thirty-five.

"Now, Anna Louise, you must tell me everything you've been up to."

"First, my friends call me 'Lou,' so you must also. As for what I've been up to, I can tell you some things that will stand your hair on end. Want to hear?"

Amanda nodded eagerly and waved to a chair, but Lou continued pacing about the room, too consumed by nervous energy to sit still.

"Don't you feel that the world's changing for the worst?" she asked suddenly. "That some unspeakable violence lies ahead?" Presuming an affirmative reply, she went on, "Well, it's not just your imagination. There's a real basis for anxiety, and anybody who doesn't feel it isn't alive."

Hearing the words fly and watching the animated gestures, Amanda couldn't help but envy the bottled lightning of youth, flashing one minute in anger, the next in contempt, but always relieved by a burst of sudden laughter. Lou punctuated her comments with explosive puffs of smoke while she explained how a recent trip to Europe had made her aware that something was in the air.

"America had better realize we've got more to worry about than internal upheaval. There's going to be war!"

"You mean because of the assassination of Archduke Ferdinand?"

"That and a thousand other reasons," she declared sweepingly. "All the young men I met in Paris are just itching to march off and fight the Germans. Can you believe they think it's noble to be sacrificed in a stupid war?"

"Will you write an article for me?" Amanda asked suddenly. "About the situation in Europe?"

Lou was delighted. Proclaiming herself antiwar, she didn't hesitate to suggest that if the United States were to embrace socialism, it could avoid the conflict which Europe was facing. "War is a capitalistic scheme to make the rich richer and the poor dead," she declared.

By a stroke of fateful timing, her article appeared only a few days before war broke out in Europe on July 28. By August 5, 1914, the fighting began with Germany's invasion of France. Everyone who had read Lou's prediction of war and her advice for avoiding involvement, now looked to the *Union Record* for guidance. Amanda saw at once the chance to capitalize on this surge of interest, and asked Lou to do a series on war from the socialist point of view. Within a month, the *Record* was converted from a weekly to Seattle's third daily newspaper, with Anna Louise Strong as managing editor.

In late August Seattle prepared once again to celebrate Potlatch Days, with Secretary of the Navy, Josephus Daniels, invited as a special guest. No sooner had this announcement been made, than the IWW asked to take an eight-page supplement in the *Record* instead of four pages, as they had the previous year.

As Amanda looked over the copy which they had submitted, she knew immediately that she had a potentially explosive situation on her hands. The main article was authored by Carl Gerhardt, the Wobblies' spirited local leader, whom Tom had denounced as a red menace. True, Gerhardt's name was becoming known for inciting riots, yet he didn't write like the usual rabble-rouser or fanatic, but like a visionary. She had never heard him speak, though she imagined that his ability to captivate an audience was more the result of what he said, not how loud he shouted. Entitled "Guilty of Murder," the article hit hard at the lumber industry in a manner disturbingly reminiscent of the days of Gus Johnson. Not since Billy Gohl's trial had such shocking practices come to light. It dwelt in unsparing detail on injuries inflicted by thugs to subdue rebellious workers—many of these thugs being "respected citizens."

The lumber trust, it said, controlled governors, legislatures and courts; directed mayors and city councils; completely owned sheriffs and deputies; and through threats of foreclosure, blackmail, the blacklist and the use of armed force, it dominated the press and the pulpit. Shocking, yes. But all the more disheartening when she thought back on her famous lumber exposé, only to realize that she had let herself be satisfied too easily that all was well. Carl Gerhardt seemed to know otherwise. He ended his article on a most disconcerting note, warning that Secretary Daniels' real reason for visiting the Northwest was to meet with the lumber trust in preparation for a wartime economy. True or not, Amanda decided that in good conscience she must run the article. In a sense, it would be perfect timing. Now maybe Daniels would be forced to answer charges that the United States was preparing for war.

The *Union Record*'s Potlatch supplement was on the newsstands the day that Daniels arrived to speak at the Rainier Club. Even from inside her office, Amanda could hear the navy band and the sound of marching feet passing by. When she went out to take a look, she was startled to see the red flag flying behind the Stars and Stripes—an army of Wobblies was bringing up the rear, hard on the heels of marching sailors.

Amanda and Lou exchanged glances. "We'd better get a reporter over to the Rainier Club—fast," said Amanda. "I think we've started something."

"Good," said Lou. "It's time we did."

At noon the reporter called in to say that Daniels had been injured by a flying bottle, and forced to flee without delivering his speech. But the trouble was far from over. A demonstration of Wobblies had erupted into violence when the Army and Navy joined forces to beat them up.

An hour later the reporter rushed in to tell Amanda that most of the Wobblies had been rounded up and taken off to the King County Jail. But the sailors and soldiers, not content to claim victory, had marched on the IWW headquarters, and while the police looked on, proceeded to demolish the building.

Amanda immediately ordered an extra edition, then began to take phone calls. George Cotterill was the first to be put through.

"I say, they're surrounding city hall," he told her. "I'm watching them from my window."

"Who? The military?"

"No, I'm afraid the Wobs," he said with calm understatement.

"I thought they'd been locked up?"

"Not all of them, apparently. I can see hundreds down there, just milling about."

The other telephone lines continued to ring persistently, while Lou, sitting at Tom's old desk, took one call after another.

Suddenly Lou began to gesture frantically. "Who *is* this?" she demanded into the receiver.

Amanda could hear her quite distinctly, for the glass partitions that had once separated their offices had been removed.

Lou covered the mouthpiece. "It's somebody who won't give his name saying that the Wobblies are going to take retaliatory action because of what happened to their building!"

"Oh, my God! George, listen, are you still there? Get out fast—I think city hall's about to be destroyed! Don't ask questions, just go!"

Amanda had no sleep that night. Order had been restored in the city, but the turmoil she felt inside could not be quelled. The damage to city hall was extensive, but though no one was hurt, Cotterill claimed that the *Union Record*'s irresponsible journalism was to blame for the IWW "uprising." Moreover, he accused Amanda of betraying him by accepting his endorsement, then using her paper to create a climate of anarchy. Heartsick, she realized that Cotterill might make good his threat to close her down—in the interests of maintaining law and order.

However, his anger was short-lived, for the next morning at seven o'clock he phoned Amanda, in urgent need of her help.

"Terribly sorry to call so early," he ventured humbly, "but I'm afraid we're having another crisis. It's Carl Gerhardt."

"Isn't he in jail?" she asked fearfully.

"At the moment, yes. But he appears to be just as violent behind bars as when he's loose."

"Don't tell me. I can guess. He's started a riot!"

"Worse than that. He's threatened that unless he and the other Wobs are released at once, the jail will be blown up. Apparently he has an accomplice on the outside."

"But that makes no sense—they'd all die!"

"Exactly. That's what we're up against—they're *prepared* to die."

"What do you want me to do, George?"

"I have no business asking you a favor, after the terrible things I said to you yesterday . . ."

"Never mind, it's all forgotten."

"I just came from the jail, Amanda, but Gerhardt refused to see me. He told the deputy that the only person he'll talk to is Firebrand."

"George, you don't have to ask me. I'll go, of course."

"I'd be most grateful."

"Are we friends again?"

"We never stopped being friends. It was just—well, I acted like a bloody fool." He sighed with relief as she forgave him.

The street surrounding the King County Jail was roped off, protecting the crowds that had gathered hoping to see the blast. As soon as Amanda identified herself, a deputy escorted her by freight elevator to the third floor where Carl Gerhardt was confined in a private cell. As they rose past the second floor, she could hear the measured clanking of tin cups against steel bars.

"The Wobs are keeping time," the deputy explained nervously, "until the bomb goes off."

"How much time is left?"

"We don't know. They won't tell us. Maybe minutes, maybe seconds." He touched a rumpled handkerchief to his brow. "Heartless bastards!"

Though Carl Gerhardt's cell was large—for "special prisoners," the deputy said—it appeared far too small to contain the explosive energy which Gerhardt generated, even as he sat on his cot, back to the bars, scribbling rapidly on a large pad.

If he heard them come in, he paid no attention, but continued to write as one obsessed.

The deputy tapped his forehead meaningfully, conveying his opinion of the prisoner, then warned Amanda not to approach within six feet of the bars, and that he would be waiting just outside the door. At the first sign of trouble, she needed only to call out.

Left alone, Amanda stared at the number emblazoned across Gerhardt's back, waiting for him to turn around. His neck was thick, and wheat-colored hair sprouting like a bristle brush reminded her of a refugee. Here she was, risking her life, while he showed only defiance and scorn. It crossed her mind that perhaps he had called for her on purpose, to be blown up with the rest of them. She had been wrong not to recognize him as a fanatic. She should have listened to Tom's warnings. It was too late now. She had walked into his trap, and her death, along with his, would start the revolution.

"I don't want to die, Mr. Gerhardt," she said at last. "I'll wait one more minute. Then I'm walking out."

Instantly the scribbling ceased, but he did not turn around at once. He raised his head slowly, listening.

"Firebrand?"

His voice was deep, commanding, but not harsh. He turned on his cot, seeking her in the dim light, then rose, conveying a sense of power. His eyes held hers, trance-like, their pupils almost transparent. High cheekbones bore the ravages of smallpox, as if stamped with the imprint of calked boots; his mouth was a jagged gash. Nose, too prominent, dominated the battered landscape. But if there was no beauty in the face of Carl Gerhardt, why did she feel caught in the relentless magnetism of his gaze? Her rapid pulse warned her that this was no man to be attracted to. Yet, he was inescapable. Suddenly she knew why. He was a flawed counterpart of Mark. Could he feel her shameless excitement, growing more intense by the moment, just knowing that her life was in his hands?

"What can I do for Firebrand?" His voice lingered, like his eyes.

His unexpected question left her without an answer. She couldn't remember why she had come. Had it been her idea, or had he asked to see her?

"I suppose you were curious to meet the notorious Gerhardt. Well, how do you find him? True, he may be an ugly brute, but I assure you that he's a man of integrity."

"I don't care what you look like or who you are," she lied, trying to recover her composure. "What about the bomb?"

"That's up to you. Come closer," he urged, "so that I can see you. Afraid?" He sounded as if he were smiling, yet his face was serious.

"Of course not. The deputy said . . ."

"Pay no attention. You're free. I'm not. Only *here*." He put a finger to his temple.

Amanda moved closer.

"There, that's better."

"What would you accomplish by blowing yourself up?" she persisted, hoping that she sounded calmer than she felt.

"If I cared about myself, the answer would be—nothing. Obviously, I have more important concerns."

"What's more important than human life?" she asked, letting herself be led.

"Work with me, and you'll find out."

"As long as I have a paper, I'll print your message. But I'll never join the IWW. Or any other movement."

Gerhardt's embattled face twisted into a smile. "Keep on printing our message. That's all we ask. And there'll be no bombs." He extended his hand through the bars. "Shake?"

Amanda reached out tentatively to meet his grasp. Their eyes locked once more.

"Damn good-looking woman," he said as though speaking to himself. Before releasing her, he slipped a note into her hand.

Amanda was so distracted by his touch, that it was a moment before she realized that she was carrying a crucial message.

"I want you to deliver this to my collaborator—this tells him not to bomb the jail."

"You've already written it?"

"I was counting on your support—even before you came. Had you refused . . ." His voice trailed off. "Well, it wouldn't have mattered, would it?"

"You know me very well."

Gerhardt shrugged. "Everyone knows what you stand for. But not everyone has the good fortune to know *you*."

Amanda's cheeks warmed to his gaze. "I think I'd better go now, Mr. Gerhardt. Where will I find your collaborator?"

"He's waiting for you at the Green Parrot Saloon." Gerhardt paused. "You won't have trouble picking him out—he has only one arm. Name's Gustav Johnson."

At that moment the door opened and the deputy came in to say that her time was up.

Amanda paused inside the doorway until her eyes adjusted to the gloom. The Green Parrot was a little shabbier than she had remembered it, but still the lively meeting spot for all who favored the waterfront. Almost immediately she was startled to see a smiling, totally unfamiliar face coming toward her from the bar. Only the lumbering gait identified him as Gus Johnson. He wore glasses, had shaved his head and grown a mustache, all of which did not appear half as striking as the fact that instead of wearing the overalls of a worker, he wore a baggy business suit. The right sleeve hung lifelessly.

"Now you *know* it's me," he said in a throaty voice, offering her the scarred stubs of his left hand.

"It's been a long time, Gus. I've thought of you often, wondering what had happened. I had just about decided that you were either dead, or had gone to Mexico to join the revolution!"

"That's what I hoped you'd think," he admitted with a hoarse chuckle. "Sit down." He gestured to a nearby table and hurried to hold the chair for her. After they were seated, she watched fascinated while he took a cigarette from his pack with one hand, struck the match and lit it, scorning her offer of assistance. He inhaled deeply. "I s-severed all ties and kept on the move. Zigzagged back and forth across the state, always ch-changing my name, taking odd jobs."

Amanda noticed that he had developed a slight stutter. She waited patiently for him to continue.

"But when I got in with the IWW, I knew that's where I belonged. So I stopped running. Besides, the law had closed their b-books on me. Now I'm a W-Wobbly bigwig!" He laughed self-consciously, ill at ease in his suit.

"It's always bothered me that I wasn't able to thank you for tipping me off about the Aberdeen saloons. If it hadn't been for you— and John Looney—I'm afraid Billy Gohl would never have been caught."

Gus passed it off with a shrug.

"Remember when you wrote, 'You'll know who your friends are— and your enemies'? Well, I'm glad that *you* turned out to be a friend. As for enemies, I don't really care. We always have plenty of those, don't we?"

They both laughed, then fell silent. Gus waved to the bartender.
"Sherry, please," said Amanda.

Gus ordered the sherry and a Coca-Cola for himself.

"No alcohol," he said, grinning, as the bartender put the glasses
on the table.

Amanda declined his offer to try a sip of the Coca-Cola, as it
looked most unappealing—a thick syrup mixed with carbonated
water. Nevertheless, he gulped it down like beer, and almost at once
his stutter became less apparent.

Amanda handed him Gerhardt's note. "Here, I almost forgot my
mission."

Gus read it quickly, then handed it back. "It's for you," he said.
"For me?"

"The only reason I needed to see it was to confirm that everything
was all right, that you had agreed to work with us."

"Now wait a minute, I agreed to no such thing!"

"Better read what he says."

Amanda stared at the note. Gerhardt had written, "Gus: Just to
tell you that the bombing will not take place. By the time you receive
this, I will have Firebrand's word that she will give us her whole-
hearted support . . ."

She looked up in dismay. "That's not true—I didn't say that!"

"Read on," said Gus.

She continued, "I'm certain that once she realizes that the U.S.
government is committed to the elimination of the IWW with the
help of local law enforcement, she will understand that the *Union
Record* is not only our most vital weapon, but crucial to our survival.
Without the backing of the press, we're finished . . ." He then gave
an explicit account of police brutality, claiming wounds to verify his
statement.

"Is this true?" she asked aghast, "about the government and the
police?"

"We've been branded as communists," Gus replied matter-of-
factly. "If they can't run us out, they'll kill us off."

"But this is a free country!"

"Free for some." He smiled cynically, leaning across the table.
"Think of this—if the government gets its way, who'll be next?"

Amanda said nothing, but she noticed the perspiration on his forehead.

"You have evidence there that can do us a lot of harm," Gus went on, watching her as she folded the note. "I'm sure C.G. trusts you not to go to the police."

"I have no intention of going to the police. You helped me once. Now it's my turn to repay the favor."

"You won't be sorry," he assured her with relief, passing his hand across his brow. "C.G. is a man who can change the world. Look at me." Gus pulled on the lapel of his jacket. "Never wore one of these till I met *him*. He gave me a new life and a big responsibility. He doesn't care that I'm missing an arm. All that counts with him is what you've got inside your head. For me, that was something new. I thought my life depended on my muscle. But he showed me a different road."

"That may be true for you, but most Wobblies have earned a bad reputation for starting riots."

"Only when we're pushed to the wall. Sometimes you have to make a show of power. Have to make noise." Gus smiled, world-weary, smoke trailing from his nostrils and between the unkempt hairs of his mustache. "Where is it all going to end? No one knows."

When Amanda left the Green Parrot, she went straight to the mayor's office, or rather to temporary quarters situated adjacent to the damaged city hall. She found Cotterill pacing nervously. He quickly ushered her past the other reporters who were waiting to learn the outcome of her visit with Gerhardt. Closing the door behind them, he turned to her expectantly.

"George, do you still trust my judgment?"

"Completely. What happened?"

"There'll be no bombing."

"We're saved! How did you do it?"

"I made them a promise—a guarantee of support, you might say. I think if the police leave them alone, we'll have no more trouble. The Wobblies don't want violence, but if they're persecuted, they'll fight to the death. Of that I'm certain." She paused. "Can you get them released?"

"You're backing them, is that it?"

"That's it."

"Our Mr. Gerhardt must possess the gift of persuasion. What's he like?"

"He's not what you would expect. He's well-educated, articulate, a man of—integrity."

"Handsome?"

"George, I resent that. You know me better."

"Sorry, Amanda. Only curious."

"Well, seeing as you've asked, he *is* handsome. Only he doesn't think so."

"A strange bird, eh?"

"Not strange, different. Like no one you've ever met."

Cotterill smiled. "I'll rely on your opinion. As for me, I have no interest in meeting him. Now, let's get him out of jail and hope he leaves town."

When Amanda arrived home that night, her thoughts were whirling in dizzying confusion. She had vouched for the behavior of strangers, had gambled the future of her paper—willingly. That was the frightening part. How easily she had agreed to Carl Gerhardt's terms. But when she sat down to reread his letter, she could feel again the compelling magnetism of his words, of *him,* and knew she could hardly have acted otherwise. Now she had only to wait for him to step into her life, bringing his revolutionary ideas to the one paper daring enough to accept them. When the doorbell rang, she hurried to answer, assuming it was Lou, who usually stopped by on her way home to discuss the next day's copy.

It was Carl Gerhardt, his hand resting on a cane. He had exchanged his prison uniform for blue denim work clothes.

"Well?" He smiled at her startled expression. "Am I to be asked in?"

"Of course," she said, recovering quickly. "I was just surprised to see you—this soon."

He came in, his cane thumping with each step. "I'm quite sure the King County Jail was glad to be rid of me."

Amanda glanced down. "You've been hurt."

"A club across the shin has given me this intriguing limp, but the doctor assures me it's only temporary."

"Is that the wound you mentioned in your note?"

"That and others. Care to see?"

"No," she said quickly. "I believe you."

"From now on, you'll call me Carl—or C.G., if you prefer. And I'll call you . . . ?"

"Amanda." No more nicknames, she thought. With this man I'll keep a safe distance. Then she added, "Perhaps you'd better sit down."

She led the way into the parlor, but when she turned around, she saw that Carl had remained in the doorway. He seemed to be studying the room with great interest.

"What I like about your house is that it's not too civilized." His eyebrow curved slightly. "It lets you breathe. I'll bet that's true of you, too."

Amanda laughed self-consciously.

Carl looked about. "No whatnots filled with curios, no china closet showing off heirlooms, no ancestors presiding, no photo gallery of loved ones." He gave her a sidelong glance. "*Are* there loved ones?"

She laughed again. "There are. But not here."

"Then we're alone. Good." He sat down at last. "I like it here. This room tells me that you don't pat yourself on the back."

"You see a good deal more in this room than most people do."

"Because I'm looking for more, demanding more." He lit a cigarette without asking permission to smoke, then got up to search for an ashtray.

Amanda quickly found one and brought it to him.

"You don't have to wait on me. I don't expect it and I don't want it. Especially not from you."

Amanda stopped, taken aback by his blunt manner. He spoke as though he were going to stay.

"Would I be permitted to offer you a cup of tea?"

"If I can follow you into the kitchen. I don't like to sit still and I hate waiting."

"Then it's a good thing you got out of jail."

"For which I thank you."

"I know that it's rude to ask, but why did you come here tonight?"

"I don't like to waste time, Amanda. A single life span is never enough for all that must be done."

She hesitated, unsure of his meaning, then asked abruptly, "Have you eaten?"

"Not since this morning."

"Me either. I'll fix something."

"No, let *me*."

"You know how to cook?"

"Naturally. Lead the way."

Carl followed her into the kitchen, then watched while she rummaged first in the pantry, then in the cooler on the back porch.

"I think I have all the ingredients for a stew," she said at last, assembling the items on the table.

"Or sauerbraten," he suggested. "Of course it must marinate for two days."

"Did you say—two days?"

"We'll cook it day after tomorrow. And tonight we'll dine on vegetable soup."

Amanda smiled uneasily. "Then, you're planning to come back?"

"No," he replied in a casual tone. "I'm not leaving."

"You need—a place to stay?"

"I guess I haven't made myself clear. When someone agrees to work with me, I place no limitations—I don't say, 'Today we work, tomorrow we don't,' or 'It's midnight, so we'll stop.' I don't say, 'This house belongs to you, so now I must go home.' There are no boundaries to time and place when lives are merged in a common cause. We're here, you and me, together—now."

Amanda felt the tremor of panic in her stomach. Carl Gerhardt was totally insane. She had opened the door to him, but he thought she *belonged* to him.

"Carl," she began, trying to compose herself, "let's be reasonable. You can't just walk in and take people over. I know you've done it with others, like Gus. But I'm not searching for my destiny—I have it."

"A newspaper? That's a destiny? A paper doesn't exist for its own sake, it's a powerful instrument to be *used*. I'm here to help you use it. I thought that's why we agreed to unite."

Amanda wrenched herself from his gaze, as if by averting her eyes she might escape.

"Look at me, Amanda. You're closed up. Tight. Trying to hide. From what? Surely not from me." He paused. "You don't want to be hurt again, is that it?"

What gall! Fear turned to anger as she tried to protect herself. "You're taking too much for granted!"

"Am I? I read an invitation in your eyes the minute we met. It was clear that you wanted me. And you didn't pull away when I took your hand."

"That's absurd! I felt sorry for you. Besides, there's someone else in my life."

"Forget about him. If he's not here at this moment, he doesn't exist."

Amanda could only stare, at a loss to protest. How could I have thought he reminded me of Mark? she asked herself. I'm the one who must be insane.

"What do you want of me?"

"The same thing you want. Look, I don't have time to court you, to sit alone in my room writing love poems to be read later by you sitting alone in *your* room. Life is rushing by too fast."

Carl let his cane clatter to the floor as he reached out to her. "There's nothing wrong with making love to someone the first time you meet. To wait only postpones the inevitable."

Words and reason fled as she waited mesmerized for his embrace. He didn't lead her up to bed to hide their nakedness between the sheets in a dark room, nor even to the parlor, dimly lit. But in the stark glare of the kitchen bulb, he taught her to scorn all pretense.

"Look at me. Claim your right to love."

His arms closed around her, their strength quieting her tension. She offered no struggle, wanted no way out. Her body was now against his, lips parting in the rush of passion, desire urging the moment to swift fulfillment. Then, lifted by a sudden burst of warmth, she knew it was too late to reject this man and the turmoil which he would bring into her life. Too late to run away.

Chapter Nineteen

AMANDA packed Emma's letters, neatly bound with rubber bands, into a cardboard box, sealed it, then pushed it aside for removal to the attic.

"I don't know why I save them," she said aloud. "They've all been answered." She was alone in the parlor, but talking to herself lightened the task of straightening up. It was hard to believe that it was spring cleaning time again, that 1915 was already five months gone.

The box looked very small to contain more than twenty years of correspondence. The early letters were the best, when life still lay ahead waiting to be explored, and Emma Goldman was her idol. In time, of course, their friendship lost momentum, and the once lively exchange became no more than an occasional duty, nostalgically performed. But though Emma's impact on her life was in the past, she couldn't bring herself to throw the letters away. After all, she and Emma had never met. There were no memories to share except what they had written, and she wondered if Emma, too, felt the same. How revealing it would be to make a trade, but maybe too painful.

Carl came in from the kitchen with two cups of coffee and sat down on the floor next to her. "It looks worse than before you started," he commented, looking about. "So why bother? Let's make love and forget the cleaning."

With Carl's eyes touching her, consuming her, how could she insist that certain things had to be done? The meshing of their lives hadn't yet resulted in complacency. She felt as excited now as the first time they had been together. He's good for me, she had reasoned. He's the only man I've ever met who could help me to get over Mark. Not because she had forgotten Mark, but because Carl loved her with the same intensity, and in a way, seemed to need her. Marriage, however, was never discussed. Nor did it seem important. All relationships were temporary, Carl believed. Just as life itself. Knowing this from the beginning, Amanda had no expectations that they would be together forever. In fact, each time she would enter the house to find him still there, it was always a pleasant surprise. Someday, she thought, I'll walk in and he'll have left a note. But having accepted his rules, she could tolerate the uncertainty.

In that May of 1915, the entire world seemed to be facing an uncertain future. Each day's news bombarded the reader with accounts of the grueling trench warfare along the entire Western Front, giving Americans cause to worry that the conflict in Europe was deepening. The *Union Record,* however, continued to pound away on the theme that the conflict at home was no less serious. The industrial depression had resulted in massive layoffs. And when employers began to use the vast army of unemployed as an ax to cut wages, the IWW moved in. Most of Carl's efforts went into mounting strikes and boycotts, tactics which made enemies not only of management, but often of labor itself. And because of Amanda's support, the *Record* was considered just as radical as Carl. She ignored her critics, however, refusing to agonize over the stand she had taken. In her mind, she, Carl and the *Record* were a trinity, irrevocably bound.

Even at home, Carl's imprint was startlingly visible, with the parlor turned into an office, which they shared. He used the library table as a desk, while Amanda preferred to work curled up in a chair or on the floor. His books overflowed the shelves, and political posters adorned the walls, their bold splashes of color and ominous messages a constant reminder that the battle would not be easily won. She often recalled his approving comment about the simplicity of her home, with the usual photographs and bric-a-brac conspicuously absent. When he had brought in his books and posters, there had been nothing to displace. Her house was still intact, only perhaps more lively now with all its space committed.

Later that morning, Lou stopped by with the mail and newspapers.

"How are things in the bunker?" she greeted, amused as always by the décor.

"If you need a poster for your office, I think I can find something suitably shocking for you," Carl offered without looking up from his writing.

"Fortunately, I don't have any walls," she quipped. "Thanks anyway."

"Have a pleasant weekend," said Amanda, walking her to the door.

"I will. I'm climbing Mount Rainier. I finally got a party together."

"In May? You could have an avalanche at this time of year!"

"We'll take our chances. With the world on the brink of war, we might as well live recklessly."

"You're too valuable to lose! So be careful."

Lou glanced toward the parlor and winked. "That's all right. You've always got C.G."

But I *won't* always have him, she thought, walking back inside. And Lou knows it. She sat down with the *Times* and *P.I.* while Carl worked on his speech.

"Our task is to rejuvenate the world!" She heard him practicing aloud. Even as she continued to read, part of her mind was absorbing his message to the workingman. It was the same message that had become the war cry of the young men of Europe. She knew that he was violently opposed to the war, yet envied the spirit of European youth. She couldn't help but think that *his* battleground was every bit as dangerous as the trenches on foreign soil.

"Only if we can save our youth from the corruption of adult values, shall we raise the worker to a level of dignity. That's what we must do!"

Suddenly Amanda's eyes strayed to a brief item at the bottom of the page. It said: "Mr. Mark Reed announced today that his wife and two children have set sail from New York bound for England to visit relatives. They will return to Cosmopolis in August."

As she stared at the page, her heart began pounding like a warning signal of danger, and Carl's words were lost.

Frightened by her own emotions, she went to him quickly and knelt at his feet.

"I want to make love."

He turned to her, his unblinking blue eyes accepting her need without question, just as she always accepted his, and touched her with unusual tenderness. It was the first time she had ever initiated their love-making, yet he showed no surprise. For a brief time, his mission was forgotten, the horrors of war ceased to exist.

When Amanda showed up at Mary Kenworthy's party in July, everyone made such a fuss that she realized her colleagues had come to regard her as a recluse. They were too tactful, of course, to pin point what they considered the reason for her withdrawal, but all knew it began about the time that Carl Gerhardt had come into her life. Erastus was a bit aloof, she thought, but too much the gentleman to scold her. Only Colonel Blethen still considered it his prerogative to offer unasked-for advice. He found the opportune moment and steered her into a corner where no one would dare interrupt them. Suffering from high blood pressure, his face grew plum-colored as he fortified himself with a straight whiskey, an indulgence which he refused to give up.

"What's all this we're hearing about you and that Gerhardt?" he demanded bluntly.

Had anyone but Blethen asked such an indiscreet question, she would have politely told him to mind his own business.

"Carl and I have a very unusual relationship," she replied, choosing her words carefully.

"To say the least," he snorted. "You've got the whole town blabbering about you like a fallen woman in a dime novel! Are you going to marry him or not?"

Amanda couldn't help but laugh at his concern. "I intend to continue as I am. That is, unless the town wants to punish me with sticks and stones!"

"Listen, the *Union Record* may be radical, but it's *established*. You and that paper have both been around long enough to make you a part of this town, whether anybody agrees with you or not. But Gerhardt just popped up. Folks want to know who he is and what he's doing here. We don't see much of him, but he certainly doesn't mind using your paper to give vent to all his harebrained ideas."

"I've always tried to provide a forum for viewpoints which can't be heard elsewhere. It doesn't mean that I endorse everything the Wobblies do. Nor does it mean that I'm a socialist. I only think that all these people have a right to be heard. As for the war, Carl's against it and so am I."

"I was just getting to that. I suppose it's all right for the Germans to sink the *Lusitania* and use poison gas on everybody! We should just sit back and twiddle our thumbs, is that it? Well, let me tell you something, young lady, you'd better watch your step. Know what they're saying about your friend Gerhardt? That he's a German spy!"

Amanda laughed again, concealing her annoyance. "Is that what *you* think, Colonel Blethen? Well, don't worry, it's not true."

"I didn't say it was. But if that's what your readers think, you're going to be in for it."

"Carl and I are aware of the anti-German feeling. But we pay no attention."

Blethen shrugged. "I've said my piece. So do as you wish." He finished his whiskey in one swallow, sending the color to the roots of his thinning hair. Two days later he was dead.

Amanda and all Seattle were shocked. It was hard to believe that this much-loved, much-hated man, who had battled through life as though he expected to live forever, would quite simply no longer be there. The question was, who could replace him? That was when everyone learned that Blethen had a son, Clarance, the product of an early marriage. Unknown to all, Clarance had been groomed from boyhood to succeed his father as publisher. Clarance Ballard was the name he had used while he worked as a relatively obscure staff reporter. Clarance Ballard! In a flash Amanda remembered that she had had two encounters with Clarance—the first in '04 on the train to Aberdeen; the second in 1912 when he interviewed her on the *Union Record*'s fifth anniversary. Amanda smiled to think that young Blethen had worked under a pseudonym. That, no doubt, had been his father's idea. She could just hear Colonel Blethen insisting that no favoritism would be tolerated at the *Times*. Clarance would have to prove himself, like everyone else. Whether or not he had succeeded would remain to be seen. But Amanda knew that without Colonel Blethen, the *Times* would never be the same.

"It can't be helped," said Carl, lighting his cigarette from the ash of the one he had just finished. "War is wrong."

"I know. And we're going to be deluged with mail."

"I'll be disappointed if we're not."

Carl was not disappointed. His article warning against U.S. involvement in the war brought a storm of protest. So widespread was the reaction that every newspaper in the Northwest took the article as a challenge to state its position on war. Only then did Amanda discover that the anti-German climate was a real danger. Blethen's last prediction, like all his others, had been on target. Patriots felt that the Germans must be punished; pacifists felt that the suppression of German propaganda in the United States would win the war for the Allies without shedding a drop of American blood. And a great segment of the public seized upon the *Union Record* as the instrument of German propaganda. It mattered little that Carl Gerhardt was an American citizen born in the United States. He had German blood. That was why he opposed the war—he knew that without America's help, Germany would be victorious. Parroting the suspicions of his late father, Clarance Blethen suggested in a *Times* editorial that Gerhardt might be a German agent. That was all it took to trigger a hate campaign.

Carl seemed to relish the upheaval he had created. Amanda was appalled.

"I'm going to answer the accusations," she declared heatedly. "We must not be intimidated!"

"But this is exactly how I planned it. I've gotten people to think." He calmly blew a succession of perfect smoke rings as though he hadn't a care in the world.

"I believe," said Amanda, struggling to maintain her composure, "there comes a time when you must put aside your concern for everybody else and worry about yourself! It's called self-preservation."

Carl crushed out his cigarette. "I prefer self-sacrifice."

In the months that followed they suffered a period of harassment unlike anything she had ever experienced. Threatening notes arrived almost daily; the *Union Record* was routinely vandalized in a manner which suggested that many of the incidents were inside jobs. Amanda replaced the pressmen and—reluctantly—the presswoman because she could trust no one. Glue had been poured into the ink on one occasion; on another, some parts had been removed which were crucial to the operation of the presses. She felt bad about losing the girl, who had done her job well, less so when the girl immediately secured a job in the pressroom at the *Times*. Furiously she told herself that such a thing would never have happened if Colonel Blethen were alive. Carl, however, felt undefeated.

As a figure of controversy, he began to attract increasingly large crowds whenever he delivered a speech. With the help of Gus Johnson and John Looney, he denounced profiteering in every lumber town in the state, thriving on the knowledge that he was feared and hated by the bosses, feared and respected by the workers. But of all the trouble spots he had chosen, Everett was the toughest.

In Everett the lumber trust remained in firm control. The UMWL was a feeble presence at best, with the majority of workers unaffiliated, playing it safe. Carl was convinced that if he could break the barrier in Everett, all the other holdouts around the state would follow suit. Back and forth he traveled, making sure that no mill escaped his wrath. But too often he'd return with a black eye or missing tooth resulting from a "little skirmish with the law," as he put it.

Knowing that he was not to be talked out of his mission, Amanda purchased a first-aid kit, which Carl called his "portable hospital."

"You have enough bandages there to bind up an army," he teased. "And what's this? Chloroform? I hope you're not planning to do amputations!"

"I won't if I don't have to," said Amanda with a straight face. "Though I'm thinking of buying a saw—just for emergencies."

She joked with him only because she dared not show the deep concern she felt in knowing that his reputation as an agitator had placed him in such grave danger.

On a rainy morning in early September Carl announced that he might be late for dinner because he was taking thirty of the boys up to Everett to support the striking shingle millworkers.

"I don't have a cold remedy in my first-aid kit, so I really wish you wouldn't march around in all this downpour getting your feet soaked," she scolded, just to let him know she cared, but not imagining for a minute that he would change his mind.

"You think rain is going to stop the revolution?" he asked in pretended horror. But Amanda knew he truly believed that nothing would stop it.

"Give my regards to Sheriff McRae," she added, pouring the coffee. "Don't be too hard on him."

"He and I will probably go out for a beer afterwards. Underneath it all, I think he wishes he could be a Wobbly, too!"

They both laughed, though Amanda knew there was nothing to laugh about.

"Is Gus going along?" she asked.

"He's already up there. I sent him and Looney ahead to size things up."

He spoke as if he were going on an outing, Amanda thought almost enviously, as she watched him shrug into his jacket. She knew there was nothing in the world he'd rather be doing than taking the train up to Everett, just to tramp about in the rain. How could she love such a man?

At noon she received a call from Gus Johnson asking what had happened to Carl. He had not shown up yet.

Amanda assured him that Carl was on his way and that the train was probably running late due to the weather. But when she hung up she decided to call the Everett station to find out what had caused the delay.

The stationmaster insisted that the train had arrived on time.

"Do you remember a group of about thirty men getting off?" she asked.

"Were they wearing badges? And carrying signs?"

"That's them," said Amanda in relief.

"There was quite a turnout to meet 'em," he volunteered. "Fellow workers, it appeared, all wearing overalls. In fact, they came with a whole string of automobiles to pick 'em up. And off they raced at top speed, one after the other. They sure went in style, I'll say that!"

Amanda thanked him for the information and hung up smiling. But then she began to think how odd it was that they would have been met with automobiles. Wobblies were not known to travel in style.

At four in the afternoon Gus called back. He apologized for worrying her, but Carl and the boys still hadn't arrived. With a sinking feeling, she told him of her conversation with the stationmaster.

Gus moaned when he heard about the automobiles. He asked Amanda not to notify the police until he had a chance to investigate, and to wait for his call.

His call never came. In agony, Amanda paced from room to room, debating what to do. Hours passed before she heard the front door quietly open and close. Then silence.

"Carl? Is that you?"

Fearfully, she crept into the hall. Carl was leaning against the door breathing heavily. He put a finger to his lips. "Put out the light," he whispered.

She hurriedly obeyed, then waited in the darkness until the creaking of the floor told her that he was coming into the parlor. He said nothing until he had gone first to the window and stood for a moment behind the curtain. Satisfied at last, he turned to her.

"I thought I was being followed," he said in a low tone.

"Are you all right?" she ventured.

He nodded, eyes closed.

"What on earth happened?"

Instead of answering, he took her by the hand and led her into the kitchen. He pulled down the window shade, then sank into a chair.

"I can't talk yet," he said, his voice heavy with exhaustion. "I've walked all the way from Beverly Park."

"But that's miles from here! What were you doing there?"

"I was driven," he replied dully.

Amanda suddenly remembered what the stationmaster had told her. "Someone met you at the train—who was it?"

But Carl had already put his head on the table. "I can't talk now." His voice faded. The next minute he was asleep.

The night passed without incident and in the morning the sun shone.

Carl was still at the kitchen table, awake now and drinking coffee, while Amanda waited helplessly, giving him the time he needed to remember what had happened.

"We were picked up at the station by a gang of drunks—all wearing overalls. I knew right away they weren't the strikers and warned my boys not to get into their autos. But the boys saw their UMWL buttons and figured they were among friends. When I tried to stop them, McRae suddenly appeared." Carl shook his head in disgust. "He was wearing work clothes, too. I told him to get the hell out of my way, so he pulled a gun—ordered me into his car. Well, in I got. It was one of those five-passenger Reos. Cyrus Clough's son was driving."

Amanda's eyes blazed. "Thank God we've got witnesses! The stationmaster saw everything and there must have been others!"

"Don't count on anybody. With the sheriff, the police and the bosses thick as thieves, we don't stand a chance."

"They kidnapped you! That's a crime!"

"That's only the beginning. They drove us out to Beverly Park. Right in the middle of nowhere. Not a soul around." He paused.

"They ordered us out of the cars and told us we were going to be shot."

"My God!"

"But instead, they kept us standing in the cold drizzle all afternoon, while they sat inside their cars passing the bottle."

"Were they deputies?"

"Oh, sure. They'd all been deputized that morning. Respectable businessmen!" he added with contempt.

Amanda refilled their cups, her hand trembling. Carl took a long sip, then continued.

"As soon as it was dark, they got out of their cars and formed two lines reaching from the roadway to the interurban tracks. They forced our boys to run a gauntlet, one at a time, that ended with a cattle guard. And while they ran, these drunken sons of bitches swung at them with gun butts, blackjacks, loaded saps and pick handles. Most of the poor devils ended up sprawled on the cattle guard, so in case they missed the blows, they got a bed of blades, razor-sharp." He stared into his cup. "That's about it."

"Miserable bastards!" She felt her rage give way to furious tears. "Was anyone killed?"

Carl shook his head. "I don't know for sure. Most of the boys managed to run into the woods, scared they were going to be finished off."

"But what about you? How did you escape?"

"I figured they were saving me for last. But I didn't feel like waiting. McRae was so drunk by then that I landed him on his ear before anybody knew what was happening. Once I took off, I never looked back."

Amanda stood up in alarm. "They'll never let you get away, not after hitting McRae and witnessing what they did! They'll come after you!"

"If they haven't come by now, I'm safe—for the moment. They had their chance to beat the hell out of me or kill me, but they didn't. Maybe they decided to teach me a lesson, instead of making me a martyr."

"It was a warning—you've got to be careful!"

He smiled grimly. "It was a declaration of war. I've got to fight back."

The next edition of the *Union Record* came off the press printed in red ink on a tinted sheet, its headlines reporting the Beverly Park attack in bright red letters, two inches high. The effect was so startling that Amanda decided to print every edition in red until the guilty were brought to justice, as a continuing reminder of the blood that had been spilled.

Public outrage earned the Wobblies a wave of support, forcing a full investigation of the slugging party. However, fearing recrimination, none of the victims would come forth to testify. With Carl as the lone witness, and Sheriff McRae denying any involvement, the case was dismissed for lack of evidence. McRae walked out of the courtroom, wearing a smile.

Carl was tired. Once McRae had been vindicated, Everett settled down. Not because anyone believed all was well, but in defeat. The shingle mill strikers quietly returned to work. Amanda sensed that Carl was disillusioned by the way it had turned out. He had geared himself to lead the Everett revolution, but it never materialized. Now she could see he was at a loss to build up momentum again. It was time for a change.

"We're having such a beautiful Indian summer this year," she ventured cautiously, watching his reaction. "Wouldn't it be nice to take advantage of it, and go away someplace for a month or so?"

Carl lit a cigarette. "Where to?"

"Endoline," she replied quickly, pleased that he was open to her suggestion.

"The end of the line," he said with a dry laugh. "How appropriate."

"You'll love it," she went on. "It's wild and remote, but not too far from town. We can relax there—and be ourselves."

"You've undoubtedly found a charming cottage for rent, am I right?"

"Of course I haven't seen it, but the ad in the paper caught my eye —it's a small farm."

Carl brightened. "I like farms. They allow you to be self-sufficient."

It was settled. The following day Amanda packed a trunkful of clothing and household essentials, covered the furniture with sheets, and hired an unemployed Wobbly to board up the windows. When Carl saw what she was doing, he became immediately suspicious.

"Are you sure we're going to be gone only a month?"

"Well, you never know how much we may like it out there. So I'm closing up the house—just in case."

"Amanda, listen to me. No matter how much we like it, we can't stay there forever." He saw her disappointment and his voice softened. "We can't just walk away."

Erastus agreed to drive them out in his new roadster. Although Amanda didn't see him often, she still considered him one of the few friends who could be trusted.

"We don't want anybody to know where we are," she had explained. "We want some privacy—for however long it lasts."

"Are you happy?" he had asked.

"I don't know," she answered honestly. "I never stop to think about it."

When they arrived at Endoline, Carl glanced about with obvious approval at the decrepit, vine-covered frame house sagging in a bed of tall grass and weeds.

"This place looks as battered as I do!" he declared in sudden good spirits. "It will be a real challenge."

"Better check to see if the roof leaks," said Erastus, surveying the shack with a skeptical eye.

Carl inhaled deeply. "Ah, fresh, clean air with just a whiff of kelp. Are we close to the Sound?"

"The owner told me we're only about a half mile from a beach where there's good clamming. See the path? Right through the blackberry bushes."

Carl led the way eagerly, and when they had gone a few hundred yards, a wedge of gray, white-capped water emerged through the high grass. But as soon as they stopped to gaze at the view, his bright mood seemed to vanish.

"It looks peaceful," he said, "but that's a deception. It won't be long before we'll be spotting enemy submarines out there, sneaking up to spy on us."

"Oh, come now, Carl, you can't be serious!" said Erastus with a laugh. "Why would the Germans want to attack Seattle?"

"Because we're going to be at war with them."

They walked back up the path in silence.

The mild golden days of Indian summer stretched to the end of October. For Carl, resting and thinking had to be accompanied by physical labor. He cleared the land—in case they decided to return in the spring to plant a vegetable garden, then made all the essential repairs. Encouraged by his enthusiasm, Amanda also set to the task of making the place livable, vowing to speak to the landlord at the first opportunity about a possible long-term lease. They worked compulsively, though no amount of scrubbing could dispel the odor of mildew, for it seeped from under the cheap linoleum that had been laid in every room to cover the worn oak floors. And no sooner was the roof patched, than a sudden rain found an even weaker spot through which to enter. The furnishings were sparse and rustic, befitting a beach cottage. But the plumbing functioned and the Franklin stove saw them through the cool evenings with some degree of comfort.

Carl had brought with him only one poster—for "inspiration," as he put it—so as not to lose sight of his objective. "STRIKE FAST, STRIKE HARD" was the one he had chosen to dominate the front room. Yet, its impact seemed lost in the tranquil isolation of their surroundings. Amanda was glad there was no telephone to ring, no friends to drop by, no deadlines, no emergencies. Her mind was at ease because Lou was in complete charge, having promised to abstain from mountain climbing until they returned.

"When we moved in here, this place was crumbling, stagnant," Carl said to Amanda one day. "But look at it now. We've given it new life. It's the same house. Only better. New life is the key."

Amanda grasped his message with a sinking feeling. Endoline wouldn't be able to sustain him for much longer. With no more improvements to be made, he would soon be ready to move on to the next challenge.

A few days later when Amanda returned from the beach with a bucket of clams, she noticed a copy of the *Times* lying on the table.

"Where did that come from?" she asked in surprise.

"Oh, some of the boys stopped by today. They wanted to let me know what was going on."

"They knew where to find us?"

"It was just Gus and John Looney and a couple of others."

"I thought we weren't going to tell anyone where we were?"

"Except close friends," he reminded. He gestured toward the paper. "Take a look."

Amanda picked it up reluctantly. The front page carried a story which maintained that the solidarity of the IWW had been seriously undermined since the "disappearance" of Carl Gerhardt. The article speculated that he had been paid off by the Everett mills to abandon the IWW for good.

Furiously Amanda crumpled the paper and stuffed it into the stove. Then without turning, she asked him, "It isn't true, is it, that the Wobblies are in trouble?"

"All I know is, they want me back. Gus can't handle it alone."

Amanda was sure that she detected a note of satisfaction in his voice. "Then we have no choice, do we?" Her tone was flat, resigned. But the tears came nonetheless. The realization that their cottage—their privacy—had been invaded, filled her with resentment. "Why can't they leave us alone?"

"This wasn't meant to be permanent, it was an interlude. Now it's over."

They returned to town in the middle of November, having arranged to keep their cottage hideaway to use on weekends, a decision which eased the move for both of them. But Amanda knew the spell had been broken. Endoline was in the past.

Carl immediately plunged into the task of pulling the Wobblies together, dismayed to discover that even within their ranks, detractors emerged to question his German heritage and whether or not he had accepted a pay-off from the mills. Carl was deeply depressed by their suspicion and mistrust.

"What do they want of me?" he finally asked in exasperation.

"They want a savior," she replied. "But their faith has been shaken. You'll have to win them back."

"I'll tell you one thing—I'm sick of being called a German agent. That's one rumor I intend to lay to rest."

"I don't see how."

"As soon as we get into the war, I'm going to be the first to enlist."

"But you're opposed to the war! How can you go against your convictions?"

"Because that's the only way to prove that I'm *not* a spy. And if I die charging out of a trench somewhere on the Western Front, so much the better."

"I don't think that's funny!"

"It's not meant to be."

"Oh, Carl, to hell with them! You don't have to be loved by the whole world—*I* love you. That's all that matters." Amanda knew that desperation had crept into her voice, that her argument was selfish.

He smiled patiently, a bit sadly. "I know you do. But life isn't that simple."

Amanda felt a sudden pang. War meant separation. "I'll feel terrible, staying behind, watching you go off to fight. Knowing I can't be part of it with you."

"You will be. You'll carry on here till I come back."

"I'm frightened, Carl. In war you have no control over the circumstances. You have to keep on fighting whether you want to or not, till you win—or die."

"That's true. Exactly like life."

She watched him blow a smoke ring and follow it with his eyes until it became a ragged trail of vapor, then vanished. Calmly he blew another. Each one a new beginning. His reaction seemed to confirm what she had known right from the start, that even her love wasn't enough to keep him.

Chapter Twenty

Amanda worked tirelessly on her Beverly Park investigation, assigning it first priority for all of her reporters. She was determined that every Wobbly who had run the gauntlet on that rainy September night would tell his tale; and that every "respected citizen" who had participated would be identified. Only by such an exposé could she hope to prove that Carl had not been paid off by the mills to abandon the IWW, but had gone to Endoline in a state of complete exhaustion.

Two days before Thanksgiving, Carl arrived home with good news. He had finally succeeded in persuading the Everett shingle-weavers to strike again.

"They're going out tomorrow," he announced triumphantly. "And when they go out, it's likely that every other mill in Everett will follow suit. Three hundred Wobs have volunteered to back them up. Everybody's with me!"

"At last!" said Amanda excitedly. "The timing couldn't be better—my first article is ready to go. I'll run a headline: '300 WOBBLIES ENTER THE KINGDOM OF EVERETT!' How does that sound?"

"Earth-shaking!" he answered, and sweeping her up in his arms, he whirled her around until they were both dizzy.

They collapsed in laughter, Amanda knowing his exuberance would turn to passion. Only this time it didn't. He slowly released her, his expression suddenly serious.

"You're risking a lot for me," he said. "But I promise you won't be sorry."

"I'm not worried. We've both chosen to live this way, haven't we? Remember when you told me that a newspaper was to be *used,* not merely exist for its own sake? Well, I'm finally learning what that means. I may lose the paper, but if we win the war—*our* war—it will have been worth it."

The penetrating blue of his eyes suddenly dimmed. He turned away abruptly.

"Will you be leaving in the morning?" she asked after a moment.

He nodded. "First thing—up and back the same day."

"Good. I'm glad you'll be home for Thanksgiving because I've invited Lou and Erastus for dinner." Then she added sadly, "I'll miss having Mary this year. It won't be the same without her. She was a good friend."

"Don't forget Gus."

"Of course not. He's invited and John Looney as well."

"They'll appreciate it."

All the lonely people always come to our house, she thought. We're the gathering place. I hope that never changes.

Carl was too restless to enjoy his dinner. After several forkfuls, he pushed his plate away and lit a cigarette.

"Do you know that over a hundred shingle-weavers are ill or dying of cedar asthma? They've promised to turn out, sick as they are, to back us up. The sins of management will be on parade and we'll bring those bastards to their knees!"

Amanda stared at her plate. "Will you be armed?"

Carl slowly exhaled. "That's an odd question."

"After what happened at Beverly Park, I'd feel a lot better if you were carrying a gun."

"If I carried it, I'd use it. Without a second thought. So we'll go unarmed, like we always do."

"And if the deputies meet your train?"

"We're not taking the train. We're going by boat."

"By boat? Why didn't you tell me?"

"Because it's a secret," he replied calmly. "So don't print anything until after we get there."

"Which boat?"

"*The Verona.* It's the only passenger steamship with regular service between Seattle and Everett, so there'll be other passengers on board besides us. This way, when we dock at Everett, all will appear normal."

"Will it?" she asked in sudden anxiety. "I don't know. I don't like the sound of it."

"Listen to me, we've got a lot of people on our side—the strikers, their families and friends. Why, that's half the town right there—a town that's ripe for revolution! There are three hundred of us, Amanda. This time we've got the 'respected citizens' outnumbered."

Amanda thought of the Chinese immigrants, remembering how their ship trapped them, became a prison. "A boat's so vulnerable. It moves so slowly . . ."

"That's all in our favor," said Carl confidently. "We'll be singing and enjoying ourselves, comrades on an outing. We'll be ashore before anybody knows what's happening."

It was no use. He was set. Amanda scraped back her chair. "I'm going to send a reporter with you."

"There's no need. I can tell you what went on."

"Carl, you'll have your hands full. This is too important not to be covered from every angle. Besides, I want to send Ida Reynolds. It will be a good opportunity for her to show what she can do."

Ida was overwhelmed by Amanda's call, thanking her profusely for assigning her to such an exciting, top-secret event. When she learned she was to go by boat, she quickly assured Amanda that she never got seasick, even though the question hadn't been raised. As she hung up, Amanda recalled with a pang of nostalgia her own youthful exuberance when she had started out so many years ago. She knew instinctively that Ida, her youngest reporter, would do a creditable job.

That night when Amanda reached to pull down the bedroom window shade, she noticed an elongated shadow lying in a pool of light from the street lamp. Quickly she stepped back.

"Carl, come here!" she called in a loud whisper. "No, wait—put out the light first."

By the time Carl reached the window, the shadow was gone.

Hours passed before Amanda closed her eyes, but Carl slept soundly.

They awakened to the dawn of a crisp, cloudless day, made to order for sailing, Carl said, eager to be off. Even Amanda had to admit the sunshine was reassuring. She put aside her fears of the night before, and tried to be cheerful.

"I'm going to bake two mince pies before I go to work this morning," she said, watching him dress. "And the grocery boy will deliver the turkey. So be sure to tell Gus and John that I'm expecting them."

Carl caught her eye in the mirror as he put on his jacket. His mood changed abruptly and he came over to sit on the edge of the bed.

"Thank you," he whispered, a gruffness in his voice concealing his emotion.

"For what?"

"For everything. You've been just the right woman for me. I'm not sure that you know how much I love you, because I don't always tell you."

Amanda couldn't remember that he had *ever* told her.

"I want you to know that you've made this day possible."

"You mean—the exposé?"

"I mean *you*. For being there when I needed you."

She blinked rapidly, but tears came nonetheless. For the first time since they had been together, she felt sure of him. Sure that they would go on.

"Do a good job today," she said, swallowing. "And hurry home. I'll be waiting."

When Amanda arrived at work Lou greeted her with a sly grin. "The chief of police just called you. What, pray tell, have you been up to *now?*"

"Beckingham?" Amanda glanced at the clock. It was seven-thirty. "He must think I work twenty-four hours a day!"

As soon as central put through her call, Chief Beckingham came on the line. "We've got trouble brewing," he announced, "and I want to know if your friend Gerhardt's involved."

Amanda felt a stab of resentment at his brusque manner. "Why should he be? He's not even in town."

Beckingham groaned. "That's just what I didn't want to hear. Gone up to Everett, right?"

"How did you know?"

"A couple of Pinkertons tipped us off. They said that a boatload of Wobs are heading for Everett—they're armed to the teeth, and are planning to invade and burn the whole damn town. So I figured you must know about it."

"It's a lie! They're not armed! They're only going to march with the striking millworkers."

"That right?" Beckingham's tone was unconvinced. "What about Gerhardt?"

"I tell you there's not going to be any violence! You have my word!"

"Well, I already alerted the Everett authorities—just as a precaution. So at least they'll be prepared."

"You shouldn't have done that. You've made a terrible mistake!"

"Simmer down, Miss Lamar. If the Wobs aren't looking for trouble, they won't find any."

Amanda hung up in a daze. She knew that Carl wouldn't deceive her. Hadn't he firmly denied that they would be armed? Then she remembered the shadow outside their bedroom window. Suddenly it was clear—the Pinkertons had been hired by the mills to spy on him, to thwart his mission!

"Who died?" Lou asked. "You're positively gray!"

"I've got to borrow a car—I'm going to Everett!"

As they drove, Gerald, the young photographer whose last name Amanda was never able to remember, held himself stiffly in the seat next to her, his camera balanced on his knees. Each time Amanda veered to the shoulder in order to pass another vehicle, Gerald would brace for a crash. He had lost confidence at the start of the trip when she had turned to ask him, "How do you shift this thing?"

With luck they managed to reach Everett's waterfront, and leaving the car, continued on foot. They hurried toward the City Dock, aware of an eerie stillness. The screaming saws were silent, freight trains sat idle on their sidings and the constant rumble of logging wagons was noticeably absent. All the mills had closed down, an encouraging sign. The greater the support for the strike, the better Carl's position.

With Everett's primary activity brought to a halt, it appeared that the entire town had gathered to watch the arrival of *The Verona*. Were they there because they knew that Wobblies were on board? Or because the weather was unseasonably pleasant and they had nothing better to do? Amanda's eyes swept the crowd nervously for any sign of deputies, or men in work clothes who didn't look like workers. But she saw no one to give her cause for alarm.

Cleaving the placid sunlit waters of the bay, *The Verona* cut her engines and glided toward the dock. One agile youth had shinnied all the way to the top of the flagpole, where he clung waving wildly, as if he alone was being met by the crowd on shore. Amanda craned to catch a glimpse of the passengers, but as the steamer came closer, her view was blocked by huge stacks of lumber, waiting on the pier to be loaded. Good. It meant the longshoremen were also out in sympathy. Suddenly Gerald tugged at her sleeve.

"Look over there!"

He was pointing excitedly at what appeared to be a gleaming piece of metal protruding from between the stacks of lumber. They moved closer. It was the handle of a rifle. And beneath it was another. And still more—an entire cache of firearms. Rifles, shotguns, revolvers, ammunition and even a machine gun had been stashed, ready for use.

Gerald whistled under his breath. "Boy, oh boy! I'd better get a picture of *that!*"

"No, don't!"

"Why not?"

Amanda hesitated. A sickening thought had crossed her mind— what if the arms were for Carl? A plan he hadn't told her about?

"Why *not?*" Gerald repeated insistently.

Before she could answer, there was a sudden rush of footsteps, and turning, they saw a stream of men emerge from an empty warehouse, heading toward them.

"Make way for the Ku Klux Klan," one of them shouted; "the bullets are gonna be flyin'!"

Amanda saw in horror that every one of them wore a gold star pinned to his lapel. They had all been deputized.

"Where's Sheriff McRae?" she demanded, blocking their path. "I've got to see him!"

In answer, she was shoved aside. Feverishly, Gerald positioned his camera, focusing on the seizure of weapons.

"Hey, who are you?" bellowed a voice nearby.

Amanda screamed her warning too late as one of the men lunged at Gerald, knocking his camera to the ground, while three others converged to smash it with their gun butts.

"Run, Gerald!" Amanda shouted. "To hell with the camera!"

It was his good fortune that no one was interested in beating up a photographer; they obviously had more urgent business. Gerald was ignored as each man armed himself, then took his place crouching behind the stacks. It all happened so quickly that most of the crowd was unaware of the drama going on behind them. Only Amanda could see what was about to happen. The deputies had no intention of warning the Wobblies to retreat. It was an ambush!

Gerald's eyes were wide. "I bet they're going to round up the Wobs and put 'em in jail!"

"Oh, God, Gerald, don't you see what's happening? I've got to find Carl and warn him!"

"You can't," said Gerald. "We're trapped!"

Suddenly a voice behind them rumbled, "Who's this woman?"

Amanda whirled around to face a hulking figure in a broad-brimmed hat wearing the sheriff's badge.

"Sheriff McRae," her words poured out, "the Wobblies are un-armed! You don't have to worry!"

"Oh, we're not worried," he drawled in a mocking tone. "We're just the welcoming committee."

His deputies joined him in laughter.

"I've spoken to Beckingham," she rushed on, "and he assured me that if the Wobblies aren't looking for trouble, they won't find any."

"Oh, he assured you, did he? Are you a girl friend of his?"

"I'll tell you who she is—she's Firebrand!" Amanda turned at the sound of a disturbingly familiar voice. It was Cyrus Clough.

"So, we meet again." He eyed her coolly, savoring the moment of confrontation.

"I might have known *you'd* be here!" Amanda flung at him in contempt.

"I don't like what you've been saying about me." His tone became more ominous. "And I don't like the trouble you're making."

"Firebrand, eh?" McRae's jowls darkened. "Looks like I'm going to get me two birds with one stone! Boys," he said, waving an arm, "escort the lady and her friend out of firing range. We've got work to do! And keep an eye on 'em." He gave Amanda a chilling smile. "I'll deal with you later."

"Let *me* take care of her," said Clough, pinning Amanda's arms behind her back. "It'll be a pleasure."

"Better handcuff her," said McRae, amused at the struggle. "I think she's going to be too much for you, Cyrus."

But though Clough was determined, it took the help of two men to apply the handcuffs, and only then was he able to drag her away.

"I've waited a long time for this," Clough warned, panting from the exertion. "I'm not going to be cheated!"

Amanda could feel his hot onion breath and smell the odor of his sweat.

"Go to hell!" she gasped, trying to wrench free.

In the background began the measured tramping of feet, then a chorus of voices rising in the spirited strike song that Carl had composed.

> "Hold the fort for we are coming,
> Union men be strong.
> Side by side we battle onward,
> Victory will come!"

Looking back, she could see the Wobblies starting down the gangplank. Carl was marching in the forefront, arms linked with Gus and John.

"Go back!" she screamed. "It's a trap!"

But Carl didn't seem to hear. His face shone with the exhilaration of the moment. Amanda continued to struggle, diverting the attention of the crowd, who began jostling one another to see what was going on.

"It's a trap!" she cried to anybody who would listen, but the curious faces closing in around her couldn't seem to grasp the situation. Her pleas were overpowered by another verse of song.

> "We meet today in Freedom's cause,
> And raise our voices high;
> We'll join our hands in union strong,
> To battle or to die."

At last Amanda broke from Clough's grasp, and ran forward. "Carl!" she screamed.

Carl turned in her direction, and with a smile, raised his arm in the worker's salute, showing no surprise whatsoever at finding her there. Then she realized in despair he was only saluting the crowd, he hadn't seen her after all. There was a warning click. She froze. In that instant the air was ripped by a sharp crack, and she looked up to see the youth who had been clinging to the top of the ship's flagpole crumple up and begin to slide. About halfway down, he threw out both arms with the grace of a winging gull, and crashed to the deck.

A moment of stunned silence was shattered by a volley of gunfire, sending the crowd stampeding to safety. But the Wobblies, trapped by the water behind them, wildly sought cover. Some dived into the Sound, others tried to retreat back up the gangplank.

"Run, Carl!" Amanda pleaded hoarsely, but there was no chance now of being heard above the panic-stricken screams surrounding her.

Carl was looking back toward the steamer in bewilderment, as if trying to understand why everyone was running. At the same moment John Looney broke away in a desperate sprint for cover, but just short of safety, he was caught in the leaden hail and sent sprawling on the pier. In a gesture of defiance, Gus raised the stump within his armless sleeve and sang out:

> "Fierce and long the battle rages,
> But we will not fear.
> Help will come whene'er it's needed,
> Cheer, my comrades, cheer!"

His words fell to a whisper as a crimson circle began to slowly consume his shirt. He staggered and reeled, refusing to fall until a fresh volley brought him down.

Carl dropped to a crouch over Gus's body, and when he raised his head, Amanda saw the crazed eyes of a soldier summoning the power to spring from his trench. She knew in that instant that he was past warning, that his mind had already transcended any concern for survival. His mission now was to embrace the enemy fire, to die gulping bullets, not go down with lead in his back. As the deputies fumbled to reload, Carl leaped over Gus's still form, zigzagged toward the barricade of lumber, and crashed through with the force of a tank hitting a wall. A cry went up from those within range as boards flew like matchsticks, exposing the enemies' hiding place.

Sheriff McRae, his face suddenly washed of color, dropped his rifle in a frantic scramble to escape. He was too late. Carl lunged at his throat, trapping it in an iron grip. Most of the deputies fled, others merely stared like paralyzed prey helpless to fend off attack.

McRae's head began to expand, his eyes bulged, as Carl brought him to his knees. Then abruptly he released him. There was a hush, everyone thinking that McRae was dead. But when the hulking form began to twitch, Carl went again for his throat, as if defying his victim to survive.

Amanda ran toward him, unmindful of the iron which bound her wrists behind her. "Carl, I'm here! Don't do it!" she pleaded. "He's got to be kept alive!"

"I don't take prisoners!" he cried out. "This is war!"

Cyrus Clough came from behind and pushed Amanda aside. Sunlight caught the flash of metal as he seized McRae's rifle, took aim and, without warning, fired point blank into Carl's face. As the single shot split the air, Carl's head burst like a rocket, showering the victors with the blood of the conquered. Amanda reeled back, feeling the hot spray on her face and neck, yet even in that moment of horror the thought ripped through her mind that Carl had won. *They* had won. The hands of the enemy were stained. And the dehumanizing ritual of warfare had ended.

Chapter Twenty-One

$\mathbb{A}$MANDA paced—six steps to the wall, turn, six to the bars, repeat —a compulsive routine of one hundred paces that had to be performed each hour, for exercise and sanity. Now, after a week of confinement, she had reached the conclusion that survival was a personal responsibility, and that it was possible to come to terms even with a shrunken world stripped of all but the barest necessities.

Sometimes she was a nun in a cloister who contemplated the sins of the human race, other times a laboratory animal upon whom an experiment in isolation was being conducted. But no matter how she imagined her situation, it was essential to believe that being in prison would somehow serve her purpose, if only to remind the public of the Everett Massacre.

At last it was time to confront the clean pages of her notebook, to commit a thousand conflicting thoughts and feelings to paper. She settled on her cot with determination, knees drawn up to support the pressure of her pen, while a single bulb stabbed her cell with a cold blade of light.

"January 1, 1917

Dear Emma:"

She paused, reaching for the words to begin. It wasn't easy to pick up the threads, for she and Emma had long ago passed the point of exchanging letters. With their every move reported in the press, there was nothing left to say to each other that hadn't already been said in print. But this was different. Emma, above all others, was the one person who knew how it felt to be deprived of freedom. She would understand how the endless days of imprisonment stirred memories of past friendships, created longings to recapture a better time and the desire to strengthen old ties. She alone could offer support without pity. Why then didn't she come forward? But of course even if she *did* write, more than likely King County authorities would confiscate the letter, regarding an anarchist as an undesirable contact for a prisoner.

There was little need to describe to Emma the horrors of the Everett Massacre, the papers had taken care of that. The public by now was sated with the details of Carl's murder and knew by name all thirty of the victims who had been gunned down with him. Still, Amanda had reached a stage in her grief where she *had* to talk about it, to unburden herself of the terrible doubts which battled against her spirit.

"Dear Emma: My calendar says it is the first day of a new year. But for me, it marks my eighth day behind bars. It was six weeks ago that my world collapsed, but only now can I begin to think about what has happened without plunging into despair. I've been suffering alternate fits of anger, defiance, self-pity—and grief. My trial, as you must know, was incredibly swift. When I told the press I felt like I'd been raped, I'm certain I shocked the world, yet I can find no better way to express my feeling of rage and injustice. Do I want revenge? *Yes!*"

Calm down, Manka. Emma won't have any patience with emotional outbursts.

"On a brighter note, however, some kind, unknown friend smuggled in a notebook and pen, which I'm using today for the first time. Being allowed to write has given me hope, though I expect it will be a while before I can sound rational enough to put my thoughts before the public. Anna Louise Strong is running the paper in my absence—a great comfort. I wasn't allowed to attend Carl's memorial service, 'for fear of riots,' so they said. But I left instructions for his ashes to be carried up the Sound and scattered among the San Juan Islands. Gus and John were taken to Aberdeen; the others back to the towns and farms which they had left."

Amanda paused, staring into the shadowy corners of her cell. Emma would tell her to rejoice—Carl had died a hero. Weren't McRae and Clough behind bars, their empires destroyed? With that accomplished, the Wobblies hadn't died in vain. She would view Amanda's one-year sentence for sedition as a small price to pay.

Yet, Emma would have to admit that Amanda would most likely not have been arrested in the first place, had she not been found already handcuffed when the police arrived on the scene. This had been the incriminating evidence which had branded her as a Wobbly conspirator, "proving" that she was stirring up trouble before a single shot had been fired.

"I know you would say I have triumphed. But I don't sleep well, Emma, for blaming myself. Each night I relive the tragedy and awaken in a cold sweat. I suffer from a nagging guilt that it was Firebrand's journalism which sent Carl to his death."

At last her fears were on paper! But if she hadn't delved into the Beverly Park beatings, hadn't identified so many prominent citizens, would Carl be alive today? Or had the Everett lumber trust been *looking* for an opportunity to get rid of him?—planning to "defend" their city against a Wobbly "invasion" to vindicate themselves?

"With equal guilt I bear the loss of my young reporter, Ida Reynolds. She was on her first important assignment, excited and flattered that I had chosen her. It's of little consolation that Ida was returned to her home in glory. How do you explain *that* to a grief-stricken family in Grand Forks, North Dakota, who had allowed their daughter to leave only six months earlier to pursue a dream? In case the papers didn't mention it, Ida was just nineteen."

Amanda put her letter aside. She could write no more. Later—sometime—she would finish it. She could still see Ida's eager, fresh-scrubbed face, full of innocence and wisdom, and already showing a promising touch of the firebrand. It was Ida's blood-spattered notebook, after all, which had been retrieved from the boat and turned over to the *Union Record*. Even under fire, Ida had continued to write, knowing that perhaps hers would be the only true account. Her frantic scribbling had affirmed that none of the Wobblies had been armed, a fact which had provided valuable evidence against McRae. Her last words had been: "We're as helpless as Indians slaughtered by the white man! It isn't a battle—it's a massacre . . . !"

"Sleep peacefully, Ida," Amanda whispered. "We won't let them forget the Everett Massacre. That I promise."

Someone was coming. Amanda was on her feet in an instant, brushing back her hair in nervous anticipation. It wasn't visitor's day, yet she could hear the sound of the elevator rising to the third floor, then stop. The opening and closing of doors was followed by an army of footsteps echoing down the corridor, drawing closer. The thought of facing a group raised unreasonable fears. She felt trapped, unable to protect herself. One person was welcome, more than one was an ordeal.

But when the cell block door swung open, she sighed in relief. It was only Anna Louise.

"I know it's the wrong day," she sang out, sounding a bit too light-hearted, "but I'm here to bring your mail and the papers."

"You're just in time to mail my letter to Emma. I finally finished after working on it for two weeks."

Lou's smile faded. "I hate to tell you this, but Emma's in prison, too. This time for advocating birth control. There's a rumor that she might be deported to Russia."

"Deported!" Amanda shook her head in dismay. "I knew something was wrong."

"I'm sure if it comes to that, she'll *want* to go back to Russia."

"I suppose so. But it's still not the same as leaving on your own terms. Oh, Lou, it seems that all the people I care about are gone—except for you and Erastus, of course. You're about the only friends I have left."

"Oh, I wouldn't say that. You have four admirers waiting right outside the door."

"*Four!* Do I know them?" Amanda asked warily.

"Well, not exactly. They've been sent by the trustees of Columbia University."

"What on earth . . . ?"

"They'll tell you what it's all about. May I show them in?"

Amanda glanced down in sudden panic at her plain wash dress and slippers. "How can I receive them looking like this?"

"Don't worry, they won't mind. But I did bring you a lipstick and rouge—just in case you get your picture taken."

"Please, no pictures!"

"Suit yourself, but you may want to change your mind."

The committee was hardly the distinguished group that Amanda had expected. The two men and two women were dressed in work clothes. The guard unlocked her cell door, allowing her the privilege of mingling with her visitors.

She shook hands awkwardly as they introduced themselves. And though she attempted a humorous apology for the uncomfortable circumstances, no one appeared ill at ease.

"We're here on behalf of the Pulitzer estate," the spokeswoman announced, and presented Amanda with a parchment scroll.

Amanda accepted with pleased surprise, wondering if she had been made an honorary member of some journalism society. "This looks like a diploma!"

She unrolled it slowly, surprise turning to amazement as she read: "The Trustees of Columbia University, as authorized by the estate of the late Joseph Pulitzer, hereby award the First Annual Pulitzer Prize in Journalism for Meritorious Public Service to the Seattle *Union Record* for its courageous exposés of the Beverly Park Scandal and the Everett Massacre by its editor and publisher, Amanda Lamar. Dated this Fifth day of January 1917."

"A gold medal goes with it," the woman continued, handing Amanda the glass case that held her prize. "Congratulations!"

Amanda was still in a daze after they had left. "I can't believe it! If Joe Pulitzer were alive today, do you think he'd approve?"

"Approve! I'm sure he ended his days wishing to hell he'd had the foresight to hire you when he had the chance!"

"I liked their work clothes. A symbolic gesture, wouldn't you say?"

"Respect, that's what it was. Appreciating what you stand for. In fact, they told me they're going to exert some pressure to try to get you out of here."

"You mean—to get the verdict overturned?"

"That's what they're hoping for. But we'll have to keep our fingers crossed. It won't be easy."

"I'm glad you told me. That helps."

"See? You *do* have friends."

"I'm very lucky. If only Carl . . ."

"Now listen, girl," said Lou firmly, "we're not going to talk about C.G. any more, remember? Let some time pass. Give yourself a chance to move on. After all, you never know what lies ahead."

Amanda detected a strange innuendo in Lou's voice.

"What I'm trying to say is, there's someone else waiting to see you. He's very nervous and has asked me to pave the way."

"Someone else?"

Lou nodded, her eyes suddenly glistening. "Good Lord, what am *I* crying for?" She turned quickly and went out.

A moment later Mark walked through the door.

"Hello, Manka." He crossed the cell block as normally as if he were in his own house. Before she could speak, his arms were around her. He rocked her gently for a moment, his cheek against hers, comforting without words, then stepped back to gaze into her eyes.

"Twelve years is too long," he said.

Amanda glanced down, biting her lip. She wanted him there, and at the same time felt humiliated to think he should see her in shapeless clothing, her hair hanging loose, and in every respect deprived of feminine appeal. He, on the other hand, appeared almost unchanged. His body was firm and trim, his hair still thick, and only the tiniest crinkles around his eyes gave any evidence at all that they were meeting after more than a decade. He no longer dressed like a logger, but wore an aviator's jacket with a white scarf flung carelessly about his neck. It disturbed her slightly to see him looking like a daredevil.

"Congratulations on your award! I'm proud of you."

"Thank you. I didn't expect it." That wasn't what she wanted to say. She wanted to tell him how wonderful it was to see him, how happy she was that he had come at last. But instead, she only made it worse by adding, "I appreciate your coming."

"Manka," he chided gently, "this isn't a duty call. It's taken me ages to get up the nerve!"

"Well, I'm very pleased that you did." The words were coming more easily now, and she was confident that in another moment she would be able to converse with him like a rational being. She would be pleasant, but restrained, mindful of the fact that their former relationship could never be resumed now that he belonged to someone else. Why, then, was he there?

"I'm glad that we can still be friends," he went on.

"You didn't have to wait twelve years to find that out," she said, covering her emotions. How foolish to think there could be anything more than friendship.

Mark smiled painfully. "Are they treating you well, Manka? Do you need anything?"

"I have everything but my freedom. Some mysterious person sent me a notebook and pen," she said with a knowing smile. "And various luxury items arrive now and then which let me enjoy a measure of dignity." Her voice softened. "I treasure them very dearly, Mark, especially the book of poetry."

"You knew they were from me?"

"I think it was the perfumed soap which made me realize that this was no ordinary stranger! But why didn't you reveal yourself?"

"I was afraid that you might resent my intrusion in your life. I didn't want to place you in a position of having to write to me."

"And yet—you're here now."

"I contacted Anna Louise first—to find out how you felt. She assured me it was safe to visit."

There was a beat of silence. Amanda took a deep breath. "Does your wife know that you came to see me?"

Mark looked as though he had been struck. "Hadn't you heard?" he asked, his tone changing. "My wife and children were aboard the *Lusitania*."

"Oh no! Were they . . . ?"

"I lost all three of them. Their bodies were never recovered."

"My God, I'm so terribly sorry! I didn't know."

"There was a mix-up. Their names were left off the casualty list. At any rate I was in too much shock to send a statement to the press."

"What a horrible thing for you!"

"I'm not really over it yet. I can't stop blaming myself for letting them go."

"But it wasn't your fault."

"In a way it was. Irene and I hadn't been getting along. I was the one who suggested she spend the summer in England, because I thought we needed—a separation. Naturally she wanted to take the children." Mark looked away, suddenly distraught.

"I know it's of little consolation, but I've been going through a similar kind of torment. I try to comfort myself by believing in destiny, so as not to feel responsible."

"I, too, believe in destiny. But I was also very selfish. In fact, that's been a problem for me all my life. It took a tragedy to open my eyes."

"Selfish?"

"You, more than anyone, have suffered because I put my own interests before all else. Why do you suppose I didn't marry you when

I had the chance? Because you weren't willing to trade your dreams for mine!"

"Please, Mark, we don't have to talk about it," she pleaded.

"We *do* have to talk about it. I want you to know why I married Irene. I never loved her, Manka. I thought she was right for me, that she would make a good wife and mother. I was sure I could grow to love her. God knows I tried. I tried by staying away from *you*. But it wasn't enough. I thought about you every day. I even continued your scrapbook—keeping it locked up in my desk."

Amanda closed her eyes. "I don't understand any of this. Why wasn't *I* right for you? What were you afraid of?"

"You overpowered me. I'd never met a woman of such determination. You were different from the others, you weren't waiting like a tree to be felled. Your destiny seemed to be within yourself. I thought that you didn't need me enough. I was afraid our marriage would never succeed. And I've paid for that decision ever since. So, here I am, the fellow who thought he had the whole world at his feet . . ."

The door opened behind them.

"Time's up!" the guard called.

Amanda looked at Mark in helpless frustration, her eyes saying, No! You can't leave so soon!

"I'll be back, Manka." He braved a smile. "If you want me."

Amanda endured the endless days, sustaining herself only on Mark's promise to return. But having no idea when that might be, she remained in a constant state of expectation, alternating between hope and despair. Perhaps his visit had been no more than an act of conscience. Perhaps, having seen her, he had found that his feelings were no longer the same. Or someone else had come into his life, which was forcing him to a decision. And as the days dissolved, one into another, she told herself that he had no intention of coming back. She tore a page from the calendar. January was gone.

A few days later, while she was pacing, she became conscious of a disturbance in the street outside. Finally it subsided, but the next day it began again, as if people were congregating right beneath her window. And although it was too high to see out, she could hear a muffled chant, "Firebrand free! Firebrand free!"

Her heart beat wildly as she realized that they had actually gathered to demand her release. The very idea of a demonstration filled her with fear, as memories of the Everett Massacre crowded her mind. But no screaming sirens came, and by the following day, all was quiet again. Her nerves settled and she prayed to be forgotten. That afternoon Mark returned.

He seemed startled to see that this time her cell door was shut, and he stood awkwardly, facing her through the bars. As before, he looked like he had just come from flying an airplane.

"How did you get him to let you in?" she asked, eyes fixed on the leather helmet that dangled from his belt.

"I bullied him, how else?" He tried to be lighthearted, but his anxiety was apparent. "Manka, there's something I've got to tell you." He paused, unsure how to continue. "I've been taking flying lessons."

"So I gathered." She smiled nervously.

He came closer to the bars and reached through for her hand. "It began with the *Lusitania*. When I saw how the Germans had killed my family, who were totally innocent and helpless, it was as though they had declared war on *me*. I thought, here we sit, waiting for them to strike again, perhaps to bomb American cities, while in France they're fighting for survival, short of men, and especially in need of trained flyers . . ."

Amanda's heart plunged. "You volunteered!"

"Do you remember some months back reading about a squadron of American aviators who had offered their services to the French government? A kind of flying Foreign Legion?"

"You mean—the Escadrille Américaine?"

"That's it. Except that their name has now been changed to the Lafayette Escadrille. Anyway, I've joined them as a volunteer."

"You're going to fly airplanes? Drop bombs?"

"Well, yes. That's about it. Look, Manka, it's only a matter of time until we get into the war anyway. So I say, why wait? Let's get it over with. Maybe our help will turn the tide, send the Germans packing." He stopped. "You don't approve, do you?"

"You think risking your life will make up for the *Lusitania?*"

"Manka, I spent too many years thinking only of myself. Risking my life means nothing—I do that every day in the woods. But this is for humanity."

She stared at him, thinking how much he sounded like Carl. Both were attracted to danger, eager to embrace the battle. Carl, needing to prove himself; and now Mark, searching to find peace. Peace on a battlefield! How do I compete with war? she wondered. Carl died fighting, as he had wished. Was that Mark's wish, also?

"If I could only make you understand! I'm doing what I have to do."

"I understand perfectly well. It's just that I seem to have the bad luck to fall in love with men who think death is the ultimate goal! I'm sorry, but *my* goal is to live!"

She turned away in tears, but when she heard the door open and close, she turned back quickly. It was too late. Despondently she listened to his receding footsteps, knowing she had sent him off to war without wishing him well, with nothing resolved. He was gone from her life again and she had no way to reach him.

"I've brought you a present!" Lou announced with forced cheerfulness.

Amanda rested her fingers on the typewriter keys and slowly turned around.

Lou was carrying a large basket of fruit tied with a bow. "I'm only the bearer," she explained. "It's from Erastus."

"That's the third basket in as many weeks. How much fruit does he think I can eat?"

"He's afraid you're not getting a proper diet."

"So why doesn't he deliver it himself?"

"He means well. He just doesn't want to be rebuffed."

"Why would he think that?"

"He knows what you're going through." Lou smiled guiltily. "I'm afraid I told him."

Amanda shrugged. "Well, it doesn't matter."

"I think he'd like to make you forget about Mark."

"I'm sure he would."

"He's got his good points. For one, he'd never stand in your way. That's something to consider."

"Lou, for God's sake, I'm not shopping for a man! And I resent your acting as go-between."

"Sorry. I should know better. But I didn't have the heart to refuse him."

"It's not your fault," Amanda relented. "If he wants to come next visitor's day, I'll be glad to see him."

"Good." Lou glanced at the typewriter. "Any letters to mail?"

"Here. I just finished writing to the Tacoma *Evening News*. Don't tell anybody, but I'm negotiating to buy it."

"You *are?* Good God! I bring you a typewriter and the next thing I know you're buying a paper!" Looking around, she lowered her voice. "Where's the money coming from?"

"No money will be exchanged—if they accept my terms. They're going bankrupt, so I'm going to save them. After that, I have my eye on a paper in Yakima and another in Olympia. Why so surprised? Isn't it time we spread out?"

"Well, yes, but—you'll still be keeping the *Record,* won't you?" she asked anxiously.

"Lou, you don't seem to understand. I'm talking about a syndication, with the *Record* as the parent publication and the others as offshoots. We'll manage the whole thing from right here in Seattle."

Lou scowled. "Sounds to me like you're turning into a regular capitalist!"

Amanda smiled in amusement. "So you think I'm hungry for power?"

"If you are, look out! Because I'll be the watchdog!" Then she asked slyly, "I wonder what Erastus will have to say?"

"He'll be shocked, of course. Like he was when I started the *Record*. But the *P.I.* won't suffer. He'll just have to work a little harder to compete, that's all."

"And so will Clarance Blethen. Bet he'll turn pea green when he finds out."

"I'll gladly tell him that I have his father to thank. Then he won't be able to say a word."

They laughed together.

"Damn, but it's good to hear you laugh!" Then Lou asked suddenly, "Amanda, when you're here alone, what do you do? I mean, do you pace around, or what?"

"I did at first. But I found that the more I paced, the more nervous I became. Now I've learned to sit quietly. Sometimes, I concentrate on the blank wall, pretending that it's a moving picture screen to project all my dreams on. This way I can be anyplace I want to be and doing whatever I please. Do you think I'm going crazy?"

"Perhaps. But it *sounds* sensible. Like you've taken a bad experience and made something good out of it."

"Funny, that's what Mary Kenworthy once said. She felt that losing her hand in that machine opened up her life to a whole new opportunity. Maybe I can do the same."

"As far as I'm concerned, you already have. So forget about my teasing. I'm glad you're going to buy up those papers. And I have every confidence that you'll give capitalism a good name!"

"Lou, wait—don't go yet. I want your opinion on something."

"Name your subject."

"What do you honestly think of the Lafayette Escadrille?"

Lou raised a brow. "Now that you've asked, I'll have to tell you—I'd join them myself if I knew how to fly."

"You? The pacifist?"

"Look, if war could be avoided, then it *should* be. But we're already past that point. I saw it coming when I was in Europe two years ago, but then nobody was ready to listen. Now I think we have to stop the Germans at any cost—before they overrun the world."

"I see." Amanda felt suddenly helpless, isolated. "Then you think Mark was right to volunteer?"

"I'd say it was the ultimate in patriotism."

Amanda swallowed, thinking how unreasonably she had behaved with Mark, all because she didn't understand what was really happening.

"And if you'd consider sending a correspondent to France," Lou continued eagerly, "I'll be happy to go."

"I'm afraid you're needed here." Amanda forced a weary smile. "But that's a good suggestion. I'll have to find someone to send, won't I?"

Amanda had just typed the date, February 27, 1917, when she heard the heavy bolt of the compound door slide back. Her fingers began to lag on the keys. Was it visiting day already? Then she remembered. Erastus. She stared at the wall thinking, I hope he's brought a bottle of whiskey and not another basket of fruit. At the sound of footsteps, she turned with a fixed smile to greet him.

"Mark!"

"Manka!" He rushed toward her as though the bars didn't exist, then stopped short.

She saw that he was dressed for combat, with a strange insignia on his leather jacket.

"I thought you had gone." Her mouth twisted in a hurt smile. "And here you are."

"We were training. That's why I couldn't come. We're shipping out from New York next week." He spoke in a rush, out of breath. "I have something to say to you, Manka." He paused to swallow. "I want to marry you—*now*. I've got to go away knowing that you belong to me!"

She stared, hearing the words but not believing them. She had lived this moment too many times. Something had to go wrong. It always did—where Mark was concerned.

"If you love me, you've got to say yes!"

"You know I love you," she answered, finding her voice. "But with you leaving and me in here, what chance do we have to be married now?"

"It's all taken care of. The plans have been made."

"Plans?"

"For our wedding!"

"Good Lord!"

"I know I should have consulted you first, but with so little time . . ."

"Then it's true? I'm not just imagining all this?"

"It's true. We're going to be married here—I got the warden's permission." He paused anxiously. "Now all I need is yours."

Her lips parted in a smile of relief. "You've had mine for more than a dozen years. I've been waiting only for the question."

Mark took her hand through the bars. The instant she felt the warming pressure of his touch, she realized that she would never have to awaken from this moment. The dream had become reality.

Lou and Erastus were waiting with the chaplain outside the warden's office. Lou was carrying Amanda's favorite green dress on a hanger. Erastus was holding a bouquet of yellow roses.

"There you are!" said Erastus with a display of cheerfulness. "The bride and groom!"

"We were beginning to think the bride had backed out," quipped Lou.

Mark looked at Amanda and squeezed her hand. "She tried, but the groom told her there was no escape."

Amanda smiled nervously, suddenly feeling like any normal bride on her wedding day.

A moment of awkward silence was broken by the distant ringing of a phone. Amanda caught Lou and Erastus looking at the warden's closed door, then exchanging meaningful glances. The ringing stopped, but the door didn't open. Lou sighed heavily.

"Come on," she said to Amanda. "Let's get you changed."

As soon as Amanda put on her green dress, she was herself again, not just a shadowy nameless creature going through the motions of living. It didn't matter that she was to be married within the gray walls of the King County Jail.

When she entered the warden's office, her transformation merited a hum of approval, which brought the proverbial blush to her cheeks. For a moment it seemed that the years had been peeled back, revealing a young girl who had yet to experience the pleasures and sorrows of life.

"I've never seen you look more beautiful," Mark whispered.

He gazed at her with such longing that she felt a sudden pang— more for him than for herself—at the prospect of the long separation ahead.

"Well?" said Lou brightly. "We all seem to be here. What are we waiting for?"

Erastus gently relinquished the roses and offered Amanda his arm. "I nominated myself to give the bride away," he said with a shy smile. "So, in the absence of a relative, I hope you'll accept an old and faithful friend."

Amanda clutched his arm to quiet a sudden tremor. The next thing she knew, the chaplain had positioned himself beneath the window and was beckoning them to come forward. He motioned Mark and the warden to his left, and Lou to his right. Everyone was smiling, as if all that mattered was this moment.

A shaft of steel gray light fell from the window illuminating the chaplain's bald head as he opened his prayer book and began to intone:

"Dearly beloved, we are assembled here in the presence of God . . ."

The room grew brighter, a sudden flood of light dispelling the gloom. Sun, at last! Warm, heavenly sun.

". . . Into this holy estate, this man and this woman come now to be united. If anyone, therefore, can show just cause why they may not be lawfully joined together, let him now speak, or forever hold his peace." He glanced up, then continued, his tone becoming more personal.

"Wilt thou have this woman to thy wedded wife, to live together after God's ordinance in the holy estate of matrimony? Wilt thou love her, comfort her, honor and keep her in sickness and in health, and forsaking all others, keep thee only unto her, so long as ye both shall live?"

"I will," said Mark. His eyes assured her that everything was going to be all right.

In a dreamlike state of disbelief, Amanda repeated her vows.

"I, Amanda, take thee, Mark, to my wedded husband, and plight thee my troth, till death us do part." She felt the ring slip onto her finger and heard the chaplain say:

"Receive this ring as a token of wedded love and troth. Join your hands. Forasmuch as Amanda Lamar and Mark Reed have consented together in holy wedlock, and have declared the same before God and in the presence of this company, I pronounce them man and wife, in the name of the Father, and of the Son, and of the Holy Ghost. Amen. What God hath joined together, let not man put asunder."

Mark was kissing her at last, and suddenly everyone was gathered around. The warden produced a bottle of champagne, but no one could find any glasses. And while they were searching, Amanda was struck by an alarming thought.

"Mark! What will happen to the *Union Record?*"

"You don't have to give it up," he said with a smile. "In fact, I was planning to surprise you with a lifetime supply of paper for a wedding present!"

"That's not what I mean. When you come back from overseas, how can I possibly live with you—four hours by train from my office?"

Mark's exuberance faded. "We'll figure out something . . ."

"Unless," she said hopefully, as her thoughts rushed to the solution, "unless I move my office to Olympia. Then I wouldn't be far from Simpson's at all."

"You mean—move the whole paper?"

"I don't need to. I just bought the Olympia *Star*. It was bankrupt. Never mind, that's a long story. I have four papers now. Lou can manage the *Record,* can't you, Lou?" She turned to her quickly, then back to Mark. "But I'll make our headquarters in Olympia. Oh, thank God, we *can* live together!"

Mark was still shaking his head in bewilderment when an automobile horn began to squawk persistently in the street below. Erastus hurried to the window, then turned to Mark in dismay.

"They're here to pick you up."

"But we haven't had our champagne!" Lou protested.

Mark held Amanda's eyes in the midst of a last frantic scramble to locate glasses. But time had run out before a toast could be made. They embraced in the confusion, not caring whether they drank or not, and the next instant he was gone, his boots echoing sharply in the vast corridor outside.

She heard distant doors open and close, boots on the pavement, finally a car door slamming and the sound of an engine starting, reaching its speed, then fading into the traffic. Everyone was suddenly still, which left Amanda feeling alone, listening only to the anxious rhythm of her heart.

She returned to her cell where the afternoon stretched away in silence. Except for the fact that she was still wearing her green dress and a wedding ring, it was no different from any other day.

I'm a married woman, she thought, yet I have no idea why my husband is gone and why I must be left behind. Left with the old familiar ache of disappointment.

It was early evening when she heard the elevator rise to the third floor. Running footsteps approached. Running? She stood up apprehensively.

When the door opened, Lou was the first to burst in, followed by her lawyer, Erastus and the warden. The guard hurried to unlock her cell.

"They did it!" Lou shrieked, laughing and crying. "They overturned the verdict! You're free!"

Amanda stood in her own front hall, like a stranger waiting to be invited in. The last time she had stood on this spot was little more than three months ago—only three months?—on the day before Thanksgiving, when she had kissed Carl good-by. Yet, it was already a dim memory.

"If you want to change your mind and stay at my place, just say so." Lou shot Amanda an anxious glance.

"No, I'm fine. This is *home,* Lou. Home at last."

"I'm so mad to think you had to be married in jail—I had my heart set on a ceremony under the totem in Pioneer Square!"

Amanda smiled. "I would have liked that."

"I knew this morning the verdict had been overturned, so just before the ceremony when that damn phone rang, I thought—this is it! But it wasn't, and of course we couldn't move until the papers were signed."

"If only Mark had known before he left . . ."

"I should have said something, but I was so afraid of getting your hopes up—just in case it fell through at the last minute."

"It's all right, Lou. He had to leave anyway." She drew a deep breath and looked about.

"I took the liberty of cleaning up," Lou ventured cautiously. "I put all of C.G.'s things into boxes. They're in the attic, out of the way, until you decide what you want to do with them."

Amanda nodded gratefully, relaxing. Now she could go into the parlor.

It was true. Every trace of Carl had disappeared, except for one poster which had been left hanging—"STRIKE FAST, STRIKE HARD."

"I didn't want to erase what he stood for," Lou explained quietly. "Or rather, what we *all* stand for. I hope you don't mind."

"No, I want it to stay. That poster went with us to Endoline."

Lou appeared visibly relieved. She took out a pack of cigarettes, offered one to Amanda, then took one herself. Amanda had never smoked, but she did so now, as they wandered from room to room.

The house seemed immense and she marveled at the amount of space she was expected to consume. "I might as well be living in an open field! Except for the doors. Isn't it ridiculous for one person to have so much—air?"

Finally they sat in the parlor, sipping brandy and talking till past midnight.

"You should be sitting here with your husband instead of me!" said Lou regretfully, crushing her cigarette into a full ashtray. "Damn the bureaucracy!"

"It's thanks to you that I'm sitting here at all! I'm so grateful, Lou, for the way you've stood by me."

"What the heck did *I* do?" Lou shrugged with characteristic disdain and refilled their glasses. "You can thank the Pulitzer committee for raising the issue."

"I do. Everybody's been wonderful." She was silent for a moment. "It's going to be hard to leave Seattle."

"What about this?" asked Lou looking around. "Your house?"

"Well, I can't very well sell it. Who would want to buy a house that's attached to a factory?"

They both laughed.

"You know, Lou, I think I'll keep it for future expansion. So remember, if Clarance Blethen comes snooping around looking to buy, tell him we're not in the market!"

That night, though exhausted, Amanda tossed sleeplessly. The bed was too soft, the blankets too warm. And when she felt the vibration of the presses against the wall, which she had missed so much in prison, she could think only of Mark speeding away from her on an eastbound train.

As the darkness faded, she got out of bed and went to the window to watch the sunrise. Why should men be the only ones compelled to fight wars? she reflected. How easily they leave their jobs, their professions. Is my work so important that my papers wouldn't survive without me? She remained at the window until the sun was above the horizon, while excited thoughts began to stir. This war could use a Firebrand—especially to cover the adventures of the Lafayette Escadrille. Isn't it really my *duty* to go?

"Your *duty?*" gasped Lou, exaggerating in horror. "Is that what happens when you become head of a publishing empire? You suddenly get the urge to go to war?"

"Lou, I'm serious! Didn't I tell you I was going to send a correspondent to France?"

"And did you forget that *I* volunteered to go? Only you said I was needed here."

"You are. Now more than ever."

"Then you've made up your mind?"

"For me, it's the right thing to do."

Lou responded with a quick, encouraging smile. "If I were in your place, I'd do exactly the same."

"I'm being selfish, you know. If anything happened to Mark while we were separated, I could never forgive myself. I want him to know that his wife will face whatever he can face. Even death."

A warm Chinook wind blew in with the March rain when Lou returned that afternoon to drive Amanda to the station. Asking her to wait, Amanda explained that she needed to make one final check to be certain that nothing had been forgotten. But as she went from room to room, her real purpose was to say good-by to a part of her life that was over. She knew that when she returned, it would be as a visitor; it would never be the same again.

Coming downstairs, her hand traveled lightly along the smooth balustrade as she savored the last moments. She lingered in the front hall for a sweeping glance, then as easily as the door closed behind them, her thoughts flew ahead, impatient to move on.

As they drove, the rhythmic pelting of raindrops on canvas filled the silence.

"I'm sure the war will be over soon," said Lou, trying to sound convincing. "Especially with all of *you* over there helping them. Probably three months at the most."

Amanda nodded. "At the most." She didn't say what they both feared, that the United States might become involved.

"Are you going to miss us?"

"I'm a little afraid to think about it. I don't want to get sentimental, but so much of me is here. I've watched this town grow up, while I grew with it. I think in the process we've all become more liberated."

Lou concentrated, frowning. "But what do you really think made us grow up? There had to be a turning point."

Amanda reflected for a moment. "It was everything," she replied at last. "From the gold rush to the Everett Massacre—our youthful dream to the grim awakening—and all the events in between that led us out of the Victorian age. And now the war. We've won and lost, and we'll win again. Because I think we have destiny on our side."

Lou waved from the station platform, her bright smile shining through the fogged window of the train, wind-blown hair embracing the raindrops, in the triumphant stance of a climber who has just reached the summit.

Amanda waved back eagerly, reassured.

They started with a lurch, laboring slowly at first, then at the outskirts gathered speed, passing factories, mills and plants for endless miles. When the chimneys and smokestacks finally ran out, they raced the new highway down through the broad sweep of the Duwamish River Valley. At the curve in the tracks, Amanda turned for a last glimpse of the receding skyline.

"Klahowya, sikhs," she whispered. "Good-by, friend. For now." But the city was only a shadow behind a curtain of rain.